A SOLID BOND IN YOUR HEART

by

Paul Dixon

WEAR WORD OF MOUTH BOOKS

Acknowledgements

I am indebted to Mandy and Stephanie for their assistance and advice. A special thank you must go to my wife, Lesley, and children Becky and Jim for their patience and support.

Dedicated to Darren Billingham

CHAPTER 1

A period of relative calm had slowly descended upon Spennymoor in the gloomy, pre-dawn hours of a new weekend. High Street, the heartbeat around which everything else revolved on a Friday evening, was now a ghost town, its vacant bars and clubs standing eerily silent. The melange of small-scale destruction and petty vandalism left behind - jagged remnants of smashed beer glasses scattered across the street and stagnant pools of urine in shop doorways – together with trails of blood at the taxi rank, told its own story of revelry gone sour.

The sated carousers had drifted away into the anonymity of the night, beyond the compact urbanity of the town's epicentre, back to their homes in the surrounding districts, a sprawling hotchpotch of post-war council housing and seventies built modern estates.

The nocturnal tranquillity of the suburbs was occasionally broken: a scavenging cat sending a dustbin lid clattering to the ground; a dog barking with sporadic disgruntlement while tethered to its kennel; an owl hooting while perched up high on the branch of a tree, its telescopic vision trained upon the ground for vulnerable prey.

On the Moss Green council estate, the foraging creatures of the night were the first to detect a disconcerting rumble in the distance. Curious ears began to prick up, intuition telling them something was amiss; nervous eyes furtively scanned their habitat to gauge the level and immediacy of any potential danger.

A sudden escalation in noise brought their survival instincts to the fore, with all activity abandoned in favour of scurrying back to the safety of the shadows.

Seconds later, an omnipresent tidal wave of sound shattered the peace.

The instigator, a mildly stoned Phil Hughes, was oblivious to the widespread bedlam the plodding Bob Marley tune was creating, turned up to maximum volume on his top of the range car stereo; he was of the opinion that the song's lyrics, espousing the virtues of love and peace, deserved to be heard by all mankind. Phil was not about to allow the inappropriateness of the hour prevent him from attempting to spread the ethos of the sub-culture he subscribed to.

He weaved his white Ford Fiesta briskly through the empty residential streets, the booming music making conversation impossible between himself and his passenger.

Turning into North Close, Phil pressed his foot down on the accelerator and tore down the straight road, harshly applying the brakes once he arrived at the end of the cul-de-sac.

Ten metres away, the eyes of Ronnie Blackburn snapped open.

He sat bolt upright in his bed, as if his body had been subjected to an electrical shock. To his ears, it sounded as if King Kong was on the rampage outside, with the beast's pounding gait trampling all nearby cars and buildings underfoot.

Once he had allowed a couple of seconds to elapse for his eyes to adapt to the darkness and his muddled mind to adjust to its rude awakening, Ronnie glanced at the red neon lighting of the digital clock radio on his bedside cabinet. He groaned as he realised his bout of slumber, achieved with an obstinate force of willpower in the tortuous cauldron of a sticky summer night, had lasted less than an hour.

Stung into action, Ronnie slid out of bed and stomped indignantly across to his bedroom window, muttering to himself under his breath while running an agitated hand through his regimentally short, bristled grey hair. Experience told him who was to blame for the offending din, but Ronnie wanted to have his suspicions rubber stamped before venting

8

his frustration. He parted the curtains and peered outside.

'Dom! I might have bloody known,' growled Ronnie, shaking his head disapprovingly as he watched his son spill out of the passenger door of the car parked outside, his outstretched palms cushioning an undignified drunken stumble onto the pavement. With a great deal of effort, Dom raised himself upright and staggered down the garden path to the front door.

Enough was enough. Ronnie turned sharply on his heels and headed for the door to the landing.

'What are you doing, Ronnie?'

The mumbled question came from his wife, Iris, who until now Ronnie had hoped would not be disturbed.

'Go back to sleep,' he said brusquely. 'I'll handle this.'

'Don't be too hard on him,' said Iris, more in hope than expectation, fully aware her husband's notoriously short fuse had been set alight.

Purposefully descending the stairs, Ronnie unlocked the front door and yanked it open in a fit of pique, startling his son who was rummaging around in his pockets for his house key.

'Get in there and wait for me,' barked Ronnie, grabbing Dom by his shirt and forcefully shoving him inside.

Switching his attention to the sole occupant remaining in the car, Ronnie strode ominously down the garden path, furiously shaking his fist and mouthing expletives.

Panicked by the sight of the patriarchal head of the Blackburn household menacingly approaching, Phil swiftly found first gear and, with a screech of tyres, escaped the wrath of his friend's father with seconds to spare.

Swearing he would have it out with Phil on another day, Ronnie returned to the house and locked the front door. Dom was nonchalantly leaning against the mantelpiece in the living room, awaiting his return.

'Sit,' ordered Ronnie, pointing at the sofa.

'What's the problem?' asked Dom, clumsily flopping down.

'The problem,' began Ronnie, the vein in his forehead pulsating, 'is that you're rolling in pissed at three in the morning after I specifically told you to be home no later than midnight.'

Ronnie paused, took a step towards his son and sniffed the air before recoiling in disgust.

'And you've been on the wacky baccy, too, judging by the smell on your clothes. Then again, knocking around with scum like that, I'd expect nothing else.'

'I can explain why I wasn't home earlier, Dad,' said Dom. 'We missed the last bus.'

'There are taxis,' replied Ronnie firmly, sitting down in his armchair.

'Me and Jonesy didn't have enough money for one, so I rang Phil, and he brought us back from Newcastle.'

Ronnie shook his head, smiling in disbelief. 'And it takes nearly three hours to drive thirty odd miles? I know he's an idiot, but even for Phil that would take some doing.'

'You don't understand, Dad. We went to drop Jonesy off first, but Phil got a puncture on the way. He managed to make it to Jonesy's house, but we had to hang around there until Jonesy's brother put the spare tyre on.'

'The phone's over there next to the kitchen door, son. Give *Jackanory* a ring,' said Ronnie sarcastically. 'They're always on the look-out for a decent storyteller.'

'It's true,' countered Dom, with impassioned denial. 'You ask them next time you see them.'

Ronnie snorted. 'I wouldn't trust those two as far as I could throw them. You're all thick as thieves, the whole bloody lot of you.'

'What's the big deal anyway? I'm not a kid anymore.'

'The big deal?' said Ronnie furiously, his eyes widening. 'In case you haven't noticed, you are supposed to be in mourning. It's your grandad's funeral in a few hours, and you're out partying as if nothing out of the ordinary is happening. You should be showing a little respect,' he said, adopting a tone of moral disgust. 'I couldn't give a monkeys if you have none for me, but what about your mother? As if she didn't have enough on her plate as it is, without you waking her and the whole street up in the middle of the night.'

'I'd never do anything to hurt Mam,' Dom fired back defiantly, riled by the accusation. 'And Grandad wouldn't have minded. He said life is there to be enjoyed when you're young because it all turns to shit when you hit old age.'

Ronnie stiffened upon hearing this retort. It was bad enough that his son was feeling sufficiently emboldened to dare to verbally joust with him and question his authority, but for Ronnie's father-in-law to be still holding sway over Dom even in death was too much to take. Ronnie was damned if he was going to concede any ground or admit defeat.

'So, that's enjoying yourself, is it? Making more noise than an invading army at an hour when most normal folk are asleep. God knows what state you're going to be in tomorrow ... I mean today,' said Ronnie, quickly correcting himself.

'I'll be as right as rain in a few hours.'

'Well, that's nice to hear,' said Ronnie cuttingly. 'What about the rest of us? After the week we've had, was it asking too much to try and get a decent night's sleep?'

Dom gazed sheepishly at the floor.

'And this isn't a one-off,' continued Ronnie, stabbing an accusatory finger in Dom's direction. 'I've lost count of the number of times I've wondered where you're at and what you're getting up to, out there in all weathers at all hours, half expecting a knock at the door in the middle of the night from the police to say something's happened to you. You need your bloody head looking at. Then, when you are here, you treat this place like a hotel, getting your clothes washed and

11

your meals cooked for you without lifting a finger yourself. Well, that's all going to change, my lad. Easy days are over for you. It's about time you started acting responsibly.'

'I work, don't I? I pay my way.'

'Do me a favour,' said Ronnie mockingly, a cruel smirk tugging at his features. 'The few lousy quid you give us barely covers what you eat, never mind anything else.'

'I'll pay more, then.'

'Money's not the issue, son,' said Ronnie. 'It's about sticking to the rules, which I make. If you don't want to obey them, you can sling your hook and get your own place. See how a spell spent living in the real world suits you.'

Ronnie sat back and drummed his fingers on the armrest, convinced his threat would be the final word in the argument.

He was wrong.

'Well, if I'm that much of a disappointment, maybe you're right,' Dom fired back, unfazed by the warning his father usually reserved for occasions like this.

'What?' said Ronnie, caught off guard.

Unbroken by his father's all-out verbal assault, Dom stood up.

'I think it's time I got out, especially if I'm that much of a burden to you,' he said.

Too shocked to formulate a suitably superior riposte, a visibly stumped Ronnie held up a stalling hand to indicate the conversation had reached an impasse.

'Let's sort this out later. We've got a long day ahead of us, and the way I feel at the minute they'll be burying me as well as your grandad, if I don't get some sleep.'

Dom, too, had found the argument draining, but he was swelling with pride at having stood his ground. With nothing further to say, he disappeared upstairs.

The unsatisfactory conclusion to the abrasive exchange of words left Ronnie feeling unsettled. Needing a few minutes to calm down before attempting a further bout of sleep, he walked into the kitchen, unlocked the back door and pulled it open. Stepping out into the backyard, Ronnie took a heavy draw on his freshly fired up cigarette. Gazing up at the clear, starry sky, he exhaled, wishing he could dispel some of his ever-growing worries as easily as the smoke leaving his lungs.

CHAPTER 2

With so much to look forward to, Ronnie had clocked in for the final shift at Murray Shipbuilding a fortnight ago, before the firm closed down for its summer break, in a buoyant frame of mind. The leaving party for Dom, the elder of his two sons, was due to take place that evening, ahead of his departure for the navy in two days' time. As an ex-naval man himself, Ronnie was immensely proud that his son had landed, with a great deal of encouragement from himself, a respectable, worthwhile career. After sending Dom on his way to a new life, Ronnie was then due to go on holiday to Bournemouth with his wife and other son, Daniel.

There had been a celebratory atmosphere among his workmates on that Friday morning as they prepared for their day's toil, exchanging earthy banter and good-humoured insults. There was nothing to suggest that the remainder of the day would not play out in a similar fashion.

Then the bombshells began to drop.

The first dark cloud to appear on Ronnie's horizon occurred when the management summoned their workforce to the canteen for an impromptu meeting halfway through the morning. As he marched down with everyone else, Ronnie feared the worst.

At the beginning of the year, unfounded rumours had surfaced that suggested Murray's was in financial trouble because the expected new shipbuilding contract that would secure the firm's long-term future had still not materialised. A large percentage of the workforce believed there could be no smoke without fire, subscribing to the theory that the government in Westminster was not interested in helping to maintain the long tradition of shipbuilding on the River Wear, but only in grinding it into the ground. As things stood, Murray's existing contracts took them up to the summer of nineteen eighty-four; beyond that, nothing major was in the pipeline. In the end, however, no official announcement from the firm's hierarchy was forthcoming, and the unsubstantiated stories soon died away.

Ronnie now had a terrible feeling in his water that the negative speculation of a few months ago was about to be resurrected.

The manager of Murray Shipbuilding, dour-faced Bill Grimes, made his entrance at a quarter past ten. To a packed room seething with malcontent, he prepared to read out a succinct statement.

A foreign shipyard company, he began, had unofficially won the contract Murray Shipbuilding had been counting on, and he was now informing them directly in case the newspapers or local television picked up the story and leaked it while they were on their holidays. There would be no immediate job losses, but in the long-term, unless there was an upturn in the firm's fortunes, he was ruling nothing out. Grimes then concluded proceedings with the guarantee he would be pressuring the local Member of Parliament to pursue new orders with the Department of Trade.

Ignoring the plethora of questions the workforce instantly threw at him, Grimes made a hasty exit.

Everyone shuffled away feeling heavily aggrieved that their livelihoods had been plunged into uncertainty, muttering disparagingly about Grimes and the government for allowing matters to deteriorate to the current position. In an instant, the promise of two weeks' worth of leisure time did not appear so alluring, and the atmosphere for the remainder of the day reflected the new spirit of dissatisfaction.

On the drive home later that afternoon with workmate and neighbour Davie Stoker, Ronnie vowed that nothing would put a dampener on Dom's leaving party and the holidays, so he made a pact with Davie to say nothing to their wives about the day's events, unless forced by the media, until their return to work.

The last thing he had expected to find upon his return home was his wife and two sons sitting morosely in the living room. Ronnie was puzzled; he had assumed Iris would be busy down at the social club putting up the banners and balloons, and setting up the buffet that she and Glenda next door had spent half the week planning and preparing.

'What's going on? Shouldn't you all be getting ready for tonight?'

No one answered; Ronnie could have heard a pin drop.

'Will somebody explain what the hell is going on?' he persisted.

Dom was gazing down at the carpet, and Daniel was looking out of the living room window.

Iris took a deep breath before speaking. 'There's been a change of plan.'

'What?'

'I'm n … n … not going to join up,' stammered a visibly nervous Dom, relieving his mother of some of the burden.

'You're not going? What's brought this on?' asked Ronnie.

'It's just not for me,' said Dom, unable to look his father in the eye.

'That's no bloody excuse. You're meant to be leaving in two days' time, and you'll bloody well be on that train. It's all arranged.'

'Ronnie,' intervened Iris, her pleading tone of voice suggesting her husband's reaction was too harsh.

'Don't "Ronnie" me, Iris,' he retorted, refusing to be soft-soaped. 'I know who's behind all of this: your bloody old man.'

'Grandad said I don't have to go, if I don't want to,' said Dom, warming to the theme of fighting his own corner.

'I knew it,' said Ronnie, throwing his arms up in exasperation, his suspicions confirmed. 'He cannot resist getting involved with things that are of no concern to him.'

'It's not Grandad's fault, Dad. I made the decision myself. The thought of moving away makes me feel sick. And … and I've got my own dreams,' added Dom tentatively.

'Dreams,' scoffed Ronnie. 'Dreams don't put a roof over your head or food on the table.'

'Let him have his say, Ronnie,' said Iris.

'I know me, Dad. I wouldn't last a week, and what if there's another war? I haven't got the stomach for it.'

'That old fu …'

'Ronnie,' interrupted Iris sharply. 'That's my father you're talking about.'

'Well, he's turned the boy's head, Iris,' said Ronnie, attempting to justify his ire. 'A week ago Dom was all set to join up, but now his head's been filled with rubbish. He's a meddling old git, that's what he is. Wait until I get my hands on him.'

'You'll do no such thing, Ronnie Blackburn. He's not well.'

'Not well? He's fighting fit the way I see it, sticking his bloody oar in.'

Ronnie spent a further ten minutes attempting to persuade his son to have a rethink; when he realised he was banging his head against a brick wall, Ronnie stormed out of the house in a blind rage.

As he paced down the street and through the estate, Ronnie had the scent of revenge in his nostrils. For fifteen minutes, he walked in the direction of Bill Armitage's home, fully intending to confront his father-in-law.

Approaching The Rose and Crown, a backstreet hostelry that was not one of Ronnie's regular haunts, he darted inside for a much-needed drink.

An hour and several pints later, he reluctantly decided to leave his face-off with Bill until his return from Bournemouth. In his current mood, Ronnie did not think he would be responsible for his actions if they were to be in the same room together. Instead, he ordered yet another drink and spent the rest of the evening ruminating upon the bad blood that had always existed between the two of them.

Too alike in personality, both strong-willed and stubborn, the pair had loathed each other at first sight two decades ago when Iris had introduced her new boyfriend to her father. Ronnie's subsequent marriage to Iris a year later did nothing to assuage the mutual animosity, and it was inevitable that the ill will would eventually transmute into physical violence.

That day duly arrived on 16 July 1966.

A chance meeting in the beer tents at the Durham Miners' Gala after a long day of heavy drinking led to an unsavoury exchange of words between the pair. The argument swiftly spilled over onto the grass outside; surrounded by a human circle consisting of friends from both sides, the two men squared up to each other.

A large man, and still physically strong for one in his mid-fifties, Bill's iron punches repeatedly hammered into Ronnie's face, putting the younger man onto his backside twice in quick succession. With any other combatant, such punishment would have been enough for them to throw the towel in. To Bill's utter astonishment, however, he watched as his son-in-law, his nose bloody and his face bearing numerous cuts, stubbornly scrambled back to his feet and defiantly raised his fists.

Felling him for a third time with a carefully executed punch, a chorus of 'oohs' reverberated around the rapidly swelling crowd of onlookers as Ronnie, as if in slow motion, began to rise gingerly to his feet once more.

It was then that a modicum of common sense prevailed as associates from both camps intervened to quell the duel, realising they were running the risk of standing by and watching a man be beaten to death, an act that would have far-reaching implications, particularly for Ronnie's young family.

From that day onwards the pair had never spoken.

In recent years, Bill had degenerated into an emphysema ridden shade of his former self, but his physical illness had failed to mellow him; Ronnie still found him to be a cantankerous old sod on the rare occasions they happened to find themselves together in the same room at family gatherings.

With the potential ramifications of the two major incidents from his last day at work swirling around in his mind, Ronnie knew the holiday in Bournemouth was never going to be anything but a sour anti-climax.

Most mornings saw him rise early to take lone walks along the coast, and to gaze despondently at the sea as he struggled to cope with a snowballing sense of fear that at times threatened to overwhelm him. It was the threat of imminent change that had shaken Ronnie to the core, of not being in control of his own destiny. Outside of the navy, being a welder in the shipyards was all he had ever known; it was his whole life, and he had thought that would be the norm until the day he retired. Ronnie knew he was too long in the tooth to learn a new trade if he was to lose his job.

His elder son's situation also weighed heavily on Ronnie's mind. Apart from the anger and disappointment he felt at his throwing away of a dream career, he had misgivings about Dom's continuing presence in the Blackburn household. To all intents and purposes, his adult son was now his equal, no longer a child where a raised voice would be enough of a deterrent to dissuade him from behaving in a manner of which Ronnie disapproved. Given that Ronnie was a stickler for rules, traits instilled in him as a child growing up in the austere thirties and war-torn forties, and further entrenched by his years in the navy, he foresaw his relationship with Dom becoming increasingly fraught.

The problem for Ronnie stemmed from his inability to empathize with Dom and the culture of contemporary teenagers. When Ronnie was eighteen years old, there had been no middle ground between the suffocating worlds of being a child and becoming a man, thrust out of one demanding and cruel world into the gleeful tentacles of the next with no pause for breath.

The holiday rumbled on uneasily into its second week, with Ronnie still detached and moody. Iris knew something was troubling her husband but did not dare probe; they were not a couple for talking through any personal problems they had.

In the early hours of the Tuesday morning, a persistent knocking at the door of their hotel room woke Ronnie. He opened it to find a fresh-faced male hotel employee, who informed him there was a caller on the reception desk telephone requesting they speak to him immediately.

Ronnie dressed quickly in the dark without stirring Iris or Daniel and made his way downstairs. The receptionist handed Ronnie the phone before disappearing into a room at the rear to afford him a little privacy.

The caller was Tel Armitage, Iris's younger brother.

Ronnie listened impassively to what his brother-in-law had to say, promised they would return home straight away, and replaced the receiver. Ronnie then returned to his room, gently shook Iris awake and broke the news of her father's death.

As Ronnie held onto his sobbing wife, no emotion stirred within him. Instead, he silently cursed Bill for having died without getting to hear some long overdue home truths.

Even in death, Bill Armitage had conspired to have the last laugh on Ronnie.

CHAPTER 3

When the funeral was over, family and friends congregated at the Blackburn family home in Spennymoor.

In the kitchen, Iris and a small army of female helpers busied themselves with the unwrapping of the sandwiches and savouries while the men drank cans of beer in the living room, making small talk about the weather and football.

Dom grabbed himself a couple of cans from the stack by the back door, declined the offer of food, and made his way through the throng out into the front garden, slumping into his father's wooden garden seat positioned by the living room window. The can hissed as he lifted the ring pull and took a much-needed drink, before leaning back and closing his eyes.

It was the first funeral Dom had ever attended and his only experience of loss on a first-hand basis. His paternal grandparents had died before he was born, and he had only been a toddler when Grandma Armitage succumbed to cancer.

The moving church service, on top of his alcohol over-indulgence the night before and the argument with his father, had left him physically and mentally drained; Dom wanted nothing more than to lie down and go to sleep, wishing that the day was over.

Dom had been extremely close to his grandad as a child. Now finding himself in a contemplative mood, many of his fond memories from that era began to flood back. He recalled, as a three or four year old, the pair of them playing football together on his grandad's front lawn on a blazing hot summer's day, with the sound of The Beatles audible from the open window of a neighbour's home. Beyond the perimeter of the garden fence, Dom pictured neighbours being out in their own gardens while older children played hopscotch in the street.

Then there were the occasions, when Dom was slightly older, when they would go off on adventures together. Usually this involved a visit to the local park, a stroll through nearby woods and surrounding farmland, or a walk to High Street. At the latter, Dom would be spoilt with an ice cream and bottle of pop, before going into the bookmakers so that Grandad Armitage could place his daily accumulator bet on the horses.

'Just imagine it, Dom,' he once proclaimed excitably to his grandson as they exited the smoky, dingy premises. 'By teatime, if all six horses come in, we could be the richest people in town. If I do win, the first person I would buy something for would be you. If you could have anything in the entire world, what would it be?'

'Anything?' double-checked the young Dom disbelievingly, having never had to stretch an imagination unused to such fantastical offers.

'Anything at all.'

'Erm …' he pondered, scratching his head thoughtfully. 'I want to be in a band like The Beatles and go on *Top of the Pops*.'

Bill Armitage roared with laughter, having expected an answer like 'as many sweets as I can eat,' or 'lots of Action Men.'

'So, you want to be a singer and become rich and famous.'

'Yes.'

'Well, we all have to have our dreams in life. Fingers crossed, one day you'll get your wish.'

A voice, in the present, punctured Dom's retrospective thoughts.

'Are you feeling OK, Dom?'

Dom opened his eyes once more to discover his uncle, Tel Armitage, standing in front of the blinding sun. Dom nodded unconvincingly, choosing not to speak in case his voice cracked and betrayed his emotional fragility.

'Never good days, these,' said Tel, reading his nephew's mood.

Dom always felt at ease in Tel's company, usually having no trouble in confiding with him over any problems he had, no matter how big or trivial. The nature of their relationship was informal and brotherly, with the pair having an understanding that Dom call Tel by his first name.

Tel sat down next to Dom on the seat, stared ahead into the distance and gave his knee an affectionate pat.

'It's the crappy bit of life they always forget to tell you about,' said Tel, 'but it's all for the best, I suppose. Dad was in a lot of pain and discomfort. I just hope he didn't suffer too much when he went. I'm going to miss the old bugger, though, even if we did fight like cat and dog most of the time.'

Sounds familiar, thought Dom.

'Still, at least he's with Mam now,' continued Tel, 'if you believe in that kind of thing. Hey, I bet they're up there now having their first barney in years.'

The briefest hint of a smile flashed across Dom's face as he visualised the surreal scenario of his grandad sitting in his favourite armchair on a cloud, Grandma Armitage brazenly scolding her husband while wagging a disapproving finger at him for some indiscretion, with the pair of them surrounded by harp strumming angels. Having no real-life recollection of Grandma Armitage, Dom could only imagine her through the only forms of connection he had available: the photographs that for years had hung on the wall in his grandad's living room, and from the stories about her that his grandad would habitually tell.

'Your old man still giving you a hard time, is he?' asked Tel, perceptively sensing there was more on Dom's mind than the day's sad occasion.

Dom nodded.

'Still giving you grief for not doing the honourable thing

and joining up?' probed Tel further.

'Yeah.'

'Take no notice, Dom. It's your life, and your dad can't live it for you. His problem is, he thinks he's always right and knows what's best for everyone else. He doesn't see things from your angle.'

'I'm fed up of living here, Tel,' said Dom sadly. 'It doesn't matter what I do, he finds fault with it. I wish I had my own flat, so I could come and go as I please without getting constant earache. Could you help get me a place? You have mates who rent property out, don't you?'

'I'd like to help you out, Dom,' said Tel, 'but your mam's just lost a father. She could do without her son disappearing, too, and God knows what Ronnie would say if I fixed you up somewhere.'

'Oh, I don't give a toss what he thinks,' said Dom boldly. 'Anyway, he even told me last night that if I don't like it, then I can get out the house.'

Tel looked surprised. 'Your dad said that?'

'In so many words. Look, I mean it, Tel,' pressed Dom. 'I need my own space.'

'Rents don't come cheap, Dom. On top of food and other bills, it might be financially beyond you, unless you have someone who could share with you.'

The only two friends Dom could think of were Phil and Jonesy, and the thought of living under the same roof with either of them did not appeal. His hopeful expression soured.

Tel looked long and hard at his nephew. 'You're serious, aren't you?'

'As serious as I've ever been about anything in my life.'

'I tell you what,' said Tel, rubbing pensively at his chin, 'the next time I see my mate, Vince, I'll have a word and see if there's anything suitable available. He owes me a favour or two. How does that sound?'

'You're not just saying that to fob me off, are you?'

'No, I promise. He would have been here today, as it happens, but he had a bit of urgent business to attend to. Just don't go mentioning it to your mam and dad, in case nothing comes of it, especially as your mam is so fragile at the moment.'

'Cheers, Tel,' said Dom, brightening up for the first time in what felt like weeks.

'Right, I'd better get back inside and see the clan before I agree to something else I'll probably live to regret. Coming?'

'Why not,' said Dom, raising himself up from the seat, his spirits instantly lifted.

CHAPTER 4

'Who's bloody banging on the door at this time of day?' bawled Ronnie. 'It's only just gone eight.'

Iris slid out of bed and peeked through the curtains. 'Oh, it's only our Tel,' she said, spying her brother's new black BMW parked outside.

'What does that flash git want?'

'I'll not know until I answer the door, will I? I can't read minds,' said Iris gruffly, putting on her dressing gown before trudging downstairs.

'Get the kettle on, Iris,' said Tel chirpily when the front door opened, giving his sister a peck on the cheek before walking through to the kitchen.

'And to what do I owe this pleasure?' said Iris, in close attendance.

'Oh, I promised Dom a day out. I thought we might have a drive up the coast to Bamburgh.'

'At eight o'clock on a Sunday? He'll not thank you for getting him out of bed. It's his last lie-in before he goes back to work tomorrow.'

'The early bird gets the worm, Iris. The roads are nice and quiet at this time of day, so there aren't many Sunday drivers out yet to get stuck behind.'

'Well, make yourself useful and put the kettle on yourself while I let him know you're here.'

'Will do,' said Tel.

'Not bad, is it?' said Tel, as he cruised down the dual carriageway towards Durham City, noting the enchanted look on Dom's face at being in the BMW for the first time.

'Too sodding right,' replied Dom. 'Beats my old Mini any day of the week.'

'How are you feeling this morning? Rough?'

'A little.'

Tel roared with laughter. 'I thought you looked a bit pale before. Never mind, we can stop somewhere for a bacon sarnie. A nice bit of greasy food always sorts me out.'

The thought of this made Dom turn more pallid.

'You said we were going to Bamburgh, Tel,' murmured Dom, attempting to take his mind off his rising nausea. 'This isn't the way.'

'We are, but first we're going to make a quick mystery stop. All will be revealed soon.'

As he drove, Tel chatted away with a cheeriness that disguised the fact he had been to his father's funeral the previous day. For all the current difficulties in the relationship between himself and his own father, Dom could not imagine being able to just get up and get on with life as easily as Tel appeared to be doing.

'Have you guessed where we're going yet?' said Tel, as they approached the city centre.

Dom's mind was blank. 'Newton Moor?' he said finally, taking a stab in the dark.

'No.'

Dom gave the roulette wheel of place names beginning to appear in his mind a second spin and decided on '... Sherburn?'

Tel smiled. 'Getting warmer.'

'Belmont?'

'Ooh,' howled Tel, suggesting a correct guess was imminent. 'Close but no cigar.'

'Gilesgate?'

Tel nodded enthusiastically. 'At last! Now, you have to guess the reason why.'

Dom looked at Tel in disbelief. 'Not a flat?'

'Got it in one,' said Tel, grinning from ear to ear. 'We're meeting Vince there.'

As Dom absorbed this unexpected piece of news, Tel

swept across Gilesgate roundabout, turned into Sunderland Road and effortlessly ascended the steep hill. When the road finally levelled out, he drove a further two hundred metres before making a left hand turn.

'This is the Acorns estate,' said Dom, surprised to find themselves in one of Durham's well-to-do residential areas.

As he drove through the tree-lined streets of three and four bedroomed properties, most of which boasted private driveways, spacious, impeccably manicured lawns and well-maintained borders, Tel noticed Dom's look of awe.

'Don't be intimidated by the plushness of the surroundings,' said Tel. 'Appearances can be deceptive. What you've got to remember, Dom, is that behind closed doors these people are no happier than you and me. In my experience, a lot of them who live here are in it up to their necks in mortgage repayments and bills. Have a guess what they've nicknamed this place?'

Dom shrugged his shoulders.

'Cornflake City,' said Tel.

Dom appeared confused, with Tel's logic not registering.

'Don't you get it?' giggled Tel. 'It's called that because that's all some of the buggers can afford to eat once they've paid all their other bills, all for the sake of telling people they live somewhere desirable. So, don't go thinking you're not good enough to live here, Dom. You're as good as anyone else in this … this …' he said falteringly, searching for the most appropriate words to express himself. '… facade of paradise.'

Tel turned into a concrete parking area, sandwiched between a three-storey block of flats and a row of residential garages.

'This is it,' he said, choosing an empty parking bay. 'Harold Wilson House.'

Dom gazed at the building. There were six flats per floor, with access gained to the first and second floors by an enclosed internal stairway on the gable end; an open gangway at each level led from the stairway to the individual front doors, with only a waist high wall protecting residents from the drop to the ground below.

A thrill of anticipation ran down Dom's spine as he wondered which flat they were going to be viewing.

'No sign of the boss, yet,' said Tel, glancing at the other parked vehicles.

'What kind of car does he drive?' said Dom.

'A silver Mercedes. It's a right beaut.'

'Really!' exclaimed Dom. 'Is your mate a millionaire or something, Tel?'

'I wouldn't have thought so,' chortled Tel. 'No, he rents a few properties out and is also a moneylender. He loans it to mugs at extortionate rates of interest, and then apes like me go knocking on their doors to collect it back. Still, I can't complain. It keeps the wolf from the door and means I don't have to get a proper nine to five job. Could you see me working in a supermarket or a bank, being told what to do and when to do it, by some little Hitler in a shirt and tie holding a clipboard?'

Seconds later, the exquisite looking automobile Tel had just been referring to glided into the car park and came to a halt next to them.

'Here he is,' said Tel. 'Right, are you ready for the guided tour?'

'Ready as I'll ever be.'

They got out of the car. Tel walked over to greet his friend and employer while Dom hung back.

Dom had heard a great deal about Vince Staveley over the years, primarily through the derogatory comments made by his father - loan shark, drug dealer, violent psychopath - that cast the man in a less than flattering light and gave the impression of someone best avoided at all costs. Finally seen at close quarters, Dom had to admit that Staveley ticked many of the boxes deemed essential for any self-respecting gangster, more than living up to the legend.

Standing well over six feet tall, with the physique of an obsessive bodybuilder, the bull-necked Staveley cut a distinct, physically intimidating figure. His predatory shark eyes glinted with roguish intent, untrusting, always on their guard. Polished white teeth, the prerogative of the working-class boy made good, contrasted vividly with a deep mahogany suntan that suggested it had not been acquired on a week's stay in Benidorm, but expensively and frequently at exotic locations. Numerous items of unashamedly ostentatious jewellery – chunky bracelet, V-shaped pendant, and three over-sized rings – completed his public persona.

'Dom,' shouted Tel, beckoning him forwards, 'come and meet Vince.'

Dom approached tentatively and shook Staveley's huge hand.

'How you doing, Dom? I'm Vince. Just wanted to say how sorry I am for your loss. He was a good man, was Bill. Proper old school.'

'Thanks, Mr Staveley.'

'Hey, none of this "Mr Staveley" crap. It's Vince to you, son. Any relative of Tel's is a friend of mine.'

With the introductions concluded, Staveley got down to the matter at hand.

'So, you fancy a place of your own, son?'

'Yes, Vince.'

'Shall we, then?' gestured Staveley with a nod of his head in the direction of the flats.

With Staveley leading the way, they entered the gloomy communal hallway and walked to the foot of the stairway.

'These flats were built about seven years ago,' said Staveley. 'The developer never bothered to fit a lift, but that shouldn't be a problem for a fit lad like you.'

On the first floor landing, Staveley pushed open the door to the walkway and ushered them through.

'This is our floor; stop at number nine,' said Staveley, bringing up the rear.

Once they arrived at the correct flat, Staveley slotted the key into the lock and pushed the blue wooden door open.

'After you, Dom,' he said.

The youth shivered in the unexpectedly chilly passageway, screwing up his nose at the musty odour hanging in the air.

'Take no notice of the smell,' said Staveley. 'It just needs a good airing. The living room's straight ahead of you.'

Dom pushed open the door at the end of the narrow passageway and walked into a room far larger than he was expecting. Décor wise, he felt it was old fashioned, with its seventies style, baroque burgundy wallpaper and dowdy brown carpet, but quickly realised the benefits of the room far outweighed any decorative faux pas on the part of the previous tenant. What struck him immediately was the quality of the natural lighting, with sunlight streaming in through a large window that ran the length of the outer wall, bathing the interior in warmth.

'Now then,' began Staveley, entering into estate agent mode, 'I think the quality of the flat we're in speaks for itself, but as your prospective landlord, I am obliged to give you the obligatory flannel. As you can see, Dom, this room is fully furnished.' His arm performed a grand sweep to demonstrate the range of furnishings. 'You've got your three piece suite, a little coffee table in the middle of the room, and curtains fitted at the window, which is east facing as you might have gathered, so even in winter if the sun's out you get some heating for free courtesy of old mother nature. Also, seeing as you'd be no ordinary tenant, a twenty-inch colour television. Now, I'm the first to admit, it's not exactly at the cutting edge of technology, and it crackles like an egg frying when you first switch it on. I can't guarantee it will last a week, but then again you might get a couple of years out of it. Whichever, it's yours while there's still life in it. The only downside is you'll have a struggle on your hands to bundle it into the cupboard if the television license van is in the vicinity, but that's not going to worry a lad of your pedigree. Water off a duck's back, eh, Tel?'

Staveley and Tel caught each other's eye and, sharing a private joke, smiled knowingly.

'If you think this is good, just wait until you see the rest of the gaff,' said Staveley effusively, guiding them out of the room into a compact corridor. 'Your bathroom's on your left there, Dom, if you want to pop your head inside. It's a bit snug for the three of us all at once.'

Dom stepped inside, with Staveley providing a running commentary from behind.

'The bathroom suite was only fitted last year, there's a shower as well if the mood takes you, and it's fully tiled.'

With the bathroom looking pretty much the same as any other to Dom, he had a quick glance around before exiting.

'Now, if you want to go into the room opposite,' continued Staveley, 'we'll show you the bedroom.'

Once inside, Staveley resumed his sales pitch. 'You've got your bedframe and an old mattress, which you might want to change at some point. In addition, there's a wardrobe and set of drawers. They're a bit old-fashioned but furniture like this was built to last, made by true craftsmen, not your self-assembly rubbish where the instructions are written in Chinese and there's a million pieces to put together. Again, the room is east facing, so you get the heat from the sun all year round.'

'OK, I'm happy with that,' said Dom, once he had politely inspected the interior.

Staveley led the way to the final room, gently pushing open the door for Dom to step inside.

'And, last but not least, the kitchen,' said Staveley. 'There's a fridge with a built-in freezer compartment, a gas oven with grill, a couple of fitted cupboards with drawers, and a small table there to eat your grub off. Everything and the kitchen sink.'

Back once more in the living room, Staveley brought the swift mini-tour to its conclusion.

'Well, that's about it. All the flat's lacking is a washing machine and a telephone line. I'm sure your dear old mother will wash your clothes for you, but there's a launderette up on High Street if you ever need one. There are some shops here on the estate, too, and if you want to use the telephone, there's a call box just out the front of the flats. See,' he said, pointing it out to Dom through the window. 'It's handy to have one on your doorstep in case of an emergency.'

Dom was impressed with everything he had just seen and heard; he could just see himself stretched out on the comfortable looking sofa without fear of recrimination from his parents for having his feet up, or watching television after a hard day at work without his brother bleating on that he wanted to watch rubbish sitcoms with canned laughter. The cherry on the cake, above all else, was he would finally be free from the clutches of his father.

However, Dom knew in imagining himself as a tenant he was running before he could walk. There was still the significant matter of the rent to negotiate.

As if second-guessing Dom's thoughts, Staveley immediately broached the thorny topic.

'Normally for a place like this, I could expect to get twenty, maybe twenty-five quid a week,' he began, his demeanour becoming more business-like. 'But, as you're a close relative of Tel's, I'm prepared to drop it to sixteen. Now, there's no need to tell me right this minute, son. Give it some thought over the next couple of days, and let your uncle know what you intend to do by Friday at the latest. OK?'

Dom nodded.

'Great. Right then, I need to be somewhere else. I'll lock

up and walk down to the cars with you.'

'Well, what do you think?' asked Tel, as, with a toot of his horn, Staveley drove away.

'I like it,' Dom said, with far less enthusiasm than Tel had anticipated.

'But?' said Tel, intuitively sensing a problem.

'But,' began Dom, 'I just don't know if I can afford it. The rent would make a big hole in my pay, and I'd still have my bills and food to fork out for.'

'Hey, don't be so defeatist,' said Tel soothingly. 'Like I said to you yesterday, Vince is a mate. Let me work on him a little. I reckon I can get him to lower his rent even further. I know how his mind works. He likes to be begged to, and to see people squirm for a while; it appeals to the sadist in him.'

Tel unlocked the car doors before easing himself into the driver's seat.

'Just suppose for one minute the rent won't be a problem,' said Dom, getting in the passenger side, 'there's still Mam and Dad to get past.'

Tel nodded in agreement. 'Aye, I can't pretend that will be easy. Ultimately, though, and maybe I shouldn't be telling you this, but what they say doesn't matter. You're old enough to make these decisions for yourself. I'd just rather you had your mother's blessing. Like I said yesterday, it's been a rough week for her.'

Dom could see the reasoning behind that.

Tel laughed as a thought crossed his mind. 'And I'd be wasting my time having a word on your behalf with your old man. He'll not have anything to do with me; he thinks I'm a bit of a gangster. I'm the first to admit that I'm cut from a different cloth to him. Everyone can see we're chalk and cheese. Don't get me wrong, Ronnie's a good man, but sometimes he can be a bit too straight-laced and principled for his own good. You can take a man out of the navy, but you can't take the navy out of the man. I sometimes think Ronnie signed away his sense of humour when he joined up all those years ago.'

Tel switched on the engine and pulled out of the car park.

'Right, next stop Bamburgh. Put the radio on, Dom. Any station will do.'

'Great,' said Dom, pleased for the opportunity to get away from the stifling atmosphere of the family home for a few hours.

CHAPTER 5

Iris was up to her elbows in dirty dishes at the sink when Dom walked into the kitchen.

'The wanderer returns at last,' she remarked. 'Did you have a good time?'

'Yeah. We went to Bamburgh first, then Holy Island, before stopping off at Seahouses on the way home for fish and chips.'

'What!' said Iris in amazement. 'Our Tel willingly setting foot on hallowed ground. That's a first. He'd be about as popular as the Vikings if they knew what he was like. I hope he behaved himself.'

Sitting down at the kitchen table, Dom smiled; it was nice to hear hints of his mother's dry wit emerging once more.

'Did you keep my dinner for me?'

'You've just had fish and chips, son,' protested Iris. 'You'll pile on the weight if you have another big meal.'

Dom looked at his watch. 'It was three hours ago. We had a look around Seahouses after we'd eaten, so I've built up an appetite.'

Iris's expression softened. 'Go on, then. It's keeping warm on a plate in the oven.'

'Thanks, Mam,' he said, retrieving it and returning to the table.

Iris watched as Dom tucked into his food, wondering where he found the room to put it all.

'I've had to guard it like a hawk,' she remarked. 'Your brother was after second helpings, and your father was all for giving it to the dog.'

The smile fell from his face. 'Is he still in a mood with me?' Dom asked cagily.

'Not as much as the other night when you decided to announce your return home to the whole of the street,' she said bluntly, attending to the remaining dishes soaking in the sink. 'I'll be pleased once the pair of you are back at work tomorrow. Things might return to normal around here once more.'

His mother's last comment filled Dom with guilt; he realised she was putting on a brave face for the family's benefit so soon after the funeral, and it troubled him to think he could add to her troubles if he opted to leave home.

'Is Dad down the allotment?' said Dom.

'You just missed him,' she replied, placing the final piece of washed crockery in the rack by the side of the sink. Drying her hands on a tea towel, she sat down at the table opposite Dom and poured herself a cup of tea from the teapot.

'Did you go anywhere else, apart from Northumberland?'

'Oh, here and there,' Dom said, in as innocent a voice as he could muster.

'Here and there, eh?' she said, with a mild hint of suspicion, scrutinising her son closely. 'It takes a lot to shift our Tel out of his bed before midday on a Sunday, especially after the skinful he knocked back yesterday. I can't put my finger on it, but I could swear you're up to something Dominic Edward Blackburn. You've got that look in your eye.'

'Mam,' moaned Dom, his mouth crammed with peas, 'do you have to call me by my full name? You know I hate it.'

'Fine. You can try and change the subject for now,' she said, holding up her hands to indicate she was backing away from the subject, 'but we'll find out soon enough.'

Common sense told Dom to concentrate on finishing his meal without saying another word so that he could disappear upstairs and not have to fend off more prying questions.

The advent of dawn on Monday morning signalled a fresh beginning for Iris. Life had to go on, and there was to be no more moping around the house; her father would not have wanted her to be miserable.

With the protagonists of the recent tensions out from under her feet and back at work, she began the day in a breezy mood, relishing the opportunity to tackle the much-neglected housework and enjoy the relaxed air of domestic normality.

Dusting and polishing the furniture and ornaments in the living room, Iris suddenly remembered one of the black and white photographs she had taken from her father's bungalow while clearing it of its possessions. Pausing to retrieve it from the box of personal effects she had placed under her bed, Iris returned downstairs and afforded it pride of place in the middle of the mantelpiece, allowing herself a moment to wallow in the happy memories the photograph evoked.

Taken during a family holiday to the Lake District one summer in the late forties, the snap featured all of the Armitage family. Estimating that the younger brother standing next to her, more intent on devouring the ice cream in his hand than posing formally, was no more than three years old at the time, Iris figured she must have been ten or eleven years of age.

Standing behind them were their parents. Her father was dressed in a pair of pinstripe trousers held up by braces, and a light coloured shirt with the sleeves rolled up. With his hair slicked back, he was puffing away contentedly on a pipe. Beside him, with her hands on her hips, was Iris's mother; she was wearing a short-sleeve flower patterned dress, its hemline falling way below her knees.

Both parents had carefree, incredulous expressions on their faces, as if they could not quite believe they were standing in such naturally beautiful surroundings. The imposing mountainous landscape, serene atmosphere and pure, lung cleansing air had been a world away from the stark reality of their grimy mining village.

In the right hand side of the picture stood her father's motorbike and sidecar, both gleaming in the bright daylight.

Iris smiled, recalling how her father had made two trips in one day in order to transport the whole family, their camping equipment and provisions. Her mother and Tel had gone first, setting off just as daylight began to push away the remnants of the night. Still in bed, Iris had remained behind secure in the knowledge that her grandmother, who had only lived three houses away, had arrived to keep an eye on her until her father returned later on that day.

Iris sighed and returned to her chores.

By mid-afternoon, she had cleaned the house from top to bottom and completed three machine washes. As a reward for her efforts, she stopped briefly to indulge herself with a fully milked coffee; there had been surplus pints left over from the previous Saturday's gathering that needed using up, so she knew Ronnie could not moan at her for wasting good milk needlessly.

After her short break, Iris began to plan the family meals and prepare the shopping list for the week ahead. In itself, this did not require a great deal of thought, but she liked to go through the routine anyway before the house began to fill up with hungry mouths that needed feeding.

Ronnie was such a creature of habit that each day was synonymous with a particular meal. Monday's saw a rough and ready bubble and squeak served up, the ideal dish to use up the abundance of vegetables leftover from the Sunday dinner; on a Tuesday, the kitchen would be filled with the aroma of liver and onions cooking; Wednesday was a comforting shepherd's pie; egg, chips and beans made up uncomplicated Thursday's. On a Friday night, Ronnie called into the chip shop on his way home from work, freeing up precious time for Iris to wash her hair and prepare for a night out with him at their local social club. Iris and the wives of Ronnie's friends would sit together to catch up on all the latest gossip while the husbands drunkenly argued about sport and politics at the bar.

An hour later, Iris was reading the local evening newspaper at the kitchen table, briefly taking the weight off her feet before cooking the evening meal, when the doorbell rang. Opening the front door, she found herself face to face with her brother.

'To what do I owe this pleasure?' said Iris. 'Three visits in as many days. Are you feeling OK?'

'I was just passing so thought I'd pop in for a cuppa.'

Tel closed the door behind him and followed his sister through into the kitchen.

'Bubble and squeak tonight, eh?' he said, glancing at the bowl of cooked vegetables on the kitchen bench.

'Yes. I can spare you ten minutes, Tel, but then I'll have to start making it.'

'My favourite. I'm sure Ronnie wouldn't mind if I helped myself to his.'

Iris laughed. 'Mind! He'd bloody kill you. He's like a bear with a sore head when he comes home on a Monday. If his tea isn't nearly ready when he walks through that door there'll be hell to pay.'

'Let him make it himself,' replied Tel mischievously, making it clear he was not afraid of his impetuous brother-in-law. 'You're always running around after him and the boys. You have to make time for yourself, Iris.'

'I'd have no flipping kitchen left if I let him loose in here. He'd be like a bull in a china shop. He's not domesticated, just as I'm not capable of building a ship. It would sink before it left the harbour.'

From the early stages of their marriage, Ronnie and Iris had assumed clearly delineated roles within their household. At Ronnie's insistence, he was the sole breadwinner, while Iris attended to all duties of a domestic nature. Nothing over the years had threatened to disturb their well-established equilibrium.

'Are the boys home?'

'Daniel's playing outside somewhere and Dom's upstairs. He's just got home from work. Shall I let him know you're here?'

'No mad rush,' said Tel, sitting down and picking the newspaper up off the table. 'I'll pop up to see him in a minute.'

While pretending to read, he mulled over how best to raise the difficult subject he had come to discuss.

Once the pot of tea was ready, Iris placed two porcelain cups and saucers on the table, sat down and began to pour.

'Ah, Iris, can I not have a proper mug?' Tel said, unable to mask his contempt for his sister's best china. 'These posh cups hardly hold any tea, and I can't get my fingers through the handles.'

'You get what you're given in this house. It's not as if you couldn't do with a little training in etiquette,' she said, raising a disapproving eyebrow as Tel took a vicious slurp of his drink.

Iris took a more refined sip from her cup and returned it gently to the saucer.

'You don't have to feel the need to check up on me every five minutes, Tel. I knew he was going to die sooner or later. It feels a little strange at the moment, not having to pop in to see him during the day, but as long as I keep myself busy, I'll cope.'

'I've not come here about that,' Tel said, before immediately realising how callous his reply sounded. 'I mean, I did want to check on how you were doing. Of course, I did.'

'But? There's always a but with you, Tel,' said Iris, raising her cup to her lips.

'But, there is something else of a rather delicate nature I wanted to talk to you about.'

Iris's cup clinked as she brought it down on her saucer harder than she had intended.

'It's our Dom, isn't it?'

41

'Oh, has he mentioned it?' said Tel sheepishly.

'Mentioned what?' said Iris, a look of horror on her face. 'He's in some kind of bother, isn't he? I bet that's why the pair of you were out yesterday, trying to sort it out without letting on to Ronnie and me.'

'Calm down, pet,' said Tel nervously, as much to buy himself a few precious seconds in which to decide how best to broach the subject as it was to reassure her. 'You're getting the wrong end of the stick. Dom's not in any kind of bother. What do you take me for?'

Iris's mistrustful expression spoke volumes.

'You'd do best not to answer that, but I wouldn't get my nephew messed up in anything dodgy,' said Tel truthfully.

'Well, if it's nothing illegal, just what is it you've come to tell me?'

Tel took a deep breath and finally came clean about his conversation with Dom after the funeral, and the reason for their disappearance the previous day.

Iris listened intently without interrupting once.

Her reaction, once Tel had finished talking, was not what he had been expecting.

'Well,' she began after a brief silence, 'I knew this day would come sooner or later, but I thought it would be in a few years' time, once he'd met someone he liked enough to want to settle down with. My only concern is can Dom afford it? I mean, flats are expensive things, Tel, and it's only Donnelly's where he works, not Harrods. He's not exactly being paid a fortune.'

'Don't worry about his rent, Iris. I've just come from a meeting with Vince, and we've come to a special arrangement where Dom will pay a lot less than Vince's other tenants. I'll owe him a favour or two in the future, that's all.'

Iris gave Tel a hard stare. 'I don't even want to know what you'll have to do to repay him.'

Tel held his hands up to protest his innocence. 'All legal

stuff, Iris, I promise you.'

Iris contemplated the proposition for a moment. 'I'm not sure, Tel,' she said finally. 'I can't say I like the thought of our Dom getting mixed up with Vince.'

'Vince is one hundred percent kosher these days,' said Tel. 'He's no angel, but he's certainly not the rogue that people make him out to be.'

'What? You call loansharking respectable, and at those interest rates. It's immoral and disgusting, Tel.'

'OK, he's nearly kosher, but he's no different from all the banks in the high street, Iris,' said Tel defensively. 'Just because they have all those glossy adverts on the television it doesn't mean they're not shafting people on mortgages and other loans. Vince is no different. He just lends it to people who the banks don't want to deal with, that's all. He's not standing on anyone else's toes and everyone's happy.'

'I don't know, Tel. I mean, it's Dom's decision, of course. He's an adult now, after all, but I'll have to talk it over with Ronnie first.'

Right on cue, they heard the front door open and close, followed by a deep, hacking cough.

'No time like the present,' remarked Tel.

'He's early,' said Iris, springing up from her chair and lighting the front gas ring on the oven.

'Tel,' acknowledged Ronnie gruffly as he stepped into the kitchen, before addressing his wife. 'Is tea ready, Iris?'

'Won't be long, Ronnie,' Iris said, placing the frying pan on top of the flame.

'Well, I'd best get washed and changed.'

'Don't go yet, Ronnie. Tel has come to tell me … us something, about our Dom.'

'Jesus, what's he been up to now?' said Ronnie tetchily, falling through the same trapdoor as his wife had moments earlier.

'I'd best let Tel explain while I get on with this,' said Iris,

43

dropping a chunk of lard into the pan and applying a masher utensil to the vegetables as she waited for it to melt. 'This bubble and squeak won't cook itself.'

Ronnie sat down on the chair that his wife had just vacated, folded his arms and looked at Tel expectantly.

Tel relayed again the events of the last two days to his brother-in-law.

'Well, what do you think?' said Tel, after he had finished.

Ronnie shrugged casually. 'It's nothing to do with me, Tel. It's up to him. He's big enough to make his own decisions now. I've found that one out to my cost these past few weeks.'

'I'll go and ask him to come downstairs a minute,' said Iris, before walking through into the living room and calling up the stairs.

An awkward silence prevailed in the kitchen while they waited for Dom.

'Your uncle tells us you've been thinking about getting a flat for yourself,' said Ronnie bluntly, when Dom appeared in the kitchen doorway.

Dom shuffled uneasily on his feet. 'I was only looking, Dad,' he mumbled. 'I haven't come to a decision yet.'

'I'm sorry, but I had to tell them about our little trip yesterday, Dom,' explained Tel. 'That's because there's been a slight change of plan that I need to discuss with you. Vince has found someone who is keen to move in as soon as possible, so he'd like to know what you plan to do. I can't leave here without getting an answer, but the good news is he will let you have it for only ten quid a week.'

Everyone awaited Dom's response.

'You'd be following in mine and your dad's footsteps,' said Tel, after a few seconds. 'We both left home early, didn't we, Ronnie?'

Dom looked puzzled. 'I never knew you served too, Tel.'

'Well, my circumstances were slightly different,' said Tel.

'I was a guest of Her Majesty for a brief while, if you get my drift.'

By the confused look on Dom's face, it was obvious he was none the wiser.

'He was banged up in the nick,' chipped in Ronnie, not missing an opportunity to stick in a verbal boot.

This was news to Dom.

'It was nothing too serious, mind you,' said Tel, 'just breaking and entering into a warehouse. Kids stuff, really. Six months in Strangeways was long enough to see the error of my ways, and look at me now. I haven't looked back since the day I walked out of those gates a free and much-changed man.'

'Aye, you're a model citizen,' said Ronnie maliciously.

'Have you made your mind up, son?' asked Iris apprehensively, returning the focus upon Dom once more.

All day at work, Dom had thought of little else. His indecisive mind had seesawed one way, then the other, then back again. Now, pressed to make a decision on the spot, he experienced a moment of clarity; the clouds of uncertainty parted. Dom now knew if he was going to leave home.

'I have,' he replied, before pausing.

'Well then,' barked Ronnie impatiently. 'What's it to be?'

CHAPTER 6

Dom walked down the garden path, went through the open front door and forced his weary limbs upstairs. On the landing, he paused at the entrance to his bedroom and leaned against the doorframe, allowing himself one final look around.

It had taken Dom over two hours to pack all of his possessions away into cardboard boxes and carry them to his car, and it now felt strange to see his bedroom looking so empty. Unexpected tears pricked his eyes as an assortment of childhood memories flashed through his mind.

'You're really going, then?'

The intrusive voice belonged to Daniel, who had sneaked up from behind.

'No,' replied Dom bitingly, taking a few paces inside the room and lifting up the last box, annoyed that his moment of poignant reflection had been disturbed. 'I just thought I'd put all my stuff into boxes and cram them in my car so I could get on *Game For A Laugh.*'

Daniel gawped at his brother, genuinely confused by his retort.

'Bloody hell, Daniel,' said Dom, shaking his head in disbelief, 'of course, I'm going.'

His sibling had never been that quick on the uptake.

A wide smile spread across Daniel's face. 'Yeesssss,' he shouted, punching the air with delight, before diving onto the bed with all the relish of a revolutionary testing out a deposed monarch's luxury sleeping quarters. 'I get the big bedroom at last.'

Daniel rolled over onto his back, put his arms behind his head and stretched out his body; he surveyed his new kingdom from floor to ceiling with wide-eyed wonder and a smug smile. Being the younger of the two brothers, Daniel had been forced to endure the smallest bedroom all of his life and had been looking forward to this moment for years.

'I bet you don't jump into my grave as fast,' remarked Dom on his way out of the door, the bulky box tucked under his chin.

'See you, pillock,' hollered Daniel, watching Dom slowly descend the stairs, bravado fuelled by the fact his brother was powerless to physically retaliate.

Dom, however, was determined to win their final verbal dispute.

'Tosser,' he replied.

'Are you two buggers at each other's throats again?' said Ronnie, as Dom walked down the garden path towards him. 'The whole street could hear you.'

'It's nothing, Dad. Just Daniel being an idiot.'

Ronnie dropped the gnarled chamois leather he had been using to clean his Ford Granada into his bucket of tepid water, and looked on with bemusement as Dom struggled to squeeze his box inside the boot of his Mini.

'You need your head looking at, son,' said Ronnie, peering through the windows of the overburdened vehicle. 'There was no need to load everything up in one go. Two trips wouldn't have hurt you.'

'I'm fine, Dad.'

'My mate Den, the decorator, would have taken you in his van. All he wanted was his petrol money and a little extra for a drink. If you have an accident in that thing, your shite will be scattered all over the place.'

Dom bit his tongue and counted to ten; he had wondered at what point his father was going to intervene and tell him exactly where he was going wrong.

'Your mate's van is full of paint and dust. I didn't want my clothes and stuff getting dirty,' he said calmly but firmly, countering the criticism.

Dom rearranged the boxes inside the boot and attempted

for a second time to close the door; to his immense relief, it clicked shut.

Unconvinced by his son's logic, Ronnie scratched the stubble on his craggy face.

'You could have put dust sheets down.'

'I'll drive slow, Dad. Real slow,' said Dom, wiping a bead of sweat from his forehead. 'Besides, there's not much traffic on the road on a Sunday.'

Ronnie shook his head dubiously to himself. He had offered his advice and assistance, and that was all he could do. He could take a horse to water but now had to let his son decide when to drink from it, to make and learn from his own mistakes.

'Are you all set, then?' said Ronnie.

Dom nodded. 'As ready as I'll ever be.'

'Right,' said Ronnie, walking purposefully down the garden path and leaning into the hallway. 'Iris. Daniel. Dom's off.'

'Do I have to come down?' replied a distant sounding Daniel.

'Yes, you bloody well have to,' snapped Ronnie. 'Now.'

Iris dutifully appeared outside, wiping her hands on her apron. She had been keeping herself busy in the kitchen, hoping in her heart of hearts that Dom would change his mind at the last minute and decide to stay at home. The sight of him standing next to his car poised to leave proved her hopes had been in vain.

'Are you absolutely sure about this?' she asked in a quivering voice, as the occasion threatened to overwhelm her.

Seeing how upset she was, and keen not to have a scene develop in public, Dom acted quickly.

'Yes, Mam,' he said, giving her a farewell hug. 'I am.'

Neighbours Davie and Glenda Stoker were approaching as Dom released his mother.

'All the best, lad,' said Davie, extending a hand to Dom.

'Ah, Dom, I can't believe you're going,' added his wife, planting a kiss on his cheek that left behind a trace of pink lipstick. 'It doesn't seem two minutes since you were only knee high, riding up and down the street on your little trike.'

'See you,' said Daniel, who had finally wandered outside.

'Enjoy your new bedroom,' said Dom.

'I will once you've gone,' Daniel replied impatiently. 'I'm dying to sort out what posters to stick on the walls.'

'Oh, have you remembered your toothbrush, Dom?' said Iris.

'Yes, Mam.'

'And don't forget to iron your shirts for work like I showed you. You'll get the hang of it if you keep practising.'

'OK, Mam. I'll have plenty of spare time on my hands.'

'And remember to read the instructions on the back of food packets before you cook. You don't want to be giving yourself food poisoning.'

Dom laughed. 'Even I can grill a burger, Mam.'

'And don't just eat fried food every day. Buy plenty of fresh fruit. You need your vitamins. You're still a growing lad.'

'OK.'

'And don't be going home drunk, switching your frying pan on and falling asleep. I don't want to be getting a knock on the door from the police to say my son's been roasted.'

'For pity's sake, woman, will you stop fussing?' interjected Ronnie, with characteristic brusqueness. 'We're going to be stood here all bloody day if you list everything that could go wrong. He's only going to be living fifteen minutes down the road. It's not as if he's emigrating to Timbuktu.'

'Dad's right, Mam,' agreed Dom, jangling his car keys while attempting to ignore the alluring aroma of roast chicken that was wafting into the street. 'I'll pop in during the week just to prove I've not gone to rack and ruin.'

'OK, son,' said Iris, reluctantly admitting defeat.

'Take care, lad,' said Ronnie, shaking Dom's hand and pressing a wad of twenty pound notes into his offspring's palm.

Dom looked at the money. 'Dad, I ...'

'Shut up and put it in your pocket. It should give you a head start for a few weeks.'

'Thanks, Dad.'

An unexpected silence fell upon the small group congregated on the pavement; the Blackburn's and Stoker's all looked at each other like actors who had forgotten who should speak the next line.

Realising the onus was on him, Dom seized the moment.

'Right, if there's nothing else, I'll be off,' he said, walking to the driver's side of the Mini.

Climbing in, he started the engine, and after a quick wave, cautiously pulled away. With all of the extra weight the car was carrying, Dom half expected his suspension to buckle and scrape along the road surface. To his immense relief, he progressed uneventfully to the end of the street.

Just before he turned right, Dom glanced in his rear view mirror. His family and neighbours were still rooted to the spot, looking down the street in his direction. To Dom, they already appeared distant and far away.

And then they were gone.

Dom drove slowly through the estate that had always been home, taking in the prominent places from his childhood. His old primary school, a Victorian structure with gothic nuances that had struck fear into him as a young child, now looked like a harmless, antiquated building that belonged in a bygone age. Beside it was the comprehensive school where he had played football, acted the fool and occasionally broken the rules; with the new academic year a week away, it stood vacant and silent.

The last place of note for Dom was the local cemetery, which he had frequently used as a shortcut to the playing fields, woods and farmland that lay beyond, places he would escape to as a youngster on weekends and during school holidays.

All those days, months and years of his past were gone forever, confined to the mists of time.

It was time to begin a new chapter in his life.

CHAPTER 7

Unceremoniously dumping the final box on the living room carpet, an exhausted Dom was sorely tempted to flop down on the sofa and put his feet up. He knew, however, if he stopped then all motivation would be lost, with his possessions cluttering up the floor space for days to come.

Deciding the best course of action was a brief break for a revitalising cup of coffee, he located the box that had 'KITCHEN' written on the side in black felt-tip pen and rifled through the newspaper wrapped contents until he located his beloved Newcastle United mug.

In the kitchen, Dom took the precaution of sniffing inside the battered and tarnished kettle that sat on one of the rear oven rings. Satisfied that there was nothing putrefying inside, he gave it a quick rinse, filled it with fresh water, lit the gas ring and placed the kettle on top of the roaring flame.

While he waited for the water to boil, Dom trawled through the box marked 'FOOD ETC' for the jar of coffee he had bought on his shopping trip to Presto the previous day.

When the whistling kettle lured him back into the kitchen, Dom suddenly realised he had no milk. Recalling that Staveley had mentioned something about shops being situated on the estate, he decided to venture out into the labyrinth estate for the first time, more in hope than expectation that he would find any open on a Sunday afternoon when the whole world seemed to shut down.

Standing by the phone box outside the block of flats, Dom had a choice of walking left or right. Opting to go right, he felt conspicuous and out of place as he walked down the unfamiliar, empty street.

As he continued on his quest down the adjoining street, Dom was just beginning to wonder where everybody was when he spotted a male head bobbing about behind a perimeter garden hedge.

As he neared, Dom saw that the man was busy trimming it with a set of shears. Their eyes met, and the suspicious, unfriendly stare he received made Dom think twice about asking directions. He walked by, head down, seething inside that a complete stranger should look at him so judgementally without knowing the first thing about him.

Thankfully, Dom soon came to two youngsters playing football on a small patch of grass who were happy to point him in the right direction.

Set back slightly from the road, Ravi's General Store was the end property in a short row of businesses that included a barber's shop, a bank and a butcher's. To Dom's relief it was open.

A bell fitted to the door chimed as Dom entered.

A middle-aged Asian shopkeeper, sitting behind his counter watching a black and white portable television fixed to the wall, glared at Dom.

'Hello,' said Dom cheerfully. 'I'm after a pint of milk, mate.'

The man pointed to the rear of the store without taking his eyes off Dom.

'Down the back,' he said impassively.

'Right, cheers,' replied Dom, picking up a shopping basket.

The shop contained a couple of aisles packed with the most common of convenience groceries and snacks: jars of coffee, packets of teabags, pot noodles, soups, tins of beans and spaghetti, as well as plentiful supplies of biscuits, chocolate bars, packets of sweets, crisps and cans of pop.

The final aisle consisted of a freezer and refrigerated section, from which Dom plucked a pint of milk from the dozen or so bottles remaining. While browsing the shelves, the pizzas, packs of bacon, and bags of chips caught his eye. With the bundle of money burning a hole in his pocket, Dom grabbed one of each and dropped them into his basket.

On his way towards the counter to pay for his goods, Dom stopped by a magazine rack and picked out the only remaining copy of *New Musical Express*. He opened it up and began to scan the contents of the issue to ensure there were enough articles of interest to justify buying it.

While working his way through its inky pages, Dom became aware of someone standing in close proximity to him, sighing loudly with indignation every couple of seconds.

'Are you going to stand there and read the whole thing or actually buy it?' the stranger eventually blurted out.

Shocked by the sheer audacity of the question, Dom turned round to find a slightly older, serious-looking male scowling at him.

What instantly struck Dom about his confronter was his distinct sense of style. Wearing dark tinted glasses, he had layered hair, parted at the centre, which offset an angular face; an unzipped parka coat revealed a grey suit, and blue check button-down shirt underneath. With a pair of black and white Gibson shoes completing the image, he was possibly the coolest looking person Dom had ever set eyes on in the flesh, and not the type of character he had expected to bump into on The Acorns housing estate.

'Well?' pressed the stranger, frantically chewing gum while peering down at Dom over the top of his glasses that sat perched on the tip of his aquiline nose.

'Help yourself, mate,' replied Dom diplomatically, closing the magazine and handing it over.

'Cheers,' said the stranger, snatching it eagerly from Dom; without another word, he walked away.

Dom chose a copy of *Sounds* from the rack, dropped it into his basket without even bothering to look through it, and ambled over to the counter once the ill-mannered male had left the shop.

Taking Dom's basket from him, the shopkeeper tapped in

the cost of the items on the keys of his antiquated till and put the goods into a plastic bag, all the while keeping one eye on the television set.

'Two pounds and sixty-one pence, please.'

Dom handed over a twenty pound note; as he waited for his change, a young boy of five or six years of age appeared from a door marked 'Staff Only', ran up to him and pretended to fire his toy cowboy gun. Dom laughed as the youngster went haring off down one of the aisles.

'Was that boy bothering you before?' asked the man, handing over Dom's change.

Dom shook his head. 'He's all right; he's only playing.'

'Not my son, Imran. I meant the boy who was in here a moment ago.'

'Oh, him,' said Dom, as it dawned on him who the shopkeeper was referring to.

'Such a rude boy,' explained the man. 'Never says hello or thank you. Good manners cost nothing. I think it is because he delivered newspapers for me when he was young, until I caught him stealing. I had to let him go. Such a shame,' he concluded, shaking his head sadly. 'But never mind him, tell me about yourself. You are new here, yes?'

'Just moved in today.'

The owner's original mistrustful expression turned into a wide smile.

'New residents. Fantastic news. My name is Ravi. You tell your parents that anything they need, Ravi is here from six in the morning to eleven at night. The customer is always right and I always do right by my customers, that is my saying. If you want something, come to Ravi. If it is not on the shelf, then tell me and I will look in my stockroom. I have many things to sell but so little shelf space.'

'Pleased to meet you,' replied Dom, transferring his shopping bag to his left hand and reaching over the counter with his other to shake Ravi's. 'I'm Dom.'

'Where have you moved to?'

'The flats. Harold Wilson House.'

'They are very small to house a family,' Ravi said, his face furrowed in puzzlement.

'Well, there's only me living there.'

'But you look so young. How old are you?'

'I'm nineteen early next year.'

'Oh, forgive me, Dom. I do not mean to pry. Tell me to mind my own business.'

'That's OK, Ravi,' said Dom.

'You are a student?'

'No, I work at Donnelly's in Durham City.'

Ravi nodded and smiled approvingly. 'I know it well. I have bought many of my household goods from there over the years. They are all good quality. There is no substitute for well-made items.'

The bell on the door rang again as a new customer entered.

'Well, I look forward to seeing you many times, Dom,' said Ravi. 'We will have plenty of opportunities to chat then.'

'OK, mate,' replied Dom, heading for the exit.

Outside on the pavement, Dom glanced at the local advertisements on display in the shop window, with one in particular catching his eye. He edged closer to read it in full:

Local band requires singer ASAP for future gigs.
Influences include The Jam, Kinks, Small Faces, Beatles,
Who, Joy Division etc. New Romantics need NOT apply.
No time wasters. Ring Matty Parker on 41226.

Not in the habit of carrying a pen around with him, Dom endeavoured to commit the name and telephone number to memory until he returned home.

He had only walked thirty metres, saying the telephone number over and over like a zealous religious disciple learning a new mantra, when shouting from behind disrupted his concentration.

'Mr Dom. Mr Dom. Wait, please.'

Dom turned round to discover an out of breath Ravi, half running and half walking, approaching him.

'I would like to give you a house warming present,' he said, handing Dom a bottle of wine.

Dom looked at the dusty bottle. The faded label was peeling away at the edges and the wine itself was hardly a vintage, but the unexpected gesture from someone he had only just met was gratifying.

'That's great, Ravi. Thanks very much,' he said.

'No problem,' replied Ravi, waving away Dom's gratitude. 'I must get back. I asked Mrs Smith to keep an eye on the store for a moment. You have a nice first evening.'

'OK, Ravi. See you.'

Once back inside his flat, Dom finally had his coffee.

His next task following that was to carry the boxes containing his cooking equipment, crockery, cutlery and food into the kitchen, where he unpacked them into the cupboards and drawers.

Ready to cook his first ever meal as a tenant in his own home, Dom placed two rashers of bacon underneath the overhead grill and put a saucepan full of tinned spaghetti onto an oven ring. While they sizzled and puttered away, he stared thoughtfully at the name and telephone number he had scribbled down on the cover of his copy of *Sounds*.

Dom had always dreamt about becoming a singer, the seeds of his ambition sown as a young child when he would grab a hairbrush and pretend it was a microphone whenever his mother played her pop records. As he moved into his teenage years, Dom would spend hours in his bedroom enthusiastically singing along to his rapidly growing record collection. In such moments of fantasy, anything had seemed possible.

In the cold light of day, however, making the transition from being an unknown in a bedroom in Spennymoor to a pop star known to millions seemed impossible to achieve. The small town, situated in County Durham in the North East of England, was a million miles away from the bright lights of London where all the main movers and shakers in the music industry resided.

In the spring of nineteen eighty, Dom had attempted to find an outlet for his musical yearnings by pinning a poster on the school noticeboard that invited all interested musicians to audition for a new band.

The response was encouraging.

Over the course of the following week, eight hopefuls came forward to demonstrate their talents. Of this initial bunch, Dom invited half to join him in forming a band.

Despite serious misgivings, Ronnie Blackburn arranged with the steward of the local social club for them to rehearse in the upstairs function room on a Saturday morning before it opened for business. Mindful that the all-important O Level examinations were a matter of weeks away, Ronnie would have preferred all extracurricular distractions to be kept to a minimum; he also did not want his good name tarnished with the club committee should anyone damage property or make a nuisance of themselves. Dom, however, swore to apply himself whole-heartedly to his revision studies in exchange for this one concession. Believing that to be a fair agreement, Ronnie gave his permission.

In the end, Ronnie need not have worried. Only three half-hearted, shambolic sessions took place over the space of a month before Dom terminated the venture, frustrated by individuals failing to turn up and the debilitating effect of personality differences. Dom consoled himself by vowing to pick up the threads of the group upon his return to school in September.

Once his examinations were finally behind him, Dom had

found a temporary part-time job as a general assistant at Donnelly's department store in Durham City, holding no great ambitions for the post beyond earning some much-needed cash; he fully believed, as did his parents, that he would resume his education come the autumn.

When Dom entered the final week of his employment in late August, he was surprised to receive the offer of a permanent full-time position. Without asking for time to talk it over with his parents, he accepted on the spot.

When Dom explained to his parents that evening what he had done, it initially produced a mixed response: his mother was supportive, but his father, predictably, hit the roof. Dom was eventually only able to pacify him by declaring he had taken the job because he was strongly considering a career in the armed forces in the next couple of years, and would rather earn money in the meantime than waste time studying. With Ronnie keen for both of his sons to benefit from a military career, this argument was enough to placate him for the time being.

Dom's unexpected career path in retail also conspired to curtail his immediate musical aspirations, removing him from the social environment he had been relying upon to nurture a new band.

Following his successful application to the navy, Dom's doubts began to deepen as his join up date loomed. He visited his grandad on the pretext of saying his farewells, as the old man was too unwell to attend the leaving party. Accurately perceiving there was something troubling his grandson, Bill Armitage managed to tease out the whole story. It was then that he gave one final piece of advice to Dom.

'Listen, son,' he began, attempting to encapsulate the experience he had accumulated over three score and ten years into a few succinct words, 'if the navy is for you, then walk out that door with your head held high and go and enjoy every bloody minute of it. However, if something else is calling you, an urge that overrides everything else, then you have to go with your heart, otherwise you might just spend the rest of your days wondering "what if". Remember what I've always said to you, son. Follow your dreams.'

Feeling fortified after his meal, Dom spent the next couple of hours unpacking the rest of his boxes, before celebrating a successful conclusion to a day that had been long and tiring by pouring himself a glass of wine.

He then put on a record, sat down on the carpet, and thumbed through his music collection in preparation for making a new compilation audio tape to mark the occasion of finally achieving his independence.

As he cogitated over which tracks to include, Dom was surprised to hear a loud knock at the front door. Who could be calling at such a late hour? He turned the music down and listened.

There it was again.

He got to his feet and walked down the passageway to answer it.

'Evening, Dom.'

'Oh, Mr Staveley.'

The last person Dom had expected to find on his doorstep was his new landlord.

'Hey, I told you not to be so formal. Just call me Vince. I was in the area, so thought I'd pop round.'

'Erm … come on in,' said Dom.

'I see you're already making yourself at home,' said Staveley in the living room, surveying Dom's houseplants and framed Athena poster of the Manhattan skyline.

'There's not a problem, is there?' Dom asked, curious as to the reason for the visit.

Staveley's booming laugh filled the room. 'No, nothing like that. I just thought I'd bring you a little house-warming present.'

He handed Dom the plastic bag he was carrying.

'No prizes for originality, I'm afraid, but your uncle told me you're fond of a drop of vodka.'

Dom removed the bottle from the bag. 'Thanks, Vince. Would you like a drink? I've got a spare glass in the kitchen somewhere.'

'No thanks, son. I'd best be on my way. My girlfriend is waiting in the car for me. She'll chew my nuts off if I keep her waiting any longer than two minutes. Birds, eh? They can be a real pain at times. Can't live with them and can't live without them.'

Dom laughed along agreeably, as if the problem of demanding females was something he, too, suffered on a regular basis.

'Madness, eh,' said Staveley, picking up and inspecting the cover of the record that was playing. 'I'm a bit more old school, myself ... Buddy Holly, The Everley Brothers, Gene Vincent ... now they're real rock 'n' rollers. They don't make them like that anymore. I can let you borrow some, if you like?'

'That's OK, Vince. My mother has a lot of those records.'

'All right, not to worry,' said Staveley, starting to walk back down the passageway towards the exit. 'Anything you need, Dom, or you're not happy with, be it a leaking tap, draughty window or damp on the walls, just let me know. I like to nip any problems in the bud. If you ignore them, they just get bigger and become a real pain in the arse. That's a little piece of philosophy I like to carry with me through life. It's always served me well up to now.'

'Will do, Vince.'

Once back outside on the gangway, Staveley faced Dom.

'Well, see you later, son. I imagine you've got a million and one better things to be doing on your first night than talking to an old fart like me. I'll be seeing Tel tomorrow. I'll let him know you've settled in.'

'Thanks.'

Dom closed the door and breathed a sigh of relief. He hoped it was, as Staveley had intimated, a one-off visit; he was not keen for their relationship to become anything beyond that of landlord and tenant.

CHAPTER 8

'It looks like you've been sleeping in some of these,' said Iris Blackburn disapprovingly, as she sorted her son's dirty laundry into piles on her kitchen floor.

Dom's mouth was too full of bacon, egg, beans and sausage to offer a coherent reply; a grunt was all he could muster.

'Don't try to talk with your mouth full,' she said, aghast at the speed with which he was consuming his late breakfast.

'Is there any tea on the go, Mam?' said Dom, once he had swallowed his food.

'I've only got one pair of hands, son,' said Iris irritably, throwing a heap of jeans into the washing machine and firmly closing the door; she turned the knob to the correct washing temperature and set the device away.

'What time's dinner?' enquired Dom, noticing the raw slab of beef on the kitchen bench.

Iris put her hands on her hips and looked at her son in amazement.

'You haven't even finished that yet. I hope you're cooking proper meals over at that flat of yours. It's important to eat a balanced diet, you know.'

His mother's cooking was the one thing he had missed most in the six weeks since he had moved out. Lacking the aptitude or inclination required to cook a half-decent meal from raw ingredients, Dom frequently chose the easy option of takeaways and convenience meals from Ravi's shop. Some evenings, he was simply content to survive on a diet of pot noodles and chocolate.

'I do my best, Mam,' said Dom vaguely, hoping that would put the matter to bed for the time being; he was in no mood for unnecessary earache on his day off.

Seemingly placated by his response, or not inclined to push

the issue, Iris prepared a pot of tea.

'Have you made any friends yet?' she asked.

'Kind of,' said Dom, 'but I've not met them yet.'

Her son's cryptic remark stopped Iris dead in her tracks.

'You'll have to explain that one to me. I may be a little slow at times, but that didn't make any sense to me at all.'

'I've got an audition with a band tonight.'

Iris looked blank. 'But you don't play any brass instruments.'

'Not a brass band, Mam. I mean a pop band. I'm auditioning tonight to be their singer.'

Dom had spent five weeks plucking up the courage to ring the telephone number from the advert displayed in Ravi's window. Finally, in mid-week he had taken the plunge. Answered by the mother of Matty Parker, she explained that her son was currently not at home, but that he would be delighted that someone had finally responded. She then gave Dom the time and location of rehearsals, and told him it would be fine to turn up at the next one that weekend.

'Don't go mentioning this to your father,' warned Iris. 'You know how touchy he is, especially after … well, you know …'

How could Dom forget? The repercussions of his decision to remain in Durham continued to resonate to that day.

'I hope it's not one of those punk groups,' continued Iris. 'So unclean and foul-mouthed they are, spitting everywhere and swearing. They should be ashamed of themselves.'

'I'm not that daft, Mam. Then again, I've always quite fancied the idea of a Mohican.'

'You get a Mohican, my lad, and you'll not set foot in this house until you cut it off,' said Iris, flaring up.

'Don't get your knickers in a twist,' said Dom lightly.

'I'm not,' screeched Iris, failing to detect she was being teased. 'Your idea of what's normal and mine are completely different.'

Dom sighed. 'I thought you wanted me to make friends, Mam. And music's my thing, just like knitting's yours and the allotment and darts are Dad's.'

'Just as long as you don't dress in clothes that will embarrass me.'

Dom leapt to his feet and jokingly saluted her. 'Scout's honour, Mam. I promise.'

'Sit down, you silly bugger,' she laughed. 'You were only in the scouts for a week until they kicked you out.'

'And I've lived with the pain of the rejection all these years,' he said.

Their good-natured banter made Dom realise just how much he missed these moments, just the two of them chatting and having a laugh.

'You're always welcome back here, you know,' said Iris seriously, changing tone. 'This is still your home, whatever your father says. I hate to think of you sitting alone every night. It's not healthy.'

'I know, Mam.'

'Speaking of your father, did you remember it's his birthday today?'

The vacant expression on her son's face told Iris all she needed to know.

'Oh, Dominic, you're on another planet sometimes. Did you not buy him a card at least?'

Dom shook his head guiltily.

'Well, it's just as well I bought a spare one, isn't it? I'll go and get it.'

Dom breathed a sigh of relief. Good old Mam, always popping up to save the day with a 'Get Out Of Jail' card when he least expected it.

'Here's a pen,' she said, upon her return. 'Write it out straight away, and then go next door to Davie's. Your father only went there to lend him a saw, and that was an hour ago. You know what Davie's like when he gets talking. Take your father down to the club for a couple of hours while I prepare the dinner. I can't be done with both of you under my feet when I'm trying to get on.'

'Oh, do I have to?' Dom protested. 'I haven't read the newspaper yet.'

'Yes, you do,' she said. 'The pair of you have been acting like a pair of kids the past month, barely speaking to each other. It's about time you had a civilised conversation.'

The dialogue was strained between father and son on the walk to the social club; Dom knew the next couple of hours were going to drag if the frostiness showed no sign of thawing.

The atmosphere inside the bustling hostelry was boisterous but convivial.

'You get them in, son. I'll be sitting over there next to old Billy,' said Ronnie, indicating a pensioner sitting alone at the back of the room, gazing thoughtfully into space.

Trade was brisk at the bar, with the two female members of staff working flat out. Having patiently waited his turn, Dom returned five minutes later with their drinks.

'Bloody hell, what kept you?' said Ronnie abruptly.

'It's heaving, Dad,' said Dom.

'You just need to have the knack to get served fast, son. Anyway, cheers,' he said, raising his pint glass. 'I thought you'd forgotten.'

Dom's face went red.

'Happy birthday, Dad.'

'Oh, I don't really celebrate them now,' said Ronnie, 'not the way I used to when I was younger.'

'And definitely not when you get to my age,' added Billy, unprompted.

'How old are you now?' said Ronnie, turning to the old man.

'Eighty-seven,' said Billy.

'That's living history sitting right there,' said Ronnie,

turning back to his son. 'Fought in the First World War, did Billy. In the trenches, in France.'

Billy nodded in agreement, but added nothing further to the conversation.

'How are things going with you?' said Ronnie to Dom. 'We've not really chatted since you left.'

'Great, Dad. I'm really enjoying it.'

'And there's me thinking you'd have come home with your tail between your legs by now.'

'There's no chance of that happening,' said Dom.

'I've heard it's a bit posh. Coppers and screws live there, don't they?'

'Not posh. It's just more … modern,' said Dom, choosing his words carefully.

'You're managing your bills OK, are you?'

Dom nodded.

'So, it's all plain sailing, eh?'

'Not exactly, but I'm coping. How about you, Dad? What's going on in the world of shipbuilding?'

Ronnie frowned.

Dom sensed he had accidentally touched upon a sensitive topic.

'Everything's up in the air at the moment, son. We've lost a contract we were expected to win, which means heads are going to roll if nothing changes.'

'Redundancies?'

Ronnie nodded. 'Them buggers in London don't give a toss about the likes of us. Hopefully, it's just a temporary blip. I shudder to think what will happen otherwise.'

'Fingers crossed then, Dad.'

'Aye, fingers crossed.'

CHAPTER 9

Matty Parker was in good spirits as he closed the front door of his parents' house behind him, clambered onto his scooter and commenced his short journey into town.

The early evening roads were quiet, and he was able to make brisk progress. Within minutes, he was tearing down Gilesgate Bank before joining the main approach road to the city centre. Veering onto the cobbled slip road off Walkergate Bridge, Matty turned left into Back Silver Street, rode down the dimly lit, narrow lane as far as it allowed and parked next to the solitary blue Ford van.

There was a spring in his step as he walked towards Gray's Yard rehearsal room, anonymously located in the middle of a row of antiquated single storey buildings that backed on to the River Wear. In recent years, most of the properties had fallen into a state of decay and dereliction, the industries that necessitated their construction in the first place long since confined to a bygone era.

As he bounded up the short flight of steps with his long, wiry legs, Matty heard from within the sound of enthusiastic drum rolls and the low rumble of a bass guitar.

He entered and strode buoyantly into the centre of the small room, hoping to discover a new face among them. When it immediately became obvious only the usual band members of Northern Circle were present, Matty gestured for silence from Mick Pearson, warming up on his set of drums, and Brian Drake, methodically tuning his instrument.

'Lads, I just might be the bearer of great news,' Matty grinned.

'What's that, then?' asked Mick, his spotty forehead peering over the top of his kit.

'What's the one thing that we've been missing all these weeks? The one thing that will finally allow us to make some much needed progress.'

'Blanko's agreed to return, has he?' said Brian.

Matty's face screwed up as if he had just sucked on a lemon.

'That tosser,' he spat, with inflamed ire. 'I wouldn't have him back if he was the last singer on planet earth.'

Blanko had been their one and only official singer to date, recruited by Matty at the band's inception at the turn of the year, together with Mick and Brian. Christening themselves Northern Circle, they had gone on to rehearse for months until they could adequately perform over an hour's worth of cover versions. When their debut gig was booked at a local pub for early June, it had appeared all of their hard work was about to pay off. The excitement and jubilation Matty and the band felt at this development, however, was short-lived; on the eve of their performance, Blanko failed to show up for the band's final rehearsal. When Matty called at Blanko's home, the missing singer's father informed Matty that his son had travelled to Spain to follow the England football team at the World Cup tournament. No one in Durham had set eyes on Blanko since; it was rumoured he had stayed on in Spain when the tournament finished to sing in the pubs of Benidorm.

Unable to perform any gigs without a singer, the three remaining members had put aside their disappointment as best they could. Matty had temporarily assumed vocal duties during subsequent rehearsals, but was under no illusion that his voice was of the required quality on a long-term basis.

As summer faded into autumn, and with no end in sight to their search for a new frontman, a disillusioned Matty had been tempted to quit, until the telephone call four nights ago that suddenly offered a glimmer of hope.

Mick's eyes widened, daring to think the unthinkable. 'Have we got a singer?' he said, raising his eyebrows.

Matty nodded. 'All that money spent on placing ads in the

national music papers with not a dicky bird to show for it, and then we go and get a response from a postcard in my local shop.'

'Well, I've actually been thinking about calling it a day,' added Brian unhelpfully. 'Pauline's been chewing my ear off for weeks. She thinks I should be doing something useful on a Sunday night like tiling the bathroom instead of wasting my time playing bass.'

'Don't be daft, Brian,' countered Matty. 'Not now we may have someone to fill Blanko's shoes. And, you work hard all week long. You deserve to enjoy yourself at least once a week.'

'You call this enjoyment?'

Matty ignored Brian's remark as he unbuttoned his parka and folded it over the back of a chair. He then removed his electric guitar from its case, strapped it on and plugged it into his amplifier.

'What's he called?' asked Mick, poised to resume his warm up.

Matty scratched the back of his head thoughtfully. 'I'm not sure, to be honest. My mother took the call.'

Matty rubbed his hands together to generate some warmth in his fingers. With the room having only a small paraffin heater, the temperature indoors felt nearly as cold as the October evening outside.

'But he's definitely coming, is he?' pressed Brian.

'Yeah, I think so. My mother told him where to come. The lad didn't leave a telephone number, so I couldn't ring him back to confirm.'

Brian was unconvinced. 'And he's never tried to get back in touch?'

'No,' said Matty softly, suddenly realising how unconvincing his story sounded when held up for scrutiny.

'So, all you've had,' continued Brian, 'is a call from someone who didn't leave a name, contact number or address, or even a firm answer that he will definitely be here tonight. That sounds more like a wind-up to me.'

'He'll be here,' retorted Matty touchily, underwhelmed by the lack of praise for achieving a potential major breakthrough in recruitment.

'We'll see,' said Brian, his reservations suggesting the guitarist and stand-in singer's optimism was misplaced.

'Let's just start and continue as normal,' said Mick, keen to avoid a bust up.' "Substitute" first?'

For half an hour, they played the same set of songs as always in the same tired order. As the minutes passed and still no one showed up, the euphoria that Matty had felt upon arrival began to dissipate until the evening bore all the characteristics of a typical Sunday rehearsal: a miserable experience with its participants just going through the motions.

Matty felt foolish for having raised the hopes of everyone based on unsubstantiated information, and was now feeling angry at the whole world. He was mad with Blanko for creating the situation in the first place, with Brian's wife for deeming domestic DIY activities as being more important than the band, and with himself for not having been at home when the caller had telephoned.

The musicians were fast approaching the halfway stage of the evening, the point when they usually had a swift break for a cigarette and a hot drink. Matty was anticipating a fresh bout of complaints about the singer's no-show, judging by the grim expression on the face of Brian.

Matty had just begun to sing the opening line of Joy Division's "Transmission" when the outside door opened, and a youth tentatively popped his head into the room. In that instant, Matty's heart leapt for joy. He stopped playing immediately and gestured for the new arrival to enter.

'Hi,' said the nervous looking male. 'I'm looking for Matty Parker.'

'That's me. Are you the lad who rang last week about the singer vacancy?'

'Yeah.'

Matty walked across the room and shook his hand warmly.

'Great to meet you. I'm Matty.'

'I'm sorry for being late.'

'You're here now, that's all that matters. Let me introduce you to the others. That's Brian on the bass, and Mick is our drummer. Lads, this is … sorry, what's your name, mate?'

'Dom.'

'This is Dom. Right then, Dom, we can chat more in a bit, but first, how about we let you sing a couple of songs? Do you know "Transmission", what we were just playing a second ago?'

'Yeah.'

'Great. OK, lads, let's give it a go. Dom, we play it in the original key, if that's OK with you?'

'No problem,' said Dom, walking over to the spare microphone resting on its stand, before switching it on and testing it with a couple of one-twos.

As Brian began to play the rudimentary opening riff on his bass guitar, Dom removed his navy Harrington jacket. With nowhere in easy reach on which to hang it, he dropped it onto the floor by his feet.

As the guitar and drums joined in the introduction, Dom attempted to compose himself. Standing alone in the privacy of his bedroom holding a hairbrush while posing in the mirror was one thing; a room full of strangers with all attention acutely focused on his every sung note was quite another.

It was now or never.

His throat felt dry and tight, as if a pair of hands had begun to throttle him; his stomach knotted, and for a split second Dom thought he was going to be physically sick.

Taking a deep breath, he closed his eyes and prepared to attempt to justify to everyone why he deserved a chance.

For all his familiarity with the Joy Division track, Dom struggled during the opening half, with the cold air and jangling nerves affecting the quality of his vocals. Towards the end, however, he began to feel more at ease; his initial worries faded and an element of confidence returned. There were a couple of bum notes sung, but in the main Dom felt he had given a good account of himself.

'Not bad, Dom,' said Matty, when they had finished playing, 'not bad at all.'

The guitarist then handed Dom a sheet of paper containing the names of several dozen songs.

'OK, the ball's in your court, Dom. Shout out any song on here that you know, and we'll run through it.'

Dom scanned the list, featuring tracks by the likes of Elvis Costello, The Doors, The Kinks, The Stones, The Beatles, Blondie, Joy Division, and The Jam. Some he knew inside out, while others were familiar enough for him to hum along to, but not to sing all the way through.

' "Break On Through",' he said finally, before adding as an aside, 'Joy Division's singer loved Morrison, you know.'

'Doesn't bode well for you, if they're your two role models,' quipped Matty, as he quickly found the notes for the riff. 'One dead at twenty-seven and the other even younger. Good for the rest of us, though. We could make a mint on all our records storming the charts if our singer dies on us.'

They began to play the song, with each member studiously immersed within their own individual role. As it neared its raucous conclusion, Matty had a huge grin on his face.

'If you can sing every song as good as that, Dom, I hope you live to at least see your thirties,' said Matty drily.

Mick laughed, and even Brian was unable to suppress a slight grin.

It was not just Matty's jokey banter that had restored a feel-good factor, but the realisation that, in the space of only two songs, the months of frustration at being a rudderless band had been instantly stripped away; all of a sudden, they sounded like a half decent act and it felt good.

As they launched into "Going Underground", Dom began to lose his inhibitions, removing the microphone from its stand and pacing the room as he sang, as if playing to a full house at Madison Square Garden instead of a near empty room in Durham City.

Two more songs followed. Dom acquitted himself well, with the occasional humorously adlibbed line drawing approving smirks and nods of the head from Matty and Mick; Brian remained locked in his own world, unwaveringly focused upon the notes he was playing.

'Okay,' broke in Matty, glancing at his watch. 'Let's take a quick break. Ten minutes, yeah?'

Brian leaned his instrument against the wall, pulled a handful of change from his jeans pocket and piled it on top of the payphone in preparation for making a telephone call; Mick wiped the sweat from his face with a beer towel, before getting up from behind his drum kit to go to the bathroom.

'Who wants coffee?' Matty shouted.

'White, no sugar,' said Brian.

The drinks machine clunked and whirred into life when Matty inserted his money and made a selection.

Dom pulled on his jacket and headed for the exit. Adrenalin was rushing through him, and he needed a cigarette.

He walked up the lane and stopped by a waist high wall that overlooked the murky river.

With a plastic cup in each hand, Matty joined him a moment later, swirls of steam rising off them into the night air.

'Fancy a coffee?' he said.

'Thanks.'

'Quick, mate,' urged Matty, as liquid sloshed from the near full container, 'it's burning my bloody fingers.'

Dom took hold of his drink and blew on it before taking a tentative sip. It was weak and scalding hot. He placed it on top of the moss-covered wall.

'Very impressive vocals in there, Dom,' said Matty. 'Sounds like you've done this type of thing before.'

'Cheers,' replied Dom, with as much humility as he could manage. 'Actually, I'm new to this. All my singing's been done in the shower up until now.'

Dom opted not to mention his brief and disastrous outing with his schoolmates.

'Really?' said Matty in amazement. 'You're as good as anyone I've ever heard in this city. I thought you must have been doing this for ages.'

Dom took another drink of his coffee. 'How long's the band been going?' he asked.

'Nine months.'

'How many gigs have you played?'

Matty looked slightly sheepish. 'None yet,' he admitted, proceeding to fill Dom in about Blanko and how the vacancy for a singer had come about.

'What are the others like?' said Dom, when Matty finished.

'Mick's a good mate and a solid drummer. Brian's shit hot on the bass, but that's offset by the fact that heavy metal is his first love. If it was up to him, we'd be doing Motorhead and Rainbow covers. Also, he doesn't think he should be told what to do by someone ten years his junior, meaning he can be a bit stroppy when he wants to be.'

'He looks old enough to be my dad,' said Dom plainly.

Matty laughed. 'He's had a hard paper round, and he's not very cutting edge on the fashion front, either, but he's still an important member. We'd be up shit creek without him, truth be told.'

'Why's that?' asked a perplexed Dom.

Pointing to the van, a wry grin lit up Matty's features.

'Because he's the one with a vehicle big enough to transport all of our gear to rehearsals and gigs, if we ever get any.'

Pausing to take a draw on his cigarette, Matty continued.

'You know, your face looks dead familiar, Dom. Are you from this neck of the woods?'

'Spennymoor, originally. I moved to Gilesgate a few weeks ago.'

'I live there. What do you think of it?'

'I've not been anywhere yet, apart from the pub on Sunderland Road once or twice.'

'Come out with us one night, if you like. I'll show you the best pubs to go to and the ones to avoid.'

'Nice one. I'd like that. Does that mean I'm in?'

'Too right, you're in.'

'Do you not have to clear it with Mick and Brian first?' said Dom, nodding in the direction of the rehearsal room from where the sound of renewed musical activity had begun to filter up the street.

'You're in regardless of what they say, but I'll go through the rigmarole of asking them, just to keep them sweet. At the end of the day, though, my decision is final. However, I need to know that you're really serious about this, and that you're going to turn up to all the rehearsals and not mess us about.'

'No sweat, Matty. I'm deadly serious,' he stated, with maximum conviction. 'I want this to be a success so that I'm not stuck in a dead-end job all my life.'

'Where do you work?' said Matty.

'In the stockroom at Donnelly's. The pay's not fantastic, but it's a proper job that just about covers my bills, and it's not a shitty youth scheme. What about you?'

'I'm still at university in Newcastle doing poxy business and finance. I've only been doing it to buy me some time to make a real go of music before I have to get a job. Hopefully things will take off soon, but I've just started my final year, so time is running out.'

Dom flicked the butt of his cigarette into the river. 'Shall

76

we go back inside?' he said, keen to complete the practice session and officially cement his position in the band. He began to walk back towards the building.

'Hang on a minute,' shouted Matty.

Dom stopped in his tracks. 'Yeah.'

'Since you walked through the door tonight,' said Matty, 'it's been bugging me where I've seen you before, and it's just come back to me. It was in Ravi's shop.'

The penny suddenly dropped with Dom. 'That's right,' he said, casting his mind back to the day he had gone in search of milk. 'You just about mugged me for the last copy of the *NME*, if I recall correctly.'

Dom grinned to show he was not being serious.

'I needed to check my advert was in that week's edition, and there was an article I wanted to read on The Jam. I would have just had a quick look and handed it back to you, but Ravi's a bit precious about people reading his stock without buying it. He watches you like a bloody hawk.'

'He doesn't speak very highly of you, either.'

Matty smirked knowingly. 'Ah, he's OK, really. I just like to wind him up a bit; he takes the bait every time. It's my little act of revenge for him sacking me from my paper round years ago.'

'He mentioned that, too.'

'Caught me slipping a *Razzle* into one of the newspapers. It was one of the perks of the job, besides the occasional Mars Bar finding its way into my pocket.' Matty threw away the dregs of his cup. 'You're right. We'd better get back inside. Brian will have a fit if we overrun and he gets home late. His missus will think he's got a bit on the side and all hell will break loose.'

Half an hour later, Northern Circle rounded off the evening with a frantic version of "Heat Wave". At the end of the song, Matty whipped off his guitar and placed it on its stand, the final chord reverberating around the room.

'Right, lads,' said Matty, wiping the perspiration from his forehead, 'before we head off, let's take a vote on Dom. All those who want him in raise your right hand.'

The vote was unanimous.

'There you go, Dom. You've just witnessed a minor miracle. We've all agreed on the same thing for the first time ever. Welcome to Northern Circle.'

'Cheers, lads,' said Dom appreciatively to the other members, already busying themselves with dismantling and packing away equipment.

Weary from his exertions, Dom leaned against the wall, palpably relieved to have passed his first test with flying colours.

'We rehearse every Sunday evening, Dom,' explained Matty, crouching down to place his guitar inside its protective case. 'Once we get some gigs lined up, we'll fit in a weeknight session, too, in order to fine tune our act. Is that good for you?'

Dom nodded. 'The more the merrier. I've got sod all else to do.'

'Right, the only other rule is everyone mucks in with carrying the instruments and equipment to Brian's van. He stores everything, apart from Mick's drum kit, in his garage during the week.'

'You go a whole week without playing your guitar?'

'No. I've got another one at home.'

It only took five minutes for them to load everything into the rear of Brian's dented and rusting van.

'Right, I've got to get going,' said Brian, hurriedly climbing into the driver's seat. 'Come on, Mick.'

'See you next week, lads,' said Mick, getting into the passenger side.

As the van sped away up the lane, Matty sat on his scooter and put his helmet on.

'Brian and Mick both live at Bowburn,' he said, 'so Mick

always cops for a lift. How did you get here tonight?'

'I've got a car but fancied the walk.'

'You're welcome to a lift if you don't mind sitting on the back.'

'No, thanks,' said Dom. 'I know it's a cool looking bike, but I'm not that keen on two wheels.'

'Suit yourself. Listen, about that night out I mentioned earlier. Me and Mick will be down town next Saturday night, so why don't you come out to celebrate joining?'

'Sounds good to me,' said Dom, who knew he would scream if he spent one more weekend alone in his flat with a four pack of lager for company while watching subtitled French films on BBC2. 'I'll give you a ring.'

'OK,' said Matty, starting the engine. Pulling away, he tooted his horn as he disappeared into the shadows.

Walking to the bus stop, Dom felt on top of the world. His evening had gone much better than expected and anything in life felt possible. All he had to do was reach out and grab it.

CHAPTER 10

It was standing room only in the crowded lounge of The Dun Calf. A crackling fireplace offered a welcoming warmth and a comforting glow to patrons upon entering the premises, a stark contrast to the biting chill of the clear November night, its air pervaded with the aroma of bonfires still smouldering from the previous evening.

The novelty of having a new terrestrial television channel available to view had failed to deter the pub's regular clientele from seeking an evening of quality beer and good conversation. Fresh-faced students, dressed in an array of rugby sportswear, Marks and Spencer pullovers, and hooded sweatshirts bearing their college insignia happily rubbed shoulders with the primarily middle-aged, smartly dressed locals.

For a number of reasons, The Dun Calf had always been a convenient venue for the members of Northern Circle to meet up at on a Saturday evening.

Its location on the periphery of the city centre suited the eldest member Brian, who found the majority of the more central pubs at a weekend tiresomely rowdy and overtly aggressive. Furthermore, he was an enthusiast with a discerning palate when it came to real ales, so felt naturally drawn to The Dun Calf because of the high standard and range of beers available.

Matty and Mick liked the establishment because its jukebox free environment allowed them to chat and catch up with all of the events of the week. Once Brian decided to call it a night and head for home, they invariably moved on to the less salubrious watering holes where loud music made only the most basic of conversations possible.

Since his arrival in the band, Dom had done his best to fit in socially by joining his new acquaintances on their weekly night out. In a short space of time, he had become good friends with Matty and Mick; he was even learning to tolerate Brian, despite their age difference and obvious lack of musical common ground.

Dom, Mick and Brian were sitting at a table situated conveniently close to the bar, speculating as to why the absent Matty was so uncharacteristically late; usually, he was the first one there.

'What time do you call this?' Mick joked, when Matty eventually arrived. 'You've wasted an hour's valuable drinking time.'

'Sorry I'm late, lads,' said Matty, squeezing into the seat that Dom had reserved for him by draping his coat over. 'I had a bit of business to take care of.'

'Oh, yeah,' sneered Brian sarcastically.

'No, seriously,' said the latecomer, protesting his innocence. 'The phone rang just as I was about to leave the house for the first bus. Then, the next bus never came, so I ended up walking down. Bloody freezing, I am.'

'Well,' said Dom expectantly, 'how did last night go?'

'Give me a second while I have a drink. I'm gagging.'

Matty took a large gulp from the now flat pint of beer bought for him in the first round of drinks, its frothy head long since disappeared, before placing it back down on the table.

'Un-bel-iev-able,' he began, slowly emphasising each syllable for good measure. 'That's the only way I can describe it.'

Matty had been extremely fortunate to get his hands on a ticket for the inaugural show of *The Tube*, which had featured the soon to be disbanded The Jam's final ever television appearance. Transmitted live from nearby Newcastle, the music programme was one of new broadcaster Channel Four's flagship attractions.

'Your mate came good with the ticket, then?' said Mick.

'He did. Not only did I get to see them live, but I also managed to grab a quick chat with them beforehand.'

'Never,' said Dom, his jealousy levels almost shooting through the roof.

'Straight up. I was hanging about outside, talking to some other fans, when they walked past. I managed to shake Rick's hand on his way into the building and wish him good luck for the future.'

'Did you get their autographs?' asked Dom.

'No. The kids next to me did. I'd be too embarrassed to ask at my age.'

'You jammy sod,' said Mick.

Brian shook his head disbelievingly. 'I watched it on the TV, and I never saw you in the crowd.'

'I couldn't get near the front because it was so packed. I was stood about halfway back.'

Matty took another thirsty drink from his pint, wounded that the credibility of his story should be in doubt.

'I watched it, too,' said Dom. 'The atmosphere looked electric.'

Matty nodded in agreement. 'When they took to the stage a shiver went down my spine. I've never been to a gig like it. It's a tragedy they're splitting up. They could have dominated British music for years,' he said sadly.

'What was the rest of the show like?' said Mick.

'Magic. All of the musicians played totally live. The whole experience has completely inspired me. That's what we must aspire to, lads. Getting onto *The Tube*, and not just shows where you have to mime like a puppet.'

Brian shook his head disparagingly and smirked.

'And what's so funny about that?' said Matty, annoyed by his condescending attitude.

'Every band in Britain will be busting a gut to get onto it, and that's just the established ones. There's more chance of Newcastle United winning the league title than *The Tube* booking a small-time set of chancers who haven't even played a gig in anger.'

'Well, then, it's just as well I've secured Northern Circle's first professional gig, isn't it? Boys,' proclaimed Matty, 'it's time for us to take our music to the world.'

'Where at?' said Mick.

'The Wild Ferret.'

'Hardly the Royal Albert Hall, is it?' moaned Brian.

'The name means nothing to me,' added Mick. 'I've never heard of it. Where's it at?'

'Newcastle,' said Brian quickly, before Matty could answer, 'and it's a right dive.'

'I can't argue with that,' replied Matty.

'So, why have you booked us in there?' said Brian accusingly. 'I played there two years ago when I was in my heavy metal band. A gang of punks smashed in the windows in the middle of our set and caused a riot. It was a right bloodbath. The police were called and the place was closed down. I'm surprised it ever re-opened.'

'I booked us there because it's an opportunity, Brian. As things stand, Northern Circle are musical virgins, and we have to pop our cherry somewhere. Granted, The Wild Ferret wouldn't have been my first choice of venue, either. It's exactly the same situation as when I had my first ever shag. The girl I did it with was bottom of my list of preferences and I blush even now when I think about her, but beggars can't be choosers. Yes, The Wild Ferret's a shithole and only the bottom rung of the ladder, but at least we can say we're actually on the ladder once we've played there. The only way is up after that.'

Brian was unconvinced. 'I don't know,' he said finally. 'The place holds bad memories for me. I needed stitches in the back of my head where a glass hit me, and the hospital had to shave my hair. It took me weeks to grow it back to its correct style.'

'So, what better way to banish your demons than to return to the scene of your humiliation in triumph,' said Matty. 'Listen, lads, it's a respectable place these days. All the troublemakers have been barred, there's no lock-ins and no drugs being sold by dealers. I got talking to the publican last night; he's got big plans for the place, and we're a part of them if we play our cards right.'

'I'll have to think about it,' said Brian, finishing off his drink and rising to his feet.

'You do that, Brian. Off so soon?' said Matty.

Brian nodded. 'I've got to be up early to drive Pauline to church in the morning. I'll see you all tomorrow night.'

Matty shook his head despairingly as Brian headed towards the exit.

'Right, now that the Cliff Richard of Durham has departed, what would the rest of you sinners like to drink?'

Upon Matty's return from the bar, discussions about the fresh development on the musical front resumed.

'This gig you've lined up, Matty,' said Dom.

'Yeah.'

'When is it?'

'In three weeks, which leaves us just about enough time to really work on our act. If we can survive in front of a crowd of pissed up Geordies, we can get through anything.'

'What if Brian doesn't play, though?' said Mick.

Matty did not appear unduly concerned by the suggestion.

'Oh, he's just making a bit of a scene. Brian's like that sometimes. He always likes to create barriers when there aren't any. He'll fall into line once we get playing properly again. This gig is just the beginning for us. I have a master plan.'

Mick laughed into his glass. 'A bloke called Hitler had one of them, and look what happened to him.'

'Listen,' said Matty seriously, 'we need to get some gigs in so that we are ready for the challenges that lie ahead. If we play our cards right, next year could be a massive one for Northern Circle.'

'Challenges?' said Dom.

'I've got it all figured out up here,' said Matty, tapping the side of his head with his finger. 'The Wild Ferret is the first step. Do well there, get a few more gigs, and we'll be ready for The Battle of the Bands competition that's being held in Langley Vale in February. Winning that will be our passport to bigger and better things.'

'How?' said Mick.

'The winner's get a free recording session at a local studio, with a tape of their songs produced. Those kinds of things cost a fortune usually. With our own songs professionally recorded, we can send them to the top record companies in London to try to get a deal. Yes,' concluded Matty, grinning confidently, 'we're going one way, lads. Up.'

Over three hours later, with last orders been and gone, the bars in Durham were in the process of preparing to close their doors. Customers were streaming out into the streets in their droves, with many heading for the nearby bus station and taxi ranks, while a long queue had already begun to form outside Q Ball, the local nightclub, for those keen to extend their night out into the early hours of Sunday.

The three friends exited The Neville pub in North Road and hovered outside on the pavement.

'Anyone fancy clubbing?' said a willing Mick, keen to take his place in the rapidly expanding line of people outside the nearby nightclub.

'No, not me,' replied Matty.

'How about you, Dom?'

'I'd love to, but I'm nearly skint. Maybe next time.'

'Well, I'm going to chance my arm. I'll see you both tomorrow night.'

Dom and Matty bid Mick farewell and began their walk home, heading back across Framwellgate Bridge to the city centre.

'I've got some blow in the house if you fancy a smoke when we get back?' said Matty, as they made the steep ascent up Claypath towards Gilesgate roundabout.

'Won't your parents mind?'

'They're pretty cool about my mates coming back, so there's no need to worry about making a noise or wiping your feet.'

'I meant about smoking in the house?'

Matty shook his head. 'I'll just light a joss stick and open the window, but we have this understanding. They pretend they can't smell anything, and I pretend I don't smoke. It'll be nice if you introduce yourself, anyway. They're keen to meet our amazing new singer.'

Dom had to admit the idea appealed; his only other alternative was to go home to a cold and empty flat.

'Go on, then.'

When they arrived, Matty snapped on the light switch in the hallway.

'I'll just go and let my parents know I'm back.'

Matty opened the door to the lounge and entered, before re-emerging a moment later.

'They're in the middle of watching a video,' he informed Dom, pulling the door to behind him. 'You can say "hi" another time.'

Dom was secretly relieved; he was extremely drunk, and feared that he would have made an idiot of himself in front of them. In the cold light of day, there would be less chance of making a bad impression when his faculties were not so impaired.

'I'll make us a coffee,' said Matty. 'Just go up to my room. It's the first on the right at the top of the stairs.'

Dom made his way upstairs and switched on the light in Matty's bedroom; looking around, he whistled in admiration when he saw the sheer volume of records contained in a

86

shelving unit on the far wall. Instantly enthralled, he began to browse indiscriminately through them.

'I'm bloody jealous at some of the records you've got,' admitted Dom, when Matty appeared a short time later carrying two mugs.

'What can I say? Music's my life. Feel free to borrow any that catch your eye.'

'I'll take you up on that, definitely.'

Matty placed the mugs down on his study desk, before dropping to his knees and rummaging under his bed; his hand emerged with a blue mini security box.

Removing a key from the record sleeve of a Small Faces album, Matty unlocked the box to reveal a small brown lump of cannabis wrapped in cling film, a lighter, filters, a box of cigarette papers and a packet of tobacco. Grabbing hold of the items and the record sleeve the key had been inside, Matty walked across the room, sat on the floor with his back against the inside of his bedroom door, balanced the record sleeve on top of his legs, and placed all of the objects onto it.

'Be a mate and open my window, Dom,' said Matty. 'And pass my coffee over.'

Dom handed Matty his mug before opening the window slightly, the resultant blast of cold air causing him to shudder.

'Stick an album on while I do this,' said Matty, already studiously at work.

Dom walked over to the wall of vinyl, selected The Gift by The Jam, put it on the turntable of the hi-fi, and placed the stylus at the beginning of side one.

Matty lit his thinly rolled cigarette when it was ready and took a long draw on it, before holding it out to Dom, now sitting cross-legged on the carpet opposite.

'Jesus, that's strong,' Dom said, taking a toke.

Matty giggled like a child. 'I get it from a mate at college. His stuff is always spot on.'

Dom took a second lungful, before allowing it to escape

87

through his nostrils.

'Just what I needed,' he said, handing the joint back to Matty.

Once the first joint had expired, Matty began to assemble two more while chatting excitedly with Dom about their impending debut gig.

At some point in the early hours, after they had finished smoking and were listening to a second album, Dom's heavy eyelids closed and his thoughts began to drift.

After what could have been five minutes or hours, Dom woke up with a start.

The room was silent. Matty was slumped to one side against the door, asleep, with his chin resting on his shoulder.

Dom looked at his watch and groaned; it was nearly three o'clock in the morning.

Gripped by a distinct feeling of nausea, and cursing himself for not having gone straight home earlier, he scrambled to his feet and held out a hand to steady himself against the wall.

'Matty. Matty,' he shouted, in a state of heightened anxiety.

'Yeah, what?' mumbled Matty, stirring slightly, his eyes still closed.

'I need the toilet urgently. Where is it?' he demanded.

'Straight across the landing,' said Matty, moving aside to allow Dom just enough room to squeeze past him and get through the door. 'Hurry up and don't puke on the carpet, or my mother will kill you and me,' he warned, before curling up into the foetal position on the carpet and going back to sleep.

Dom lurched blindly onto the landing, before crashing through the bathroom door with all the grace of a drunk being ejected from a nightclub by overzealous bouncers.

With the bathroom sink mercifully close, Dom gripped hold of its sides, bent over and began to vomit profusely.

Once the first wave of burning liquid forcibly leaving his insides had eased, he rested his forehead against the cold wall mirror in front of him.

'What the bloody hell's going on?' demanded a startled looking, middle-aged man perched on the lavatory in the corner of the room, his navy pyjama bottoms down by his ankles and his hands doing their best to cover his modesty.

In his blinkered desperation, Dom had failed to realise the bathroom was already occupied.

For one split second, the speechless youth hoped it was all just a bad dream; he closed his eyes tight and gave his head a violent shake.

Re-opening them, Dom peered back across the room. The man, with his distinguished nose, slightly extended facial features, and tall, slim frame, was still there and had not moved, frozen by a combination of shock and embarrassment.

This was actually happening.

'Mr Parker, I presume? Pleased to meet you,' slurred Dom, before painful spasms in his stomach caused him to double up as a fresh tide of vomit erupted from him, curtailing the most unorthodox of introductions both of them had ever experienced.

CHAPTER 11

Dom woke up on the morning of the gig at The Wild Ferret a nervous wreck. Unable to eat any breakfast for fear of bringing it straight back up, and having already cut himself shaving, he drove to work full of trepidation at what the evening had in store for him.

With Christmas only a month away, Donnelly's was extremely busy. Tasked with ensuring the shelves of the store remained as full as possible, Dom spent all day transporting new stock onto the shop floor as soon as gaps began to appear. It was only towards the end of the day when the rush was over that he was able to fully return his thoughts once more to his pending debut performance, now only hours away.

Loading a consignment of portable audio cassette players onto a trolley in the stockroom in preparation for transferring to the top floor, Dom began singing to warm up his vocal chords.

Once the trolley was full, Dom pressed the button for the staff lift and waited. When it arrived and the doors opened, he was about to enter the interior when a voice suddenly called out from behind.

'Excuse me.'

Dom nearly jumped out of his skin with shock.

He turned round to find Katy Taylor from the finance office approaching him. Dom was surprised to see her; it was rare for administration staff to stray into the basement area.

Katy was struggling to stifle a giggle at the fright she had given the unsuspecting Dom.

'Sorry, I didn't mean to give you a heart attack.'

'That's OK,' said Dom, attempting to mask his embarrassment.

'I never knew you were a singer,' she said. 'I was standing

listening to you back there for a minute.'

'Sorry for inflicting that upon you.'

'Don't be silly. You sounded really good.'

'Thanks,' said Dom meekly, when he realised Katy was being genuine in her praise. 'I'm just getting some last minute practice in. I'm in a band, and we have a gig tonight in Newcastle.'

'Wow. You're a dark horse, aren't you?' she said, visibly impressed.

Dom shrugged his shoulders. 'It's only a hobby. It's not as if we're good enough to be giving Paul Weller sleepless nights or anything. To tell you the truth it's the first time we'll have played in public, and I'm bricking it.'

'I wouldn't have minded coming to see you play, but I'm babysitting my little sister tonight. Maybe another time?'

'OK, I'll let you know,' said Dom, not believing for one second Katy was remotely interested in someone like him; he assumed, instead, she was merely being polite.

'The reason I'm here,' said Katy, 'is because Deidre from our office has just had a baby girl. You know Deidre. Brown hair, glasses, has a loud voice. We thought it would be nice to send her a card and some flowers, so we're having a collection. All contributions appreciated.'

Dom was unable to recall Deirdre Tomlinson ever attempting to say a civil word to him in all the time he had been working at Donnelly's. Whenever they passed each other in the store, she would turn her nose up in the air and not even acknowledge his presence. Dom thought she was a stuck up, arrogant cow and was the last person he would normally donate money to, but it was a willing compromise to make if it put him in Katy Taylor's good books.

He put his hand into his pocket and pulled out the only cash he had: a five pound note.

'Five pounds,' said Katy, wide-eyed. 'Are you sure?'

'Good old Deidre. She deserves it,' said Dom, through

gritted teeth, an inane grin on his face as he dropped the money into the collection tin.

'That's so generous of you. The card will be doing the rounds on Monday, so make sure you sign it,' she said.

'Will do,' said Dom.

'Good luck for tonight. Let me know how it goes.'

'OK.'

When the store finally closed, Dom dashed home to shower and get ready for the evening.

Waiting for the band to pick him up, he paced up and down his living room like a caged tiger, drinking from a can of lager and anxiously smoking his packet of cigarettes at a furious rate.

When the blue van pulled up outside the flats and honked its horn, Dom quickly made his way outside.

'All right, mate?' said Mick, through the wound down window of the passenger door.

'You're in the back,' shouted Brian, drumming his fingers impatiently on the steering wheel.

'Welcome to first class,' said Matty sarcastically when Dom pulled open the rear doors and climbed inside; the guitarist was half buried in amongst all of the musical equipment.

For the majority of the thirty minute drive to the venue, everyone was uncharacteristically silent, the apprehension in the air so thick it was almost palpable.

Once there, they parked at the rear of the building. Dom and Matty freed themselves from the constrictive interior to announce their arrival, while Brian and Mick remained with the vehicle.

With Matty leading the way, the duo entered the pub. It did not take long to spot the publican, standing at the bar with his back to them.

'Evening, Vic?' said Matty brightly.

Matty was unprepared for the sight that greeted him when Vic turned to face him: he had two black eyes, with severe bruising and swelling to his face.

'What in God's name happened to you?' said Matty.

Vic mumbled an incoherent, barely audible reply.

'Eh?' said Matty, failing to understand a single word.

'I'm Gloria, Vic's wife. How can I help you?' intervened a steely looking blonde from behind the bar.

'We're the band for tonight,' explained Matty. 'Northern Circle from Durham.'

Vic nodded at his wife, silently verifying Matty's claim.

'Oh, yes,' she smiled, her manner instantly more welcoming. 'We've been expecting you.'

'What happened to Vic?' said Matty.

'He was set upon by a couple of scumbags in the function room last week. They dislocated his jaw and left him with concussion. He's on a diet of soup for the next month. He was lucky, though. It could have been a lot worse.'

'How?' said Dom.

'Well, pet, at least he can still drink his beer. Admittedly, it's through a straw, but it still goes down the same way. Come on,' she said, walking round to the customer side of the bar, 'I'll show you where to go.'

'I thought you said this was a respectable pub now,' whispered Dom to Matty, as they followed the landlady out of an internal side door and up a narrow, wooden staircase.

Gloria held open the door of the function room at the top of the stairs and ushered Dom and Matty inside.

'That's where you'll be playing,' she said, pointing towards a small wooden stage at the far end of the room.

'It's filling up already,' remarked Dom, surveying the tables that took up two-thirds of the floor space, most of which were occupied by a predominantly middle-aged, male clientele.

'It is, pet,' replied Gloria, 'but I'm afraid it's not because the whole of Newcastle is eagerly waiting to hear you play. It's because you're sandwiched in between Sylvia and Brenda, our two strippers. They have quite a following in these parts.'

'So I see,' said Matty.

'Our female artistes also have sole use of the dressing room, so you'll have to make do with the toilets, I'm afraid.'

'No need for that, Gloria,' said Matty. 'We're already dressed.'

'Well, if you've got no further questions, I'll leave you to get set up and do your soundcheck,' she said, heading back towards the exit. 'Just to reiterate: Sylvia goes on at eight o'clock, Northern Circle at half-past eight, and Brenda at quarter past nine. And make sure you're off five minutes before Brenda's due on. If you overrun, we'll have a riot on our hands. Brenda's fans travel from all across Tyneside just to see her and like to get their money's worth. Is that clear?'

The friends nodded.

'Hey, Gloria,' said Dom, following her out onto the landing at the top of the stairway. 'What happens if they want an encore?'

Gloria looked at him and cackled. 'I don't think you need worry about that, pet.'

'Why not? They might like us.'

She shook her head, as if pitying Dom for his youthful naivety.

'Who do you lot think you are? The Police?' she laughed. 'No, pet, I don't want to sound harsh, but it would be a first. There's only one thing that lot are here for. Right,' she said, beginning to descend the stairs, 'once you get set up, come into the bar for a drink. First ones are on the house.'

The applause at the end of Sylvia's act was clearly audible in the downstairs bar.

'Chop chop, boys,' said Gloria, clapping her hands

together. 'That's your cue.'

'Right,' said Matty, standing up from their table and heading to the door. 'It's now or never. Let's go and do it, lads.'

Dom, Mick and Brian duly followed the guitarist.

Walking across the small dance floor situated in front of the stage, Dom glanced at the audience. As underwhelming entrances went, he reckoned Northern Circle's just about topped the lot. There was no rapturous ovation, screaming or chanting of their names, just the drone of dozens of voices ordering drinks at the bar and chatting among themselves. No one was giving them a second look.

While Matty, Mick and Brian readied themselves for the performance, Dom ensured his microphone was working. Despite the inauspicious reception they had received, he felt a thrill of anticipation sweep through him.

'Everybody ready?' said Matty, tensely gripping his guitar, before giving Mick the nod to count everyone in with four hollow taps of his drumsticks.

'Good evening, Newcastle,' said Dom, removing his microphone from its stand and pacing around the stage as Matty struck up the opening chords to "Substitute". 'We are Northern Circle. It's great to be here tonight at The Wild Ferret.'

As Brian's thunderous bass line caused the stage to shake, Dom fixed his attention upon the rotating disco ball hanging from the ceiling, before delivering a below par, unconvincing vocal.

The reward for their efforts at the end of the song was a wall of indifferent silence. A frustrated Dom turned his back on the spectators.

'Told you we'd be rocking them,' Matty quipped to the band. 'OK, Mick, let's see if we can wake some of these fuckers up with this one.'

Mick held up his drumsticks and counted everyone in for

their second song.

'One two three four …'

As the band played the introduction to "Oliver's Army", Dom addressed the audience, desperate to shake them out of their apathy.

'I'd like to dedicate this next song to our glorious Prime Minister and her jingoistic, trigger happy cronies,' he said caustically. 'The blood on their hands will never wash away.'

A determined Dom proceeded to give as passionate a rendition as he could muster. When the band finished the track, there was a smattering of appreciative applause. Heartened slightly, they continued their short set with raw avidity.

Any lingering anxiety within Dom had eased over the course of the first two songs, and he began to sing with a mastery that had been missing in all of their rehearsals to date. Matty, with his jerky, Wilko Johnson inspired stage movements, stared intensely ahead while playing his combination of chords and riffs. Mick pounded out the frantic tempo of the songs, grinning non-stop with the sheer pleasure of finally playing to an audience. Only Brian remained impervious to the joyousness of the occasion, his face a portrait of aloofness as he stood rooted to the spot.

All too quickly, Dom was introducing their final song of the evening, ironically dedicating "When You're Young" to everyone present in the room, the vast majority of whom were over fifty years of age.

Gloria had appeared at the rear of the room to watch them complete their set, holding up her arm and pointing at her watch to ensure they clearly got the message.

'Well done, lads,' she said, approaching them when they finished. 'You all did champion.'

'Thank you,' said Dom, sweat dripping from his nose.

'Come and have another drink downstairs once you've cleared your stuff away, and we'll try and slot you in for another gig.'

'OK,' said Matty.

They quickly packed up their equipment and carried everything down to Brian's van, before returning to the ground floor bar. Everyone ordered pints of lager apart from Brian, who was content to drink coke.

Behind the bar, Gloria, a pair of black-rimmed spectacles now perched on the tip of her nose, was flicking through the pages of her diary.

'Come on, Brian,' said Dom, still pumped up with adrenalin, 'get yourself a real drink.'

'Someone has to be sober enough to drive us home,' responded Brian, sounding like the world's biggest killjoy, 'and I can't see anyone else offering.'

The disparity between Brian and everyone else had really begun to irritate Dom lately: in terms of age, musical tastes and personality they were poles apart. Dom thought the band would always lack credibility while they had someone who looked like a roadie for Black Sabbath in their ranks.

Matty flung an arm around Dom, distracting him from his disaffection.

'That was fucking great tonight, mate. Your singing was spot on.'

Dom brightened up. 'Cheers, Matty. That's one of the best feelings I've ever experienced. Words can't describe it. My heart's still going like the clappers.'

Gloria removed her glasses and looked up from her book. 'Is the seventh of January OK, lads? That's the only date free until February.'

'That's fine with us,' said Matty. 'Pencil us in, Gloria.'

'OK, you're booked,' she said. 'I'll see you all then.'

Gloria walked back behind the bar and resumed serving.

'Just going to the bog,' said Mick.

Brian finished his drink and placed the glass on the counter.

'Shall we think about getting off home?' he said. 'I've got an early start in the morning.'

'I was just beginning to get warmed up,' said Matty. 'I fancy another drink.'

Brian's face twisted in annoyance. 'Twenty minutes and no longer,' he said begrudgingly. 'I'll just go and call Pauline to let her know we'll be setting off soon.'

'What a misery,' said Dom, once Brian was standing at the payphone out of earshot. 'Best get the drinks in sharpish, then, and make the most of it.'

'Not very rock and roll, I have to admit,' said Matty.

A couple of minutes later, Mick returned.

'There's a pint there for you, Mick,' said Dom.

'Have you been at the bog all this time?' asked Matty.

Mick had a wide grin on his face. 'Dom, do you see those birds sitting at that table next to the toilet door?'

Dom peered across the room. 'I can't see any lasses. Just a few old women drinking in the corner. Why?'

'That's them. One of them's took a right shine to you.'

Catching sight of the females Mick was referring to, Matty laughed into his drink, sending foam spraying in all directions.

'Which one?' said a horrified Dom, conscious the women were staring back across the room at them.

'The one with the long black hair and clunky earrings who looks like Cher's mother. She's just asked me if you fancy going back to her place in Benwell.'

'Do me a favour. She's nearly as old as my mother. I bet she's got cobwebs on her knickers it's that long since anyone went down there.'

'Get yourself in there,' Matty managed to say, struggling to speak in between howls of laughter. 'You don't look at the mantelpiece when you poke the fire.'

A worried looking Dom raised his pint to his mouth and drank it off in one go.

'She'd eat me alive,' he said. 'Mick, go and tell Brian we're ready to go now. I'll wait for you all by the van.'

Matty and Mick collapsed into hysterics as they watched Dom make a hurried exit, all the time glancing warily over his shoulder in case his would-be groupie trailed and cornered him.

CHAPTER 12

'OK, everyone,' said Dave "The Hitz" Brown, music reporter for local newspaper The *Durham Echo*, and one of the judges for the 1983 County Durham Battle of the Bands competition, 'after three, everyone say "sex, drugs, and rock and roll", and give me a smile brimming with star quality. OK, one, two, three …'

'Sex, drugs, and rock and roll,' bellowed the competition entrants in unison, gathered together outside the Langley Vale community centre for a publicity photograph.

'Great stuff,' said the reporter. 'OK, it's time to go inside to draw lots to decide the running order for this evening. After that, you'll all be allowed a quick soundcheck with Ben, our soundman for the day. Then, it'll be doors open at six-thirty and first group on at seven sharp.'

The acts followed Brown back indoors, pleased to escape the February chill.

The day of reckoning had finally arrived for the musical talent of County Durham. In a few hours' time, one lucky act from the seven short-listed entrants would claim the title, as well as the highly coveted prize.

Ever since their entry - a rough and ready version of "Heat Wave" recorded on a portable cassette player at Gray's Yard - had deemed them worthy of advancing through to the latter stages of the competition, Northern Circle had been excitedly preparing for the day. Keen to hone their act and give themselves the best chance of success, Matty had managed to secure a handful of additional gigs in recent weeks, on top of their sporadic appearances at The Wild Ferret.

The competition rules stipulated that entrants had to perform one original composition and a cover version. The prospect of writing a song had thrilled and horrified Dom in equal measure. He knew that creating a tune good enough to win would instil within him the self-belief that he had what it took to forge a successful career in the music industry. On the flipside, he knew a failure to compose something would prevent Northern Circle from taking part and dent their ambition to become serious artists.

Between Christmas and New Year, all four members had attempted to see what they could come up with individually, before reconvening at Gray's Yard on a bitterly cold and snowy Sunday evening in January to share their ideas.

Up first, borrowing Matty's guitar, Brian thrashed his way through a power chord driven song. Littered with references to Lucifer and the Devil, it was so far away from the sound and image Matty was seeking to project that he would have sacked Brian on the spot there and then, van or no van, but for the more pressing matter of the need to stay together for the competition.

Shaking his head despairingly at the first effort, Matty turned next to Mick. The drummer smiled and was honest enough to admit that he had been unable to think of anything, adding he was more than content to let someone else take the lead when it came to songwriting.

With two members down and two to go, it swiftly became apparent to Matty on whose shoulders responsibility was going to rest.

All attention then focused upon Dom, who self-consciously produced a sheet of folded up A4 paper from his coat pocket and opened it out. Lacking the ability to convey his ideas with an accompanying musical instrument, Dom sang a cappella the song he had prepared, titled "I Want You".

Stating that Dom's contribution held promise, Matty went on to play the band some fingerpicked chord sequences and riffs that he had been toying with.

For the remainder of the evening, Dom and Matty worked

together to combine their musical efforts until they had a semblance of a song on which they could build upon. Mick and Brian sat playing cards in a corner of the room.

The following week's rehearsal had been a more integrated affair; in the days leading up to it, Matty had fine-tuned the song's chord sequences and decided upon a medium tempo. It was then a relatively straightforward process for Brian and Mick to add their respective instruments to the song until, slowly but surely, Northern Circle emerged with their very first original composition.

Predictably, Brian was far from happy, grumbling that it sounded like a million other songs from the sixties; on the contrary, Mick declared himself pleased with the fruits of their labour, as did Dom, who thought it sounded both current and retro at the same time.

Having taken the comments of everyone on board, Matty came up with his own interpretation on the new song that, miraculously, just about managed to appease everyone. In acknowledging Brian's view that it was never going to win any prizes for musical originality, Matty claimed that very factor could only work in their favour. To be too original or arty, he argued, might alienate the support of judges who were basing their judgement on one or two hearings only; for once, Matty surmised, familiarity would not breed contempt.

With the original song completed, the question of which track to cover had unsurprisingly proven to be a drawn out affair, as each member had strong opinions on what they thought would be the perfect choice. Dozens of popular songs were considered, spanning the rock and roll era of the fifties, British pop and American soul of the sixties, glam, punk and disco of the seventies, and contemporary eighties numbers. Eventually, they decided upon "Heat Wave", the song that had secured them a place in the competition line up, its brisk Motown beat offering a suitable contrast to their slower paced original composition.

While Matty went off to represent the band in deciding the running order for the evening's proceedings, Dom, Mick and Brian trooped into the backstage area. Each band had a table allocated to them that contained an assortment of nibbles and soft drinks, and while everyone began to enjoy the limited hospitality afforded to them, Dom took the opportunity to cast an eye over his rivals at close quarters.

Skol Warriors, a shaggy haired, heavy metal outfit from Consett, occupied the next table along; they were wearing metal studded denim jackets emblazoned with the words 'Kings Of Hell' on the back, and skin-tight jeans that accentuated their sparrow-like legs.

Then came Blazing Saddles, an ensemble of heavily bearded, tousle haired forty-somethings who specialised in parodies of current hits.

Next to them was punk group Doomed Youth, a baby-faced bunch of sixth form students from Newton Moor, who had shyly closed ranks around their table.

Modern Vogue, consisting of teachers and various other white-collar workers, had tailored their style on the playboy look of pop act Duran Duran, right down to their tinted, finely crafted coiffures, headbands, pastel-coloured suits, sunbed tans and hints of androgynous mascara; impatient for the show to begin, the New Romantic pretenders stared loftily at their fellow competitors.

Two members of rockabilly trio The Straw Men, with their matching quiffs and chambray shirts, had elected to stand in one corner of the room, busying themselves with tuning their acoustic guitars.

The home band was the Langley Vale Trojans, a skin-headed collection of rudimentary musicians. They were an intimidating sight, swearing loudly, belching, spitting, and snarling 'what the fuck you looking at, like?' to anyone brave or stupid enough to be caught looking in their direction. Lead singer, Nails, a twitchy, hyperactive bundle of negative energy with narrow, hate-filled eyes that suggested violence was never far from his thoughts, wandered the room like a creature of the wild ensnared against its will, wearing a permanent expression of belligerence.

'Well?' said Mick, when Matty reappeared a short time later.

'Second last.'

'I'm happy with that. It'll allow us to hear most of the other acts and show us what we have to do to win,' Dom reasoned.

'Who's playing last?' asked Mick.

'The Trojans,' said Matty.

'The judges won't dare give it to anyone else in case they don't get out alive,' said Brian.

'No way,' protested Mick. 'It can't be a fix. Respectable judges are involved.'

'Ha,' said Brian cynically. 'A third-rate hack whose dream of writing for the national music papers is all it will ever be. Pat Shingle, a DJ who plays utter garbage on a Mickey Mouse local radio station, and a third judge who I've never even heard of.'

'He's the manager of an independent record shop, apparently,' added Mick.

'Well, I rest my case,' concluded Brian. 'If they're not ripe for corruption and intimidation, then I don't know who is.'

'Well, even if the Trojans do try to nobble them, they're hardly the Mafia, Brian,' retorted Matty. 'I'd expect them to be instantly disqualified, otherwise the competition has no integrity whatsoever. The judges might not be household names, but we have to have faith in their honesty, as they are the ones with the power to get us onto the next rung of the ladder.'

'You mean we're actually on the bottom rung,' said Brian drily. 'I never realised we had scaled such dizzy heights.'

'Stop taking the piss,' said Matty heatedly.

'Matty, you're taking all of this far too seriously,' said Brian. 'I've got more chance of marrying Princess Diana than we have of getting anywhere with the band. You've got your head in the clouds with these daft ideas. In ten years' time, I'll still be a painter and decorator, and you'll be an accountant with a nice little house, two kids and a wife. The sooner you face reality the better.'

'Ah, I'm off to watch the run-throughs,' said a disgruntled Matty. 'I'll come and give you all a shout when it's our turn.'

Tiring of the bassist's negativity, Mick drifted away to chat to some of the other musicians.

Fearing he would throttle Brian if he had to listen to his drivel a minute longer, Dom went off in search of Matty. He found him standing at the back of the main hall watching Skol Warriors set up their instruments for the first soundcheck of the day.

'So, is that the common consensus, Dom?' he began angrily. 'We're all wasting our fucking time playing at something we'll never be.'

'Take no notice of Brian,' said Dom, attempting to placate him. 'He doesn't speak for me. I wouldn't be here if I didn't believe in myself or the band. This is life and death to me.'

Dom's words failed to have the immediate soothing effect he was anticipating; it was clear Brian's cynicism was getting under Matty's skin, as well as planting a seed of doubt.

'But he's right, in a way, as much as I hate to admit it,' said Matty. 'If we don't win tonight, in a little shitty community centre a million miles away from the bright lights of London where the real action is, then what chance do we have of mixing it with the real McCoy?'

'We'd better not lose, then,' said Dom emphatically.

When the heavy metal group finished playing their two songs, they trudged off stage.

'Any sign of the other judges?' asked Dom, noticing the

vacant chairs and table with a reserved notice displayed on it.

Matty shook his head.

Dom looked at his watch. 'I tell you what. Once we're done here, how about we escape for a bit? I'm sure we can find a pub that does an afternoon lock-in.'

'Good idea. If I hear much more crap out of Brian, I'll have to plant him one.'

'Good evening, good people of Langley Vale, and welcome to the 1983 County Durham Battle of the Bands competition,' proclaimed Pat Shingle, with a grandiosity that the host of the Grammy Awards would have struggled to match.

For the occasion, the bronzed Shingle was wearing his trademark attire of orange Hawaiian shirt, white jeans, blue pod shoes, and oversized, red-framed glasses.

'Let's hear some noise,' he implored, his shoulder-length, bleached blond hair lighting up the room like a beacon, as he paraded and bounced around the stage with the microphone held out in front of him towards the audience. Instead of the excess of adoring screams and good-natured whoops that his efforts normally produced, Shingle received a unanimous torrent of abuse. Ever the professional, the DJ remained unperturbed.

'I'm sure you are going to enjoy watching and listening to all seven of the acts who are backstage as we speak, eagerly awaiting the opportunity to perform. It really is fantastic to have the cream of County Durham's musical talent all gathered together under one roof, and I am, indeed, honoured.'

As Shingle paused for breath, a lone taunt pierced the brief silence.

'Crap shirt, tosser.'

The self-proclaimed 'man of the people' ran a hand through his mane and ignored the catcall.

'Before we let battle commence,' he informed the audience

in his honey-toned voice, 'I would briefly like to introduce you to my two colleagues at the back there, who will be helping me to judge the competition. Stand up, fellas.'

A spotlight lit up the faces of the two men sitting at the table near the rear wall, who now bashfully rose to their feet.

'First, we have Mr Dave "The Hitz" Brown from local newspaper The *Durham Echo*, and next to him is Mr Pete Fryer, the owner of Pete's Records in Durham City. Best stay on your feet, fellas, otherwise you'll not be seeing a great deal.

'OK, now that the formalities are over, without any further ado, I would like to introduce our first act of the evening. They're heavy, they're metal, they are Skol Warriors from the steel town of Consett.'

Backstage, everyone went deathly silent, desperate to hear the type of reception Skol Warriors received.

As they took to the stage, the majority of the partisan crowd greeted their arrival with a chorus of boos, before following up with a relentless chant of 'Trojans, Trojans'.

Nails looked around at his rivals and laughed with the kind of confidence that suggested he had expected nothing else but such devout loyalty from his supporters.

The members of Modern Vogue attempted to alleviate their nerves with some last minute checking of appearances in their handheld mirrors, aware that they would soon be following Skol Warriors on stage.

When the opening act finished playing and returned backstage, the despondency the experience had inflicted upon them was apparent for all the other competitors to see; no words were required as to how they thought their performance had gone.

'And now, a five-piece New Romantic group from the very exclusive and sophisticated Neville's Cross. They've even brought their own fan club with them,' said Shingle, gazing with unsavoury lust at their congregation of girlfriends pressed up against the stage. 'Please give a big hand for Modern Vogue.'

Exaggerated screams of an adulatory nature, from the female contingent Shingle had been referring to, attempted to drum up some excitement as Modern Vogue breezed onto the stage, their assured demeanour designed to portray themselves as pop heirs in waiting.

As they plugged in their instruments an impromptu chorus of 'get your tits out for the lads' began to ring out; directed at Modern Vogue's vocal followers, it punctured the intended sense of purpose the band's entrance had attempted to convey.

They launched into their first song, an original tune titled "Martina's On The Rocks". The deliberately mumbled, deep-toned crooning emanating from vocalist Roger was barely intelligible as he casually prowled the stage, devoting more attention to ensuring the sleeves of his lemon jacket remained rolled up to his elbows, and to constantly flicking his floppy fringe out of his eyes, than to his Bowie influenced singing.

Two youths standing at the right-hand side of the stage treated Barry, the posturing bass player, to a volley of well-directed phlegm, with one particularly venomous spittle missile scoring a direct hit in his left eye; he paused playing to wipe away the offending sputum with his sleeve.

Unaware of the reason behind Barry's decision to stop playing, Roger glared angrily across the stage as the missing bass notes threatened to halt the song in its tracks. Barry quickly resumed, but the impact of the song had been lost and it stuttered to a limp conclusion.

As Roger began to introduce the second song, a voice shouted out from the dark sea of heads, 'Get on with it, yer poof.'

A fresh wave of derisory laughter echoed around the hall.

Roger immediately stopped talking and pointed his finger at the crowd as if about to remonstrate with them for their rudeness, before thinking better of it. Instead, he carried on with his introduction, before the band recommenced with a shaky version of "Hungry Like The Wolf".

'Bloody peasants,' hissed Roger backstage after Modern Vogue had just finished playing, tearing off his headband and throwing it to the floor in disgust.

'What's that you just said?' said Nails accusingly.

Roger suddenly realised there was a good chance many of those disapproving boos had emanated from family and friends of his.

'Erm, nothing,' he said softly, displaying all the ferocity of a kitten as opposed to the wolf he had just been singing about.

Without wishing to think himself as being uncharitable, Dom had to admit to not minding seeing Modern Vogue, the spitting incident aside, have their cockiness deflated with such a public display of vitriol. He had watched them earlier on in the afternoon during the run through, when they had been the epitome of the highly pompous, all-surface but no depth musical charlatans he so vehemently despised.

In terms of who was in with a realistic chance of winning the competition, Dom knew that the odds on Skol Warriors and Modern Vogue had severely lengthened after their below-par performances.

With a foreboding look on their faces, The Straw Men stood at the stage door as Pat Shingle began to introduce them, before disappearing through it to meet their fate.

Doomed Youth and Blazing Saddles swiftly followed.

As the latter's routine, which included a musical pastiche of Madness, Bucks Fizz and Human League songs, garnered some unexpected belly laughs and warm applause from the audience, Northern Circle hovered anxiously backstage. Dom's throat felt as rough as sandpaper; Matty was checking the tuning on his guitar for the tenth time in five minutes; Mick was restlessly playing a beat against the wall with his drumsticks.

'Your turn, lads,' said a glistening, round-faced member of Blazing Saddles as they returned backstage after completing their set.

Northern Circle's moment of destiny had arrived; it was make or break.

As Pat Shingle gave his penultimate introduction of the evening and beckoned them on stage, Matty addressed his bandmates.

'Right, let's get out there and show them what we can do,' he said determinedly.

As the rest of the group prepared their instruments, Dom approached the front of the stage to go through his customary ritual of ensuring his microphone was in working order. Before he could do so on this occasion, a stinging object bounced off his forehead. Annoyed, Dom looked down at the floor to see if he could find the offending item, but as Matty began to fingerpick the opening chords to "I Want You", he put the incident to the back of his mind and composed himself for the performance.

'We're Northern Circle,' announced Dom, 'and this is the very first song we've written together as a band.'

He closed his eyes, and once the instrumental introduction was over, began to sing the opening verse: 'She knows, you know, that this is not a game …'

Concentrating fully upon ensuring each word was note perfect and delivered with the required emotion, Dom temporarily forgot all about the aggressive element in the audience, ambling around the stage making eye contact with the individuals in the crowd he believed were genuinely enjoying the song.

He also allowed himself a quick look at the judges standing at the back, and was heartened that all three appeared to be paying close attention, particularly Pete Fryer, who was nodding his head along with an approving smile on his face.

'Thank you,' said Dom, when the song ended.

Without pausing for breath, Matty struck up the punchy riff to "Heat Wave". As Mick kicked in with his drum roll and Brian plucked at his bass, Dom leapt into the air before energetically bouncing up and down on the spot, feeding off the excited urgency of the music; only when it was time for him to start singing did he become less animated.

Approaching the end of the second verse, Dom felt as if things were going too well; they had not had to endure any taunts from the crowd or the vile spitting that Modern Vogue had suffered.

An object suddenly whacked off Dom's forehead again, just above his left eye. Castigating himself for being lulled into a false sense of security, he just about managed to maintain the flow of his singing without missing a word.

Almost immediately, a second item was hurled. This time it bounced harmlessly off his shirt; a second later, another ricocheted off his leg.

He glanced over to Matty to see whether he was the sole victim, just in time to witness a small glass capsule shatter against the face of his guitar. Within seconds, a familiar, acrid smell permeated the air: stink bombs.

Encouraged by their initial success, the perpetrators continued their attack, with more objects raining down on the band.

Dom and Matty, being closest to the edge of the stage and the most vulnerable targets, reacted in their own unique manner.

Dom, with acute deftness, dodged the missiles by repeatedly jerking and twisting his body in an effort to be a more difficult target to hit. The judges and a large percentage of the audience at the rear of the hall interpreted his swaying body as being an eye-catching, original sequence of dance moves.

Matty's approach was more obstinate, staring defiantly ahead as if to say 'you can throw what you like at me because

I don't give a shit', all the while swinging the arm of his guitar backwards and forwards and performing his usual irregular stage movements.

Battling on gamely, they made it through to the end without it upsetting their performance too much. Leaving the stage, Dom and Matty brashly raised their fists into the air.

'Bloody tossers,' shouted Matty, kicking a chair across the floor in the backstage area, giving full vent to his feelings. 'My clothes are minging. It'll cost a fortune to get my suit cleaned.'

In the main hall, there was a thunderous reception for Langley Vale Trojans as they took to the stage.

'Listen to that,' said Brian. 'What chance has anyone else got?'

'Ah, come on,' said Dom, reasoning with his bass player as a badly out of tune Nails began to sing. 'They're crap. Any half-normal person can see that.'

'I know that, but which judge will want to vote against them, knowing they have to get out of town alive afterwards?'

'We were great, Brian,' said Dom confidently. 'Any judge worth his salt will see that. I saw it in their eyes. They liked us.'

Before Brian could respond further, Dom was surprised to see an unexpected group of visitors entering the room: his uncle Tel, accompanied by Vince Staveley and a third man who Dom had never seen before.

'What are you doing here, Tel?' said Dom.

'Your mother mentioned you were playing here today. We were working in the area, so thought we'd come and check it out.'

'Have you been here long?'

Tel nodded his head. 'We've watched the whole show. I'm no Hughie Green, but as far as I can tell, you haven't got anything to worry about.'

'You boys have got talent,' chipped in Staveley. 'Not like

112

that lot out there now. Dear oh dear, call that singing?' he said, shaking his head. 'It's rattling my bloody fillings.'

'That's Langley Vale Trojans,' said Mick. 'They're the favourites.'

'Over my dead body will they win,' said Staveley. 'They're a bloody shambles.'

'Aren't you going to introduce us to your mates?' said Tel.

'Of course. This is Matty, Mick and Brian,' said Dom, pointing to each member in turn. 'Lads, this is my uncle Tel, Vince and …'

'Billy,' said the third man.

'Billy,' repeated Dom unnecessarily.

'Pleased to meet you all,' said Tel warmly.

The sound of rowdy cheering and clapping from the main hall signalled the end of the Trojans' first song.

'Well, good luck, lads. We'd best be on our way,' said Tel. 'No rest for the wicked.'

Dom said, 'Aren't you staying to hear the results?'

Tel shook his head. 'No need. If it's based on talent alone, then it's a foregone conclusion. See you later, lads.'

'Who the hell was that Vince bloke with the sheepskin?' said Matty, once the trio had left the room. 'I wouldn't want to get on the wrong side of him in a hurry.'

'Vince Staveley.'

Everyone's mouths dropped open in shock.

'What, the Vince Staveley?' said Mick, in astonishment. 'I've heard he knows the Krays.'

'It's only a rumour. I don't think there's anything in it,' said Dom. 'Tel works for him, and I even rent my flat off him.'

'Really?' said Mick.

'At a preferential rate,' added Dom.

'Wow, Dom the gangster,' said Matty jokily. 'Bloody hell, we'd better watch what we say in front of him, lads, otherwise he'll have us fitted with a pair of concrete boots and dropped in the Wear.'

Fresh applause, followed by the appearance a moment later of Nails and the rest of his group, signalled the end of the competition.

Pat Shingle popped his head into the room. 'Well done everyone. That was a fantastic show you've just put on. The other judges and I have been really impressed by what we've heard tonight. We're just going to confer for five or ten minutes now. Once we've made a decision, we'll call you all back onstage for the announcement of the winner.'

While they waited, the bands all remained within their individual cliques. Nails and the Trojans swigged from cans of cheap lager and high fived each other as if the result was a mere formality.

'The way they're acting, we may as well go home now,' said Mick dejectedly. 'It's obvious they know something we don't.'

Five minutes later, everyone was still nervously awaiting the result.

'What are the judges doing?' said Matty impatiently.

'Maybe it's not as cut-and-dried as we thought,' said Dom. 'If it was going to be a fix, they'd have called everyone back by now.'

'Then again, they could just be trying to make it look convincing, before naming them as winners,' Brian added, ever the pessimist.

A further fifteen agonising minutes elapsed before Shingle returned to summon everyone back into the hall. As they walked onstage, the majority of the audience struck up once again the chant of 'Trojans, Trojans'.

Once all of the acts, together with the judges, were present, Shingle grabbed the microphone and turned to address the audience. As he appealed for quiet, the tension in the air reached fever pitch.

'Ladies and gentlemen,' he began, with all the

114

showmanship of a boxing ring announcer at Caesar's Palace, 'we, the judges, have arrived at a decision and it is unanimous.'

This remark elicited several 'oos' and a great deal of murmuring.

'In reverse order, the act to come third this evening is … Blazing Saddles. In second place, close but no cigar … Langley Vale Trojans.'

As the crowd voiced their dissatisfaction, Dom and Matty looked at each other in surprise, aware the dream was still alive. Everything hinged on the next few seconds.

'It is my great pleasure to announce that the act crowned County Durham Battle of the Bands champion for 1983 is … Northern Circle.'

Dom and Matty's eyes widened in sheer joy; they threw their arms around each other and jumped up and down on the spot, revelling in the glorious moment of victory.

Aware of the unpopularity of the decision, Shingle promptly congratulated Northern Circle, before hastily thanking the audience for turning up and bidding them a good night.

As all of the groups made their way backstage to collect their possessions, a sizeable minority of the crowd continued to express their displeasure with the result, hurling invective and numerous objects in the direction of the musicians.

Once safely out of sight in the rear of the building, Shingle asked Northern Circle to remain behind to collect the details of their prize.

As the disappointed bands slowly left the community centre, Nails, disconcertingly, began to head butt the wall in frustration like a rabid woodpecker. Along with some death stares from the other Trojans, it all made for an uncomfortable couple of minutes for Northern Circle until Pete Fryer led them back into the hall.

By now, a modicum of sanity had returned to the near

empty room. It was the calm after the storm, the only noise coming from the competition crew packing away the sound equipment, while the caretaker silently swept up the vast amounts of litter from the floor.

The three judges posed with the group for the obligatory victory photographs, with Shingle grinning inanely and giving the thumbs up sign to the camera. Afterwards, Brown scribbled down some quotes from Matty and Dom for his article in the next edition of his newspaper.

After the record shop owner and disc jockey had shook the hands of the victors, wished them good luck for the future and bid them farewell, Brown remained behind to hand over a large brown envelope to Matty.

'Here's your prize. In there are the details of your recording session, including time, date, and location. Enjoy the day, and I look forward to interviewing you all when you are at the top of the charts. If you ever need any help in the future, just pop into the paper's offices for a chat.'

'Thanks, Dave,' said Matty.

'Well, I'd best be off. I'm sure you are all keen to go out and celebrate.'

The reporter shook everyone's hand and left, leaving the foursome to shuffle away to collect their belongings and equipment.

As the others began to pick up their coats, an impatient Matty was unable to wait any longer and tore open the envelope.

'Read it out,' said Dom.

To The Successful Artist,

Congratulations on winning the 1983 County Durham Battle of the Bands competition.

Your prize is a four-hour recording session at JT Recording Studios, Cookson Terrace, Bearpark, to be held on

Saturday 30 April 1983 at 12pm. A cassette tape of your recordings will be produced free of charge.

Please ring the studios two weeks in advance to confirm your attendance.

I would like to wish you every success with your future musical endeavours.

Yours sincerely,
Ed Turnbull (Editor)
The Durham Echo

'I don't want to spoil anyone's good mood,' said Mick, peering out of a rear window, 'but it looks as if we have company.'

'What do you mean?' said Matty, folding up the letter and shoving it into his pocket.

'Come and have a look for yourself,' said the drummer.

The window looked out upon a now near empty car park. By a low perimeter wall at the far end of the tarmacked area, over a dozen youths had gathered under a neon street light.

'There's loads of them. What do you think they want?' asked Mick, struck by fear.

'Well, I should hardly think it's to congratulate us,' said Matty.

'That bloody head case singer's there, too,' said Dom.

The unmistakable figure of Nails was sitting on the wall, staring intently in their direction.

'What're we going to do?' said Mick.

'Why don't we have a cup of coffee from the drinks machine over there and toast our success?' suggested Matty calmly. 'It's nice and warm in here, and freezing out there. They'll soon get bored and disappear. Come on, the drinks are on me.'

Fifteen minutes passed; Matty, Mick and Brian were sitting at their table, coats on and instruments packed, waiting for the signal from Dom, on lookout duty, that it was safe to leave.

'Coast clear yet?' said Matty.

'Not exactly,' replied Dom. 'If anything, there's more of them now than before.'

Dom wiped away the bead of sweat that had begun to run down his face. He knew now how the British soldiers in the battle of Rourke's Drift, as depicted in the movie *Zulu,* must have felt: outnumbered, surrounded and with nowhere to go.

'Look, this is crazy,' piped up Brian. 'We can't stay here all night. Pauline will be wondering where I'm at. She'll think I've got another bird. Again.'

'Brian, Pauline is the least of your worries,' said Mick, failing to stifle the rising panic in his voice. 'Compared to this lot, she's a pussycat.'

'It's lights out, I'm afraid.'

Everyone looked around to discover the caretaker standing in the doorway, a bin liner of rubbish in one hand and his broom in the other.

'Haven't you all got homes to go to?'

'It'll be lambs to the slaughter, mate, if we leave here with that mob out there,' said Mick plainly.

The caretaker gazed through the window. 'Take no notice of that lot; their bark's worse than their bite. I've known them all for years.'

'He's right. We're being silly,' said Brian, standing up and walking towards the exit.

'Well,' added Matty, following Brian's lead, 'there's only one way to find out, I suppose.'

Mick followed tentatively, with Dom bringing up the rear.

As soon as they left the sanctuary of the community centre and stepped out into the night air, the caretaker swiftly locked the main doors behind them.

There was no going back.

As they walked warily towards Brian's van, the waiting group of youths fell silent and stared menacingly at them.

'Shall we make a run for it?' whispered Mick.

'We'll never outrun them with the instruments,' said Dom. 'Just keep your nerve, Mick. They want to see you shitting yourself.'

'I've got my looks to think about,' moaned the drummer.

'Whatever you do everyone, don't stop walking,' said Matty. 'Just keep moving towards the van. Brian, have you got your keys ready?'

'Yes.'

Arriving unhindered at their vehicle, Brian unlocked the rear doors and placed his instrument inside; before any more could follow suit, the pack headed across to confront them, with Nails at the fore.

'Evening, lads,' said Matty brightly.

Nails stood nose to nose with Matty, staring coldly into his eyes.

'Was there something, as we're in a bit of a hurry?' said Matty. 'It's my old mum, you see. If I'm not home before she goes to bed, she worries.'

'This won't take a minute,' said Nails ominously.

Matty swallowed hard; the time for fast talk and being diplomatic appeared to be over.

Nails jabbed a bony finger into Matty's chest. 'We've got a problem here that needs to be sorted out before you go anywhere. I want that recording session.'

'But we won,' said Matty stubbornly.

'Tell the judges you no longer want to be the winner. Withdraw, and then the Trojans will be promoted to first place. That way nobody gets hurt and we all go home happy.'

'That sounds reasonable to me,' said Mick, panicking and losing his nerve. 'We can do that, can't we, Matty?'

Nails smiled maliciously. 'One of you is showing some common sense. That's what I like to hear. So then, Beaky, does pretty boy here speak for the lot of you? Are you going to withdraw?'

The drummer of the Trojans, an overweight youth with a squat neck, produced a bike chain and began to smack it off the palm of his hand, pure hatred bulging in his stony eyes.

Beginning to feel like a fly trapped on a spider's web, Dom threw caution to the wind. He took a step forward so that he was standing shoulder to shoulder with Matty.

'Listen, you morons,' he began, 'my whole life depended on us winning tonight. I'd rather die than give it away to you. End of story.'

'Is that your decision too, Beaky?' said Nails, probing for a hint of weakness in Matty's armour.

Matty took a deep breath and looked up to the heavens.

Before he could respond, everyone's heads turned as one, as a car driven at a reckless speed turned sharply into the car park and accelerated towards them.

The gathering of youths splintered, some running off down the street while others retreated to the safety of the perimeter wall. Only a hard core of six remained rooted to the spot in support of Nails.

'Who the fuck's this, *The Professionals*?' said Nails nonchalantly, as the car screeched to a halt yards away.

The doors swung open, and from within Tel, Staveley and Billy emerged.

'What's going on here, Dom? Are these toe rags threatening you?' said Tel.

It was the turn of Nails to be apprehensive, uncertain how to react to this unexpected development, but well aware that the odds had just taken a significant swing out of his favour.

'What exactly do you think you're going to do with that, son?' said Tel, taking a step towards the Trojan brandishing the chain.

Without waiting for a response, Tel planted a head butt onto the bridge of his nose. The thug collapsed to the ground, rolling around squealing and clutching his face.

'Any of you other fuckers fancy some of that?' spat Tel,

pointing to the stricken figure.

Realising how seriously out of their depth they were, all but Nails vanished into the shadows.

For the first time since they had intervened, Staveley sprang into direct action. From inside his coat, he removed an object and pressed it hard into the chest of Nails.

'You obviously don't know who you're messing with, son,' he hissed. 'So, for that reason alone, I'm willing to give you the benefit of the doubt on this occasion.'

Staveley grabbed hold of the back of Nails' head and pushed it downwards so that he could see what was being held against him; immediately realising how dangerous a situation he had become embroiled in, Nails' cockiness disintegrated.

'Yes, son, you do right to look scared. I bet the only time you've ever seen one of these is in the movies. Now, let's get one thing straight between us. If I ever hear of you bothering these lads again, I personally will come looking for you. And when I find you, one dark night when you're walking home alone, me and the boys here will take you somewhere nice and quiet, and hurt you so badly you'll be begging for me to put a bullet into you to put you out of your misery. Do we have an understanding?'

Whimpering uncontrollably like a child, Nails eventually managed to nod his head.

Staveley pushed the broken figure contemptuously to the ground.

'You see, Dom, bullies are all the same. Together they think they're invincible, but give them a taste of their own medicine and you find they're just cowards underneath. Finish packing your gear up and get yourselves off home.'

Dom was initially unable to move, too shocked by what he had just witnessed.

'Best do as Vince says,' said Tel, noticing the caretaker staring out at them from inside the community centre. 'Just in case the old bill turn up.'

'OK,' said Dom.

While his uncle and two friends kept watch from their car, Dom and the others quickly shoved the rest of their instruments into Brian's van, climbed inside and drove off.

Everyone was heavily relieved to have gotten away so lightly from the angry mob, but the manner of the reprieve had been deeply unnerving to witness first hand.

While musically there was much to celebrate, the atmosphere within the van was still extremely subdued as they headed home.

CHAPTER 13

When the persistent knocking finally roused him from his state of deep slumber, Dom groaned when he realised he had overslept.

'All right, all right, I'm coming,' he shouted, rolling out of bed and tottering through the flat to answer the front door.

'Are you not ready yet?' said Matty, impatiently standing on the gangway, guitar case in hand.

Without responding, Dom turned round and walked into the living room, leaving Matty to enter and close the door himself.

Dom collapsed onto the sofa and held his head in his hands.

'God, I feel terrible,' he complained.

'Hey, you weren't on the piss last night, were you?' said Matty accusingly. 'You know how important today is.'

Dom held up a protesting hand to halt Matty in his tracks.

'No, I wasn't,' he said crabbily. 'The new bloke in the flat above had a party until five for the third night in a row. I'm lucky if I had an hour's sleep with all the racket he was making.'

'That's a pity. I slept like a log,' said Matty.

'Lucky bloody you,' said Dom.

'Tell your mate, Staveley, about him. I'm sure he could easily sort it all out.'

Matty held his hand up like a gun and rattled off a *Dirty Harry* quotation in his best Clint Eastwood impersonation; the incident in the car park at Langley Vale was destined to remain firmly embedded in his memory for a long time to come.

Dom shook his head. 'I'd rather not get him involved.'

'Please yourself,' said Matty. 'Anyway, forget about your neighbour and shake a leg. We don't want to be late for our big day.'

'It's too early in the day to be making music,' Dom moaned. 'It's not natural.'

'Now, now. You can't look a gift horse in the mouth. It's not every day we get the opportunity to record in a professional studio for free.'

'I know,' conceded Dom, wearily rubbing his eyes as he rose to his feet and headed towards the bathroom. 'Look, make yourself useful and put the kettle on. I need a strong coffee with a tiny drop of milk and two sugars. I'm just going to grab a quick shower.'

'It's your other servant's day off, is it?' quipped Matty.

'I'm not in the mood for your sarcasm,' said Dom.

'OK. No problem. I can take a hint,' said Matty. 'But if your vocals are crap because of that tosser, then I'll be knocking on his door to give him a piece of my mind. We've got too much riding on today.'

'I've already tried that without success. You should see the size of him up close. He's built like a brick shithouse.'

'The bigger they are, the harder they fall.'

'He could take the pair of us on without breaking into a sweat.'

'Bollocks,' said Matty defiantly. 'You usually find with blokes like that their bark is worse than their bite. If it was me, I'd be sorting it out straight away before it escalates. I'd complain to the authorities about the noise or give the cops an anonymous tip-off about certain illegal substances being consumed on his premises. That would sort him out.'

'Oh yes. Apart from the fact that I have no proof whatsoever to corroborate that last claim, what if he decides to grab hold of me and interrogate me over who grassed him up? I don't fancy hobbling around on crutches for the next six months.'

Matty made his way into the kitchen, willing to pamper his singer if it ensured he made it to the recording studio on time in a fit physical and mental state.

Dom undressed in the bathroom, stood in the bathtub, turned on the shower and pressed his forehead against the wall tiles, willing the hot jets of water to soothe away the lethargy that three nights of interrupted sleep had produced.

The day Northern Circle had been waiting for since they had won the competition was upon them.

To make the most of the rare opportunity to have their music professionally recorded, the band had added a further two original songs to their repertoire. As was the case with their debut composition, the creative impetus had come from Dom and Matty, both driven by a fierce determination to prove to themselves and the world at large that they possessed the necessary talent to cut it in the music industry.

Over the long Easter bank holiday weekend the pair had locked themselves away in Matty's house while his parents were on holiday, spending hours slowly developing their scraps of musical ideas and words into potential songs. By the time dawn broke on the Tuesday, the weary but proud tunesmiths had two new songs: "Not A Day Goes By" was an acoustic ballad, whereas the second, "Planes, Trains and Taxis", was a medium-paced track with an infectious guitar riff layered over a standard three-chord structure.

Demonstrating to himself that he had the ability to create songs out of thin air was a huge weight off Dom's shoulders; the nagging self-doubt that he was nothing but a musical charlatan had hung over him during gigs that consisted of nothing but cover versions. Even after coming up with "I Want You" for the competition, Dom had wondered if that had been a fluke; he had worried that he and Matty would be unable to replicate the process and write more songs.

But ever since Easter his fears had eased. Creatively inspired, snippets of melodies and lyrics constantly swamped his mind, sometimes at the most inopportune of moments;

frequently, he would find himself in the bath, sitting on the lavatory or lying in bed at night, only for an idea for a song to present itself. Dom had learnt from bitter experience that it was best to have a pen and paper handy by his bedside at all times to jot them down, as on a couple of occasions he had awoken next morning to discover his ideas had vanished with the night.

Dom turned into Cookson Terrace, an unassuming street in the small village of Bearpark, and drove down it until he came to the end property.

'This is it,' said Matty, spying the JT Recording Studios sign by the main entrance.

Dom pulled up outside and peered through the car windscreen.

'Hardly Abbey Road, is it?' he said acerbically, noting its lacklustre appearance: the black paint on the front door was flaking, and a pair of shabby green curtains were hanging in the grimy downstairs window.

'Looks like we're the first ones here,' said Matty, scouring the area for Brian's van, before undoing his seatbelt and opening the passenger door. 'Come on,' he said, 'let's go and introduce ourselves.'

They walked up to the door, rang the bell and waited.

A moment later, Dom and Matty detected signs of life from within: the sound of heavy footsteps approaching, a jangling security chain, and a key turning in the lock.

The front door then opened to reveal a plump man in his thirties, wearing loose-fitting jeans and an undersized Pink Floyd t-shirt that failed to conceal a protruding stomach.

'What?' he snapped, staring suspiciously at his visitors through long strands of unkempt ginger hair.

'We're Northern Circle,' began Matty. 'We have a session booked for today.'

A thin, humourless smile curled the sides of the man's

mouth.

'Oh, the freeloaders,' he said sardonically.

'We're the competition winners, if that's what you mean,' said Dom, irked by his disrespectful manner.

'Just the two of you, is there?'

'No,' said Matty. 'The others will be here any second.'

'Well, by my reckoning your session just started. You've got four hours, and then you're out on your arses. We've got another group booked in after you lot.'

'Right, I'll fetch my guitar then,' said Matty. 'Give me a hand, Dom.'

'Some afternoon this is going to be with that stroppy sod,' muttered Dom, lifting Matty's guitar case off the back seat. 'I thought people like him were meant to be cool and not tossers.'

Dom's lack of sleep had made his temperament as fragile as an eggshell.

'Whatever he calls us, that session is still paid for, just the same as if we'd handed over the money ourselves. Just keep your temper in check and don't go giving him cause to boot us out of there,' said Matty, attempting to placate his singer. 'I'll crack a few jokes to lighten the mood. He'll be putty in our hands.'

Walking through the open entrance into the hallway, they discovered their greeter had vanished.

'Hello,' shouted Matty along the corridor.

'Up here, lads,' a male voice boomed down at them from somewhere on the first floor.

Dom and Matty walked up the staircase and paused on the landing.

'Hello,' said Matty again.

'In the back room.'

The friends continued down a narrow corridor and entered a large, windowless room, in which were positioned various microphone stands and stools; in the corner of it was a much smaller room, from which a voice within called out.

'Hi. Come through into here and mind you don't trip on the wires. They're an occupational hazard, I'm afraid.'

Dom and Matty squeezed through the second doorway into the confined space.

Judging by the futuristic-looking black console that contained a mind-blowing array of knobs and coloured buttons, and a windowpane that offered a view into the outer room, Dom deduced that the narrow booth was the producer's work area.

From underneath the desk a male in his late twenties, with an unruly mop of dark hair, emerged; he stood up and dusted down the knees of his jeans.

'Just fixing a loose cable,' he said cheerfully, before introducing himself. 'Jez Turner. I'm the owner, and I'll be working with you today.'

Dom and Matty both shook his hand.

'Oh, you're the producer,' said a visibly relieved Matty. 'I thought …'

'… that Bruce was the producer. No, Bruce doesn't really have a proper job here. He just likes to help out with things in return for free recording time.'

'So, this is it, then?' said Matty, impressed by the surroundings.

Jez's smile conveyed a mix of pride and affection.

'Welcome to my world. This is my own little piece of paradise.'

'Have you been here long?' said Dom, keen to establish a rapport with Jez from the off.

'I picked it up cheap three years ago. It belonged to an old lady, but when she died, she had no family to leave it to. The estate agent said she'd been lying in this very room for weeks decomposing.'

Dom and Matty looked uncomfortable at hearing this piece of news.

'Just as well I don't believe in ghosts and all that stuff, otherwise I'd be bricking it sitting in here alone until the early hours. It's perfect for recording music, though, built before the war when they preferred substance over style. It's got real solid foundations, not like the dolls houses they're building on these new estates where you can hear your next door neighbour fart in his living room while you're sat watching *Crossroads*.'

Jez ceased talking and peered beyond Dom and Matty. 'I thought there'd be more of you. I wasn't expecting a duo.'

'Our drummer and bassist should be here any minute,' explained Matty, putting his guitar case down on the floor.

'I'll just give you a quick rundown of what to expect on the session while we wait. Basically, I'm at your beck and call. If you want, we can run through as many of your songs in one take as you like, with the best ten tracks being put onto tape. Personally, though, I think it would be more beneficial to only concentrate on a couple of songs, maybe three at best. That way, I get to know the tracks better, can suggest improvements and choose everyone's best performance. Another plus point is I'll have more time to spend mixing each track if there are only a few.'

'That option sounds good to me, Jez,' said Matty. 'Go for it.'

From downstairs, the sound of the doorbell suggested the two missing band members had arrived; a moment later, Mick and Brian duly appeared.

'All right,' said Mick, a drum carry case in each hand; Brian loomed in the background.

'And then there were four,' said Jez.

'Who the hell was that ignorant git who let us in?' complained Mick.

Jez laughed. 'Take no notice of Bruce. His bark's worse than his bite.'

'He seemed OK to me,' added Brian.

Jez stared at Brian in astonishment. 'Well, bugger me, that's a first. A musician who Bruce hasn't pissed off within a minute of meeting them. The pair of you weren't separated at birth, were you?'

Jez quickly introduced himself to Mick and Brian, and ran through the itinerary once again for their benefit.

'Right, lads,' he said in conclusion. 'I'll leave you to bring the rest of your stuff inside and get set up.'

'No worries, Jez,' said Matty, before addressing everyone. 'You heard the man. Let's get cracking.'

'That's what I like to see,' remarked Jez drolly, following them down the stairs and out into the street. 'Good, honest, working-class lads not afraid of hard work. You can quote me on that in the chapter entitled "I knew them when they were shite", when you've all become millionaires and they come to interview me for a book about you.

'Right, I'm just popping to the shop for some milk, so we can have a brew. Can one of you stick the kettle on when you get back inside? The kitchen's downstairs at the back of the house. There's no point in asking Bruce, as he'll be playing on the space invaders machine I've got. He's desperate to beat my score. Any preference on biscuits from the shop?'

'Jaffa Cakes,' said Mick.

'I said biscuits, not cakes,' said Jez lightly.

'Eh,' replied a confused Mick.

'Kit Kats,' said Matty.

Jez stared at them all in exaggerated disbelief. 'Fucking hell, they're making outrageous demands before they've recorded a note,' he joked. 'Listen, my commitment only stretches to squeezing something musically legible from you lot between now and four o'clock. The refreshments are provided from the goodness of my heart, so the options are Custard fucking Creams or Digestives. At least until you sell a few records. Bag me a top ten and you're definitely in Kit Kat territory.

'I'll be five minutes. Take the kettle off the ring when it starts to boil and switch the gas off. And try not to rile Bruce while I'm out. He's like the Incredible Hulk if you push him too far.'

'The Geordie David Banner,' said Matty.

'That's a good one,' said Jez, laughing to himself as he walked up the street.

Each member of Northern Circle had agreed beforehand to put aside for one day the petty arguments that usually arose in rehearsals, to pull together in a unified effort to produce the best music possible in the short time available to them.

For the most part, they were true to their word, with not a raised voice or a harsh glance exchanged all afternoon.

When their allotted time was up, they had managed to commit to tape their three songs written to date.

Everyone was in good spirits as they began to pack their equipment away. Leaving them to it, Jez returned just as the band were poised to depart.

'I've just had a telephone call to say my next session's cancelled,' he began. 'The singer has a grumbling appendix apparently, which means their misfortune is your good fortune. I've got the evening free if you want to hang out a bit longer.'

'We'd love to Jez, but we can't afford it,' said Matty.

'Don't worry about that,' replied Jez, casually disregarding the monetary problem with a wave of his hand. 'I don't do refunds so close to a booking, so my time's already been paid for.'

Matty grinned. 'If that's the case, I'm game.'

'And the rest of you are OK to stay?' said Jez, turning to the other three members.

'Fine with me,' Mick said.

Dom concurred. 'Cool with me, too.'

'I'll have to check with my Pauline,' said Brian. 'Can I use

131

your phone?'

'Sure. There's one downstairs in the hallway.'

Brian shuffled out of the room.

'Is he always like this?' said Jez.

'He's under the thumb, Jez,' said Matty. 'He even needs to ask permission from his missus to go to the toilet. Don't worry, though. If he goes, I can play his bass parts.'

'Well, that being the case, I suggest we take half an hour's break,' said Jez. 'There's a chip shop on Front Street if you want to grab something to eat.'

Brian re-entered a minute later. 'Pauline's happy for me to stay.'

'Hallelujah,' said Dom.

'Coming to the chippy, Brian?' asked Mick.

Brian shook his head. 'No, thanks. I'll just go and have a chat with Bruce,' he said, exiting the room in search of the cantankerous assistant.

'Yes, your bass player's definitely found a soul mate in Bruce,' said Jez, causing the whole room to erupt in laughter.

'OK, everyone. Time to call it a night,' said the jaded producer, rubbing his eyes. 'I'm dead on my feet here.'

It was after nine o'clock, and the bonus time granted to the band had been productive, enabling them to finish writing and recording one of their incomplete songs.

'I just want to say, though,' said Jez soberly, 'how much I've enjoyed working with you all today. You should be proud of yourselves.'

'When will the tape be ready?' asked a hoarse Dom.

'I'll work on it over the next few weeks, and give you a call to come and collect it once it's done.'

'Let me write my number down for you,' said Matty, scribbling it onto a sheet of paper. 'I'll pop over when you call.'

'Give me a shout next time you get some gigs lined up

locally. I'd like to see you play live.'

'Will do, Jez,' said Dom.

'I'll keep my ears open for anything further afield, too,' said Jez. 'It won't do you any harm to try different audiences out. I've got a friend in the industry in London who sometimes gets to hear which venues the talent scouts from the record company he works for are going to be at.'

'You could get us into those types of places?' asked Matty eagerly.

'Perhaps,' Jez said cagily, 'but you're getting a little ahead of yourselves. Let me work my magic on these songs of yours first, and then we'll take it from there. But you'll need to have at least an hour's worth of original material if you're going to be taken seriously in those kinds of places.'

'Jez, you're fucking incredible,' said Matty.

'Just as long as you don't forget me when you're in the music charts, and I'm still wading through the pretentious shite of every kid in Durham who wants to be the next big thing.'

Once their equipment was loaded in the van, Dom and Matty said their farewells to Jez, Brian and Mick.

'I don't know about you, mate,' began Matty, as they got into Dom's Mini, 'but I'm still buzzing. I don't feel like going home just yet.'

'I'm too knackered to go for a drink, Matty. Anyway, I've got the car.'

'I meant go somewhere quiet to clear our heads.'

'Go on, then,' said Dom, too weary to argue.

'Good lad,' said Matty, as Dom started the engine. 'Right, just drive down towards the city centre and I'll direct you from there.'

Five minutes later, Dom was driving cautiously down North Road, not wishing to hit any of the drunken revellers staggering like zombies up and down the street.

Turning into the quieter, more salubrious South Street,

with its residential three storey townhouses facing the cathedral across the river, Matty instructed Dom to continue a little further down the narrow cobbled lane.

'Pull in here,' said Matty a few seconds later, as they approached a small parking area.

Dom did as requested. 'Now what?'

'You're going to love this,' said Matty, exiting the car and quickly disappearing out of sight down an unlit footpath.

'For fuck's sake, Matty,' muttered Dom, getting out and locking the car.

Unseen thorny branches clawed at his face as he blindly followed his friend in the darkness.

'Where are you?' he shouted, struggling to keep his footing on the steep descent.

'I'm over here,' replied Matty.

With his eyes slowly adjusting to the gloom, Dom was just able to make out the tall figure of Matty in the distance, walking in the direction of the river.

'Sit yourself down on here,' said Matty, once Dom had caught up with him, indicating a set of wide concrete steps that led down from a large storage hut to the water's edge.

'This is where a local rowing club keep their boats and equipment,' explained Matty. 'Whenever I need some real peace and quiet, to be alone with my thoughts and unclutter my mind, I often come down here. I look up at the stars in the sky and sometimes wish I was up there, so far away. It makes everything down here on earth seem so small and trivial.'

'You come here by yourself, at night?' said Dom.

'Of course.'

'You're out of your mind. Don't you get scared?'

Matty shook his head. 'No. I just ask myself who else would be mad enough to be walking late at night down here. I mean, you get the occasional couple necking on in the trees or the odd pisshead, but nobody really hassles you. Murders and things like that don't happen here.'

'There's always a first time,' warned Dom.

'This is Durham City, Dom, not New York. Go on, take a good look around you. It's beautiful.'

Dom had to agree it was a captivating spectacle. Perched atop the peninsula across the river was the illuminated, towering cathedral, visible for miles to the naked eye; above it, a plump moon was hanging in the dark sky, its luminosity reflected in the gently rippling water.

'You see what I mean, don't you?'

'I suppose so,' admitted Dom, although he would have preferred to have the more alluring Katy from Donnelly's with him in such a romantic location.

'One day we'll be able to afford one of those houses we just passed, if our tape does the trick with the record companies,' said Matty.

'We could buy four next to each other, just like The Beatles in the *Help* movie,' Dom joked.

Matty smiled agreeably. 'It's a nice dream to have.'

'Hey, we'll have to remember this moment when someone comes to tell the story of the band,' said Dom, resuming Jez's theme from earlier of how Northern Circle's formative years might one day be chronicled if they went on to achieve fame.'
"After they finished their first professional recording session, Blackburn and Parker wandered the riverbanks of Durham City late at night with the conviction that fame and fortune was a heartbeat away". How does that sound?'

'Much better than, "They went down town to get pissed on cheap lager and to try and pull a couple of slappers",' laughed Matty.

Matty stood up and patted down the seat of his trousers.

'Come on, let's go for a pint. I'll get piles if I sit on this cold surface much longer. We've just got time before last orders. This will probably be my last opportunity for a good night out until after my exams.'

The band had agreed to take a brief hiatus from rehearsals

and gigs once they had completed their recording session, allowing Matty the time to concentrate fully on revising for his final year exams. The hope was that by the time Northern Circle reconvened in July a string of record companies would be eagerly banging on their door, desperate to sign them up.

'Go on, then,' said Dom, unable to resist the temptation.

'Good lad. Just leave the car where it's parked. I'll fetch you down in the morning to collect it.'

'We're only having a couple, though, aren't we?' said Dom, raising himself up.

'Well, we can always go clubbing afterwards if the mood takes us,' said Matty mischievously, as the pair began to walk down the riverside path in the direction of the city centre.

'I suppose we could,' laughed Dom.

CHAPTER 14

It was lunchtime on the last day in May, a full month since their recording session, when Matty finally received the telephone call from Jez informing him the results were available for collection.

Matty tore himself away from his revision notes and excitedly sped over on his scooter to Bearpark. Admitted by Bruce back into the inner sanctum of JT Recording Studios, he was feverish with anticipation as he waited in the downstairs lounge.

The forthright producer appeared a couple of minutes later, carrying a tray containing mugs and Bourbon biscuits.

'Matty, good to see you, mate. I took the liberty of making you a drink. Is coffee good for you?'

'Fine, Jez.'

'Right, I'll not say a word more until we've had a listen,' said Jez, placing the tray down on the coffee table. 'I'm sure you're dying to listen to the fruits of your labour after all these weeks.'

Matty attempted a smile of confidence, but was so nervous at what he was about to hear that it materialised more as a grimace.

Jez slotted a tape into his hi-fi system and pressed play; the pair sat in silence as they listened, with Jez poker-faced throughout.

When the tape ended, Jez ejected it and handed it to Matty.

'I've got to admit it, Matty,' said Jez, picking up his mug and settling back into his armchair, 'when I first clapped eyes on you lot, I thought it was going to be a waste of everybody's time. But I have to admit you've really surprised me; there's definitely some rough talent there in that group of yours. Dom's got a good set of lungs on him, and you're not so bad yourself on guitar. And the pair of you can write a tune or two, which doesn't hurt, so it's obvious you've got the necessary tools. However, I'm sure the thousands of amateur groups all over the country have similar opinions of themselves. It just boils down to how much you really want success. The difference between the likes of those who have the smash hits, and the rest bubbling below the surface, is hard work, a hell of a lot of hard work. It also involves one other ingredient that you just can't buy or predict.'

'Yeah,' said Matty, 'what's that?'

'Luck,' Jez stated emphatically. 'Take The Beatles. Initially rejected by every major record company, who knows what would have become of them if George Martin hadn't taken a shine to them when they couldn't get the lickings of a dog off anyone else? They got lucky. And let's face it, you're going to need all the good fortune you can get without an obvious heartthrob to attract the girls. Let's be honest about it, Matty, none of you are going to give George Michael or Simon Le Bon a run for their money in the looks department.'

His pride dented, Matty noticeably bristled at this last remark.

'Got many friends, have you?' he said tartly.

'No offence intended,' laughed Jez. 'I'm just trying to tell it as it is. Honesty's what you want to hear, isn't it?'

'None taken,' said a slightly pacified Matty. 'Anyway, we're not in this for teenyboppers throwing their knickers at us and groupies who want to bed us.'

'You're telling me you're not shallow?' smirked Jez. 'I'll believe you respect them when you're actually turning the girls away, if you become famous.'

'Like I said, that's not what we're about,' said Matty categorically. 'We're serious musicians.'

'Getting back to the band, anyway, how are things with you all? Are you still gigging hard?'

'We don't have anything pencilled in at the minute. I'll let you know where we're playing once we book something after my exams are out of the way.'

Matty began to blush, aware that his reason for keeping a low musical profile did not exactly portray him as being one hundred percent committed to the cause.

He stood up and shook the producer's hand.

'Thanks again, Jez. You've done a really good job with our material. The other lads will be over the moon when they hear it.'

'All part of the service,' said Jez modestly.

On his way back home, Matty stopped off at Woolworth's in the city centre to buy a packet of envelopes, several books of stamps, four packs of blank audio cassette tapes and a writing pad.

Back in his bedroom, Matty set to work making multiple copies of the master tape while writing out letters of introduction to twenty London-based record companies.

Once these tasks were completed, he popped a letter and tape inside each envelope, before sealing, addressing and stamping them; all that remained was for him to make the short walk to the nearest post box.

With one spare recording of their sessions in his pocket, Matty made a detour to Dom's flat on his way home; he climbed the flight of stairs, walked down the gangway and pushed it through his letterbox with an accompanying note, before heading back home for another evening of mind-numbing revision.

Over the ensuing fortnight, Matty did his best to forget about the tapes on their journeys to the heart of the British music industry, with revision, exams and sleep dominating his time. Only on the occasions when the telephone rang at home and he dashed downstairs to answer it, did Matty allow his thoughts to return to his musical aspirations. However, rather than the head of EMI phoning to offer Northern Circle a seven figure recording contract, the caller always ended up being a relative or a family friend.

Postal deliveries also proved to be a momentary, twice daily distraction. Matty would impatiently flick through the fresh pile of bills and junk mail that landed on the doormat, hoping to discover the dream letter inviting them to an audition.

When the eve of his final exam came around in the middle of June, Matty had still not received a single response; this was a sobering reality check and real food for thought. His days of freedom were dying one by one, and all that stood between him and his reluctant admission into the real world was the holiday in the Lake District he and Dom were due to embark upon the following week.

While Matty was revising late into the night for the last time, Dom was grappling with troubles of his own.

Ever since mid-April, the excess noise emanating from the flat above had been a problem. Through chatting to other residents, Dom had discovered some facts about his neighbour from hell: he was a divorcee called Doug, and worked on the oil rigs in Scotland.

The nature of Doug's occupation meant that for two weeks at a time while he was away, Dom was able to return home every evening to a tranquil atmosphere. The counterbalance to this, however, was the fortnight of sleepless nights when Doug was in residence, when the sound of indefatigable party antics filtered down through the floorboards. Loud music, drunken voices and heavy footsteps would commence late in the evening and continue until four or five o'clock in the morning; at times, it sounded to Dom as if he was living below a nightclub.

And now, for the fourth night in a row, the sound of rock music playing had just woken Dom up at two in the morning.

'Jesus Christ,' he shouted, tears of frustration welling up in his eyes.

Severely disgruntled, he sprang out of bed and went into the living room. As the latest shindig raged on above his head, an exasperated Dom paced up and down in the dark, his fortitude smashed to pieces. Sleep deprivation had left him feeling constantly moody and drained all week, and with less than four hours to go before he was due to get up for work, Dom was now at breaking point.

He sank down to his knees in a corner of the room and futilely clamped the palms of his hands over his ears in an attempt to snatch a fleeting respite from the racket.

As the unrelenting barrage of noise continued, Dom was powerless to prevent his mind from dipping for the first time below the marker where sanity temporarily ends and madness begins; the mental ticking bomb inside him had detonated.

With a plan instantly formulated in his mind, and beyond the point of caring about the consequences of his actions, Dom went into the passageway, returning a moment later with his amplifier and microphone. He knew it was impossible to match Doug physically, but was willing to take him on in a war of decibels.

Plugging his amplifier in at the wall, Dom switched it on and turned the volume up to maximum.

It was time to fight fire with fire.

He clasped the microphone with both hands, held it up to his lips and unleashed weeks of pent-up anger in one swift primal scream.

'Doug, you noisy bastard. Will you shut the fuck … upppp? Just shhhuuutt ... uuuupppppp.'

Many of the residents of Harold Wilson House immediately woke up in a heightened state of shock and confusion, believing that an earthquake had struck or that there had been an explosion nearby.

Dom switched off the amplifier. Suddenly drained of energy, he sank onto the sofa, his ears sore and ringing.

As his hearing gradually cleared, Dom realised that all was now silent upstairs; he smiled to himself, enjoying the moment of triumph. If he had known that such drastic measures would produce the desired effect, he would have taken action weeks ago.

The sweet taste of victory soured abruptly a couple of minutes later when a fist pounded against his front door, shaking Dom out of his complacency. His letterbox snapped open, and an irate voice shouted down the passageway.

'Come out, you cheeky bastard. I know you're in there.'

Dom's heart nearly stopped, as he instantly recognised the voice that had haunted him for weeks.

'If you don't show your face, I'm going to kick in your front door and drag you out myself. You've got one minute.'

'Shit, shit, shit,' cursed Dom.

With the clock ticking, Dom swiftly weighed up his limited options: he could remain inside the flat and hope that Doug's threat was an idle one, or go to the front door and attempt to reason with him, man to man.

When the minute was up, the disturbing sound of a body forcibly throwing itself against the door suddenly made both of these choices less appealing.

This left one further alternative: run like hell.

Dom grabbed his car keys off the top of the television set. He then tore the curtains apart, opened the front window and climbed out onto the window ledge. With his right hand clutching the window frame, Dom reached across to the drainpipe that was mercifully nearby, wrapped his free arm around it and held on for dear life while he established a firmer hold with both feet and his other hand. The drainpipe groaned under the strain of his body weight, but held firm long enough for him to descend to the communal gardens.

Dom peered around the side of the building. To his relief, the public entrance to the flats and the car park just beyond were both clear.

Realising that the chances of him being seen and apprehended increased the longer he remained rooted to the spot, Dom decided to leave his position of cover and sprint towards the car park, wincing as his bare feet swapped comforting grass for concrete.

As Dom arrived at his car, he heard an angry voice behind him call out.

'There he is.'

Dom glanced over to the block of flats in time to see three men haring along the first floor gangway towards the stairwell. Estimating he had approximately thirty seconds before they would be upon him, Dom got into his Mini and pulled the door shut.

In the dark interior, his first attempt at blindly slotting the key into the ignition was unsuccessful; a task he would usually perform automatically under normal circumstances had suddenly become unexpectedly difficult.

Precious seconds elapsed as, with shaking hands, he tried again; for a second time, he failed.

Dom imagined the vengeful mob now tearing down the stairs, smelling his fear.

He took a deep breath, peered in the gloom to where he estimated the ignition slot was, and stabbed with the key again.

It slid mercifully in.

Dom started the engine, put the car into reverse and shot backwards, braking sharply when the rear bumper was centimetres away from the row of garages.

The hunting pack was on the grass verge, a matter of metres away, baying for his blood.

Frantically turning the steering wheel and accelerating away, Dom heard a fist thud against his side window, but the pursuers' efforts were in vain; he had evaded their clutches by the briefest of margins.

Breathing a heavy sigh of relief, Dom left the housing estate and made his way to the safety of the nearby dual carriageway.

CHAPTER 15

'That was some entrance this morning,' remarked Ronnie Blackburn gruffly, sitting down at the breakfast table next to Daniel and pouring himself a cup of tea.

Sitting opposite, Dom sipped sheepishly from his mug of coffee.

'You ring the doorbell in the middle of the night with nothing on but your Y-fronts, and then go to bed without a word of explanation. What's going on? I'm all ears.'

'I had to leave the flat in a hurry, Dad.'

'Why, for Christ's sake?'

Dom explained the events of recent weeks that had led up to the flashpoint incident hours earlier.

'Eeh, you expect people like that on some of these rough estates, but I never expected them to be where you're living,' said a shocked Iris, keeping an eye on the bread toasting under the oven grill. 'Well, that's settled it, son. I'll make up the bed in the spare room with proper sheets tonight instead of that old blanket. You can stay here for as long …'

'Ah, give over, Iris. It'll all have blown over by now. He can stay here one more night, if he wants, but then it's back to his own place.'

Her husband's suggestion horrified Iris.

'Don't give me that look, either,' said Ronnie. 'He made his own bed when he moved out of here in the first place. He needs to learn to be a man and to cope with situations like this.'

Ronnie drained the contents of his cup and placed it back down on the table.

'Right, if that's all it was, I can get off to work now,' he said. 'I'll see you all later.'

'Some help he was,' said Dom, at the sound of the front door closing. 'I think he'd be happy for me to get torn to

144

pieces by that psycho, just as long as I don't let down the family honour by being a wimp.'

Daniel, who up until now had been silently eating his breakfast cereal, began smirking to himself.

'I thought you'd find it funny,' complained Dom. 'Daddy's blue-eyed boy.'

'No, I'm not,' whined Daniel, his pained expression implying he was mortally offended by such a suggestion, although everyone present knew there was more than a grain of truth in the accusation.

'It's not that your father doesn't care, son,' said Iris, trying to remain loyal to all parties. 'It's just that he's got a lot on his mind at the moment. There's more redundancies looming at the shipyard before the end of the year, and he's convinced he'll be one of those given his cards. He would never admit it, but he's a worried man at the moment. Come to think of it, I'm worried. If we lose his pay packet, then I don't know how we'll make ends meet.

'But I have to say that I'm not happy about the situation you're in. This neighbour of yours sounds like a right lunatic, braying on your door in the middle of the night.'

Daniel finished eating his cereal, slid off his chair and headed for the door.

'Put your bowl in the sink, Daniel, please.'

'I'm coming straight back. I'm just fetching my magazine from the living room.'

'Sink,' insisted Iris.

Daniel tutted to express his displeasure, but knew better than to disobey his mother and risk the wrath of her temper.

'Shall I have a word with your uncle?' said Iris, returning to the matter at hand while placing the last batch of fresh toast into the rack on the table. 'I'm sure he could sort something out.'

Dom shook his head. 'As much as it pains me to say it, Dad's right. I can't go running to someone else whenever

145

things go wrong. I've got to learn to fight my own battles.'

Iris moved over to the sink and began to run the hot tap. She gazed thoughtfully out of the kitchen window into the backyard, troubled by the prospect of Dom attempting to resolve his dilemma unaided. She recognised her son had his pride, but was not prepared to sit back and watch him gamble his health and risk a heavy fall just to keep it intact.

In that instant, Iris knew the most appropriate course of action to take. She also realised that it was best to keep her scheming to herself.

'Look at you,' said Iris, changing the subject and adopting a lighter mood, 'sitting there in your pants and nothing else. The last time I saw you do that you were about six years old.'

Dom blushed; in the cold light of day, he recognised how ridiculous he must look.

'A full set of clothes and packing my toothbrush was the last of my worries with that maniac on my tail.'

Iris nodded understandingly. 'You grab some more toast, son, and I'll go and dig out some of your washed clothes so that you can get to work. They'll just need a quick iron. You can borrow a pair of your father's shoes.'

'Thanks, Mam,' said Dom gratefully. 'You're a star.'

Once he was dressed and on his way to work, Iris picked up the kitchen phone handset.

'Who're you calling, Mam?' said Daniel, staring dreamily at a poster of Bananarama in his copy of *Smash Hits*.

'Uncle Tel, so not a word to your brother or father.'

'Why not, Mam?' asked Daniel curiously, unable to appreciate the delicate nature and complications of family politics.

'Because your father wants your brother to sort this mess out himself, and your brother is too stubborn to ask for help. The way things stand, Dom will end up being beaten to a pulp by some gorilla who doesn't care about the knock-on effect of his actions.'

Daniel put down his magazine, a look of astonishment on his face.

'Dom's gonna fight with a monkey?'

'Oh, son, just read your music … thingy,' she said in exasperation, not in the mood for his madcap teenage humour at that time of day.

CHAPTER 16

'You're quiet today, Dom. I thought you'd be ecstatic, what with going off on holiday next Monday. Is there something up?'

His downbeat mood had been troubling Katy all hour as they strolled around the city centre on their lunch break.

Dom shook his head. 'It's nothing,' he said unconvincingly, his face a mask of unease.

All morning, Dom had thought about nothing else but his impending return that evening to Harold Wilson House, and the type of reception that awaited him.

Katy grabbed hold of his hand and gave it a supportive squeeze.

'If you were in any sort of trouble, you would tell me, wouldn't you?' she said earnestly.

Dom looked at Katy and briefly considered coming clean about the events of the previous evening, knowing that to do so would reveal his cowardice.

He quickly discounted the thought; the couple were still in the honeymoon period of their relationship, and Dom was not keen to reveal any weakness of character to her.

'Of course, I would,' he said, hating himself for lying so blatantly and convincingly.

The one major benefit of the recent cooling in band activities had been the additional time it had allowed Dom to spend in Katy's company.

He still had to pinch himself to believe that he had ended up courting the attractive young woman from Accounts, much to the displeasure of several of his male colleagues. Their brief chat in the stockroom towards the end of the previous year had acted as an icebreaker in the workplace, but Dom had never expected her to follow-up on her promise to

148

attend a Northern Circle gig. She, however, had proved as good as her word, and had been there to offer enthusiastic support when the band next played in Durham City.

In the weeks that followed, their mutual shyness had receded as they discovered how much they enjoyed each other's company.

Finally, in early May, they had become an official couple. Walking Katy to her bus stop after a work's night out, a gibbering Dom had attempted to explain the depth of his feelings for her. Fortunately, for him, the attraction was mutual, and Katy had pulled him into the shaded seclusion of a shop doorway to share a tender kiss.

Their relationship had now gotten to the stage where Dom would occasionally sleep over at Katy's when her flatmate was away. He had also spent a lot of his spare time there in recent weeks, watching videos and hanging out, finding it a particularly welcome haven when the neighbour from hell was around.

On the short walk back to Donnelly's, the toot of a car horn caught Dom's attention.

'Got time for a quick chat?' smiled his uncle, popping his head out of the window of his BMW.

Dom sighed; he had a hunch as to why Tel had suddenly appeared out of nowhere, guessing it was more than mere coincidence.

'You go back to work, Katy,' he said. 'I'll just have a word with my uncle.'

'All right, son?' said Tel, once Dom had joined him inside the vehicle. 'How's the band going? Are you still playing your shows?'

'We haven't played any for a couple of months.'

Tel looked aghast. 'You haven't split up already, have you? I've been telling everyone my nephew's destined for *Top of the Pops*.'

'No, it's not that. Our guitarist has been tied up with exams, but we hope to be playing again in a couple of weeks.'

'Not very rock and roll, that. I can't recall Elvis ever putting off a show because he had a maths exam the next day.'

'It's not Matty's fault. He's under a lot of pressure from his parents.'

'So the dream's still alive?'

'Yeah,' said Dom, waiting for Tel to cut to the chase.

'I hear you're having problems?' said Tel, looking straight ahead, his voice suddenly quiet and business-like.

Dom, too, stared out of the windscreen, saying nothing.

'It's nothing to be ashamed of, son,' continued Tel. 'The world's full of bullies. You just have to know how to handle them. But before I can do anything, I need to know the full story.'

Put on the spot, and realising Tel would not take no for an answer, Dom briefly recapped his version of recent events.

When he had finished talking, Tel said, 'You've tried everything possible to resolve this in the correct manner, so don't be ashamed that things got a little out of hand when you lost your temper. Every man has his breaking point, Dom.'

'So, what happens now?'

'Well, if you think this neighbour of yours will be around for the next week, that means I can get this sorted out as soon as possible. Until then, it's best if you stay away from your flat.'

'I'm off on holiday on Monday until next weekend, though. I need to get stuff that I'm taking with me.'

'That's no problem, son,' said Tel. 'There's a notepad and pen in the glove compartment. Write down what you need and I'll pop over to get everything, and drop it off at your mother's house for you. Then, when you return home next week, this idiot will be long gone and your life returns to normal.'

150

'Are you sure you'll be able to handle him? He's built like Rambo.'

'Rambo?' said Tel mockingly, unfazed by the comparison. 'He'll be more like Dumbo by the time we've finished with him.'

Dom began to scribble down the list of items he required for his trip.

'That lass of yours is a right looker, isn't she? You certainly know how to pick them.'

Dom reddened.

'What's her name?'

'Katy.'

'Katy, eh? Your mother's never mentioned her.'

There was a simple reason for that: Dom had kept her existence a secret. His love life was not something he cared to discuss when he returned home for his Sunday dinner and weekly exchange of dirty for clean laundry. Now that Tel had spied her, Dom felt sure it was only a matter of time before his relationship became public knowledge.

'She's not really my girlfriend,' said Dom, unashamedly telling a white lie. 'We're just good friends.'

Tel laughed at his nephew's visible unease. 'Whatever she is, Dom, you make sure you look after her. You've landed on your feet there.'

'OK, I will. Anyway, I'd best be off,' said Dom, handing the notepad over. 'My boss will read me the riot act if I'm late.'

Tel gave the list a quick once-over. 'Yeah, I'm sure I can sort this lot out for you.'

'Thanks, Tel,' said Dom, opening the car door.

'No problem. Enjoy your break, and give me a call when you get back. I'll take you for a curry or a chinese. It's ages since we've had a good night out.'

'Will do.'

He got out of the car and waved as Tel bolted up Neville

Street.

Dom had mixed feelings about this latest development. On the one hand, it was reassuring that Tel had offered his support, but on the other, Dom worried over what "sorted out" would involve and whether Staveley would have a role to play. With the Langley Vale car park incident still fresh in his mind, it troubled Dom that his landlord was a character who thought it acceptable to carry unlicensed firearms around with him.

CHAPTER 17

'Oh, I wish I was coming with you,' said Katy, glumly nibbling on a slice of toast. 'You'll be out in the countryside in all that fresh air while I'm stuck inside the office doing boring accounts.'

'There are downsides, though, Katy. Imagine having to share a tent with Matty and his smelly feet. I'll be ringing the Samaritans for help by Tuesday.'

'Don't lie to me, you sod,' she responded lightly. 'You can't wait to get away from here and booze it up.'

Dom laughed out loud at Katy's perceptiveness.

After the stresses of the previous week, Dom's weekend had turned out to be much better than expected. Having reconciled himself to reluctantly spending a further three nights back in Spennymoor, Katy had come to his rescue at the eleventh hour on the Friday evening, by inviting him to stay over at her flat for the weekend. Her housemate had unexpectedly had to travel to Sheffield to see her sick mother, so Katy had the place to herself.

'Me and Matty have had this planned for ages, Katy,' he reasoned, 'long before I knew you properly. Things will be different once we get home next Saturday. Matty has his job searching to keep him busy, so I'll be all yours.'

'Do you mean that?'

'Of course, apart from band practice on Sundays and Wednesdays, and the occasional gig.'

'Dom, I know how important that is to you,' said Katy seriously. 'I would never come between you and your music.'

'And Saturday night is lads' night out.'

'Well, you could maybe cut back on them a little, so we could have the occasional night out.'

'And Tuesday, don't forget Tuesdays,' said Dom, acting as if he had not heard Katy's previous response.

153

This last remark puzzled Katy. 'What happens on a Tuesday?'

'Nothing yet,' said Dom, struggling to maintain a straight face, 'but I'm working on it.'

The look of genuine hurt on Katy's face was all too much for him to take; unable to maintain the pretence any longer, he burst out laughing.

'You bastard,' she said. 'I knew you were winding me up.'

'Maybe we can get away ourselves later on in the summer,' said Dom tentatively, once Katy had stopped playfully whacking him.

Katy smiled. 'Do you mean that?'

'Of course, I mean it. I wouldn't have said it otherwise.'

'On one condition,' said Katy.

'What?'

'I get to choose the location. Agreed?'

'As long as I get to choose the one after that,' countered Dom.

Katy nodded. 'Deal. Right,' she said, rising from the breakfast table, 'I'm going for my shower, otherwise I'll be late for work. What time is Matty picking you up again?'

'Half twelve.'

'And he knows how to get here?'

'Yes.'

Alone in the living room, Dom switched on breakfast television and stretched out on the sofa, savouring the prospect of a whole week spent away from the dingy stockroom at Donnelly's.

CHAPTER 18

'Goodbye Durham, hello Cumbria,' whooped Dom, as they crossed the county boundary.

With a golden sun reigning supreme in a clear blue sky, the Style Council playing on the car stereo, and the promise of long, leisurely days ahead of them, all was good in the world of Dom and Matty, as they travelled to their holiday destination in the brown Volvo Estate Matty had borrowed from his father.

When Matty had first broached the idea of going on holiday, in the midst of a drunken night out in March, Dom had swiftly agreed; the only point of discussion in the ensuing weeks had been to decide upon a destination.

Dom's top choice had been London, having never previously visited the capital city; however, a visit to the local travel agent to browse through their brochures led to him reluctantly ruling it out, as it proved far too expensive for their limited budget.

Brighton had been Matty's preferred choice; as a mod from the north, he had long dreamt of making a pilgrimage to the South Coast resort. However, once the high cost of the return train journey and a week's stay in a hotel was calculated, the pair had dropped the idea. Matty was disappointed but philosophical, vowing to make the journey on his scooter on a future bank holiday weekend when he had more funds at his disposal.

From the initial list of four possibilities, only two had remained: Blackpool and the Lake District. The former had held some appeal for the friends, namely for its prolificacy of pubs and seaside attractions, but as they had both visited the resort on so many occasions in previous years, they ruled it out on the grounds of familiarity and predictability.

Dom had never visited the Lakes, and Matty had only been once as a teenager. Besides being the last choice remaining, the decisive factor was its economic viability: there were dozens of cheap camping sites to choose from, and it was a relatively short drive away, so travel costs would be manageable.

Dom was also attracted by the region's literary connections. Although ignorant of most of the romantic works of Wordsworth, Coleridge and other related pillars of English literature, he was aware that some of the most memorable stanzas ever committed to paper had been inspired by the unspoilt natural beauty of the Lakes. Dom became convinced that the experience of sitting atop mountain peaks, or relaxing by campfires next to awe-inspiring lakes, would trigger a fruitful spell of songwriting.

'Jesus, my head's pounding,' complained Matty, when they had been on the road for fifty minutes.

'Were you out last night?'

Matty nodded gingerly. 'I was through Newcastle having a farewell drink with some of the lads from my course. God, I was hammered.'

'What time did you get home?'

'I slept through there on my mate Gav's floor.'

Dom absorbed this information. 'What time did you stop drinking?'

'Search me. The last thing I remember was Gav buying a kebab sometime after two on the way back from the disco, and then everyone drinking vodka at his place. It must have been at least four when I crashed out, but I can't be certain. It's still all a bit hazy.'

'Pull over, Matty,' said Dom suddenly.

'What?'

'Pull over.'

'I can't. There's no laybys to stop at, and this truck behind me is right up my arse.'

'For fuck's sake,' shouted Dom, 'if we get stopped by the coppers, they'll lock you up and throw the key away if you get breathalysed.'

'Stop getting your knickers in a twist. I had probably two vodkas at best, and they'll be out of my system by now. That'll explain the thumping hangover I've got. Anyway, you do know where we're going, don't you?'

Dom was confused, not following Matty's logic.

'The Lakes. Why?'

'Exactly,' said Matty, as if his, as yet unspoken, theory was obvious. 'They're country bumpkins up there, aren't they? Their coppers aren't exactly in the same league as *The Sweeney*. They're more relaxed about life. A crime wave for them is a spate of Mars Bar thefts or a sheep shagger on the loose.'

Dom shook his head disapprovingly at his friend's patronising attitude, although he figured Matty was simply being deliberately mischievous with his comments. Dom was also realistic enough to know that, bar ploughing into a herd of cattle walking across the road, they stood little chance of attracting the attention of the local constabulary. For all of that, he still preferred to err on the side of caution.

'Next café we come to, pull in, please. I'm ready for a coffee anyway, and it won't do you any harm to have a strong black one.'

'If it makes you happy, I'll pull over and have a coffee,' replied Matty. 'Now, will you please relax, mate? We're on our holidays, with no parents, no lecturers and no bosses to tell us what to do. The world's our oyster. Well, until next weekend at least.'

The pair did not speak until several miles later when Dom spotted a sign for a hotel.

'This one will do, Matty.'

'OK, no problem.'

Dom let out a sigh of relief when they were finally stationary in the hostelry's car park.

'Right, I'm just going to the gents,' he said, getting out of the Volvo.

'I'll go and see if they're serving food,' said Matty.

When Dom found his friend a couple of minutes later, he nearly had a coronary at the sight that confronted him: Matty was at the counter of the bar, staring lovingly at two freshly pulled pints of lager.

'Matty, what are you doing?' hissed Dom.

Matty looked at Dom as if he had suddenly grown two heads.

'Getting the drinks in. What does it look like?'

'I thought we were stopping for a coffee? Not a drop of the local sheep dip.'

'Hair of the dog, that's what I need,' said Matty. 'I'll be as right as rain after this.'

'On top of all the booze still swilling around inside you from last night?'

'Don't fret, mate. I've got a high tolerance factor when it comes to alcohol. I'm not a lightweight.'

Conscious that he was beginning to sound like an old bore with his nagging protestations, and that he was running the risk of falling out with Matty before they had even arrived at their destination, Dom decided damage limitation was the best course of action.

'Well, make sure you order something to eat. A big meal should soak some of it up,' he said, more in hope than belief.

'Now you're talking,' said Matty, brightening up. 'I can't remember the last time I had a decent meal.'

'Nineteen eighty, by the look of you.'

After squeezing in an hour's nap in the car after his lunch, Matty declared himself rejuvenated and ready to commence driving. As they headed off on the second leg of their journey,

Dom decided to raise the subject of the band.

'So, what's the plan for Northern Circle when we get home?'

Matty thought for a moment before answering. 'I think we need to get working on more new songs, so that we can push Jez to get us a gig at one of those talent-spotting places in London he was telling us about. Especially if the tape we made doesn't do anything.'

'There's still been no interest from any of the record companies?'

'Not a sodding thing,' said Matty darkly.

'Have you written anything new in the last few months?'

Matty shook his head. 'Been too busy with my revision. What about you?'

'I've been working on a few ideas.'

'Oh well, that can be the starting point. Now that I've got a bit of free time on my hands, I'll get cracking too, so between us we should be able to come up with plenty of new songs.'

'Have you started looking for any jobs yet?' said Dom.

'I've applied for a couple and have some interviews to attend next week, but I can't see me being successful as there will be hundreds of people in for them.'

'You never know.'

'Anyway, what else have you been up to? I feel like I've been on a desert island for weeks. Are you seeing that lass from your workplace who came to a couple of our gigs? What's her name again?'

'Katy.'

Matty snapped his fingers. 'Katy. That's it.'

'We've been going steady for a while. She's got a flat over Newton Moor, so I've been spending a lot of time over there.'

'Really? You jammy bugger. You've done all right for yourself there, mate.'

'Cheers.'

The pair chatted for a further thirty minutes, until Matty

noticed how close they were to their destination.

'Bloody hell, we're almost there,' he said, pointing at a sign at the side of the road. 'Keswick fifteen miles. We'll have the tent pitched and our beans bubbling away in the pan before we know it.'

'I hope those clouds clear,' said Dom, peering through the windscreen at the now ominously black sky.

'I wouldn't take too much notice of them. The weather's extremely changeable over here. Rain one minute; sun and blue skies the next. You did bring a coat?'

'No.'

'Always come prepared, young Dominic,' joked Matty. 'I'll have to get you schooled into the Parker code of conduct. When in Cumbria, you need a pac-a-mac in your bag and a johnny in your wallet.'

Dom laughed. 'You're optimistic.'

Matty smiled confidently. 'I've got form up this neck of the woods. I pulled the last time I was here with my parents. The summer of '77. It was a vintage year.'

'Bollocks.'

'It's the truth. A family from Leeds was in the tent next to ours. They had a daughter called Jeanette. While both sets of parents were sat around the campfire getting pissed, the two of us were getting it on up a mountain.'

'The whole way? At fifteen?'

'No, but everything else. And now that the shackles have been unlocked after my brief academic exile, who knows what's in store? One thing's for certain: the mothers of Cumbria had better lock up their daughters because Matty's coming to town.'

'Dear God,' said Dom, shaking his head.

An hour later, Dom and Matty had still not arrived at their campsite. Having come off the main road at the correct junction, a wrong turning on one of the unfamiliar local roads had led to them completely losing their bearings. Eventually tiring of driving aimlessly and wasting valuable petrol, Matty pulled over on the narrow country lane.

'So,' began a frustrated Matty, gazing at the unfolded well-worn map in his friend's hands, 'where exactly do you think we are, Dom?'

'I'm not sure. It's difficult to tell on the map which turn-offs are proper roads and which are footpaths or dirt tracks.'

'Great. We could be anywhere, then,' grumbled Matty.

'This sodding rain hasn't helped,' remarked Dom, gazing miserably at the heavy downpour that had begun just as they had entered Keswick and which was showing no sign of easing.

'Well, we have to make an educated guess because I don't have that much petrol left in the tank. The last thing we need is to conk out miles from anywhere. OK, give me a closer look,' said Matty, taking hold of the map and resting it on the steering wheel.

As Matty occupied himself with planning their next move, Dom noticed in the rear view mirror a blue swirling light, quickly followed by the sight of a police officer getting out of his vehicle and walking towards them.

'Copper,' warned Dom.

A look of panic struck Matty. 'Where?'

'Behind us.'

Matty glanced over his shoulder. 'Act natural and let me do the talking,' he said quickly.

'What's the panic? We're doing nothing wrong, apart from having got lost.'

'I'm not bloody insured, Dom.'

'What?'

'My parents are abroad on holiday, so I borrowed my Dad's car without telling him. It's only been sitting on the drive doing nothing.'

'Jesus Christ,' said Dom.

The knuckles of the policeman rapped on Matty's window,

terminating their conversation.

Matty wound it down and greeted him with a cheery smile.

'Good afternoon, officer,' he said. 'Is there a problem?'

PC 637 Thorn squatted down onto his haunches so that he was face to face with Matty.

'Just doing the rounds, sir. I saw you parked up here, so thought I'd say hello and lay down a few rules about the do's and don'ts of driving in this area.'

'Rules,' said Matty, feigning puzzlement.

'Yes, rules, sir. I gather you are visitors here?'

'That we are, officer,' replied Matty. 'And you are just the person we need.'

This response flummoxed the man in uniform; typical initial reactions to his presence tended to range from the fearful to the downright obnoxious and aggressive. This, however, was a first: a member of the public declaring they were pleased to see him.

'And why would that be, sir?'

'Because, officer, we are a little lost. We are meant to be staying at a local campsite but appear to have missed our turn-off. Perhaps you can show us the error of our ways,' he said, turning the map for PC Thorn to inspect.

'OK,' drawled Thorn, in a heavy Cumbrian accent, 'you are here.' He planted his finger onto the top of the map. 'And which campsite is it you're staying at, sir?

'Pine Tree, officer.'

'In that case, you need to continue in the direction you are going for approximately two hundred metres, take your first left, and drive down that road for about a mile until you come to a junction; turn left at the junction, and you will come to it at the end of the lane.'

'That's jolly decent of you, thank you very much, officer,' said Matty, in his best model citizen voice that left the policeman unsure if he was being made fun of.

'Think nothing of it.'

A sudden flash of lightning, followed by a rumble of thunder and an increase in the ferocity of the rainfall, offered an incentive for the now extremely wet Thorn to conclude the conversation as swiftly as possible.

'Well, I'll let you lads get on your way. Remember to drive carefully; you're in the countryside now, not on one of your fast city roads. The rules are a little different here, what with tourists walking on the road and more cyclists about the place.'

'We certainly will, officer,' said Matty, restarting the engine. 'Thank you for your time.'

Matty pulled away and began to follow the directions he had been given.

'That's the way to act under pressure, Dom,' said Matty smugly. 'I called his bluff. He was expecting me to be evasive and on my guard. They don't know what to do if you act as if you're glad to see them.'

'You are bloody unbelievable,' said a severely annoyed Dom. 'If I'd known you weren't insured, I would have taken the Mini.'

'Don't be daft. It isn't big enough to fit all of the camping gear into, is it? Quit worrying and relax. There's been no harm done,' said Matty.

Finally locating it a short time later, Matty turned off the main road and drove down a gravelled lane until he came to the site reception, a humble-looking brown wooden hut. The shutter was pulled down and a sign hanging on the door said, 'Closed For Tea – Back Soon'.

'What do we do now?' asked Dom, watching torrential rain bounce off the windscreen.

'I'm not waiting here. It's not like checking into a hotel where we need a key to get into a room,' said Matty. 'We'll just find a space, park up, and pitch the tent once this bloody weather brightens up. We can let them know we've arrived when they re-open. Right, there's an arrow sign pointing the

163

way to the site, so if I just drive this way ...'

Following the road around a wide sweeping bend, the gravel soon gave way to rain-sodden grass, but tyre tracks worn into the ground indicated the correct direction to take.

Coming to the bottom of a short, sharp hill, Matty pressed hard on the accelerator; the furiously spinning wheels of the Volvo scattered mud in all directions as he struggled to negotiate the boggy incline.

'Jesus, this is like one of those rallies you see on *Grandstand,*' he shouted.

As they gradually neared the summit, to Dom and Matty's horror the car unexpectedly gained traction and propelled forwards with rapid velocity over the peak of the hill onto the treacherously slippy surface on the opposite side.

'Hey, slow down a little,' warned Dom, as they found themselves on the margins of the main camping area, a downward sloping field congested with tents.

Matty worked hard to prevent the vehicle colliding with the birds' mouth fencing on his left-hand side. Veering sharply to his right, he slammed on the brakes, causing the Volvo to skid precariously close to the outer line of tents.

'Shit,' screamed Matty, wrestling frantically with the steering wheel; it was as if the car had a mind of its own, refusing to adhere to his desperate efforts to regain control.

Straightening up just in time to avert a major disaster, Matty was unable to prevent the car from ploughing through the outstretched guy ropes of half a dozen tents, ripping out pegs and sending the canvas habitats into a state of semi-collapse.

The Volvo continued to hurtle downwards, leaving the camp and a trail of chaos behind in its wake.

At the bottom of the field, they crashed effortlessly through a wooden fence as if it was made of matchsticks. Bouncing and sliding for twenty metres further, they came to a halt as the ground levelled out.

'You OK?' said Matty, his head sore from banging against the roof interior on their bumpy descent.

'I … I think so,' replied Dom, in a state of shock.

They slowly got out of the Volvo to assess the damage it had sustained: steam was gushing ominously out from underneath the bonnet, and the front end had several large dents.

'Look at it. Dad's going to kill me, Dom.'

'Matty, you've just wiped out a load of tents and nearly half of Keswick's entire tourist trade,' blazed Dom, noticing the number of disgruntled campers in the distance angrily inspecting their property. 'Your dad's car is the last thing you should be worrying about.'

'Ah, get stuffed.'

Matty's unrepentant response was the final straw for Dom; unable to contain his fury at Matty's irresponsibility a second longer, he flung himself at his friend and grappled him to the ground. Matty fought back, and the pair began to brawl and flail around in the dirt.

'Hey, you two? What the bloody hell are you playing at?' shouted the ruddy faced site manager, half-running down the slope towards them.

His question fell on deaf ears, as the two youths continued to exchange punches with each other until, totally exhausted, they rolled onto their backs, their heaving chests gasping for breath.

CHAPTER 19

The two female members of staff in the Keswick Lakes Café looked on in amazement as their latest customers, caked from head to foot in mud, entered and occupied the table beside the main front window. The taller of the two new arrivals proceeded to stare moodily outside at the inclement weather while his companion, with folded arms, gazed disconsolately down at the floor.

Given the erratic regional climate, owner Sue Birtles was used to the sight of inappropriately dressed tourists entering her premises soaking wet from having been caught out by a sudden downpour, but she had never witnessed the sight now before her.

'If I was a complete bitch,' said Sue to Monique, her assistant, as the pair watched from behind the counter, 'I could just pull rank and insist you take their order. But, just to prove I'm a fair boss, why don't we toss a coin for it?'

'Toss?' said a baffled Monique.

Sue took a ten pence coin out of her pocket and demonstrated to Monique what she meant.

'Ah, yes, I see,' Monique laughed. 'OK, can I have heads, please?'

Sue placed the coin on her thumbnail and flicked it up, snatching it expertly out of the air as it began to descend.

'Ready?' she said, giggling as she prepared to unveil the result.

It was tails.

With a heavy sigh, Monique approached the table, her notepad at the ready.

'Good afternoon, gentlemen. Are you dining with us today?' she began, displaying a professional cheeriness that had greeted many a disgruntled customer that summer.

'Erm … I'm not sure at the moment,' said Matty, diverting

166

his gaze from the washed out street. 'Can I have a drink while I decide, please?'

His polite manner and warm tone of voice surprised Monique, having prepared herself for the complete opposite; she allowed herself to relax, satisfied they were not about to cause any trouble. Curious to discover the circumstances behind their current sorry appearance, a mixture of shyness and propriety prevented her from prying.

'We have English tea, coffee or hot chocolate.'

'Tea, please, pet.'

'And for your friend?'

'Coffee,' said Dom flatly.

'Canny lass,' commented Matty, watching admiringly as the attractive peroxide blonde assistant busied herself with their order. He lit a cigarette as his mood brightened. 'Where do you think she's from?'

'I thought we weren't meant to be speaking to each other,' said Dom coldly.

'I'm offering the olive branch here, mate. I said I was sorry, didn't I?' said Matty, wounded that his attempt to heal the bad blood between them was falling on stony ground.

'Sounded French to me,' muttered Dom eventually. 'Not that I'm an expert on linguistics or anything.'

Matty grinned, pleased Dom's frostiness had thawed a little.

'Or Scandinavian, maybe?' mused Matty. 'She has that look about her.'

'What? Because she's got blonde hair, blue eyes and a pale complexion? You've been watching too many dirty movies, Matty. No, definitely French.'

'Bollocks.'

'Only one way to find out,' challenged Dom. 'Ask her.'

'Me?'

'Not scared are you?' Dom teased, unable to be mad at Matty for too long.

'OK, then. I will,' said Matty defiantly, keen to humour Dom and play the idiot if it meant getting him back onside.

When Monique returned with their drinks, Dom sat back in his chair, fully expecting Matty to make a fool of himself.

'Thank you, pet,' boomed Matty, flashing his most winning smile as she placed the mugs down in front of them; for a second, he had forgotten how ridiculous his personal appearance was.

'Would you like to order some food now?'

'Yes, but before we do, I wonder if you would care to settle an argument. My friend and I were just trying to guess which country you are from. We have narrowed it down to France and the Scandinavian region.'

'Well done,' smiled Monique. 'I am half-French and half-English.'

To Dom's immense confusion, Matty leapt triumphantly out of his seat and punched the air.

'I win,' he said. 'I told you she was French, Dom.'

Before a surprised Dom could publicly dispute his spurious claim to victory, Matty wiped his soiled hand quickly on his serviette and thrust it towards the surprised assistant.

'I'm Matthew, by the way, but my friends call me Matty. This here is my good friend, Dom. We are musicians in a pop group.'

'Really?' said an instantly impressed Monique. 'Like Duran Duran and Wham?'

'Yes, if you like,' said Matty, prepared to temporarily put aside his hatred of all pop acts he considered teeny bop, in order to curry favour with her.

'Pleased to meet you, Matty. I am Monique.'

'Monique,' repeated a transfixed Matty, looking deep into her eyes. 'What a beautiful name.'

'Thank you. So, you guys, you have made a record?'

'Not yet, but it's only a question of time,' declared Matty confidently. 'We're waiting to hear back from one of the

168

major record companies, actually.'

'Really? I will look out for you on the radio and television. What is your band's name?'

'Northern Circle. Dom is the singer and I play guitar.'

'Are you here to play your songs, or are you on holiday?'

'Holiday, but who knows? If the opportunity presents itself to play an impromptu gig, I'm sure we could oblige.'

'Please, can I ask you another question now?' said Monique.

'Fire away,' said Matty, pleased that her English was so good; his grasp of the French language had never been that impressive.

She gesticulated at their appearance with her hand. 'Your clothes. Why are you so dirty?'

'Well, it's like this, Monique. We … we had a car accident. I took a bend on a country lane too fast and ended up in a muddy field.'

'Oh no,' said the horrified looking waitress.

'My car's been towed to the local garage, and we are stranded in town until it can be repaired.'

'You have a hotel booked?'

'No, pet,' said Matty. 'The plan had been to drive around until we found a campsite, but we're a bit stuck now without any wheels.'

Matty thought it best to avoid telling Monique the whole story: that they did have somewhere booked originally, but the owner had evicted them before they could hammer in a tent peg following an eventful arrival. He figured her sympathy for their plight might recede somewhat if all of the facts were aired.

'So, you have nowhere to stay?'

'Not at the moment,' admitted Matty. 'And we're nearly skint because of what it will cost to repair the damage to my car.'

Without the safety net of car insurance, the mechanic's

estimate, as well as the fee to have it towed to the garage from the campsite, had wiped out in an instant the vast majority of his and Dom's spending money.

'We are closing in an hour,' said Monique. 'Afterwards, perhaps I can help you try and find somewhere, although I do not hold out much hope. It is always busy here, regardless of the time of year, and the cheapest rooms will have been booked weeks ago.'

'It's very kind of you to offer, Monique,' began Dom, 'but …'

'… that would be greatly appreciated,' intervened Matty quickly, fearing Dom was about to decline any assistance.

'OK, now that is decided, let me take your food order.'

'Fish and chips for me,' said Matty.

'And me, please.'

Monique smiled at them sympathetically before disappearing through the door leading to the kitchen.

'Dom,' said Matty, 'I am going to marry that girl.'

Dom found this bold statement of intent to be the most ridiculous thing he had heard in a long time and began to laugh raucously.

'What's so funny about that?' said Matty touchily.

'Don't talk crap, Matty. You've only just met her. And anyway, she's way out of your league.'

'It's fate, I'm telling you,' continued Matty, undeterred by Dom's less than supportive reaction. 'If we hadn't crashed and been chucked off the campsite …'

'I beg your pardon?' interrupted Dom, staring daggers.

'OK, OK, if I hadn't got us thrown off, then we wouldn't have come in here to lick our wounds, and I wouldn't have fallen head over heels.'

Dom could see by the glazed, dreamy expression on Matty's face just how smitten he was.

'Put your money where your mouth is, then. What's the bet and how much?'

'A fiver says she'll be my girlfriend by the time we go home,' snapped Matty.

'Make it ten, if you're that confident.'

'You're on,' Matty said, without missing a beat.

The pair sealed the bet with a firm handshake.

Dom smiled to himself; this was going to be the easiest bet he had ever won.

While they ate their meals, Sue and Monique prepared the café for closing, wiping down the surfaces of the tables and tidying up in the back kitchen.

Returning to their table when they had finished eating, Monique pulled up a chair and joined them. She looked thoughtful, biting her bottom lip as if battling with an inner conflict.

'I have been chatting to Sue about your problem,' she said finally, 'and we would like to help you.'

'Yeah,' said Matty. 'How?'

'Well, if you wish, we would like to invite you to stay at our flat. It is very late to begin searching for somewhere else tonight, and you both look as if you could do with getting cleaned up and your dirty clothes washed.'

'Monique, we'd love to take you up on your offer, wouldn't we, Dom?' said Matty, staring insistently at him.

'I suppose so,' said Dom.

'Great. Get your belongings together, and I will go and let Sue know. I will take you back to the flat now while she finishes off here.'

'Best get that tenner of yours ready, mate,' said Matty, grinning from ear to ear.

Two hours later, Dom and Matty were sitting in the intimate surroundings of a minimally furnished lounge, sipping red wine by candlelight and enjoying the hospitality of their female hosts. Hot showers had cleaned away the mud, soothed some of the pain caused by their self-inflicted cuts

171

and bruises, and elevated their spirits. With the heavy rain outside reminding them just how close they had been to spending a miserable night camped out on a desolate piece of land, they could not quite believe the sudden turnaround in their fortunes.

By the time the fifth bottle was uncorked, the group had paired off; unsurprisingly, Matty had gravitated towards Monique, with the twosome sitting cross-legged on the carpet at the rear of the room, engrossed in each other's company.

A weary Dom was happy to chat to Sue at the other end of the room, stretched out, at her insistence, on the sofa.

With the fraught and eventful day finally catching up with him, he struggled to stay awake as Sue told the tale of how she had come to end up running her own business in Keswick, having relocated there from her native Norfolk in the late seventies. Powerless to prevent his heavy eyelids from frequently closing, Dom eventually drifted off into a blissful slumber.

With an early start at the café ahead of her the next morning, Sue found a spare blanket to place over Dom, before bidding Matty and Monique goodnight and heading off to bed.

'So, what are your plans for tomorrow?' said Monique to Matty.

He was unable to prevent himself from laughing uncontrollably at her question.

'What is so funny about that?' she followed up, clearly baffled by his reaction.

'Sorry, but I think it's best if I just see what the day brings. I had everything planned out for today, but cocked things up to the point where I fell out with my best friend.'

'I don't follow.'

'Look, Monique, I think it's time for me to come clean. Most of our injuries weren't caused when I crashed the car; it was because of what followed.'

172

Matty went on to reveal the real version of events, describing in detail the accident at the campsite and the ensuing punch-up that culminated in ejection by the owner, with the promise ringing in their ears that every local campsite proprietor would be made aware of their existence, to prevent them finding alternative accommodation. The only detail Matty omitted to mention was his lack of insurance.

'So, we were basically homeless when we first saw you this afternoon, stuck between a rock and a hard place; banned from pitching a tent anywhere in the whole of the Lakes, but lacking the money to stay in a bed and breakfast, or even a hostel.'

'You tell me all of this now,' said Monique coldly.

Matty held up his hands by way of an apology, acknowledging he had secured a roof over his head by being extremely economical with the truth.

'Look, I'm sorry, Monique. We'll get up first thing in the morning and get out of your hair. I can see we've taken advantage of your good nature.'

'Don't be silly,' said Monique. 'What I mean is, you should have told me all of this earlier. Of course, it was an accident. I am sure you did not mean to cause so much trouble. When will your car be repaired?'

'By Thursday morning, hopefully.'

'In that case, you can both stay here as our guests until then. I travel back home to France on Friday morning for a family wedding, so that will work out nicely.'

'Ah, thanks, Monique, but …'

'No, I insist. My word is final.'

'Well, if you put it like that, how could I refu …'

Monique leaned over and planted her lips forcefully onto Matty's, halting him in mid-sentence.

A couple of minutes later, they extinguished the candles and wandered off hand in hand to her bedroom.

Dom and Matty slept in late the following morning. By the time they finally did surface, there was no sign of Sue or Monique in the flat. All they found was a note on the dining room table explaining that they were at work all day, but would see them later on that evening.

Helping themselves to cereal and coffee, an ecstatic Matty gave Dom a blow-by-blow account of the previous evening, causing his friend to splutter in disbelief.

Eventually, Dom managed to steer the conversation around to more pressing matters, such as what amendments needed making to their original holiday plans in light of the events of the previous twenty-four hours.

Once Matty had filled Dom in on the proposal put to him by Monique, the pair decided they had no choice but to cut short their break and return home on Thursday.

Over the next two days, they explored the region's mountainous terrain and lakes during the day, and went out to the local pubs with Monique and Sue at night. Dom and Matty's brief falling out was all but forgotten as the familiar sense of camaraderie that had always existed between them returned, although Dom's patience was tested at times by Matty's non-stop rhapsodising about Monique.

The visit to the garage on Thursday morning to collect the Volvo went without a hitch, clearing the way for them to prepare for departure. Dom volunteered to pack all of their belongings into the rear of the car, allowing Matty to squeeze every last second out of his remaining time with Monique.

After a light lunch in the café, they all gathered outside to say their farewells. Dom gave both Monique and Sue a quick hug, thanking them for coming to the rescue when he had been at his lowest ebb. If they ever happened to visit Durham, he told them, they were more than welcome to stay at his flat for as long as they wished.

Matty's act of valediction, in comparison, was predictably elongated, prompting Dom after ten impatient minutes spent waiting in the car to give a couple of timely blasts on the horn as a reminder.

With so much to do before her own journey back home, a teary Monique eventually prised herself away from Matty's embrace, apologising for her overspill of emotion.

After one final flurry of kisses, Matty joined Dom in the car and reluctantly started the engine; his face was a picture of despondency as he pulled away from his newfound love.

'Can you believe it, Dom?' said Matty softly, as they left Keswick behind. 'She said she's going to miss me. Incredible.'

'Sounds like a typical holiday romance to me, mate,' said Dom.

'Come on, give me a break. After what you've just seen these last few days, what further proof do you need?'

'I'm sorry to appear so sceptical, but I just don't want you to build your hopes up too high. I'm talking from bitter experience here. You meet somebody on holiday, wonder how you've lived without them all your life, think you'll never be apart and then, wham, you get home, and they don't respond to your letters or answer your phone calls. I just think you need to have a bit of a reality check.'

'You're wrong, Dom,' said Matty, with impassioned defiance. 'This is different. It's love.'

The tone of Dom's hefty sigh suggested time would soon prove his cynicism was well-founded.

Annoyed by his friend's attitude, Matty pushed the cassette tape of music that Monique had compiled for him into his car stereo. He turned up the volume to a level that quelled the possibility of further conversation, allowing him to relive his whirlwind romance through the songs that had been the soundtrack to his time in Keswick.

Dom sat back in his seat and closed his eyes. Now that they were homeward bound, the temporarily forgotten spectre of his neighbour, Doug, reappeared to unsettle him.

175

Had Tel sorted the situation out?

If so, how far had his uncle's act of persuasion had to go to ensure he could return home without constantly having to look over his shoulder for fear of reprisals?

Dom's thoughts then turned to the potentially detrimental impact of Matty's infatuation. On several occasions over the course of the week, he had overheard Matty remark to Monique about how easy it would be for him to travel up to the Lakes on a weekend to spend time with her. Dom foresaw the problems this would generate for Northern Circle: rehearsals would suffer, momentum would be lost and gigs would dry up.

Dom was also worried about the influence Monique would have upon his and Matty's friendship. Up until Matty's recent exams, they had been virtually inseparable ever since he had joined the band the previous October; their mutual love of the same genre of music, as well as their ability to be able to compose songs together, had established a solid bond stronger than any other friendship Dom had ever known.

Matty's parents, despite the eventful incident with Mr Parker in the bathroom, had always treated him generously, frequently inviting him over to their house to dine with them.

From an entirely selfish viewpoint, Dom wished Monique had not met Matty and put a spoke in the wheel.

Dom's eyes opened suddenly.

Sitting upright, he peered out of the window. Unsure whether he had fallen asleep or just been lost in deep thought, more time had elapsed than he had realised as the next signpost revealed them to be approaching Barnard Castle; already, they were back in County Durham and nearing the end of their journey.

Turning to his passenger, Matty picked up the thread of their conversation from before, as if there had been no gap in it since leaving Keswick.

'Admit it though, Dom,' he said gently. 'She's something

special, isn't she?'

'She sure is,' said Dom, honestly.

'Are you jealous?'

'Yes, you jammy bastard.'

CHAPTER 20

It had taken less than half an hour that Thursday morning for Doug Rafferty to empty his flat of his few possessions and load them into his Capri. Clothes pulled off coat hangers and removed from drawers had been crammed haphazardly into two battered suitcases, while boxes gleaned from the local supermarket had sufficed for his hi-fi system and record collection; his brand new video recorder, unplayed and still inside its original packaging, was furtively placed inside a black bin liner.

Three plastic carrier bags had been sufficient to mop up his remaining items: two overdue library books he had no intention of returning, an adult magazine, toothbrush, toothpaste, soap, aftershave, razor and bedside clock. Everything else within the flat, with the exception of the chipped crockery and tarnished cutlery he had chosen to abandon, belonged to his landlord Billy Arrowsmith.

Given the paucity of notice he had been granted to vacate the property, Rafferty's lack of personal effects to pack away and transport was the one blessing in the bizarre affair that had begun the previous Sunday, when Arrowsmith had paid him an impromptu visit to inform him his tenancy was being terminated. The landlord, when challenged for the reason by a characteristically belligerent Rafferty, had said it was, 'Nothing personal, but I've just received a visit from the type of blokes it's not worth upsetting.'

Elaborating further, Arrowsmith said he had been instructed to pass on the message that, should he still be resident in Harold Wilson House in five days' time, everything Rafferty owned would be smashed to pieces. Once they had finished destroying his possessions, Arrowsmith concluded, they would focus their dissatisfaction upon him personally and ensure he spent the remainder of his days taking food through a straw.

This news stunned Rafferty, filling him with something he had not experienced in many years: raw fear.

The very next day an anxious Rafferty had set out to resolve his accommodation problem, ringing his workmate from the rigs, Jock, who had always said there was a room available at his place should the need ever arise. Thankfully, for Rafferty, Jock was as good as his word, informing him that he could drive up to Dundee that Thursday if he wished.

With his short-term housing problem solved, Rafferty had proceeded to spend his final days as a resident of The Acorns estate propping up the bar of his local pub, The Grapes, seething at the predicament fate had unexpectedly imposed on him against his will. He pondered over whom he could have upset to such an extent that they would go to so much trouble to drive him out of his home, his gut instinct telling him the incident with the kid from the flat below was at the root of the problem. Rafferty believed his disappearance off the face of the earth since that night was no coincidence, adding further credence to his theory.

At one point, towards last orders on the Tuesday evening, some of Rafferty's natural pugnacity had re-established itself as he drunkenly toyed with the idea of calling the bluff of his anonymous adversaries and telling Arrowsmith he was staying put. In the cold light of day the following morning, however, sentiments formed in the midst of an inebriated binge lost all solidity of conviction. Nursing a thumping hangover, common sense prevailed, with Rafferty reluctantly deciding to stick to his original plan. He realised that if a confrontation did not immediately occur come Friday, to remain in Durham meant he would always be vulnerable: in the shadows of the car park, the isolation of Harold Wilson House's dank stairwell, or on the lonely walk home from the pub, the threat of physical harm would always be a mere breath away.

On the Wednesday night, the eve of his departure, Rafferty had said his farewells to the pub regulars before commencing the walk home for the last time.

Entering the main entrance to the flats, Rafferty heard the sound of a vehicle approaching, breaking the silence of the late hour. Before the door closed behind him, he caught a glimpse of a white van pulling into the car park.

Rafferty's curiosity was aroused further when, peering surreptitiously through the second floor landing window of the stairwell, he saw that the van had parked in an empty bay; its headlights were switched off, with the two occupants still inside. Not recognising it as belonging to any of the residents, Rafferty remained where he was.

For several minutes, nothing happened.

Suddenly, the passenger slipped out of the vehicle and moved quickly across the expanse of the car park to the row of garages. Rafferty's eyes widened with interest when he saw whose door it was that was opened: the kid's.

The van then burst into life, reversing towards the open garage until its rear end was barely inside.

Two minutes later, the driver pulled forward sufficiently to allow his accomplice to exit the building and lock it back up; once he climbed back into the vehicle, it left with a degree of urgency.

Still Rafferty lingered where he was, watching and waiting, itching to know what had just taken place, but loath to wander across to investigate further in case the men returned and discovered him nosing around.

After ten minutes spent frozen to the spot, Rafferty walked back outside. When he was satisfied his movements had not attracted unwanted attention, he swiftly moved across to the garage door and attempted to turn the handle.

Unsurprisingly, it was locked.

Undeterred, Rafferty removed his Swiss army knife from his trouser pocket and opened out its smallest straight-edged blade. He had long since lost the original key to his own garage door, but had discovered his trusty utensil was an able substitute when it came to unlocking it; if it worked for one garage, maybe it would for another.

He poked it into the lock, jiggled it for a few seconds and tried the handle again.

This time it turned.

He opened the up and over door just enough to allow his crouched figure to gain access, before standing up to his full height once inside.

With visibility poor and the light switch not working, Rafferty took a tentative step forward and unwittingly knocked his shin against a heavy object.

Lowering himself down, he discovered a cardboard box. Blindly feeling around the surrounding area, he found many more packages of a similar size that had been dumped on the floor.

Realising he was pushing his luck with every passing moment, Rafferty picked up one of the boxes, slipped back outside and pulled the door shut. Without wishing to further risk detection by spending precious seconds attempting to relock it, he scurried back unseen to the safety of the residential building.

Back inside his flat, Rafferty switched on the living room light and placed the package onto the floor. Dropping to his knees, he tore impatiently with his penknife at the tape that sealed it.

When he saw what was inside, Rafferty smiled; a glimmer of a plan began to form in his mind, a method of retribution that would allow him to leave Durham with a degree of pride intact.

And now, hours later, at the moment of departure, it was time for him to make his move.

Closing the door on his flat for the final time ever, Rafferty walked down to his car. Before he got inside, he glanced across to the garage he had broken into the previous night and smirked. The door handle was at the angle he had left it, indicating it was still unlocked; more than likely, deduced Rafferty, no one had yet returned to empty it of its contents.

Rafferty got into his Capri and drove the short distance to the telephone box at the front of the building. He stopped the car, got out and went inside. Picking up the receiver, he dialled nine three times.

'Hello. I'd like to report something suspicious that I think you may be interested in ...'

CHAPTER 21

When the friends arrived back at Harold Wilson House late in the afternoon, Dom sighed with relief when he saw the Capri was absent from its usual parking bay.

'Do you think he's gone, then?' said Matty.

'Fingers crossed,' replied Dom. 'Tel promised he would be out by the weekend at the latest, but we've returned home two days early, haven't we.'

Dom glanced up warily at his flat; all appeared normal, but he was still anxious about setting foot inside again.

'Look, I'll come up with you if you're worried he might be hiding in your cupboard waiting to pounce,' offered Matty.

'OK, thanks.'

'Look, there's a cop car out the front,' remarked Matty casually, as they walked down the footpath up to the entrance of the building. 'Probably a pensioner's cat has got stuck up a tree somewhere.'

Safely inside his flat, Dom picked up the pile of letters that had been accumulating on the doormat and dropped them onto the sofa in the living room.

He put his hands on his hips and gazed around the room; the amplifier and microphone were still where he had left them in the middle of the floor.

'I'll just go and check the other rooms,' said Dom nervously.

'Make sure you look under the bed,' said Matty, slumping down on the armchair. 'That's the place all psycho intruders hide in the movies when the victim returns home.'

'Bollocks,' retorted Dom, from the bedroom.

Matty giggled to himself.

'Everything appears to be OK,' said Dom, when he returned.

'Told you there was nothing to worry about. He's probably

long gone by now. I'm sure I would be if your uncle and his mate put the frighteners on me.'

'I suppose you're right,' Dom conceded.

Before he could sit down himself, three thunderous knocks at the front door made Dom flinch; the blood drained from his face.

They stared uneasily at each other.

'He must have been lying in wait for me,' said a panicking Dom, instantly jumping to conclusions. He imagined his neighbour standing outside on the gangway, thirsty for revenge.

Before he could decide how to respond, a further series of heavy, intimidating thumps carried down the passageway into the living room.

'Look, it's broad daylight and there's two of us,' reasoned Matty. 'What's the worst he can do that we haven't already done to each other?' The cuts and bruises from their own fight were still fresh and tender. 'Unless you want to keep running all of your life, it's probably best if you go and answer it.'

'I hate to admit it, but I think you're right. You will come and visit me in hospital, won't you?' said Dom, with what he hoped was misplaced prescience as he walked to the front door.

'I'm right behind you, so I'll probably end up in the bed next to you,' said Matty.

Dom grabbed hold of the handle, took a deep breath and yanked the door open.

Standing on the spot where he had expected to see Rafferty were two police officers. The elder of the two - tall, slightly overweight and jowly, with a bushy moustache and world-weary expression - addressed Dom.

'Mr Dominic Edward Blackburn?' he said.

'Yes.'

'What a stroke of luck to find you here, sir,' continued the

184

officer humourlessly. 'We've just been conducting door to door enquiries with your neighbours to establish your whereabouts, as you weren't at home an hour ago, and then old Mrs Dodds on the end there informed us she saw you arrive a couple of minutes ago. I wish all collars were this easy, eh, Pete?'

'Yeah,' snarled his stony-faced, junior partner.

'Right, I'm afraid I'm the bearer of bad news,' continued the more senior of the pair. 'A short time ago a large amount of stolen video recorders were retrieved from your garage across the way there, so you're going to have to accompany us to the station for some questions.'

'What?' said Dom, mystified.

'What he means, Mr Blackburn,' said his colleague bluntly, 'is you're nicked. Can I cuff him and read him his rights, Roger?'

'Go on, then.'

The police officer overzealously pushed Dom face-first up against the passageway wall, pulled his hands behind his back and slipped handcuffs on them.

'Dominic Edward Blackburn, I am arresting you on suspicion of burglary and the theft of ...'

As Dom was frogmarched out of the flat, the remainder of the officer's words went unheard as he struggled to understand what was happening to him.

As they reached the bottom of the stairwell, Dom heard the voice of Matty call out to him.

'Dom, can I ring someone for you to tell them what's happened?'

Dom looked up to see his friend leaning over the first floor landing railings.

'Ring my uncle,' he shouted. 'His number's in my address book in the bedroom.'

CHAPTER 22

Upon his arrival at the police station, a confused and frightened Dom went through a formal arrest procedure, culminating with his detention in a cell.

As he sat in isolation and attempted to make sense of the peculiar sequence of events, Dom prayed that Matty was being persistent in his efforts to get in touch with Tel. The last thing he wanted was to have to involve his parents, hence the reason why he had attempted, with no success, to contact his uncle when offered the opportunity to make a telephone call.

As the hours passed with still no word from Tel, Dom became increasingly worried at the predicament in which he found himself.

Eventually, his prolonged period of confinement ended when an officer arrived to escort him down a series of well-lit corridors into a sparsely furnished interview room for questioning.

Awaiting his arrival were two men dressed in plain-clothes, sitting next to each other at a table situated in the middle of the room. A file was open in front of them, with pages spread out all over.

The more senior of the two, silver-haired and with a neatly trimmed beard, spoke first.

'Sit down, son.'

He indicated the vacant chair opposite them with a nod in its direction.

'So then,' continued the officer in a chirpy tone of voice, once Dom had done as requested, 'how would you like to be addressed, son? Dominic, Dom, Ted, Edward or Teddy?'

'Dom's fine.'

'OK, Dom. I am DCI Hodgson, this here is my colleague DS Smith, and we are the officers who have been assigned to your case. Just before we commence questioning, I believe that you declined the option of a legal adviser when you were brought in. Is that correct?'

'Yes.'

'Now that you've had some time to dwell upon the reason for your being here, would you like to rethink your decision? I mean, this is a serious situation you have on your hands here. A little legal representation wouldn't do you any harm.'

'No, thank you.'

Despite his growing anxiety, Dom still had faith that Tel would not leave him high and dry, and would be there soon to help clear up what had obviously been a horrendous misunderstanding.

'Have it your way,' said a bemused Hodgson, pressing the record button on the tape recorder situated in the middle of the table. 'It's 10.33pm on Thursday, 23 June 1983. DCI Bill Hodgson and DS Terry Smith are commencing interview with Dominic Edward Blackburn on suspicion of the theft of thirteen video recorders from Ridley's Electricals of Darlington, on the evening of Wednesday, 22 June 1983.'

Hodgson sat back in his chair, crossed his arms and stared at his suspect, as if weighing him up.

'OK, Dom,' he began finally, 'following an anonymous tip-off received at this station earlier today, we had reason to suspect that stolen goods were being stored at an external garage which forms part of 9 Harold Wilson House, Gilesgate, where you currently reside. Following a thorough search of the garage, a dozen brand new video recorders, stolen last night from Ridley's Electricals, were retrieved. Taking all of the facts into account, the question I would like to pose to you, Dom, is simple. Did you break into that shop, steal those items, and store them at your home address for the sole purpose of profiting from them at a later stage? Or should that be, seeing as one video recorder is missing from the thirteen stolen and was not found following a subsequent search of your flat after your arrest, profit immediately from them?'

'No,' said Dom earnestly. 'I was still on holiday in Keswick last night and only arrived home this afternoon.'

'There long, were you?' asked Hodgson.

'I went on Monday and was meant to return this Saturday, but I came home early.'

'And you have witnesses who can confirm all of this?'

'Three.'

'OK,' said DS Smith soberly, pen poised at the ready, 'names and addresses, please. We'll have to check them out.'

Once Dom had given the details, Hodgson resumed talking.

'Let me get this straight. You're telling me you've just returned home from holiday today completely unaware that four thousand pounds' worth of video recorders had miraculously appeared in your garage?'

Dom nodded.

'I'm afraid I don't buy that, son,' said Hodgson. 'It just doesn't add up at all. If you're not involved, that would mean someone has gone to all the trouble and risk of breaking and entering into premises, stealing property and transporting it twenty odd miles down the road, before dumping it inside a random garage. It doesn't sound plausible.'

'Put like that, I have to agree,' said Dom. 'I don't know why someone would do it, but in this case they obviously have. I'm innocent.'

'Hmmh,' said Hodgson thoughtfully, leaning back on the rear two legs of his chair. He turned to his associate. 'Looks like we'd better get a brew on, Terry. I thought this was going to be a dead cert five minute job, but it looks like we'll be here for the long haul. Mine's a tea, two sugars and plenty of milk. Dom. Coffee or tea?'

'Coffee, please.'

'Milk and sugar?' asked Hodgson.

'Oh, I'll just bring it all in on a tray,' intervened Smith

moodily, scraping his chair back sharply. 'Obviously at the moment he likes it black and unsweetened, but by the time I return he'll have changed his mind and say he prefers it with milk and sugar. You know these scallies; they don't know their own mind from one minute to the next.'

'DS Smith has left the interview room,' stated Hodgson for the benefit of the tape, before turning his attention back to his suspect. 'You'll have to forgive my colleague. He gets a little ratty sometimes. He's only just married, you see, and when he read the report on the burglary half an hour ago, he was convinced everything would be wrapped up in time to get back home for a cup of cocoa and a cuddle. Lucky man, he is. Myself, I have no one waiting for me at home. Either way, we're both prepared to stick this out right to the bitter end, if need be,' Hodgson warned, hinting at a tough streak lingering below his amiable exterior.

CHAPTER 23

Tel had arrived home from his weekly snooker night a little before ten o'clock.

Switching on the light in his living room, he dumped his Chinese takeaway on the coffee table, and went to fetch a plate, fork, and can of lager from the kitchen.

Upon his return, he tuned in his radio to the local late night talk show before sinking wearily into his armchair.

Lifting the lid off the foil container, swirling steam wafted up to the ceiling as he served his food up on the plate.

He had only taken three hungry mouthfuls when the telephone began to ring.

'Typical,' he muttered, leaving his fork standing upright in the mound of rice as he went to answer it.

'Yes,' he said irritably.

'Is that Tel?' said the voice at the end of the line.

'Who is this?'

'It's Matty. I'm a friend of Dom's. I met you in Langley Vale earlier on this year when we won the music competition.'

'That's right,' said Tel, recalling the name but unable to picture Matty's face.

'I've been trying to reach you for hours. Dom's in a spot of bother.'

'Bother?' said Tel.

'Yeah. He's been arrested for suspected theft.'

'Bloody hell. Tell me everything you know about it, son.'

Matty hurriedly imparted the chain of events in as much detail as he could recall, beginning from the moment the police officers had knocked on Dom's front door.

'Let's get this straight,' said Tel, once Matty had finished. 'Did this all happen at his flat and not on holiday?'

'Yeah. We came home today instead of Saturday.'

'What time did the police take him?'

'About four this afternoon.'

'Right, Matty, thanks for letting me know, son. Leave it with me.'

Tel hung up, grabbed his car keys and headed for the door.

Ten minutes later, he was outside the home of Vince Staveley, impatiently pressing the button on the intercom at the gated entrance to his property.

'Yes?'

'Vince, it's Tel. I need a word.'

A second later, the gates swung open and Tel drove up the long driveway.

'It's a bit late for a social visit, Tel,' growled Staveley, standing at his front door in a navy dressing gown. 'I've just had my nightcap.'

'This isn't social and it can't wait,' replied Tel firmly, pushing past Staveley without waiting to be invited inside.

'Best come through to the lounge, then,' said Staveley, beckoning to Tel to follow him.

'What's going on, Vince?' began Tel heatedly, once Staveley had closed the lounge door behind them. 'I've just had a telephone call informing me that my nephew's been arrested because stolen property was found at his place.'

Staveley went ashen-faced as he absorbed the news.

'Arrested?' he managed to say finally.

Tel nodded.

'Ah,' said Staveley.

'Vince, why are you storing knock-off gear in the lad's gaff? It's his home, for Christ's sake. I thought those days were behind you, anyway?'

Staveley sat down on his black leather armchair and drummed his fingers thoughtfully on the armrest.

'Me and Billy turned over a shop in Darlington last night,' he began. 'Just for laughs, you understand.'

'For laughs?'

'We'd had a few after work, you know how it is, and we were walking past this shop in the town centre, a bit off the beaten track, when we saw all of these video recorders stacked up inside. Well, we began egging each other on, didn't we. Neither of us was willing to bottle out, so we went through with it. We parked the van outside, did the old smash-and-grab routine and helped ourselves. So far, so good.

'But on the journey home, we suddenly found we had a cop car behind us. It could have just been a coincidence, but I didn't want to take the chance of being caught red-handed, so I managed to lose them before heading straight over to the lad's place to put them in the garage. It was the only option I had, Tel, as I was only a minute away. I couldn't see what harm it would cause leaving them there because he was on holiday, like you told me the other day. I sorted a buyer out this morning and was going to shift them tomorrow. Nobody would have been any the wiser.'

'Well, somehow it's all gone tits up, Vince, and now Dom is taking the rap.' Tel sat down on the sofa. 'The one positive thing is he'll be completely in the dark about what's going on, so there's nothing the coppers can force him to confess to. But the way I see things, that's not the main problem. Dom's as honest as the day is long, and sooner or later they will realise this, if they haven't already. The lad even has a cast iron alibi: he was miles away. My worry is they'll use him to reel in bigger fish, as well as charge him with being an accomplice to last night.'

A twitchy Staveley stood up and walked across the room to his mini-bar. He filled two glasses with generous measures of whisky and handed one to Tel, before sitting back down with the other.

'I think you might have a point there,' said Staveley, pensively nursing his glass. 'The lad knows nothing about last night but plenty about my business activities in general, no doubt through conversations with yourself.'

'I've told him a few things.'

'Enough to give us all a serious problem if they put the squeeze on him?'

Tel knocked back his drink in one go. 'Yes, which means there's only one thing to do, the way I see it. I need to get the lad out of this mess as soon as possible. He's got a good job and a clean record. Getting implicated in something like this will put him on the scrapheap for good, and it'll crucify our Iris.'

'So, what are you proposing? I walk into the station and confess.'

Tel shook his head. 'I'm saying that I put myself in the frame for this, get Dom off the hook and divert any attention from you.'

'You'd take a bullet for me?' said a shocked Staveley.

'Maybe not if Dom wasn't mixed up in all of this, but at the same time, I do owe you. You gave me a job when no one else wanted to know me after I came out of the nick all those years ago. I've had a good run, but my luck had to end sometime, didn't it? But it's not like I'd be up for murder. If you put Morty on the case, he'll be able to cut a deal. I reckon if I cop for handling stolen goods then all I'll get is a couple of years maximum, and I'll be out in around half that with good behaviour. That's a lifetime for a kid like Dom. For me, it's a mere siesta in the sun. Of course, we'll have to come to some agreement over adequate compensation to make it worth my while, for lost earnings and the like.'

'There'll be no trouble on that score, Tel. You know me; I've never quibbled over money. I await your instructions on how much and where you want it putting.'

Staveley picked up the phone receiver from the table by the side of his armchair and dialled.

'Morty? It's Vince … yes, I know it's late, but something urgent's cropped up that I need you to deal with straight away … you're in bed? Well, get yourself back out of bed, grab a cold shower and get yourself down to the city centre cop shop to meet Tel. He's in a spot of trouble … yes, it's serious. He'll explain it all to you once you get there. Okay, mate. Bye.'

Staveley replaced the receiver and looked across to Tel.

'You're definitely sure you want to go through with this?'

Tel nodded. 'No choice, have I?'

Staveley sighed wistfully. He stood up, carried the two empty glasses back over to the mini-bar and refilled them. He handed Tel his drink, and held his own up in readiness for a toast.

'End of an era.'

'End of an era,' repeated Tel, again draining his whisky in one gulp. He rose to his feet, handed Staveley the glass and walked to the door.

'Thanks, Tel,' said Staveley.

Tel looked back, smiled grimly, before leaving without saying a word.

CHAPTER 24

Hodgson leaned forward and stared intensely at Dom.

'Come on, son,' he said softly, his voice barely a whisper. 'I can tell just by talking to you that you're no master criminal. You strike me as being a decent sort, which is why I'm going to give you my theory on what's going on here. It might not be one hundred per cent accurate, but let's see what you think. Ready?'

Interpreting the ensuing silence as a green light to continue, Hodgson rose to his feet and pressed both hands on the table.

'I think that while you've been away someone has taken advantage of this; someone with a key who has the freedom to enter and leave your property with no questions asked. So who does that give us? A friend? A relative? A landlord? Do you know of anyone who fits that category who you think we should be talking to?'

Dom hesitated slightly, glanced away and shook his head.

Hodgson sat back down in his chair and contemplatively nibbled the top of his biro.

'Let's be a little more specific,' he continued. 'I know of at least two names that fit the bill: Terence Armitage and Vince Staveley, who are your uncle and landlord respectively, I believe, and a pair for whom the phrase "thick as thieves" could have been invented.'

Dom stayed silent.

'Your uncle's a contender, it has to be said. Ex-jailbird, and the crime fits his previous conviction, but perhaps too neatly.

'Which brings us to our second chief suspect. Hypothetically, let's assume that Mr Staveley stole the video recorders and put them in the garage. He fully intends to have them sold before your expected return on Saturday and collect his little earner. But something has gone wrong. For whatever reason, someone close with an axe to grind has grassed him up. We'll probably never discover who made that call, and to be honest, I don't care.'

Hodgson's expression was now deadly serious; sensing blood, he moved in for the kill.

'Dom, the predicament you are in is almost like a game of Cluedo, the most critical you are ever likely to play, so I want you to think long and hard about what answer you give to my next question. Before I ask you it, let me just add that I've seen the devastating effect a custodial sentence has on people. They can lose everything: their job, house, car, the lot. I've seen families disown them, turning them into social outcasts. I've seen it happen, son, to young men the same age as you.'

Hodgson paused for a moment to allow the gravity of his explicit warning to worm its way into Dom's subconscious.

The door to the interview room opened and Smith walked back in, balancing a sugar bowl, milk jug and an assortment of mugs on the tray he was carrying; he placed it down carefully on the table.

'DS Smith has re-entered the room,' said Hodgson clearly, before picking up a Newcastle football mug from the tray and taking a loud, conspicuous slurp from it. 'Ten out of ten tonight, Terry. Your tea making skills are improving.'

Smith smiled thinly as he sat down in his seat.

'I was just in the middle of telling our friend here, Terry, about the implications of a spell in prison.'

'Bird can do terrible things to a man,' said Smith, a grim look on his face. 'Some take to it like ducks to water: the hard nuts, the fairies, the persistent offenders. They're prepared to eat their porridge and do the time because they got caught doing the crime. Whereas for others, those who've had a decent upbringing, who come from nice families …' Smith paused to shake his head and chuckle knowingly to himself. '… I've seen them shrivel up like bollocks dipped in the North Sea in January. What do you think, Bill? Is he made for

196

stir, or will it eat him alive? Personally, I don't think he'd last a fucking week.'

Hodgson turned back to Dom. 'I must admit, I have to agree with Terry on this one, Dom. Usually, we don't see eye to eye on anything. Complete opposites, we are. He says Eagles; I say Sinatra. He says Sunderland; I say Newcastle. He says coffee; I say tea. But on your chances inside, it's obvious we both agree that you'd struggle to go the distance, alongside the muggers, rapists, sex cases and murderers. Even the open nicks will scare the living shit out of you. They're not the holiday camps they'd have you believe in the newspapers.'

Dom shielded his face in his hands; he was feeling lost and way out of his depth.

'OK, getting back to my original question, Dom, this is the moment of truth,' said Hodgson. 'I have the crime's location, the retrieved stolen goods, but no name. If you deny being involved one more time or refuse to answer, then I will interpret that to mean you are pointing the finger at Staveley and your uncle, and you are free to go. If you admit your guilt, then I will throw the whole book at you, and all the alibis in the world won't save you.'

Dom began to physically shake under the intense pressure, aware he was in a lose-lose situation. Either he owned up to a crime he had not committed, or effectively grassed up Staveley and his own flesh and blood, the consequences of which were just too horrific to contemplate.

'Who stole those video recorders?' said Hodgson.

Starting to hyperventilate, Dom was unable to think clearly.

'For the second and final time, Dom. Who stole those video recorders?'

There was a loud knock at the door, and a uniformed officer popped his head inside the room.

'Sir, can I have a quiet word, please?'

'Not now, Jenkins. I'm busy, as you can see,' replied Hodgson.

'I'm afraid it can't wait, sir.'

Hodgson cursed under his breath and walked out into the corridor.

'This had better be good, Jenkins,' he said, closing the door behind him.

'There's a Derek Mortimer in reception, sir, who insists he is representing your suspect and wishes to speak to him immediately.'

'Morty,' snorted Hodgson.

The DCI had crossed swords on numerous occasions over the years with Staveley's legal man in his never-ending cat and mouse pursuit of the loan shark. Morty's presence at the police station indicated to Hodgson that he was on the right track and had Staveley worried.

'Stall him for five minutes. I've nearly got a result here. I've been waiting for this day for a long time. A very long time.'

Hodgson knew how close he was to claiming the scalp of Staveley; if successful, he knew it would be the feather in the cap of his career in the force.

Jenkins remained where he was, an uncomfortable expression on his face.

'There's more, sir. He has a client with him, a Terence Armitage, who admits to handling the video recorders. He says the lad we're holding was on holiday and knew nothing about it.'

At this revelation, Hodgson ran a frustrated hand through his hair. This was not what he wanted to hear: he wanted the organ grinder, not the monkey.

'Bollocks,' said Hodgson, hammering the wall with his fist before pressing his forehead despondently against it.

After a short silence, Hodgson turned to address the constable.

'Jenkins.'

'Yes, sir.'

'Please inform DS Smith that the lad is free to leave. I will go and speak with Mr Mortimer.'

'But …'

'Just do it, Jenkins,' insisted Hodgson.

'Yes, sir.'

As he walked down the corridor towards the public reception area, a beaten and depressed Hodgson wondered, not for the first time in recent months, whether it was time for him to get out of the force, retire and let a younger man fill his shoes.

CHAPTER 25

'Where shall I put this, Dom?' said Matty, labouring under the weight of the cardboard box he was holding.

'Anywhere will do.'

Matty gratefully dropped it down onto the carpet with a thud.

'What's in there? It weighs a bloody ton.'

'My music magazines.'

'I think I've done my back in,' grumbled Matty, standing up to his full height and rubbing a soothing hand down his spine. 'I would have burnt them last week when the kids were collecting for the bonfires, if I was you.'

Dom looked at him with incredulity. 'I can't part with them, mate. There's an encyclopaedia of musical history contained in there, and I've been collecting them for years.'

'I felt the same way with a lot of my old stuff when I moved in with Monique,' said Matty, 'but there was no way she would entertain unnecessary clutter. It was a small sacrifice to make.'

Matty surveyed the total sum of Dom's possessions that they had just transported from Harold Wilson House to Katy's flat.

'So, is that everything or do you have anything else left to fetch, like a vintage collection of *Razzles* you've been keeping under the bed all these months?'

'No, Matty, we're done, so to thank you for helping me move, how about I buy you a pint at my new local pub? There's no time like the present to show my face and try to ingratiate myself with the locals.'

'The Newton Moor pub? I wonder how long it took them to come up with that name?' he said sarcastically, clearly uninterested by the proposition. 'I went there with my dad once. I swear to God there was no one there under the age of fifty.'

'Well, if that's the case, we'll be bringing the average age down a little.'

'I'd like to, Dom, but I promised Monique I'd take her to the cinema tonight.'

'That's no problem, mate. Just ask her to come over, too.'

'No, she's wanted to go and see this film for ages but hasn't had the chance, what with her studying and me working.'

'Hey, Matty,' said Dom, 'if I didn't know better, I'd say you were well and truly under the thumb.'

'Piss off,' said Matty light-heartedly.

'You are. When was the last time we had a rehearsal?'

Matty's face went blank. 'Can't remember,' he shrugged.

'July. Or the last gig we played?'

'That one I do know. April at The Wild Ferret, just before we recorded our songs with Jez.'

'Correct. Seven months ago. What was it you said when you told me Monique was moving to Durham? "Don't worry, Dom, it won't affect the band". Next thing, you'll be telling me you've stopped going to the match.'

Matty's look of guilt told Dom all he needed to know.

'I might have known,' said Dom, in exasperation. 'She's taking over your life.'

'That's not fair, Dom. You've got to remember that she's a stranger here. She came down to Durham to be with me. What am I meant to do? Say to her, "Oh, I'm sorry, pet, but I'm just going out for the day for a skinful and to watch a few overrated hairy blokes kick a bit of leather about, so I hope you can find something to entertain yourself with while I'm out". If I start acting like that, she'll be on the first flight back to France, and I wouldn't blame her.'

'I'm sorry,' Dom sighed, disappointed for allowing his frustration to surface. 'I don't mean to get at you or Monique. It's just annoying that we've hit a brick wall with the band, just when things looked so promising after we won the competition.'

'Like I said to you last week on the phone, it's not just been the arrival of Monique that's changed in my life. There's been the new job, too. With this heavy training schedule they've got me on, I'm coming home knackered after a nine hour day only to have to start all over again by studying for a stack of work exams.'

'Sounds like you've got your hands full every hour of the day.'

Matty had transformed his life beyond recognition in the space of a few short months. The initial spark of attraction with Monique that had materialised on his sojourn in the Lakes that summer had quickly blossomed into something altogether more serious. While she was away in France, Matty had telephoned her every day, and upon her return to the Lakes, he had immediately driven up to Keswick to be with her. Three weeks elapsed before the news he had been successful in a graduate job interview forced him to return home.

To Matty's surprise, the thought of spending a single day without him was so heart wrenching to Monique that she suggested accompanying him. Once there, she was so enamoured with Durham that she made the decision to stay permanently, enrolling on a philosophy course with a local college and renting a small house on the outskirts of the city centre with Matty.

Matty had begun his new job with a prestigious accountancy firm in August. They had offices all over the United Kingdom as well as overseas, and he would have his pick of work locations to choose from once his graduate trainee program was completed. With a first class degree in business and finance already safely acquired, the world was now his oyster.

'Do you see much of the others?' said Matty.

'Mick's joined a new band. He said he was getting bored of not knowing if we were ever going to play again. And Brian's retired permanently from music. Pauline found out about my trouble with the police and put her foot down, saying no man of hers was going to be associated with gangsters.'

Matty laughed hysterically. 'You? A gangster? Do me a favour. You had nothing to do with those stolen goods.'

'Apparently, she told him that there's no smoke without fire and all that rubbish.'

'Has your uncle had his trial yet?' said Matty.

Dom grew sombre. 'Yeah. He got a year and ten months.'

Matty winced. 'So, he really did nick those video recorders.'

'No,' jumped in Dom defensively, 'he was convicted of handling stolen goods. I heard he bought them from a bloke in a snooker hall on the Thursday morning.'

Matty was dubious about how true this account actually was, but thought it best not to dispute Dom's explanation.

'I'm not condoning whatever your uncle's been up to, but at least he had the decency to come clean, exonerating you from any of the blame.'

'In hindsight, that's true, but at the time I was really bricking it when I was being held in that police cell. I didn't think I'd see daylight again.'

'What about his mate, Staveley? Was he not involved?' said Matty.

'Apparently not.'

The disappearance of Vince Staveley from Durham, so soon after Tel Armitage's arrest, had been the one curious footnote of the entire episode, with an unexpected upshot for Dom. Shortly afterwards, he had received a letter from Staveley's lawyer, stating that his uncle had negotiated a deal that allowed Dom to live rent-free in the property.

On visits to his parents' home in the immediate aftermath of Tel's imprisonment, Dom's mother had been the angriest he had ever seen her, verbally lambasting Staveley and making protestations such as, 'It isn't right. He should be the one locked up, not our Tel.'

Given the level of contempt Ronnie and Iris Blackburn jointly felt for Staveley, they had been understandably keen for Dom to move out of his flat and permanently sever his ties with the absent businessman. The problem this had posed for Dom was that it was not simply a case of going out and renting a similar flat elsewhere, because the below-market value rent he had been paying when he had first moved in would only find him accommodation in a less well-heeled area of the county. Neither that, nor the option to return home to Spennymoor, held any appeal whatsoever. The fact that he had benefitted so greatly from the financial arrangement made between Staveley and Tel meant Dom had been in no hurry to move, but he had known that the constant parental pressure would soon bring matters to a head.

Expressing to Katy the dilemma he faced, on a recent night out to celebrate her getting a new job with a national banking firm, she had responded with a proposition that, immediately, he knew made total sense and was the ideal solution: move in with her.

Wondering why he had not thought of this himself – after all, her flatmate had just moved out, they had been going steady for months, and Katy had been a rock during his recent troubles – Dom had eagerly set about planning his departure from the home that had seen an eventful fifteen months.

Although more than capable of transporting his few possessions himself to Katy's flat, Dom had enlisted the services of the elusive Matty, using it as an excuse to catch up with his best friend and to see where the land lay in terms of the inactive Northern Circle.

Matty glanced at his watch. 'Oh well, I'd best be getting back. I need a shave and a shower before I go out; I bloody reek. Monique will be cooking, too. You want to taste her food, Dom. Exquisite is the only word I can use to describe it. All that rubbish about the French eating only frogs' legs and snails is way off the mark.'

'I already have, Matty. In the Lakes, remember?'

'Ah, I'd forgotten about that,' said Matty, opening the front door. 'It seems a lifetime ago, doesn't it?'

Dom was crestfallen by how impatient Matty was to leave without having a proper chat.

'Fancy a few pints one night?' asked Dom, an air of desperation in his voice. He had the distinct feeling that if his friend walked out of the door without them making any concrete plans to see each other again, then their musical adventures, and possibly their friendship, would be well and truly over.

Put suddenly on the spot, Matty was non-committal. 'We'll see, mate. I'll have to run it past Monique first.'

Dom did his best not to appear hurt by this unconvincing response; it was not so much what he said, but the uninterested look in Matty's eyes as he said it, that made Dom suddenly believe he was wasting his time in pursuing a rekindling of the musical dream that had once been a mutual obsession.

'OK, whatever,' snapped Dom. 'If you're out, I'll be in the club in Durham at eight o' clock next Saturday.'

'The club? That's only five minutes' walk away from where I live. OK, I can't promise, but I'll do my best to make it. I'll be seeing you.'

'See you,' said Dom, with a heavy heart.

Not one part of him believed Matty would show up.

CHAPTER 26

Arriving early to ensure he secured a seat ahead of the expected bustling Saturday night crowd, Dom bought a drink and sat by himself in a corner of the social club's lounge.

Eight o'clock came and went, with the absent Matty still to show his face.

Swiftly sinking pint after pint, his initial hopes for the evening degenerated into morose, drunken self-pity as the prospect of Matty not turning up grew stronger by the minute.

Feeling painfully conspicuous among the carefree groups of friends who had met up for their weekend night out, Dom was unable to endure it any longer as nine o'clock approached. He unsteadily got to his feet, walked past the bar and descended the short flight of stairs into the games room. A pool table in the far corner of the room was unoccupied, so Dom decided to play a frame. He slotted his money in and pulled the lever to release the balls; racking them up inside the black plastic triangle, he chalked a cue and bent down to break off.

'Hold your horses, Blackburn,' a voice from behind called out.

Dom span around.

'Matty.'

'Who were you expecting? The Queen of Sheba?' quipped Matty, as he swaggered in, drink in one hand and cigarette in the other, as if none of the previous four months had happened.

Dom's mood soared instantly. 'I could bloody well kiss you.'

'Steady on, Blackburn, what would the committee members think? That type of thing is frowned upon in here, you know,' Matty said drily.

'Fancy a game?' said Dom.

Matty nodded. 'Just give me one second to put my drink down and grab a cue, and then I'll give you a beating you won't forget in a hurry.'

Matty made his choice from the collection of warped pool cues that had seen better days.

Dom stooped back over the table and broke off, smashing the white cue ball into the striped and spotted balls; two dropped into pockets.

'Two stripes, you jammy sod. I see some things never change,' said Matty.

'That was skill, mate.'

'Skill my arse. You've always been lucky,' said Matty.

'So, Monique's allowed you out to play, has she?' said Dom, relishing being in the company of the Matty of old: jokey and uncomplicated.

'Now now, don't be sarky. No, she's knee deep in college work, and there's something I need to talk to you about, so I thought I'd kill two birds with one stone and have a look down. The bloke on the door wasn't going to let me in, though. He said I wasn't an affiliated member. I had to bung him ten bob, the thieving old sod, which went straight into his own pocket. Did you have to do the same?'

'No. I've got my club cards from Spennymoor; they get you into any working men's club for free.'

'Oh well, sort me some out for next time. I'm buggered if I'm getting screwed every time I set foot in the place, cheap beer or no cheap beer. I thought these places were supposed to be founded on socialist principles.'

'Next time?'

'Why aye. I'm back in the game, Dom. Northern Circle mark two is ready to rise from the ashes and finish off what it started a year ago.'

Dom stared at Matty in disbelief; he had anticipated a difficult and protracted discussion over many drinks in order to persuade Matty to resume with the band, particularly after their previous conversation.

'What about Monique?'

'Monique? Oh, I put my foot down and told her that I need to have my own interests and friends, otherwise we'll smother each other.'

'Very assertive of you,' said Dom ironically.

'Well, you have to be with women, otherwise they walk all over you.'

'Matty, I've got dozens of new ideas to try out,' said an enthused Dom.

'Me, too. I've written quite a few songs recently. Being with Monique has unleashed all these thoughts and feelings I never knew I had.'

'Fantastic.'

'But if we do this all again, Dom, then I want to freshen things up a little.'

'In what way?' said Dom.

'Nothing too radical, just add a keyboard player to colour the songs a bit more.'

'Sounds good to me, Matty.'

Over the course of the evening, the pair reminisced about the band and filled in the gaps from each other's lives over the past few months.

All too soon, the bell was ringing for last orders. Matty quickly bought a fresh round of drinks, and by the time they finished all of the other customers had left.

'God, I'm bladdered,' muttered Dom.

He glanced at his watch. The last bus had long gone; it was either a taxi, or a one and a half mile walk home.

'Come on back to mine, if you like,' suggested Matty outside. 'We can celebrate our blissful reunion over a few bifters and a little whisky. I've got a bottle of Wild Turkey just begging to be opened.'

'Are you sure, Matty? Won't Monique mind being interrupted?'

'By you? Don't be daft, Dom. You can't do any wrong in her eyes.'

'Why's that?'

'If it wasn't for you, me and Monique wouldn't have met. If I recall rightly, I was all for making the pilgrimage to Brighton.'

'I know that, but I never specifically said we should go to the Lakes. Just that Brighton was too expensive.'

'Granted, but you sold it to me: the whole poets thing, the mystique of the landscape, and the chance to recharge our batteries, and write new songs.'

'Which we never actually got around to,' added Dom.

'No, but I'll forever be indebted to you. So, come on.'

Too drunk to argue, Dom acquiesced.

The pair staggered through the residential city centre streets, arms slung unashamedly around each other, singing snippets of Jam songs at the top of their voices.

'You live here?' said an impressed Dom, when Matty stopped outside a property in a terraced street close to Neville's Cross traffic lights.

'Take your shoes off in the hallway, mate,' said Matty. 'I only hoovered up earlier today.'

Dom followed Matty inside, welcoming the wall of heat that hit him. Entering the living room, a sleepy looking Monique lifted herself up from the sofa, smiling as she recognised Matty's guest.

'Dom,' she said, with genuine affection. 'It's really nice to see you again. How are you?'

Dom kissed her on the cheek. 'I'm in fine fettle.'

'Fine fettle?' she asked, visibly confused by the local dialect.

Dom smiled. 'I'm on top of the world,' he explained.

'That is nice to hear.'

'Sorry, pet. I thought you'd be in bed by now,' apologised Matty.

209

'I should be. The essay has taken me a little longer than I thought it would.'

'Maybe you'd better leave, Dom,' said Matty softly, no longer talking in a strident tone of voice.

'Don't be silly,' Monique said, gathering up the books and papers spread out on the carpet and sofa. 'It doesn't have to be handed in until Monday. I will finish it tomorrow. I am too tired now anyway.'

'Are you sure, Monique?' said Dom. 'I don't want to be in the way or anything.'

'Of course, I'm sure. It's nice to have a visitor at last other than Matty's mother and father.'

An hour later, Dom leaned forward in his armchair to pour himself a fresh glass of Wild Turkey from the bottle on the coffee table, before clumsily flopping back. On the sofa was Monique; next to her, Matty was fast asleep, snoring heavily.

'Matty was telling me how much you like Durham, Monique.'

'Yes, it is so lovely. He give me a guided tour when I first arrived. I took many photos and sent some to my family. They are so jealous.'

'Are you enjoying your course?'

'Yes. The staff and students are amazing. I have never felt so alive these past few months. Life could not be better for me at the moment.'

'Look, I'm sorry for dragging Matty away from you tonight, but it's been such a long time since we had any kind of crack; I just wanted to catch up with him properly.'

'Do not apologise, Dom. I have been telling him for weeks to get in touch with you, but each time he said to me, "Monique, I just want to be with you". I said to him, "Yes, Matty, I love you also, but if we are under each other's feet all the time, we will end up strangling each other".' She giggled to herself. 'I kept telling him, "Go see Dom, do your band again and have some fun. You are still young and not an old man. I have my own life to live, too". He can be so jealous and possessive at times.'

Dom did a double take at this piece of information; obviously, Matty had been economical with the truth earlier when they were out, but he was prepared to overlook a little white lie if it meant the resurrection of their friendship and the band.

'It's only because he cares for you an awful lot,' said Dom.

'I know he does, and I care for him. Anyway, enough about us. I am interested in how you are. Matty told me you have had a rough time lately with the police.'

Dom felt himself going red. 'It was just a misunderstanding. It's all sorted out now.'

'And how is your new home with your girlfriend?'

'It's great. You and Matty must come and visit us sometime for a bite to eat.'

'Oh, you cook?'

'Well, not exactly, but my girlfriend Katy tries. Failing that, there's a cracking takeaway just up the road.'

'Of course, we will visit. And you must come here, too, with your girlfriend.'

'We will, thanks.'

Monique yawned. 'I am sorry, but I must go to bed. My eyes are beginning to close. Would you like to sleep over?'

As tempting as the offer was, Dom did not relish the thought of waking up with a blinding hangover in someone else's house. He stood up and began to put on his jacket.

'Thanks, but I think I'll get off home. It won't look good if I stay out just after I've moved in with Katy. She'll think I'm seeing someone else.'

'Of course, how silly of me to ask. Can I call you a taxi?'

'No, thanks, Monique. I fancy the walk.'

She gave him a perplexed look. 'Are you sure? It is so cold and so far.'

'It won't take long,' he said, zipping up his bomber jacket

in readiness for facing the elements. 'It'll clear my head anyway, if nothing else. Well, goodnight.'

They hugged, before Monique showed him to the door.

'Goodnight, Dom. Take care.'

'See you, Monique.'

CHAPTER 27

Buoyed by the knowledge they had Monique's blessing, Dom and Matty fervently threw themselves back into musical activities in the run-up to the Christmas period, with a creatively fertile series of songwriting sessions producing eight new songs.

At the same time, they began to recruit new group members. The first person to receive a charm offensive was their ex-drummer Mick; his previous band had just folded, so he was conveniently available. Dom and Matty met up with him for a drink one weekend, and plied him with free alcohol until he agreed to join. An added bonus was that Mick knew a keyboard player, Tom Davison, who also happened to be at a loose end; he, too, without even auditioning, was swiftly signed up. Mick's trusted word was good enough for Dom and Matty.

The final piece in the jigsaw arrived in the shape of sixteen-year-old bass player John Peters, a friend of Dom's brother. After a nervous but passable audition, the sixth former was welcomed into the fold. Less accomplished musically than Brian, their previous bassist, John's raw and youthful image more than compensated for any musical inadequacies he possessed.

As 1984 dawned, the new-look Northern Circle convened at Gray's Yard for their first rehearsal. With Dom and Matty dictating proceedings, over the course of January they assembled a set-list of original compositions, as well as a handful of cover versions.

A crucial breakthrough for the band came in early February with the securing of a weekly residency at local pub The Bison Head. It was a far from ideal location in which to play live music – a converted cellar with a low ceiling that, when crammed with customers, had condensation dripping down the walls and became overbearingly hot – but proved crucial in helping the new band line-up to gel, and was the perfect forum in which to test their new material on audiences.

In the first two weeks, their Thursday night performances only attracted a small crowd, mainly comprising Monique, her circle of friends from college, and Katy with some of her workmates.

Slowly but surely, as the winter snow began to thaw and spring reared its head, the band began to notice fresh faces appearing in the audience, returning week after week, until they had a small but loyal following of approximately sixty people, a respectable showing for a non-weekend evening.

At the end of one show in late March, Jez Turner, the producer who had briefly worked with Northern Circle the previous year, walked over to speak to them.

'Well, well, well, do my eyes deceive me? I thought it was an early April fools' joke when Bruce told me you'd left a message to say you were playing here tonight, but I take it all back. Obviously the rumours weren't true after all.'

'What rumours?' said Matty.

'That the prickly thorn of love had sunk you new wave boys for good. I was beginning to think I'd never see you play live. Where the hell have you been? It's been nearly a year since I last saw you.'

'We took a sabbatical from gigging until we could come up with a new set of songs, just like you advised, Jez, if my memory serves me correctly,' said Matty.

'That I did, and it's been heeded. You've gone from being a shower of shit to something approaching what a real band should be, with a new bassist and keyboard player if I'm not mistaken. Very Style Council.'

'Well, we're back and hungry to make up for lost time,' said Dom.

'How did the tape go down with the record companies? No

takers, I'm guessing.'

Both Dom and Matty shook their heads.

Jez grinned mischievously. 'Bloody hell, I'm not cheering you two up, am I? But don't be despondent. All it proves is that you needed to have a rethink about the direction you were heading in, which you've obviously started to do, but are you doing enough?'

'Enough?' said Mick.

'I mean, have you tried your hand a little further afield? This place is all right for fine-tuning your act but it's hardly The Marquee. If the big boys won't drag their arses all this way north to hear your talent, then maybe you need to take the fight to them until they can't ignore you. Remember I told you about my connection down south?'

'Yeah,' said Matty.

'Well, it wasn't just a piece of bullshit I said to try and impress you with; there is actually a grain of truth in it. I have a mate who works for a small record label down in London. Nothing too exciting, just office admin stuff. But the perks of the job are he gets to meet a few of the artists, gets his records for free, and gets to hear which venues the talent scouts are going to be at on certain nights. If he was to tip me off far enough in advance, then I might, just might, be able to book you lads a spot where a scout is expected to attend. Now that's the type of opportunity money can't buy.'

'Why would you go to all that bother for us?' asked Matty suspiciously.

'Because I've always thought, despite my comments to the contrary at times, you lot have something, as per our conversation, Matty, last year when you picked your tape up. You just didn't have the required number of original songs or the correct line-up at the time. Now, in my humble opinion, you do.'

Matty cast his mind back to the previous May when he had gone to Jez's studio.

'He's right. He did say something along those lines,' confirmed Matty.

How could he forget? The remark Jez had made about him being no heartthrob still festered.

'What I'll do is give my mate a ring first thing tomorrow. With a bit of luck, he'll be able to sort you out. Oh, all I ask is that you take me along for the ride. I haven't been down to the capital for months. Deal?'

'Too right it's a deal,' beamed Matty.

CHAPTER 28

On the Thursday morning before Good Friday, the band squeezed their instruments, overnight bags and themselves onto their hired minibus, and excitedly set off for London with high hopes.

Mick was on driving duties and Matty was navigating, armed with nothing more than an A to Z guide and alcohol.

The plan upon arrival in the capital was to locate the club they were playing at, The Shooting Star, in order to deposit their instruments, before finding a bed and breakfast for the night.

On the first leg of the journey, Dom became increasingly concerned at the quantity of alcohol Matty was consuming. By his reckoning, the guitarist was on his fourth can of lager.

'Go easy on that stuff, Matty,' said Dom. 'We need to have our wits about us tonight.'

'It calms my nerves,' said an unusually tense Matty.

'Calms your nerves? We're not due on stage for hours. If you're not careful, you'll be unable to play because you're that paralytic.'

'Ah, don't fret yourself, Dom. You're not my mother.'

'Lucky fucking me.'

'Here we go, lads,' said Matty, in a sardonic tone of voice that demanded the attention of everyone on the bus. 'A lesson in morals delivered by the Right Reverend Blackburn.'

'Come on, people,' intervened Jez, keen to soothe any fractious behaviour. 'This is the biggest day of your lives and you're acting like The Krankies. I don't understand it.'

'Fan-dabi-fucking-dozi,' muttered Dom, not so easily placated. The memory of their disastrous arrival in the Lakes the previous year was still fresh in his mind. Matty might not be driving on this occasion, but Dom knew the potential for things going pear-shaped increased dramatically when Matty

217

toyed with excess amounts of alcohol.

The remainder of their journey south passed uneventfully. Once they arrived in London later that afternoon, it took them over an hour to locate the venue, making a mockery of Matty's comment that they would easily find it because it was on a street close to the King's Road. Little had he realised that the famous street, synonymous with the swinging sixties, was nearly two miles long.

It was nearly six o'clock by the time they found The Shooting Star club, an inauspicious looking building situated on the gable end of a street in Chelsea.

They all bundled out of the cramped interior of the bus, eager to stretch their legs and give the venue the once-over.

'Doesn't look like much,' Mick commented.

Dom pressed his face up against the window, but there was no sign of activity from within the gloomy interior.

Matty tried the main door, only to discover it locked.

'I'll have a walk about, see if there's another door or something,' he said.

'Don't be put off by its sedentary nature at the minute,' said Jez, to no one in particular. 'All these places look the same during the cold light of day. Come nightfall it'll be a different kettle of fish.'

Matty managed to locate the manager, who opened up the premises for them.

Given that they were running late, the band decided to ignore their hunger for a little while longer in order to unload their equipment and do a more important than usual soundcheck. By the time they finished, the bar staff had arrived for their evening shift, and the first customers of the evening were beginning to wander in.

With less than two hours to go before their scheduled performance, the group decided to split up in order to try to find some reasonably priced accommodation, and to grab a bite to eat along the way; they agreed to reconvene back at

The Shooting Star in one hour.

Outside on the pavement, Dom, John and Jez headed left up the street, while Matty, Mick and Tom went in the opposite direction.

'Any joy?' asked Matty, when they met up at the agreed time.

Dom grimaced. 'Everywhere's way out of our price limit. It's just our luck to be playing in one of the most exclusive parts of the most expensive city in England. How did you lot get on?'

'No luck at all,' said Mick.

'There's always the Sally Army,' joked Tom.

'You've got to be kidding,' snapped Matty, taking the keyboard player's suggestion literally. 'I'm not sharing a room with a smelly old dosser. Let's go and get a drink. Tonight will look after itself.'

'Good evening, ladies and gentlemen,' said the club DJ into his microphone while fading out Frankie Goes To Hollywood's "Relax" mid-song to a chorus of groans from the multitudes on the dance floor. 'It gives me great pleasure to introduce you to five talented lads who've travelled many miles to entertain us tonight. So, let's give a warm Chelsea reception to Northern Circle.'

The band walked on stage to a lukewarm reception. Matty strapped on his guitar and checked its tuning, keen for everything to be perfect from the first note. The others readied themselves for playing.

Dom had put on a flat cap and placed a rolled up cigarette into his mouth prior to slipping through the stage curtain. He walked towards the microphone stand and raised his half-full pint glass to a bemused audience.

'Good evening, Chelsea. We are Northern Circle, and we are from County Durham in the North East of England, as you can tell by my flat cap and woodbine. I never leave home without them.'

Dom's attempt to inject some humour into the evening and establish an early rapport with the audience fell flat on its face; a dropped pin in the room would have been audible.

He drained off his drink and put the glass down on the stage.

Mick's drumming mercifully broke the awkward silence as he began playing the introduction to the first song of the evening.

Dom tore off his cap and threw it over the heads of the audience as if he was skimming a pebble on the surface of a river, before dropping his cigarette to the floor.

'We are excited to be playing for the first time in your fantastic city,' he said, gripping the microphone stand for support as a sudden bout of nerves threatened to paralyse him. 'We certainly hope it won't be the last. This song is our homage to a band you may have heard of called The Who, and it is called "Planes, Trains and Taxis".'

A hyped up Matty tore into the opening jagged riff, walked towards the edge of the stage and instinctively metamorphosed into his Wilko Johnson persona; the keyboard and bass guitar swiftly added musical muscle to the song.

As soon as Dom began singing all of his worries vanished, as they always did, replaced by a glowing self-assurance that had been a feature of his recent performances in the revamped group.

It was a gradual process, but, as song followed song, Dom gained the impression that the majority of the crowd were enjoying the show.

'Thank you for your generous support,' said Dom, as they prepared to play their penultimate song of the evening. 'If any of you would like to extend some southern hospitality to us, we are a band without a roof over our heads this evening. We came to this lovely city thinking we could get a room for ten shillings and sixpence. I'm not sure what that is in your pounds and pence as decimalisation is yet to reach our neck of the woods, but we are quiet, civilised human beings, and we promise to clean up after ourselves. This next song is called "The World That Taught You How To Cry".'

As encouraging applause and shrill whistles filled the room at the end of the song, Dom took to the mic for the final time.

'Thank you for making us feel so at home tonight. This is our last song, it's an old Jam classic, and it's dedicated to all of you who later on will find yourselves "Down In A Tube Station At Midnight".'

The crowd roared their approval as the band summoned all of their energy for one final show-stopping performance, playing as if their lives depended upon it.

Within seconds of Northern Circle finishing their set, the DJ occupied his position behind the turntables, wasting no time in getting the second half of the disco under way.

When the band had first took to the stage an hour earlier, Jez had remained near the bar at the rear of the room in an attempt to locate Piers, the representative from PDL Records, who was believed to be in attendance.

Despite having never set eyes upon Piers in his life, within seconds, based on the description given to him by his acquaintance in the record company, Jez had identified a prime candidate: a slim male, in his early forties, leaning against the counter of the bar. Dressed in nondescript jeans, white polo shirt, and casually sipping from a bottle of lager, he had the appearance of a divorcee out for the evening to enjoy a quiet drink and escape his mundane one bedroom flat, and not someone with the power to determine the fate and fortune of aspiring pop stars.

For the duration of the show, Jez had stayed rooted to the spot, keeping one eye on him in an attempt to gauge his reaction to the music.

At the end, unable to resist any longer, Jez walked over to

221

ascertain if he was there in a professional capacity.

'I most certainly am, Jez,' said Piers amiably, once they got chatting after initial introductions were made. 'And I'll say this for them: they certainly know how to put on a show.'

Jez nodded agreeably. 'That's as good a gig I've seen them play in all the time I've known them,' he said, withholding the fact that it was only the second time he had seen them perform live in public.

'Yes, they're very interesting indeed,' said Piers. 'I like the guitarist's attitude and stage presence, musically they are very tight and accomplished, and the singer is excellent. He's a top front man in the making. They're still very raw, but those rough edges could be knocked off.'

'They were my thoughts exactly when I produced them last year.'

'Ah, an insider and not just a fan,' chuckled Piers. 'Would you mind pointing out their manager to me, so I can arrange to see them play again? I never make a decision on the basis of one show.'

'They don't have one at the minute. You can talk to me, if you like. I'm sort of acting in an advisory capacity for them, as I arranged tonight's gig. There's nothing else pencilled in for London as this was just a flying visit to test the water. But I'm sure another can be arranged soon.'

'It doesn't have to be in London. I've been looking for an excuse to go up north for a while now to see the Highlands, Edinburgh Castle, York et cetera. I'm sure I can schedule my trip to coincide with a visit to your neck of the woods, if you let me know their itinerary.'

'I'll post it to you as soon as I return home, if you give me an address.'

Piers handed Jez his business card. 'Well, I must be going, Jez,' he said, finishing his drink and shaking the producer's hand again. 'I've another gig to cram in before I can call it a night.'

'Sounds like you've got the dream job.'

'It's not all it's cracked up to be. You wouldn't believe the amount of drivel I have to wade through, but it's an essential part of the job if I'm ever going to uncover the next big thing.'

'In the meantime, while you're driving from gig to gig, you might want to give this a listen,' said Jez, handing over an envelope containing the band's recording from the previous year. 'Just so they stay fresh in your mind.'

Piers slipped it into his jeans pocket. 'Will do,' he said, before bidding Jez goodnight.

A couple of minutes later the members of Northern Circle, pumped up with adrenalin and soaked in sweat, joined Jez at the bar. As they thirstily drank their pints of lager, the producer informed everyone about his positive conversation with the representative from PDL Records. At this news, a joyous round of hugs, high fives and handshakes ensued. It appeared the gamble to travel hundreds of miles for one gig might just have paid off against all of the odds.

'Well, seeing as it looks as if we'll have to make the gruelling trek home tonight, how about we all have a few more drinks to celebrate?' said Jez, wanting them to enjoy the moment. 'Mick, I'll drive back if you want a few, too.'

Unanimously agreeing to his suggestion, Mick and the rest of the band cheerfully sat down at one of the nearby vacant tables.

When the friends were on their third drink, a clean-cut, ginger haired youth approached their table; he appeared ill at ease as he waited for a pause in the conversation in which to speak.

'Hi,' he said eventually, shyly raising a hand in greeting.

'All right,' replied Matty neutrally, before turning away to continue his chat with Mick.

The stranger stayed where he was.

'Was there something?' Matty demanded brusquely a few

seconds later.

'My name's Rupert. I just wanted to say that set totally blew me away.'

'Thanks very much,' said Dom, overhearing his praise. 'We're pleased you enjoyed it.'

'You did say you were from Durham, didn't you?'

'Born and bred, pal,' said Matty, with drunken pride.

Rupert laughed politely and continued. 'I love it up there, what with its delightful cathedral and amazing countryside.'

'Cathedral? Can't say I've ever noticed,' said Matty sarcastically. 'Listen, Rupert, it's been really nice to talk to you, but you are preventing a bunch of thirsty musicians from getting to their beer. Where I come from that's looked upon as an act of provocation.'

'There is one further thing. I actually study in Durham at the university. In my spare time, I assist with student entertainment. If you are interested, I can request that your band is booked.'

'Those would be paying gigs?' said Matty.

Rupert nodded. 'Of course.'

'Erm, would that be just the one or something on a regular basis?' asked Matty softly, suddenly dropping his caustic attitude.

'There would be the possibility of further dates if you are deemed suitable after your first gig.'

Matty laughed. 'Rupert, pull up a seat, give me a minute to get another round in, and then we're all yours, mate.'

Upon his return from the bar, Matty gave the newcomer his undivided attention.

'So, you're a Rupert, eh? I've never known a Rupert who wasn't a bear. Have you, Dom?'

'No. They don't exist on the council estate at Spennymoor where I grew up. I knew a Jerome once. Years ago, when I went to Sunday school. He was a nice boy.'

'Are you a nice boy, Rupert?' teased Matty, in an

effeminate tone of voice and with a Kenneth Williams-esque exaggerated rolling of the 'R'.

Rupert blushed but laughed along with them, taking their sarcasm in good humour.

'Please, there's no need to be so formal. Everyone calls me Rupe.'

At that moment, an extremely attractive dark haired female walked towards their table, instantly distracting the two Northerners from the conversation.

'Aye, aye, another fan,' muttered Matty.

'Hey, eyes off, Parker. I saw her first. You're bloody spoken for,' said Dom.

'So are you,' replied Matty. 'Anyway, she's way out of your league, not like some of the slappers I've seen you with in your time.'

'I'm not fussy, if that's what you're saying. I don't fall in love just because I get my leg over, unlike someone else not a million miles away from here.'

'Jealousy rears its head in so many guises,' said an unaffected Matty.

Rupe stood up and greeted the young woman. 'Sara, come and meet the band. Guys, this is my girlfriend.'

At this revelation, Dom spluttered on his drink.

'Pleased to meet you, pet,' said Matty, laughing at Dom's reaction. 'Mind, you're a dark horse, Rupe. I thought we had just acquired our first southern groupie.'

'Anyway, Rupe,' said Dom, keen to get back to the matter at hand before they completely offended their new acquaintance. 'Tell us a little more about what you have in mind for the band.'

'As you may well know, there are numerous colleges at the university, many of which like to stage events on campus at the weekend for the students. It's the usual run of the mill stuff, discos mainly, but also entertainment such as comedians, theatre and live music.'

'Unbelievable,' remarked Matty. 'We come all the way down south looking to spread our popularity and crack the big time, and we end up getting new bookings for Durham.'

'It's a small world,' smiled Rupe.

'It certainly is, Rupe,' agreed Dom. 'So, what exactly are you studying at uni?'

'Politics and economics.'

'Ah, laudable subjects, Rupe,' said Matty. 'They will hold you in good stead in the outside world. I'm a graduate myself. Business and finance is my field. Not like my friend here. He didn't get much beyond Peter and Jane.'

'Student of life, me,' said Dom unashamedly.

'It's incredibly dull,' said the undergraduate modestly. 'Nowhere near as grand as it sounds. Actually, my real passion is music. I have a weekly radio show at the local hospital in Durham.'

'Really?' said Dom. 'I had my tonsils out there when I was a nipper. I'll never forget Ward Thirteen. It was paradise to a twelve-year-old. Beautiful nurses and as much ice cream as I could eat. Magic.'

'Hospital radio, eh?' said Matty. 'I bet you've got the Radio One disc jockeys shitting themselves.'

'I know it's not that glamorous; I accept that. But we all have to start somewhere, don't we? DJs on hospital radio and unknown bands in tatty clubs.'

Dom smiled at Rupe's broad shouldered ability to be able to dish it out as well as take it.

'Aye, we've played in a few of those,' Dom conceded, 'but if you can get us on at the campus, Rupe, I think this might be the start of a great friendship.'

'Don't get carried away by his Bogart impression,' said Matty. 'He gives that line to everyone.'

'*Casablanca*?' interjected Sara enthusiastically, suddenly breaking her silence. 'That's one of my favourite films. Such a groundbreaking production for its time, its influence continues to resonate today. And what an opening sequence, all filmed in one take.'

Dom was open mouthed at the depth of knowledge pouring out of Sara.

'You've stumped him there, love,' cackled Matty. 'He only likes it because he fancies Ingrid Bergman. Got a thing for older women has our Dom.'

'Don't listen to him, Sara,' butted in Dom, keen not to be upstaged by Matty. 'Bogey is the greatest actor that ever walked this planet. I've seen loads of his films: *Casablanca*, *Maltese Falcon*, *The Big Sleep* ...'

'Sara's a massive film buff,' explained Rupe. 'You name it, she's seen it. She even writes reviews for magazines and newspapers.'

'Bet she hasn't seen *Electric Blue*,' muttered Matty, before recoiling in pain as Dom kicked his shin under the table.

'I beg your pardon?' asked Sara politely.

'I said, what is it that you do?'

'Ah, I study at Durham, too, for my sins. English Literature. Sorry for mishearing you just then. It's your accent combined with the loud music,' she said apologetically. 'I have trouble following the Geordie accent when it's spoken so fast.'

'Don't worry about that, Sara,' said Dom, keen to impress her. 'Even I have trouble following Matty at the best of times.'

'We're not proper Geordies, pet,' said Matty plainly. 'You have to be born north of the Tyne Bridge to qualify for that privilege. I don't think we have a nickname, us lot from Durham, do we, Dom?'

'No, we're so cool they haven't thought a name up for us yet,' said Dom, immediately inwardly lambasting himself for his weak attempt at humour.

'Hey, Dom? Matty?' interrupted Jez, pointing at his watch. 'We've got five hours travelling ahead of us. I'd like to make

227

a start soon.'

Matty glanced at his own watch. 'Jesus, it's that time already. Well, Rupe, Sara,' he said, rising to his feet, 'it's been nice talking to you both, but as you can see our chauffeur here is dying to whisk us back home to our mansions and page three wives.'

'Oh, that's the other thing I wanted to mention,' said Rupe. 'My parents' house is not far from here in Twickenham. You're all welcome to stay over. I heard you say you didn't have anywhere to sleep tonight.'

'Won't they be a bit upset if us lunatics show up expecting bed and board?' Dom asked.

'Not at all. They're in America at the moment in Florida Keys. The old man's tracing Hemingway's footsteps; he's a bit of an anorak over that type of thing. Anyway, the house is just about big enough to accommodate everyone.'

'Well, I'm game,' said Matty. 'Monique isn't expecting me back until tomorrow.'

'Me, too,' said Dom, the idea of extending the evening with their new friends holding more appeal than travelling through the night staring at the cat's eyes on the motorway.

Matty spoke to the rest of the group, who gave a resounding thumbs up to Rupe's offer.

The matter was settled. Twickenham it was.

CHAPTER 29

Located in a leafy suburb of Twickenham, Withersall Place contained ten palatial, detached dwellings. Set well back from the tree-lined main road, each property had the added security of an eight feet high perimeter wall and gated driveway to help protect the privacy of its residents.

As the band alighted from their minibus, Rupe unlocked the front door to the house and merrily ushered everyone inside.

'Make yourselves at home,' he said, as they entered the spacious hallway.

With its expensively tiled black and white flooring, walls adorned with silky cream wallpaper, and opulent light fittings hanging from the elevated ceiling, one or two of the guests felt as if they had walked into a stately home.

'There's a bathroom just there to the left and another on the landing straight ahead of you at the top of the stairs. The kitchen is just down the corridor here. Help yourselves to beer from the fridge, but don't touch the drinks cabinet in the lounge. My father's a little precious about his vintage wines.'

'Nice place,' said Tom, whistling appreciatively.

'Two bogs. Classy,' said Jez.

'It's bloody paradise,' added Matty. 'Hey, Rupe? What does your dad do for a living? Rob banks?'

Rupe laughed with the easy manner of someone well versed in dealing with such questions.

'Nothing as exciting as that. He works in the city as an investment banker.'

'I guess he's doing all right for himself,' said Dom. 'If he ever needs a personal assistant, I'm available.'

'I'll let him know,' said Rupe playfully.

'Before we do anything, you have got to give me a guided tour,' said a visibly impressed Jez. 'This place reminds me a

229

lot of where Lennon recorded the *Imagine* album.'

'Yeah, sure,' said Rupe coolly. 'Just let me nip to the bathroom first.'

'So, this is how the other half live,' mused Tom, wandering into the huge lounge.

Following him in, Dom instantly made a beeline for the vast record collection housed in a glass-fronted storage cabinet, on top of which was a hi-fi system. He pulled out a Motown Greatest Hits album, slid the flawless vinyl record out of its cover and carefully placed it on the turntable. As "You Can't Hurry Love" filled the room, Dom continued with his browsing, musing to himself that the angelic voice of Diana Ross had never sounded so impressive.

Once he had finished, Dom stood up and turned around to discover the room deserted. In the kitchen, he found Sara sitting at a large circular table, rolling joints and chatting to John and Tom, both of whom were clearly over-awed at being in the company of such a charming and beautiful female.

'Where're the others?' asked Dom, taking a bottle of lager from the fridge.

'Rupe's showing them the house. I thought I'd get busy with these,' smiled Sara, indicating the sum of her efforts on the table.

Dom sat down on a vacant chair. 'Mind if I get started on one?'

'Be my guest,' beamed Sara. 'I'm pleased someone has asked at last.'

As Dom busied himself with lighting one of the spliffs, the host and remaining guests returned downstairs.

'What? You've got a swimming pool as well?' they heard Matty say, as the impromptu tour party approached the kitchen from the hallway.

'Just a small one,' said Rupe modestly.

'Hey, boys, this place is amazing,' gushed Matty, to the

three band members sitting down. 'There's a gym, music room, Jacuzzi, and a pub style pool table with a Wurlitzer jukebox in the games room. I think I've died and gone to heaven.'

'Wow, can we play a game of pool?' said John.

'Of course,' said Rupe obligingly.

'I'll play, too,' said Tom.

'Anyone else up for a game?' asked John, sliding off his chair.

'Yes,' said Mick.

'I'll be there in a second,' said Matty. 'I'm just going to check out the swimming pool. I'm sorry, Rupe, you must think I'm like that bloke off breakfast television who goes nosing about inside famous people's houses.'

Rupe laughed politely.

'I'm going to try out the jukebox,' said Jez. 'I've never heard an authentic Wurlitzer.'

Jez removed a couple of bottles of lager from the fridge and headed upstairs with Mick, John and Tom. Rupe and Matty went off in the opposite direction, leaving Dom and Sara alone at the table.

'Boys and their toys,' sighed Sara, fixing her alluring hazel eyes upon Dom. 'You're not going to leave me too, are you, Dom, to indulge in some male bonding with your fellow musicians?'

'I'll just sit here and relax if that's OK with you,' replied Dom equably, handing the spliff to Sara. 'It's been a long day and I'm knackered.'

She paused her rolling duties to take a quick hit.

'Rupe likes me to do this before everyone gets too stoned. He says I roll the best joints in London.'

'I'll not disagree with that,' smiled Dom.

'Be a love, Dom, and pour me a gin and tonic, please, while I finish off here,' requested Sara. 'The drinks cabinet is at the rear of the lounge.'

231

'No problem,' said Dom.

When he returned a couple of minutes later, Dom discovered she had enigmatically vanished like a genie in a bottle.

'Sara?' he called out.

'Out here,' came her muffled response.

Dom glanced around the room, attempting to figure out where she had gone. Spying a set of open patio doors at the far end of the kitchen, he headed towards them and stepped outside, finding himself on an illuminated flagged area in the back garden.

'Here's one place your friend hasn't seen yet,' said Sara, sitting on a triple-sized garden seat situated at the rear of the house. 'Come and join me,' she said invitingly, patting the empty space next to her. 'Don't be shy.'

Dom handed Sara her drink before sitting down at the opposite end, leaving the middle section free for reasons of propriety. The last thing he needed was for Rupe to come outside, discover them sitting cosily side by side and proceed to get the wrong end of the stick. Dom realised his popularity would hit a record low with his friends if they found themselves homeless for the night, just because he had been unable to prevent himself from making overtures in Sara's direction.

'I really enjoyed your show tonight. You have real talent,' said Sara, gazing up at the stars.

'Thanks,' he said, self-consciously.

'Take it from me, love, the students at Durham are going to adore your act. I cannot wait for you to play there. In years to come, I will be able to say I saw the incredible Dom from Northern Circle sing live before he was famous.'

Dom leaned back and stared up to the heavens, trying to guess which particular star had attracted Sara's attention.

'I hope you're right. It's been so difficult trying to get record companies interested in us.'

'You'll get there, love. You just have to keep persevering until you get a break.'

Sara handed him the nearly expired joint.

Dom sucked hard upon it, enjoying it as much for the intoxicating aroma left behind by her perfume and lipstick than for any hallucinogenic qualities.

'So, Dom. Tell me a little about yourself. What does your world consist of back home?'

'There's not much to tell, really. I work in a general department store lugging stuff from the stockroom to the shop floor; outside of that, I play in the band and go out for the occasional drink. That's my life in a nutshell.'

'Do you ever go to the city centre?'

'Most Saturday's. What about you?'

Sara shook her head. 'Rarely at the weekend. I prefer to stay on campus. Sometimes I go to the student nights at the local nightclub during the week.'

'That's why our paths have never crossed. I only tend to go down town on Saturday's, but sometimes I wonder why I bother. It all gets a bit wild west in North Road when the pubs spill out, which can freak you out a bit.'

Sara laughed. 'Yes, I know exactly what you mean. Just after I'd arrived at the university, I went out one Friday to some pubs in that street. Do you know, I saw a girl in a shop doorway urinating while crouched down. Urggh. And when I walked past a taxi queue the most horrendous fight broke out. It spread all across the street. It was so vulgar.'

'Not all the pubs are like that, though,' said Dom. 'There's one or two on the margins of the city where you can have a bit of crack in peace, such as The Dun Calf.'

Sara shot him a look of puzzlement. 'Crack?'

'I mean conversation,' explained Dom. 'It's great to have all types of people in one place – students and locals – without any trouble. I hate all of this so-called town versus gown animosity. It's a load of bollocks.'

233

'I don't go to that pub very often, but my friends and I sometimes go to The Oak Tree. They have a quiz every Wednesday evening.'

'I go there sometimes, but I've only been on a Wednesday on a couple of occasions. General knowledge isn't my greatest forte, unless the subject is music.'

Dom decided not to relay the tale of the evening he and Matty had entered the quiz for a bit of a laugh, and had embarrassingly come last with only ten correct answers to show for their combined efforts over ten tortuous rounds. The hapless duo had found the categories of Greek Mythology, Politics, Science, and the like, too highbrow. It was only in the Sports round where the pair scored most heavily, with Matty taking great pride at knowing the name of the dog that had discovered the stolen world cup football trophy in England in 1966.

'Bloody *Guardian* reading wankers,' Matty had so succinctly concluded afterwards of the other quiz teams. 'I'm not going back there again. They take it far too seriously, as if it's a dress rehearsal for *University Challenge*.'

'Do you have a girlfriend, Dom?' asked Sara, snapping him out of his thoughts.

'I do actually. Katy.'

'Do you love her?' she said, scrutinising him closely for his response.

Dom shrugged. 'I've never given it that much thought, to be honest.'

'Are you living with her?'

'Yes.'

'You seem too young to be at that stage of a relationship. You should be enjoying yourself before settling down. She must be very trusting of you, given that you are a singer in a band. That must put all manner of temptations your way.'

'The only offer I've had to date was a woman my mother's age,' confided Dom, shaking his head and laughing at the

234

memory of Northern Circle's debut gig.

'Really?' said a highly amused Sara, placing a hand over her mouth to contain her astonishment.

'But, to be serious for a moment, moving in with Katy wasn't something that I planned. There was a lot of pressure on me at the time to move out of my previous flat, and Katy offered to put me up. But … oh, it's complicated and boring. I'll tell you about it some other time,' he said, reticent to dredge up the events of the previous year.

'So, is it fair to say you are a serious couple, or is your relationship more like that of flatmates?' probed Sara further.

'Truthfully,' he began, 'we're definitely not flatmates, but, that apart, I don't honestly know. We get on well together and enjoy each other's company, but where it will take us in the future, I really couldn't say. The future to me is, well, like a different planet that I don't want to travel to yet. I just want to live for now.'

'Very poetic,' said Sara. 'You strike me as being a lover of poetry.'

'I haven't read anything since school.'

Sara looked aghast upon hearing this admission. 'God, you really are missing out. There's a treasure trove of works out there just waiting for you to discover them. I can firmly recommend the Romantics. Shelley's words capture the essence of love and the whole human condition far greater than any other poetry has done to date, in my humble opinion. Wordsworth and the other Lake District poets do come a close second, however.'

'Speaking of the Lakes, Matty met his girlfriend there last year when we were on holiday. They're living together now.'

'Really?' said Sara, her eyes widening in amazement. 'I wish something exciting like that would happen to me. I live in hope that somewhere out there is the man who will sweep me off my feet and be my eternal soul mate.'

Dom's forehead crinkled in confusion. 'But you have

Rupe.'

'Yes, I do,' she said, with elongated weariness. 'We are almost like brother and sister. I can't remember the last time we had sex. I have known him since I was five years old, when we would play together because our parents were good friends.'

'Were you at school together?'

'No. Rupe was at a boarding school. I only saw him in the school holidays, when we practically lived in each other's pockets.'

'How does Rupe feel about you?'

Sara gave the question brief consideration. 'Do you know, I really couldn't say. All I know is that we have never talked about marriage, kids, or even what we'll be doing after we graduate.'

Sara's candidness took Dom by surprise.

'Ooh,' she shivered, 'do you mind if I move closer? It's turning chilly, and I can't be bothered to fetch my jacket from inside.'

Before Dom could answer, Sara shuffled up so close that he could feel the warmth of her body pressing against his. He instinctively recoiled, not that he found being in close proximity to her undesirable, but because he was acutely aware of how it would look should a third party suddenly appear in the garden.

'I hope I see more of you back in Durham, Dom. Only if you want to, of course.'

'Won't that be a little awkward?'

She laughed. 'I mean when you play on the campus. You will see what it's like to hang out at the academic end of town. It will be fun. Rupe will be there too, as well as our other friends.'

'Oh, well. Yes, of course,' muttered Dom, simultaneously relieved and disappointed by Sara's clarification of her initial statement.

'Fantastic,' said Sara cheerfully.

'What's fantastic?'

The new voice belonged to Rupe, posing the question as he emerged from the house.

'That we have made a new bunch of friends,' said Sara.

He stopped in front of them and stared.

For one excruciating moment, Dom feared Rupe was going to react negatively to Sara's overfriendly behaviour, particularly if he had been in the kitchen long enough to overhear any of their recent conversation. To his immense relief, however, Rupe's overall demeanour displayed no indication that anything was seriously amiss.

'Anyone fancy another beer?' he asked casually, offering up a bottle from the three he was holding.

'Thanks, Rupe,' said Dom awkwardly, taking it from him.

'Mind if I join you?' he said, before sitting down on the end of the seat and accepting a freshly lit joint from Sara.

'What are the others up to?' asked Dom.

Rupe grinned. 'They are having the most competitive pool tournament I've ever seen. I thought I'd just leave them to it and come out to grab some air.'

Sara now gave Rupe her full attention, abruptly turning her back on Dom.

As the couple chatted, an alienated Dom felt intense waves of jealousy stir within him. With an aching heart, he closed his eyes and listened to Sara's voice, wondering if such an ideal opportunity to be alone with her would ever present itself again.

CHAPTER 30

'Hello, sleepyhead,' said Katy, to the figure sprawled out on the sofa.

'What?' blurted out a startled Dom, his eyes snapping open.

'Sorry, I didn't mean to scare you,' said Katy, standing over him.

'What time is it?' said Dom, rubbing his eyes.

'Half past five,' replied Katy, perching herself on the edge of the sofa. 'So then, what have you been doing in London to make you feel this tired, hmm?' she asked mock-accusingly.

'Wouldn't you like to know?' he fired back.

She leaned over and kissed him. 'How did the show go?'

'Pretty good.'

'Meaning?'

'A scout from an independent record label turned up. Jez spoke to him, and apparently he liked us enough to promise to come and see us play again.'

'That's good news. It was well worth the trip, then.'

Dom nodded.

'Did you find a good hotel to stay at?'

'Not exactly. Everything was way out of our budget. We were going to drive home straight after the gig, but the son of a millionaire took pity on us, and put us all up for the night in the most amazing house I've ever seen.'

Katy stood back up. 'Pull the other one, Dom.'

'Honestly.'

'Really? This I must hear, but it'll have to keep. Helen's picking me up for a game of tennis, and then we're going out afterwards for cocktails.'

'Dressed like that?'

Katy was wearing her usual sports kit of white skirt and sky blue polo shirt.

'No, silly, I've got my jeans and stuff in my bag to get changed into afterwards. Have you eaten since you got back?'

'Not if you don't count three digestive biscuits and a packet of crisps. Ah, do you have to go out? I was looking forward to a night in.'

'Yes,' she said firmly. 'I came home two hours ago from my mother's and have been doing my best to wake you up ever since, clattering cutlery and slamming cupboard doors, but you were dead to the world.'

'Yeah, it was a bit of a late night.'

Dom thought it best to spare Katy the details of the intriguing girl he had met, and who had been uppermost in his thoughts ever since.

'You'll have to get yourself something out of the freezer or go for a takeaway,' said Katy, pulling on her trainers. 'Helen's here. I'll see you later. Don't wait up.'

Once Katy had left, Dom switched on the television set and flopped back down on the sofa. As the uninspiring bank holiday television shows began to unfold in front of his eyes, he was unable to concentrate properly upon what he was watching; all Dom could think about was the night before. The beguiling spell Sara had placed upon him continued to weave its magic from a distance of three hundred miles. Less than nine hours since he had said his farewells to her, he was feeling the ache of separation, longing for the day when he could see her again.

Feverish from craving her company, Dom went into the kitchen and switched on the kettle.

While waiting for the water to boil, he began to hear the spark of a melody in his head. Not recognising it as belonging to any particular song, Dom felt compelled to capture it immediately. Fetching his portable cassette player from his bedside cabinet, he pressed record and began to hum the tune into the microphone.

Fully immersed within the sudden burst of creativity that

had unexpectedly struck, Dom grabbed a pen and notepad, and began scribbling down the words spilling from his mind as fast as his hand would allow.

Reading the verses back to himself once he had finished, it struck Dom how openly they articulated his current state of mind and the crushing vacuum he was experiencing in Sara's absence.

Dom then commenced the usually difficult process of attempting to match his lyrics to the melody; astonishingly, after only a couple of minor amendments, he discovered both components fitted seamlessly together.

Within thirty minutes, Dom had completely finished the musical piece that he was calling "Obsession", instinctively sensing that this was way and beyond the best song he had ever written.

CHAPTER 31

For the second time in just over a year, a potential major step forward for Northern Circle proved to be a false dawn. Just as victory in the Battle of the Bands competition and the subsequent recording of their songs had failed to attract any interest from record companies the previous year, so the euphoria generated by their London gig soon died away when Piers inexplicably failed to follow up his initial interest.

More bad news swiftly followed in May. To rub salt into already inflamed wounds, Rupe informed them that Northern Circle would not be playing at the university that term as all of the weekend band slots were fully booked, forcing them to postpone their debut appearance until freshers' week in the autumn.

As well as being a collective blow for the band, this fresh development was personally devastating for Dom. The powerful crush his initial meeting with Sara had triggered had shown no sign of alleviating, and he had been secretly counting the days until he could see her again.

Reeling from this series of setbacks, Dom initially drew solace from the thought of having the band to preoccupy him in his time of anguish, but he was stunned shortly afterwards when Matty announced a hiatus on band activities with immediate effect. The opportunity of a twelve-week work training placement in Birmingham had arisen, one that he felt obliged to accept, to be followed by a holiday in France visiting Monique's family.

With the feeling that history was repeating itself for the band, a sullen Dom reconciled himself to a summer of musical stagnation and frustration.

CHAPTER 32

With Jez by his side, Dom strutted purposefully into Gray's Yard on the first Sunday in September.

The last to arrive for band practice, Dom cheerfully greeted the rest of Northern Circle, all of whom were in various stages of assembling and tuning their instruments.

Jez's unexpected appearance raised a couple of eyebrows.

'Right, everyone, can we quieten down a moment?' said Dom, in a brisk, business-like tone of voice. 'I'd just like to say a couple of things.'

Everyone stopped what they were doing and gave Dom their undivided attention.

'First things first, let me introduce you all to the newest member of Northern Circle, Mr Jez Turner. I've been working with him over the last couple of weeks on the initial stages of a new band project, which I'll come to in a moment, and he has offered to join us as a rhythm guitarist.'

'Nice one, Jez,' shouted Mick.

'Is that OK with you, Matty?' said Dom, realising he had broken band protocol by making a major decision without consulting his absent friend.

'Yeah, of course,' Matty replied.

'Cheers, fellas,' said Jez.

'What was the other thing, Dom?' said Tom.

Dom took a deep breath and began to explain.

For weeks, he had been obsessed with making a fresh assault on the music business, but had been unsure as to what route to take. And then, a couple of weeks ago while reading a music magazine, he had chanced upon an article about a Durham band who had released their first single independently, from which a major record deal followed.

It was a eureka moment.

Dom had put down the magazine and wondered how such

a simple and obvious idea had not occurred to him previously; almost immediately, he had begun to think about the logistics of such a plan.

'Are you mad?' said Matty, once Dom had ceased talking. 'Release a record ourselves?'

'Why not?' Dom shot back.

'Because it'll cost us a bloody fortune, for a kick-off,' moaned Matty.

'Most of us are working. We can all chip in, can't we?' Dom reasoned.

Matty shook his head. 'Some of us have bigger outgoings than others.'

'What's that supposed to mean, Matty?' snapped Dom.

'Some of us aren't being put up by our girlfriends.'

Dom was indignant. 'I pay my way with Katy.'

'But you have two wages coming in. I pay all of the bills in our house. Monique only has her student grant.'

'Boys, boys, let's not lose our heads,' said Jez amicably, keen to restore a cordial atmosphere to the room. 'Let's not argue over money. That's only allowed once you've become a bunch of playboy millionaires who can't stand the sight of each other for longer than two minutes at a time. We can discuss this in a calm and civilised manner.'

'What do you think, then, Jez?' asked Mick. 'You've got more experience of the industry than the rest of us put together. Is it doable on a shoestring budget?'

As all eyes turned to the newest band member, Jez took a moment to do some rudimentary mental calculations.

'It won't be cheap, lads, but we can cut some corners to get the ball rolling musically. For a start, I'll waive all of my usual up-front costs for the use of the studio, and clear my schedule so that we can concentrate fully on recording and producing two songs. For the practical side of things, I'll have to ring up some of the local independent labels and see where they get their records pressed, and then try and get some

243

quotes. I'll also contact some record shops and make enquiries about getting the single stocked on a sale or return basis.'

'You make it sound so easy,' said Mick.

'It's not a difficult process when you think about it,' said Jez. 'The hard part is getting radio airplay and people to buy it. There are hundreds of new releases every week competing with each other for kids' pocket money, and the major companies have the finances to employ pluggers to promote their acts to television and radio stations. That's what we'd be up against.'

John, the youngest member of the band, timidly raised his hand.

'Yes, mate?' said Dom.

'Before we get too involved with planning the release of a record, aren't we missing something obvious?'

'What's that?' Dom said.

'Well, we don't have a song to record that's good enough, do we?'

All eyes returned once more to Dom; the youngster had made a fair point.

Much to everyone's surprise, Dom wore a smile as wide as the River Wear.

'While you sun worshippers were swanning off around Europe last month in search of slappers and cheap lager,' he said, 'yours truly was doing what he loves and knows best.'

'What do you mean?' said Mick.

'Jez,' said Dom, throwing their latest recruit a cassette tape. 'Put this on.'

Jez inserted it into the portable cassette player he had brought with him, and everyone listened intently to the demo version of "Obsession".

'Wow, that's good,' said Mick, once the song had ended. 'Did you write it, Dom?'

'Yeah.'

244

'I like it,' added John.

'Me, too,' chipped in Tom.

'For what my opinion's worth, lads,' began Jez, 'I reckon it could be a massive hit. It's the best song I've heard in all my time as a producer. So, I propose, if it's OK with you lot, to go away and come up with an approximate overall cost of releasing it ourselves. I'll also book us some studio time. We've got nothing to lose by recording it. Are we all in agreement?'

Everyone, including Matty, gave their consent.

'Right, let's get some serious practice under our belts,' said a fired up Dom, relieved by the positive reaction to his song, and the fact his proposal had survived the crucial first hurdle. 'Our all-important gig at the university is less than a month away.'

CHAPTER 33

'How many does this place hold, Rupe?' asked Matty, surveying the empty hall from the rear.

'Oh, about five hundred, maybe more at a squeeze. It'll be fairly full tonight, I can promise you that.'

'Is that because words got around we're playing?' said Mick.

'No, it's because it's the first Saturday back and there's cheap beer,' grinned Rupe, walking slowly towards the stage, closely followed by the six members of Northern Circle.

Mick's expression turned gloomy at Rupe's frankness.

'Don't look so crestfallen, Mick. I'm sure you'll go down a storm. And there'll be plenty of girls.'

'Ah, that's what I like to hear,' said Mick, rubbing his hands together, instantly cheered.

'They'll need a bloody translator to understand you, though,' chipped in Matty mischievously, playfully nudging the drummer.

'Piss off. Handsome looks are a universal language, so that's you screwed, Matty.'

'You're forgetting something,' retorted Matty buoyantly. 'The likes of me and Dom have beautiful girlfriends already.'

'OK,' resumed Rupe. 'You are scheduled to play at eight o'clock sharp for one hour, before the disco takes over for the remainder of the evening. I'll leave you to get on with your soundcheck, and will see you all later on tonight. Oh, before I forget, here are your VIP passes. These will enable you to get past the rugger lads who act as doormen. Try not to lose them, please, as they're under strict orders to allow in only those with tickets. We're constantly plagued with townies trying to get in to cause trouble.'

Once Rupe left, the musicians began to set up their instruments. When they were ready to run through some numbers, they all assumed their positions on the stage.

'Shall we play the new one?' asked Mick.

'No,' said Dom swiftly, fearing the song they had been rehearsing for its debut performance that evening would lose its intended magical impact should Sara happen to be in the vicinity and overhear. 'Let's do "Planes", "I Want You" and finish with "All Or Nothing".'

A problem free soundcheck put everyone in good spirits ahead of their first show in months. Now left with nearly two hours to kill until show time, they briefly went their separate ways: Jez, Tom and John went off to explore the campus; Matty dashed away, saying he was going home to check up on an off-colour Monique; Mick, never short of personal self-confidence, declared he was going to find some female students to chat up.

Unsure how best to fill in the chunk of time at his disposal, Dom was the final one to leave the hall. With the ground floor of the adjoining halls of residence resembling a near ghost town, he meandered aimlessly through its maze-like corridors, stopping now and then to read the notices and posters pinned to information boards, or to peer through the windows at the well-maintained grounds. At one point, he chanced upon a student bar where a small army of staff were busying themselves in preparation for the first major social event of the academic year, but there was no sign of Sara.

Finding himself at the main reception area, Dom went outside for a cigarette, standing on the set of wide steps at the entrance to the building. After a couple of minutes, a van belonging to the disco company hired for the evening pulled up outside.

'Where does the gear need to go, mate?' shouted the driver from his wound down window, obviously mistaking him for one of the organisers.

'Down this corridor in here,' replied Dom.

'Cheers. OK, Phil, let's get cracking,' said the man to his

colleague in the passenger seat.

While Dom loitered in readiness for pointing them in the direction of the hall, two warm hands covered his eyes.

'Guess who?'

Although they had only met just the once, nearly half a year ago, Dom instantly recognised the voice and the smell of perfume.

'Sara.'

'Did I scare you?' she asked playfully, releasing her hands.

'Terrified me,' he joked, turning to face her.

'How are you?'

'Erm … you know. OK. A little nervous about tonight.'

'Oh, don't be,' she said, assuming Dom was referring to his impending performance. 'Rupe and I have been banging the drum for you all week. Lots of our friends are coming to see you, and I can promise they will be incredibly supportive. You'll get no one being rude and shouting out. What do you call people like that again?'

'Hecklers.'

'Yes, hecklers. No, Dom, people are just here to have a great time. I'm sure you will be fine,' she said, giving his arm a reassuring rub with her hand.

'Is there anywhere we can sit and chat, Sara?'

'Sorry, Dom. I'm afraid I'm on entertainment committee duties at the minute. Maybe later if I'm not too busy we can find time.'

'Of course, for sure,' Dom said quickly. 'I'm sorry if I disrupted your work.'

'Don't be silly,' laughed Sara. 'It was I who inconvenienced you. I'm the nuisance.

'Well,' said Dom awkwardly, 'see you later then, maybe.'

As he watched Sara disappear back inside, Dom wondered if he had misread the signs from her all of those months ago; the possibility suddenly crossed his mind that she was never going to reciprocate the strong feelings he felt for her.

When the band took to the stage at the allotted hour to begin their set, Dom gazed over the sea of heads as he adjusted the microphone stand, estimating Northern Circle were about to play to their largest audience yet.

The show got underway, and the musicians hit the ground running with no sign of nerves or rustiness, displaying an eagerness to perform after so many idle weeks.

The audience were initially polite but restrained in their applause at the end of each song. Gradually, however, the committed performance began to win them over.

Dom had never felt such elation; back doing the thing he loved, his old confidence returned in abundance, plainly visible in the ease with which he chatted to the audience between songs, and his trading of in-jokes with Matty as they played.

When it was time for them to perform "Obsession", Dom waited for the audience's lavish show of appreciation for their previous song to subside before addressing them.

'As a band, we've enjoyed going to lots of different places these last few years, where we've met many new and interesting people. Some people you know you'll never meet again, and some you hope will become pivotal figures in your life. This next song was written earlier on this year about one such very special person. This is called "Obsession".'

Mick counted in with four taps on his drumsticks, before Matty started playing the slow tempo three chord introduction and main riff, the spine around which the song was structured.

Dom closed his eyes, wrapped his arms around himself, and began to sing with all of his heart the first verse and chorus.

> I can't get you out of my brain
> I can't get you out of my heart

Stopped me from thinking straight
I can't begin to start
To get you out of my mind
Oh yeah, I've got a kind
Of Obsession
Obsession
Obsession
Obsession

The second verse saw the remaining instruments introduced, adding further layers of depth and feeling.

Soaring breathlessly into the frantically paced middle eight section, Dom's lyrics articulated with unbridled passion the turmoil of unrequited love as the music built up to a powerful emotional peak, before coming to an abrupt halt.

After a pause of three seconds that just about managed to stay on the acceptable side of showmanship, Dom's vocals slid with weary resignation into the final verse, with the backing instruments once more restrained and sedate.

Entering the song's simplistic but effective outro - the one worded title sung recurrently - each instrument gradually faded away, leaving Dom's lone, whispered voice and Matty's riff to finish in unison.

As the audience voiced its approval, Dom glanced anxiously in the direction of his student friends at the front of the stage: Rupe was leading the applause, while Sara stood next to him, a pensive expression on her face.

Aware that now was not the moment to dwell upon the potential repercussions of the public airing of his feelings, Dom addressed the crowd for the final time.

'We are going into the studio to record "Obsession" in a couple of weeks' time and are planning to release it as a single next year, so please look out for it in your local record shops. I promise, hand on heart, that if it ever makes the top forty chart we will come back and play for you again, donating all proceeds to charity.'

The crowd boisterously endorsed his offer.

'We hope you've enjoyed the evening as much as we've enjoyed being here,' continued Dom. 'Let the entertainment committee know if you have enjoyed the show, and hopefully we'll be back soon. This is our last song this evening, and I want to see you all dancing and singing along to "You Really Got Me".'

With the thunderous applause from the hall ringing in his ears, Dom flopped into an armchair in the dressing room, swiftly followed by the rest of the jubilant band.

'Man,' shouted Mick. 'Listen to that.'

'Woo hoo,' screamed Jez ecstatically.

Matty was beaming with delight. 'Well done everybody. I'm proud of you all. We put on a show and a half out there.'

'OK if I pop in?' said Rupe, his head peering around the door. 'I thought you might like a drink to cool down after your efforts. Compliments of the house.'

'Get yourself in,' said Matty gregariously.

Rupe entered, carrying a small crate of bottled lager, with Sara close behind. Placing it down on the floor for the band, they eagerly grabbed one each.

'Just what the doctor ordered,' said Tom, taking a thirsty swig.

'Lads, that was incredible,' said Rupe. 'You've got yourselves an instant fan club out there. Loads of the students are dying to meet you all. I said I would make some introductions once you've had a chance to catch your breath.'

The sound of "Teenage Kicks" by The Undertones playing in the disco was the spur for Mick to spring to his feet.

'I'm ready now, Rupe,' he said, bursting with uncontrollable energy. 'Point me in the right direction. Anyone else coming?'

'Count me in,' said Tom. He downed his drink with

consummate ease before grabbing a second.

'This way, chaps,' said Rupe, exiting the room.

Jez and Matty followed their bandmates, with John bringing up the rear.

'You coming, Dom?' asked the shy teenager.

'Sure, John. Just give me a minute or so.'

Sara hovered tentatively in the doorway. 'Do you want to be alone?' she asked.

'No, Sara. Stay,' he implored.

Sara walked into the middle of the room; an uncomfortable silence hung in the air, with neither sure how to begin.

'You sang really well tonight,' Sara said eventually.

'Thanks,' replied Dom meekly.

'Did you …' she began hesitantly, 'did you write that song for me?'

Dom nodded dolefully, preparing himself for the disappointment of rejection.

'Thank you. It was beautiful,' she said.

He looked away, too embarrassed to meet her gaze.

'I think there's something you should know, Dom. Rupe and I, we're not together anymore. Over the summer, we came to an amicable decision that our relationship had run its course and that we would go our separate ways but remain friends. So, I'm footloose and fancy free.'

Hearing this unexpected piece of news, Dom seized the moment.

Standing up, he walked swiftly towards her. Sara wrapped her arms around him and pulled him in close. They embraced tenderly and stood as if frozen, neither wanting to be the first to break the spell.

An hour earlier, acting upon a moment of impulse, Katy had picked up her car keys from the dining table, pulled on her black leather jacket and driven to town.

Her relationship in recent months had been unsettled, with

Dom appearing distant and unhappy. Knowing how important the university gig was to him, Katy hoped that turning up unannounced would act as a gesture of support and go some way to bridging the divide that had wedged itself between them.

Her knowledge of the exact location of St Paul's, the university campus she needed to find, was sketchy, knowing only that it was located at the southern end of Durham City. Ten minutes of driving down the quiet, leafy lanes that branched off the long thoroughfare of South Road were required before she found the venue.

After parking in one of the vacant bays outside the building, Katy quickly checked her appearance in the rear view mirror before hurriedly walking towards the two burly, tuxedo-wearing males standing at the entrance. Effortlessly charming her way inside, despite the fact she was ticketless, Katy paced down the ground floor corridor towards the unmistakable sound of Northern Circle playing in the near distance.

Pushing through a set of double doors, Katy found herself in the rear of a dark, crowded hall. Being small in stature, she had no desire to force her way through the throng of students blocking her path to the stage, opting instead to find a space against the back wall from which to watch the remainder of the gig.

Like everyone else around her, Katy was enjoying the band's performance until the moment her boyfriend's brief speech at the beginning of "Obsession" set alarm bells off in her head. After listening to what Dom had to say, and the song that followed, Katy instinctively knew the reason for his recent moodiness and change in character; suddenly, it all made sense. How could she have misread the signs?

When Northern Circle departed from the stage after the final song, a stunned Katy remained where she was. She knew she had a choice to make: immediately seek Dom out and confront him over his comments, or disappear, leaving him none the wiser that she had attended.

The latter option, she figured, after a brief deliberation, would only delay the inevitable.

Regaining her composure, Katy walked slowly through the clusters of dancers, seeking out Dom. Within seconds, she spied Matty leaning against the stage talking to a couple of students, but Dom was nowhere in sight.

'Katy?' a surprised Matty said. 'Dom never said you were coming down.'

'Bit of a last minute decision,' she said coldly. 'Where is he?'

'He was just having a rest backstage the last time I saw him. You know what these singers are like, always have to be different from everyone else,' he laughed briefly, until he realised Katy did not appear to be in the mood for wisecracks. 'I'll take you there if you like.'

'That's OK. I can see you're busy. Just tell me where to go, and I'll find him.'

Matty pointed to a door at the side of the stage. 'Go through there, turn left, and there's a room at the end of the corridor on your right. He should be in there.'

'Thank you.'

Once through the door, Katy found herself in a narrow, gloomy passageway. A chink of light up ahead, however, intimated she was on the right track.

Approaching the room to which Matty had directed her, she paused outside to peer through a thin vertical gap sandwiched between the half-opened door and doorframe.

What Katy saw stopped her dead in her tracks; she clasped her hand over her mouth to contain a gasp of horror. In that moment, her world crumbled.

She retreated, undetected.

Back in the packed hall once more, Katy kept her head down and bolted towards the exit.

CHAPTER 34

Dom gingerly opened his eyes and raised his spinning head a few inches to survey the unfamiliar, curtain-drawn bedroom he found himself in, before resting it back down on his pillow.

Piecing together his movements of the previous evening to ascertain how he had arrived at his present location, Dom recalled surreptitiously slipping away from the disco with Sara back to her home in the city centre, only to discover an even livelier party in full swing.

Beyond that, Dom's recollection of events was hazy. He could vaguely remember Sara introducing him to dozens of smiley, intoxicated students, before then sitting with her on the backdoor step for a heart to heart, the outcome being she would officially become his girlfriend, but only after he had done the honourable thing and broken off his relationship with Katy.

Dom then remembered feeling ill, and Sara taking him upstairs to the bedroom where he had just woken alone; she had explained she would not spend the night with him until he was legitimately available.

After half an hour's inertia spent futilely willing his hangover to dissipate sufficiently to be able to function on a basic level, Dom swung his feet onto bare floorboards and unsteadily stood up. It was only at that moment, wondering where he had left his clothing, that he realised he had gone to sleep without bothering to undress.

Opening the bedroom door and walking across the landing to the summit of the stairs, Dom became aware of just how silent the house was. Apart from the sound of muffled snoring emanating from one of the other rooms, there was no sign of life; Dom guessed everyone must have carried on partying long after he had bowed out of the action, and were still sleeping off the previous evening's excesses.

Staggering out into a bright and mild autumn day, Dom made his way to the bus stop in North Road, attempting to focus his mind on the unpleasant matter at hand. When it came to events that involved emotional confrontation, Dom knew he had history of conducting himself in a less than chivalrous manner, on numerous occasions preferring to employ the services of a third party to break bad news to a soon to be ex-girlfriend. It was not something he was proud of, but Dom much preferred that method than to have to suffer tears and hysteria first-hand. On this occasion, however, Dom was determined to do things correctly, however much the inner coward in him begged to differ; he owed Katy that much.

Dom alighted from the bus at his stop and began the dreaded walk home, each step becoming increasingly difficult the closer he got.

Turning into his street, Dom noticed Katy's car was missing, but figured she would not be too far away.

He opened the front gate and walked down the short path to his door. Glancing up at the window of his neighbour's upstairs flat, Dom saw the familiar silhouette of Mrs Higgins staring down at him from behind her twitching lace curtains. He gave her a wave of acknowledgement, before rooting through his pockets for his house key. Before he could locate it, his elderly neighbour was at her front door.

'Hello, Dom.'

'Hi, Mrs Higgins.'

'Look at the state of you,' she said, in a concerned tone. 'You look like you've been sleeping in a skip all night.'

Mrs Higgins never minced her words.

'Where've you been?' she continued. 'I've got something here I need to show you. You'd better come in a second, dear, and have a cuppa. No point in letting the whole street know your business.'

Intrigued by Mrs Higgins's words, Dom followed her inside.

'Tea or coffee?' she shouted from within the bowels of her kitchen, as Dom waited in the living room.

'Coffee's fine, thanks.'

'And would you like a headache tablet with that?'

'That would be helpful,' he admitted.

'Take the weight off your feet. I'll not be a moment.'

Dom sank into the welcoming comfort of an armchair and waited for Mrs Higgins to reappear.

Entering a short time later, she placed a tray containing drinks, biscuits and paracetamol onto her coffee table. Walking over to her sideboard, she picked up a sealed envelope and handed it to him.

'This is for you,' she said, before perching herself on the edge of her sofa.

Addressed to him, Dom immediately recognised the handwriting. He slid his finger under the seal, removed and unfolded the letter contained within, and began to read:

Dom,

As you well know, things between us have been difficult lately. I came to see you in Durham last night, but from what I saw it was obvious I was the last person you would have wanted to bump into.

Under the circumstances, it's best I move out immediately. If you wish to take the flat on in your name, I am more than happy for you to do so. The rent is paid up until the end of the year when the current contract expires. I will let the landlord know I no longer wish to be registered as a tenant.

I'm sorry I wasn't enough for you. I hope you find with her what I was obviously unable to offer.

Please do not attempt to contact me. It's for the best.

Well, there's not much left to say apart from have a great rest of your life, and I hope you'll be happy.

Love always.
Katy

'She had a van here first thing this morning,' explained Mrs Higgins, once she surmised Dom had fully read the letter. 'I'm sorry, Dom. It must come as a complete shock to you.'

Dom put the letter down on the table and sat back for a few moments, silently sipping at his coffee.

'I'd best be off, Mrs Higgins,' he said, when he had finished.

When Dom opened his front door and entered the living room, he was not surprised to discover it stripped bare of Katy's possessions, but was still shocked at what he witnessed: the television set, three piece suite, fold-down dining table, houseplants and framed Van Gogh reprints were all gone; all that remained were his hi-fi system and record collection.

The pattern repeated itself in every other room.

In the main bedroom, Katy had taken the double bed, bookcase, bedside cabinets and chest of drawers; the fridge freezer, oven, washing machine, kettle, crockery and cutlery were all missing from the kitchen.

Feeling ashamed for allowing his relationship to end on such a messy note, but guiltily slightly relieved that he had avoided a full-on confrontation, Dom removed his camping sleeping bag from the built-in wardrobe in the bedroom, unfurled it on the carpet and crawled inside. Curling his body up into a ball, he swiftly drifted off into a deep sleep.

Sleeping off his hangover in the empty shell of his flat, Dom was not the only one to be having an eventful Sunday; at home in Neville's Cross, Matty was receiving the most surprising news of his life.

All day, he had suspected something was amiss; Monique

had been red-eyed when he had risen out of bed mid-morning and uncharacteristically subdued in the hours that followed.

'Matty,' said Monique weakly, breaking the early afternoon silence in the living room. She was reading her course notes for her latest assignment, while Matty lay stretched out on the sofa, wishing the self-induced ache in his head would go away. 'I have something I must tell you.'

Matty opened his eyes and peered across the room at her.

'Can it wait, darling? I'm cream crackered here.'

'No,' she replied ominously. 'This cannot wait.'

Sufficiently alarmed by her tone of voice, Matty sat up and gave her his undivided attention; it was then he noticed the tears flowing down her cheeks.

Matty assumed the reason she was so upset was due to his returning home later than planned the previous evening. Did she still not believe him after he had already explained that morning the reason for doing so? How, lost in the euphoria of the moment and a little worse for wear, he had accepted Rupe's offer of a few drinks back at his place. He had seen little harm in it, particularly as, unlike the others who had to get a taxi home, he had been only a five minute walk away. Maybe she believed he had been cheating on her with a younger student more than willing to share a one-night stand with a passing musician.

'What is it?' Matty asked anxiously, guessing he was not going to like what he was about to hear.

He closed his eyes, bracing himself for the emotional pain he felt was about to be thrown his way.

'I'm … I'm … '

CHAPTER 35

When the persistent knocking at the front door woke Dom up late in the afternoon, at first he hesitated from answering, fearing in his groggy, paranoid state of mind that Katy had sent around a mob of bloodthirsty vigilantes to dish out a brutal form of revenge.

A minute later, the letterbox snapped open. 'Dom, are you in there? Open up.'

It was Matty.

'What's up?' said a dishevelled-looking Dom, when he finally opened the door.

'The most incredible thing's happened, Dom,' said Matty euphorically. He was brandishing an unusually large bottle of whisky, the type usually associated with football manager of the month presentations.

'You've won the pools?'

'Better than that, mate.'

'You'd better come in, then.'

Once inside, Matty did a double take when he saw how starved of furniture the living room was.

'Bloody hell, Dom. Have you had the bailiffs in?'

'Katy's dumped me. Upped sticks and taken everything with her, just like that.'

Matty was flabbergasted. 'When?'

'She was here when I left for the gig yesterday, but when I got back today this is what I returned to.'

'But I thought you saw her last night.'

'What?'

'Katy … just after the gig. She was looking for you, so I pointed her towards the dressing room.'

Dom cast his fuddled mind back to the previous evening when he had been with Sara. In the light of this new piece of information, Katy's letter and actions now made perfect sense. Obviously, she had spotted the two of them together.

'And you didn't think to tell me this last night?'

'When did I have the chance?' protested Matty. 'You were nowhere to be seen at the disco.'

'Ah, I've made a right mess of things,' admitted Dom.

'You sound like a man in need of a drink. Tell you what, grab hold of this bottle and I'll see if she's left anything remotely resembling a cup or glass that we can use.'

Matty rummaged around in the kitchen cupboards, returning with Dom's football mug and a pint glass.

'Better than nothing, I suppose,' reasoned Matty, taking the bottle back from Dom. He squatted down onto the carpet to pour two generous measures.

'Go canny, mate,' said Dom, aghast at the generous amount of alcohol glugging from the bottle.

Matty handed Dom the mug and grabbed hold of the glass.

'Well, I don't quite know how to say this,' began Matty, 'so I'll just come out and say it. I'm getting married to Monique.'

'Well, I didn't think it would be to the milkman,' muttered Dom flatly.

It was obvious from Matty's expression that his friend's underwhelming response had stung him.

'I thought you'd be a little happier for me.'

'I am, really. It's just come as a bit of a surprise. How long have you been keeping that under your hat?'

'A couple of hours. I'm still in shock.'

'But you've only been seeing her for five minutes.'

'It's been over a year,' Matty said, correcting his friend. 'That's long enough to know if you want to spend the rest of your life with someone.'

'Still, it all seems a bit drastic unless ... she's not?'

'She is. Pregnant,' he declared. 'I'm going to be a father. Me, Matty Parker. I can't take it in at the minute. It feels like a tidal wave's swept me off my feet.'

Dom knew he should have been excited for his friend, but a selfish thought immediately struck him.

'This won't affect the release of the single, will it? You'll still be putting in your grand?'

Matty went extremely pale and failed to reply, his silence speaking volumes.

'Oh fuck, Matty,' shouted Dom, in frustration. 'Why now? Just when things are happening for the band again. Every time we take one step forward, something happens to knock us back. Couldn't you have worn a bloody johnny for a few months longer?'

Matty was indignant. 'I'm not saying we'll never bring a record out, Dom, just not right at this minute. We want to have the ceremony before Christmas; nothing too extravagant, just in a registry office, but there's still the rings and dress to buy, and the reception afterwards to sort out. That, together with the baby, is going to have a massive financial impact. Monique's going to have to abandon her course, and she'll not be able to work anytime soon, so my pay is going to be stretched to the limit.'

'Well, we've got the studio time booked now. Jez had to clear a week of evenings to accommodate us.'

Dom knew his attitude was self-serving, but he had set his heart on seeing his musical plan through to fruition; for it not to happen now would be soul destroying.

'We'll still do the recording sessions and send the song to the record companies,' said Matty, looking to appease Dom. 'Who knows, we might get lucky.'

Dom shook his head passionately in disagreement. 'We'll just hit a bloody stone wall again like last time, and end up sitting around on our arses for months waiting for a poxy phone call that's never going to come.'

'Try and be pleased for me, mate. This is the best day of my life I'm trying to share with you here,' Matty said gently. 'Monique means everything to me, and I want to do all I can to make her, and the baby, happy. And I'm going to need a best man, so the job's yours if you want it.'

Dom sank his whisky in one go. 'What the hell … why not?'

'Great. Monique will be so happy you've agreed to do it.'

'Well, you may as well pour us another round of drinks, now the bottle's open.'

Immediately regretting his lack of grace in his reaction to Matty's news, Dom decided to rein in his bitterness. It had been a crazy couple of days all round, and all he wanted to do now was to work on another mind-numbing hangover.

CHAPTER 36

'Dom, darling, would you mind turning your music down?' said Sara. 'I'm trying to work here.'

With the hand-in date for numerous assignments less than a week away, the undergraduate had been working furiously all day at the small coffee table to meet her pre-Christmas deadline.

Dom reached over to the hi-fi from his horizontal position on the sofa and pressed the off switch.

'Thank you, darling,' said Sara, unable to prevent a slight edge from creeping into her voice.

Dom said nothing, but sprawled himself out once more and stared at the ceiling.

For the next ten minutes, Sara attempted to focus on her work, but the sight of a listless Dom in her line of vision was affecting her concentration.

'Go out if you like,' she said finally, as much for her own sanity as Dom's. 'I really don't mind, especially as I'm going to be tied up all evening with this.'

'I'm skint,' he muttered sulkily, 'and even if I wasn't, I've no one to go out with. Matty's been too busy playing happy families since the wedding.'

With Monique now two-thirds of the way through her pregnancy, the newly married Matty had taken to impending fatherhood like a duck to water, to the detriment of their friendship. Dom's regular Saturday nights out with him had faltered, with Matty always having an excuse as to why he was unavailable: the spare room needed decorating; he was tired from shopping all day for baby accessories; Monique was tired, so he was doing all of the housework.

Dom switched on the television and flicked through the channels with the remote control, before settling on a weak sitcom. As he contemplated having a bath and an early night, the doorbell rang.

'If this is a double glazing salesman, I'll bloody swing for him,' grumbled Dom, getting up to answer the door.

Nothing prepared him for the surprise he was about to receive.

'Tel.'

'All right, son. How you doing?'

'Erm … fine, just fine. I thought you were still inside?'

Tel chuckled. 'I've been let out on parole for good behaviour.'

'Great. Well, come in,' said Dom, conscious he was allowing the heat to escape out of the room. Sara was always complaining about how cold it was in the flat, berating him for allowing draughts in by not closing doors properly.

'It's a nice place you've got here,' said Tel, hovering in the middle of the living room and surveying the interior. 'A little bigger than your previous flat.'

'Thanks, Tel. Sara, this is my uncle Tel.'

'Pleased to meet you, pet,' said Tel warmly, before turning back to Dom. 'I thought we could go for a pint, if you're not doing anything. I've got an hour or so to kill.'

'That's a fantastic idea,' said Sara enthusiastically. 'I would really appreciate some peace and quiet in which to finish my work.'

'Sounds like you've got permission from the boss,' said Tel wryly.

'I'll just grab my coat,' said Dom, glaring pointedly at Sara as he left the room.

Tel placed his nephew's drink down on the table in front of him, before sitting down opposite.

'Well, cheers, son,' he said, raising his own pint before swigging from it.

'Aye, cheers,' repeated Dom.

Tel placed his glass down onto a beermat.

'You forget how good a decent pint of beer tastes when you've been denied it for so long. I really missed it when I was inside, as well as sex and proper bog roll.'

'How long have you been out?'

'Just a week or so.'

'Mam never said anything last week when I phoned her.'

'I told her not to, son. I just needed a little time to myself to readjust to the outside world again. After being behind bars for over a year, everything appears alien for a while when you first get out.'

Tel cast a disapproving glance around the sparsely populated lounge of The Newton Moor.

'Is this your local, Dom? I had more exciting evenings playing draughts in the games room at the nick.'

'It's a bit livelier in the bar if you want to go through there. There's a pool table and a jukebox.'

'No, I'm fine here. I don't think my ticker could cope with the excitement,' he joked, before taking another large gulp from his glass. 'So,' he continued, becoming more serious, 'there's been some big changes for your mother and dad this last year, hasn't there? How's he coping?'

Ronnie Blackburn, having been on tenterhooks for two years, had finally had redundancy forced upon him in the autumn.

Dom grimaced. 'With difficulty. His temper's even worse than it was when he was working. Mam says he's driving her crackers.'

'Don't take any of that personally, Dom. His pride's hurt, and he's lost at the minute. All his life, he's needed to feel useful, from joining the navy to coming home and starting work as a welder. Suddenly, that's all been taken away from him, and he's been put on the scrapheap along with the other three million. The dole can play strange tricks on the mind. It's a bit like prison, really. Until you experience it personally, you don't quite know how you'll react to it.'

'He's trying to keep himself busy with the allotment and his darts matches, but he's not used to having so much free time on his hands.'

'We may not see eye to eye on a lot of things, me and Ronnie, but I sympathise with him over this. I'm finding out for myself what it's like to be out of the loop, too, at the minute. It's not an easy thing to deal with.'

'I thought you'd be OK. Vince Staveley can give you a job, can't he?' said Dom.

A shadow crossed Tel's face at the mention of his old friend.

'No. Vince is out of the picture at the minute, still lying low abroad.'

'Where at?'

'Probably best for you if you don't know the answer to that, son, in case any of the local constabulary come sniffing around. Anyway, let's not dwell on that. It's obvious there's been a lot going on with you that I need to catch up on, such as a change of home and living with a new lass. She appeared a bit spiky when I showed up just now. I hope I didn't come at a bad time.'

'No,' sighed Dom. 'She's under pressure to finish her essays before Christmas, and I'm just getting under her feet.'

'What happened to your last girlfriend? Your mam seemed to think the pair of you were really happy.'

Dom shifted uncomfortably in his seat. 'It didn't work out, but that's all in the past.'

Tel took the hint and moved the conversation forward. 'And I see our Daniel's been busy. Can you imagine the shock I got when your mother told me he's going to be a trainee copper next year?'

Dom's brother had recently successfully applied to join the local police force as a cadet.

'He'll be giving the family a bad name,' jested Tel. 'God knows what my mates will say when they find out.'

'Well, there was no chance of me ever joining the police, so Dad pinned all of his hopes on Daniel.'

'You and your brother have always been like chalk and cheese.'

Dom nodded grimly in agreement. 'I'm definitely the black sheep of the family.'

'Ha. Join the club,' laughed Tel noisily, standing up to fetch a fresh round of drinks.

Upon his return, Tel steered the chat to a topic both men knew would arise at some point.

'About last summer, Dom,' he began awkwardly. 'I want to clear the air with you and to try and make amends.'

'Tel, it's OK, there's no need to …'

'No, let me explain,' interrupted Tel firmly. 'You got the thin end of the stick with all that business, and it wasn't right that you got dragged into it. It couldn't have been nice being banged up in a cell and grilled by the coppers like a grade A criminal. So, I want to look you in the eye, tell you how sorry I am and ask your forgiveness. Do you accept my apology?'

'Of course, Tel. You're family.'

'You genuinely don't hate me?'

'No,' Dom said.

Tel sat back, wiped his brow and took a drink from his beer.

'That's a relief. You know, I've been thinking about life a lot these last few months, and I've decided that the time has come for me to go straight once and for all. No more mixing with the likes of Vince, and no more knocking on doors trying to extract money from pensioners and single mothers who can't afford to pay back their debt. Even if I have to stack shelves, I'll do it, as long as it's an honest day's work for an honest day's pay.'

As Tel spoke, there was a steely determination in his voice.

'And while we're on the subject of money, there's one last thing I want to do. Your mother was telling me about the problems your band's been having financing this record. What's going on there?'

Dom filled Tel in about why Northern Circle lacked the monetary power to press on with their plans to release a single.

'Well, if that's the case, I'd like to help,' Tel said, when Dom had finished. 'How far short are you?'

Dom scratched his head. 'I'm not sure, to be honest. At least a thousand, maybe more.'

'I think I can cover that for you,' smiled Tel.

'Really?' said Dom, disbelievingly.

'Yes, really. Look, you have to follow your dreams in this life, as your grandad used to say, while you're young enough to do it. And I don't want you ending up a bad one like me. That road only leads to one place. The nick.'

Dom was staggered. 'I don't know what to say. That's fantastic news. The others won't believe it.'

Tel glanced at his watch. 'Well, I've got a date in fifteen minutes, so I'd best be getting a move on. Can I drop you off somewhere, or are you going home?'

'Home will do, Tel. I'm too skint to go out.'

Tel drained his glass and stood up. 'Do you need a sub?'

'It's OK. You've just agreed to give me …'

'That's for your band.'

Tel removed a bundle of money from the inside pocket of his overcoat, peeled off half a dozen notes and handed them to Dom.

'Here, son. Get yourself a drink, and take that beautiful girl of yours out somewhere nice for Christmas.'

'Thanks.'

'Right, if there's anything else I can do to help out, just let me know.'

'Will do.'

'OK, see you later, then.'

'Enjoy your date.'

Tel smiled. 'I intend to, son. It's been a long time.'

CHAPTER 37

The light was fading rapidly on the cold March day as Dom, Matty and Tel loaded the last of the boxes into the rear of the van, before going back indoors.

'I've got the delivery list here somewhere,' said Dom, searching through the pile of paperwork scattered over the carpet; he located it and handed it to Tel.

Tel gave it a cursory glance before rolling it up.

'Right, I'll be off. I need an early night if I'm going to be hitting the road at the crack of dawn.'

With only three days to go until the release of Northern Circle's debut single, Tel had volunteered to deliver fifteen thousand copies of "Obsession" to seventy record shops, beginning with Glasgow and Edinburgh in Scotland, before gradually working his way down to South Yorkshire.

'Hey, Tel?' said Matty. 'Thanks for this. It means a lot.'

'No problem, Matty. Just remember who your friends are when you're at number one on *Top of the Pops* and selling records by the lorry load.'

'We'll make you an honorary backing singer the first time we appear on television, Tel,' said Matty.

'I'll hold you to that,' said Tel lightly. 'Oh, and congratulations on becoming a father. A boy, wasn't it?'

'It was. Francois,' said the proud parent, producing a photograph from his wallet and handing it to Tel.

'He's a little belter. How old is he now?'

'Three weeks. He was a little underweight to begin with because he was slightly premature, but he's piling it on now.'

'I'm chuffed to bits for you, Matty,' said Tel, returning the photograph. 'Right, I'll see you both later.'

'I think I'll turn in early myself once I've had a bath,' said Dom, once he had waved Tel off. 'It's going to be a long week.'

Matty yawned. 'Me, too, although I doubt I'll be getting much sleep tonight because it's my turn to feed the baby when he wakes up.'

'Just make sure you're ready to be picked up at eight o'clock in the morning. Our public awaits.'

'It's exciting, isn't it?' said Matty, putting on his coat. 'To be doing all of this at long last, like proper musicians.'

'We were born to do this, Matty. Just think, in a month's time we might be able to leave our jobs behind forever.'

'Fingers crossed,' said Matty.

Over the course of the next week, Northern Circle left no stone unturned in their promotion of "Obsession". Days passed by in a blur of personal appearances at local secondary schools and radio stations; likewise, there was no let-up in the evenings, as they dashed around the region to fulfil a string of live bookings.

They were able to stick rigidly to their tight agenda thanks to the invaluable assistance of Rupe. His position with the students' union had enabled him to borrow a van so that the band could transport themselves to their engagements. Keen to be involved further, Rupe had also volunteered his services as driver and roadie.

On the final evening of an exhausting but exhilarating campaign, Dom was walking through the centre of Durham City on his way to the showpiece event, the official "Obsession" launch party gig at Bodie's, a local nightclub, when he was stopped dead in his tracks on the icy cobbles of the Market Place by three teenage boys.

'Mister, can we have your autograph, please?' said the tallest of the trio, brandishing a pen and piece of paper.

Dom was dumbstruck. 'I've never been asked for it before.'

'We saw you singing at our school last Monday,' said the second youth.

'Which one do you go to?'

'Framlington Hall.'

'That was my favourite show,' said Dom truthfully. 'You lot nearly raised the roof on that hall. But I'm biased, as I live on the Newton Moor estate.'

The third youth, yet to utter a word, waited until last to receive Dom's signature.

'Would you like it dedicated to yourself?' asked Dom, seamlessly adopting the persona of a professional pop singer.

'Yes, please. Can you make it out to Pete Davies?'

Dom signed and returned his paper. 'There you go.'

'I'm going to buy your record tomorrow,' added the youth, losing some of his inhibitions. 'I hope it gets into Tuesday's chart.'

'You and me both,' said Dom. 'Are you all coming to the show tonight?'

'Yeah,' they all replied enthusiastically in unison.

'Make sure you make plenty of noise, lads, but no drinking any alcohol,' he gently warned. 'I don't want your parents blaming me for leading you astray. OK, enjoy the night.'

Dom continued on to the venue.

When Northern Circle took to the stage at a sold-out Bodie's, they received a deafening reception from a predictably partisan home crowd. Dom did a heartfelt bow of appreciation, a lump catching in his throat at the sight of all the people who had turned up to support him: Sara, his mother, Daniel, Tel, a couple of aunts and various cousins. The only person conspicuous by his absence was his father.

The band proceeded to give their all to an energetic performance that defied their recent physically punishing schedule. As had been the case all week, they ended with "Obsession".

As he soaked up the prolonged applause at the end of the song from family, friends and followers, Dom felt, after so many false dawns, that he had finally arrived.

'Bloody hell,' said Jez backstage, grabbing a towel and

wiping the glistening sweat off his face. 'They're going potty out there.'

As one, the crowd was chanting: 'WE WANT MORE, WE WANT MORE, WE WANT MORE.'

Dom opened a can of lager and took a satisfying swig.

'That,' he began, 'is the best gig we have ever done. It was perfect.'

'Just listen to that,' noted Mick incredulously. 'I've never heard anything like it. We have to do an encore. What do you think, Matty? Matty? Where's Matty?'

'Don't know. Maybe he's gone to ring Monique,' said Dom. 'Anyway, I must go to the toilet; I'm bursting. But I'm game for going back on.'

Dom swiftly made the short walk down the draughty corridor to the gents. As he stood at a urinal, he heard the door open behind him and the sound of footsteps clacking across the concrete floor. They stopped at the adjacent receptacle.

'All right, mate?' said the new arrival, in a confident southern accent. 'You're the singer, right?'

'Yeah,' said Dom, staring straight ahead, struggling to empty his bladder now that he had company.

'That was one hell of a performance you've just put on. Top class. You've improved one hundred percent from the last time I saw you, and you were decent then.'

'Cheers, but we might not be finished yet. Hopefully, we'll be going back on just as soon as …' Dom indicated as subtly as he could with a nod of his head in the direction of the urinal.

The man chuckled to himself as he walked over to the sink to wash his hands.

'I'm the same myself. Sometimes when I'm absolutely desperate for a piss, if someone's stood looking over my shoulder, I could be there all night waiting for the floodgates to open. Mind if we talk a little business?'

'Business?' said a confused Dom. 'Here?'

'Why not? It's quiet and private. I've made some of my best deals in rooms like this.'

Dom joined the stranger by the line of washbasins. 'Go on.'

'I'm Piers from PDL Records. I was at The Shooting Star in London when your band played there. Your mate, Jez, let me know about tonight, so I thought I'd come unannounced and give you a second viewing. Better late than never.'

'But that was nearly a year ago. I thought you'd just forgotten about us or thought we were shit.'

'No, Dom. It's the first chance I've had to get up this far north. I've had a hell of a year, first breaking my leg skiing and following that up with a messy divorce. But I'm here now, and I've just witnessed a new star in the making out there, so why don't we go for a drink afterwards and I'll explain more?'

Dom could not believe what he was hearing. 'Great. Just give me a second, and I'll let the rest of the band know.'

'That won't be necessary, Dom. My record label is after a solo artist, and you, alone, fit the bill. We'll have to get you into some snazzy suits, cut your hair and give you a team of songwriters, but you could, with a bit of hard work and some luck, be a top ten artist by the end of the year.'

Dom was nonplussed. 'But I'm not a solo singer. I'm in a band with a record out.'

Piers shook his head, smiling, as if he had heard such futile expressions of loyalty before.

'Sorry, son, but it's you or nothing. It's a tough enough business as it is without having hangers-on to complicate matters. Look, I can see this isn't the time or place. You've got an audience out there waiting for you, so why don't you finish off here, sleep on it and meet me in the morning at the café down the road. Say eleven o'clock?'

'So, you've decided on the basis of two gigs that I'm good

275

enough?'

Piers took out a cassette tape from the inside pocket of his jacket and held it up.

'Jez gave me this last year. The songs are average, but you've got a good voice and you're a chirpy character. Personality is as important as anything else in this line of business, something that kids can relate to.'

Dom took a moment to consider the proposition. 'OK,' he said, hesitantly. 'I'll be there.'

Piers smiled brightly. 'Now you're thinking smart, son. Golden opportunities like this don't come around very often in life.'

Walking towards the exit, Piers held the door open and ushered Dom through first.

As the sound of their voices gradually faded down the corridor, Matty emerged from the solitary cubicle, seething with anger at the act of betrayal he had just heard with his own ears.

Once the encore was over and the van was loaded up with their instruments and equipment, the band hung around in Bodie's to have a few drinks and to socialise with their extended entourage.

Dom introduced Sara and a subdued Matty to his family, with the singer doing his best to put the unexpected offer from Piers to the back of his mind for the moment. The record company scout was now nowhere to be seen; given that Jez had failed to pass comment about him being present, Dom assumed his attendance that evening had gone unnoticed.

After an hour, Mick, his girlfriend Wendy, and Tom were the first to leave. Rupe, once he had reminded the others to pick up their instruments from his garage the next day, also bid everyone goodnight and headed for the exit.

'Well,' said Iris, finishing off her drink, 'I think we'd better be making tracks, too. Ronnie will be wondering where we are.'

'Relax, Iris,' said Tel. 'This is the first time I can ever remember you having a night out that doesn't involve that bloody club of his, so you make the most of it. Anyway, he'll be too drunk to notice what time it is when you get home, I expect, judging by the bottle of whisky he had in his hand when we left.'

'You're winding me up, Tel. He never touches a drop in the house, usually,' said Dom.

'It's nothing, son,' said Iris, giving her younger brother daggers, 'just a bad patch he's going through, what with losing his job and everything, and me having to get a cleaning job to make ends meet. Maybe if you came around a bit more often and had a proper conversation with him that might cheer him up.'

Dom's Sunday visits back to Spennymoor had become increasingly irregular since Sara had moved in with him the previous November; the seemingly permanent black moods of his father, combined with his constant petty sniping, had deterred Dom from bothering to make the effort on his day off.

'You're kidding, aren't you, Mam?' said Dom bitterly. 'I'm the last person who could make Dad happy. He thinks I'm a waste of space. Why doesn't the boy wonder detective here have a go? He's the one with a proper career.'

'Come on, son, that's not fair now,' said Tel.

'I'm sorry, Daniel. I didn't mean that,' apologised Dom.

'That's OK,' said Daniel.

At that moment, Wendy re-entered the club, a look of panic on her face.

'Someone help,' she wailed. 'The lads have been jumped.'

'Daniel. John. You two stay here with Mam,' said Dom, leaping out of his seat and bolting towards the exit, closely followed by Tel, Jez and Matty.

Outside, amidst a heavy sleet shower, Dom saw the skirmish involving his friends still in full motion on the opposite pavement. Taking the lead, he ran across the street.

The first person he came to was Tom, lying on the ground groaning, while two men, their backs to Dom, had Mick pressed up against a shop window and were punching him freely; an additional two thugs were kicking Rupe, curled up protectively on the pavement with his arms around his head.

Dom and Jez tore into the two men assaulting Rupe, rugby tackling them around the waist, their momentum causing all four of them to collapse into a tangled heap.

Scrambling to their feet, the two assailants took off down the street, not fancying their chances with the sudden change in odds.

Dom picked himself up in time to see Tel single-handedly pull the two men off a semi-slumped Mick, before meting out a head-butt and a flurry of punches that forced them into a hasty retreat.

As Rupe, Mick and Tom slowly got to their feet and had their injuries assessed by the rescue party, a distressed Sara came running towards them.

'Dom, it's Matty. Come quick.'

He followed Sara back across the street to discover, to his horror, Matty lying motionless on the pavement outside the entrance to Bodie's.

'What happened? Has he been attacked?'

'No. He slipped on the ice and banged his head,' said Sara.

Dom crouched down beside his stricken friend. 'Matty. MATTY!'

Getting no response, he yelled at Sara to go and ring for an ambulance.

Much to everyone's relief, Matty had regained consciousness by the time medical assistance arrived a few minutes later. Attempting to sit up, he appeared confused as to how he had arrived at his current predicament.

Matty's concerned friends crowded round as the ambulance crew conducted an examination, before placing

278

him on a stretcher and carrying him into their vehicle.

'He looks as if he's just had a nasty bump to the head,' one of them explained to Dom. 'He should be fine, but we're just going to take him in to keep an eye on him overnight. Would you like to accompany him?'

'Yes,' said Dom immediately.

'What about Monique?' asked Sara.

'I'll call her from the hospital once Matty's seen a doctor. As the man's just said, it looks as if there's nothing to be worried about.'

Once Dom had hopped into the rear of the ambulance, it set off on the short journey to the local hospital less than a mile away, leaving a shocked and battered group behind in its wake.

CHAPTER 38

On the day of reckoning, Dom was awake from five in the morning.

With a fluttering feeling of excitement in his stomach making the prospect of further sleep impossible, he climbed out of bed and switched on the kettle in the cold kitchen.

Waiting for it to boil, Dom lit his first cigarette of the day, gazed out at the hard March frost in the back garden and for the millionth time that week mused over the two possible outcomes to the day.

The first was by far the preferred option: Northern Circle's debut single would crash into the charts, leading in the short-term to a merry-go-round of television appearances, newspaper interviews and national airplay on the radio. Dom had estimated that the lower reaches of the chart was the best position they could achieve. He doubted whether the number of copies they had distributed to record shops, even in the unlikely event that all of them had sold out, could propel them any higher.

Such success would thus leave the band well placed to earn a recording contract with a major record company.

The flipside of the coin was inglorious failure, forcing Dom to return to Donnelly's as anonymous as he had been on the day the promotional campaign began, with the record an expensive flop and his musical ambition in tatters.

There could be no in-between – it was Monte Carlo or bust.

By noon, the band, including a patched up Matty, as well as Rupe, Sara and various other friends, had packed inside Dom's living room, all eagerly awaiting the new chart countdown on the Gary Davies lunchtime radio show.

A tense hush fell upon the room as one o'clock arrived; anxious glances and nervous smiles were exchanged as the familiar countdown theme of Prince's "1999" began to play, and the presenter announced that there were nine new entries, fifteen songs going up, fourteen going down and two non-movers.

'This is it,' exclaimed Jez. 'In the next few minutes we'll know whether we've made it or not.'

'God, this is torture,' moaned John.

'I feel sick,' muttered Mick, already on his sixth can of lager.

'Shush,' said Sara.

In a flash, Davies announced positions forty down to thirty-one: a quarter of the new chart gone and no mention of Northern Circle.

Seconds later, the atmosphere in the room hit rock bottom with the declaration of the final new entry. The realisation swiftly sank in that the dream was over; their lives were not going to change overnight after all.

Dom switched off the radio; the looks of despondency on people's faces matched his own.

No one spoke for several minutes.

Ever the optimist, it was Rupe who eventually broke the silence.

'Maybe, if we've just missed the cut this week, some radio stations will pick up on that fact and give the song some airplay. That will give you some bragging rights to approach record companies with, at least. I'm off now, so I'll ring up the chart compilers later on and find out where you got to.'

'Cheers, Rupe,' said Dom flatly.

'Come on, lads,' said Jez defiantly. 'OK, we may have lost the battle today, but don't let your heads drop. Like Rupe said, if we're hovering just outside the top forty then we have a platform to build upon.'

Although Jez was attempting to put on a brave face in an effort to bolster flagging spirits, in his heart of hearts he knew that the moment for them had passed; Northern Circle simply lacked the financial budget to recover from such a setback and continue to sustain a comprehensive marketing campaign. It was all but over.

'Well, I expect we'd all better say our farewells to Dom,' said Matty sharply, rising to his feet and staring accusingly at his friend, 'seeing as he's about to jump ship and piss off down to London.'

Everyone's attention focused upon Dom and Matty.

'What're you talking about, Matty?' asked a startled Dom.

'What I'm talking about is a conversation I overheard on Sunday night in which you agreed to meet that record company bloke from London to discuss a solo career. So, whatever happened today didn't matter to you, as obviously you couldn't lose. To think the mate who I've treated like a brother these last few years would even think about swanning off by himself.'

Dom sighed, knowing his decision to say nothing about the secret meeting with Piers had always had the potential to backfire. Now that Matty had forced his hand, he decided to come clean.

'Yes, I met him, but it's not what it looks like.'

'Bollocks,' Matty retorted. 'You're going to do the dirty on me and the boys, and leave us behind, aren't you?'

'It's never been my intention to go solo,' protested Dom earnestly. 'I thought I might be able to persuade him to change his mind and sign the band as a whole. I figured I had nothing to lose by trying. As it happens, I pissed him off for wasting his time, but so what?'

Dom had not reckoned on just how tough a nut to crack Piers would prove to be; in hindsight, he figured the scout had not gotten to where he was in such a cutthroat business without being ruthless and single-minded.

Matty's pained expression made it clear he was not convinced by Dom's version of events.

'You can believe what you want, but that's the truth,'

snapped Dom irritably. 'You should know me after all this time.'

'I know the Dom of old wouldn't have met him and tried to keep it to himself. Well, you're welcome to go and sign for him, and become another tosser of a pop star who sells his soul and integrity for a few quid. I hope it makes you happy.'

Matty picked up his coat and stormed out, slamming the front door behind him.

'I was going to tell you about it, lads,' said Dom, to the rest of the room. 'I just wanted to get through today first.'

No one said a word.

'I believe you, Dom,' said Mick, finally.

'You do?'

'Of course, we do,' added Jez, 'and if you had accepted his offer we couldn't really have held that against you. Let Matty cool off for a while. He'll see sense eventually. I guess he's just annoyed after hearing the crap news.'

The room fell silent again.

'What now?' said a red-eyed John, staring down at the carpet.

'For the band?' said Jez.

'No, I mean, what are we doing now? I don't think I can face going home yet.'

Jez sprang to his feet and rousingly clapped his hands together to grab everyone's attention.

'I propose that we pick ourselves up off the floor and get bloody pissed. Where we're headed can wait for another day.'

Heeding his bandmate's advice, Mick fetched a box of lager from the kitchen and began to hand the cans out.

'Put some music on someone,' said Jez. 'No one leaves until we've drunk the flat dry.'

For four hours, everyone attempted to cushion the crushing disappointment with a bout of defiant partying. However, a telephone call from Rupe informing them that Northern Circle had failed to reach the top seventy-five knocked the wind out of their sails. Too bitter a pill to swallow on a day of extreme lows, the band and their friends shuffled off home, leaving Dom and Sara with nothing else further to do but retire to their bed.

CHAPTER 39

The next morning, a dejected, tired and extremely hung-over Dom walked into Donnelly's staffroom for the first time in two weeks knowing it was going to be a very long day.

'Ah, Mr Blackburn,' sneered Ramsgate, the store manager, sitting at a table reading his morning tabloid. 'So, you've decided to grace us with your presence. I wasn't expecting to see you ever again.'

Dom bit his tongue as he switched on the kettle and spooned a heap of coffee into a mug.

'Well, now that your ridiculous fantasies are over, and you're not going to be rubbing shoulders with the likes of Wham and Duran Duran anytime soon, maybe you can knuckle down, concentrate on your real job and put all of this pop star nonsense behind you. It is this company that pays your wages, after all.'

Dom inwardly fumed but did not rise to the bait. He knew a verbal retaliation would just be playing into Ramsgate's hands, sensing there was nothing his manager would like more than to haul him up on a disciplinary charge for foul language.

Dom poured the boiled water into his mug and walked downstairs to the cold, morgue-like stockroom.

Declining to switch on the radio, usually his first action on a morning, Dom sat down at his desk and began to work his way through the large pile of delivery notes that had been steadily accumulating in his absence.

The following Sunday evening, Matty was conspicuous by his absence when Northern Circle congregated at Gray's Yard for band practice. Jez filled in for the missing main guitarist on this occasion, but when Matty failed to show again the following Sunday a crisis meeting was held.

'I know it was Matty who had a go at you, Dom, but enough's enough,' began Mick. 'We may as well rap it all in if he's not going to show up again. Will you go to his place and offer an olive branch?'

In the sudden silence, all eyes fell upon the singer.

'Why me?' said Dom stubbornly, still hurting from Matty's stinging accusation. 'I've nothing to apologise to him for. I know my reasons for meeting Piers that day.'

'And so do we,' agreed Jez, 'but he'll not listen to any of us. I'm sure he'll have calmed down a bit by now and see reason.'

Reluctantly, Dom acquiesced, realising that the longer Matty refused to return, the greater the chance of the band collapsing for good.

'If I don't hear from him this week, I'll pop around to his place before our next practice.'

The weekend duly arrived and still Matty had not surfaced from his self-imposed exile. Making good his promise to the rest of his bandmates, Dom drove down to Matty's home on a wet and windy Saturday evening.

Pulling up outside, Dom got out of his car, rang the doorbell and waited; when no one answered, he crouched down to peer through the letterbox for signs of life.

'Can I help you, young man?'

Letting the letterbox snap shut, Dom stood up to find Mrs Beattie, Matty's elderly next-door neighbour, standing in her illuminated open doorway, eyeing him warily.

'Oh, hello,' he said, walking over to speak to her. 'Do you know when Matty and Monique will be back?'

'Back? Why, they've moved away, dear.'

Dom's heart skipped a beat. 'Moved?'

'Yes, dear. Matthew's been transferred down south somewhere. Milton Keynes, I think it was. You've only missed him by a couple of days.'

A dumbfounded Dom could only gape at her.

'Thanks,' he muttered eventually, realising she was waiting for him to leave before closing her front door.

Dom returned to his car and sat motionless, stunned by this unexpected development.

CHAPTER 40

Dom walked into The Bison Head, bought a drink from the upstairs bar and sat down at a vacant table. Picking a beermat up and nervously tapping it against his glass, he looked around for a familiar face among the current clientele.

When Mick Pearson had unexpectedly telephoned earlier that week inviting him to attend the debut gig of his latest band, Dom had been non-committal, telling his affable ex-bandmate he would try to make it but could not make any promises.

In the end, with nothing else better to do on the evening of New Year's Day, Dom decided to turn up to lend his support. He had always gotten on well with the former drummer of Northern Circle, but had not spoken to him or the rest of the band since Matty had left Durham the previous spring. The sour end to what had begun as an exciting musical adventure still haunted Dom, to the extent that he had lost all of his enthusiasm for singing.

Thirstily finishing his drink, Dom glanced at his watch; with Mick's band due on stage soon in the basement room, he decided to go to the bar for a second beer before heading downstairs.

While waiting to be served, Dom felt a tap on his shoulder. He turned around to find the familiar face of Mick grinning at him.

'Dom, you came. It's great to see you.'

'How're you doing, Mick?'

'Great. Still working in the factory making televisions and still going out with Wendy. What about you? Still living with Sara?'

The smile dropped from Dom's face. 'Actually, no,' he said. 'She returned home to London when her course finished last summer.'

'Oh, I'm sorry, mate.'

'Don't be, Mick,' said Dom lightly. 'We were chalk and cheese, but unfortunately it took over half a year of living together for me to find that out.'

'So, what have you been up to all this time?'

Dom shrugged. 'Not much really. I still live at Newton Moor, and I still work in the stockroom at Donnelly's.'

'What about music?'

Dom shook his head. 'Not sung in anger since we split up.'

'What a waste. You've got real talent,' said Mick, with genuine sadness. 'Do you regret not signing for that record company? You could have been raking it in by now.'

'Listen, Mick, that's all history, so let's not talk about it. I'd rather concentrate on the present and that begins with an apology for not returning your phone calls last year. I just couldn't bear to speak to anyone at the time.'

Mick responded in typically cordial fashion. 'There's no bitterness on my behalf, Dom. Shit happens. It's just one of those things. Bands split up, always have and always will. I've been in a few others since then, as it happens. Nothing as good as Northern Circle, obviously. The one I'm in now isn't looking much beyond playing cover versions at weddings and birthday parties.'

'Nothing wrong with that, Mick. If it makes you happy and puts a few extra quid in your pocket, then where's the harm?'

'Speaking of which, I'd better go downstairs and get ready. We're due on in a minute. I'll see you down there.'

'Of course,' replied Dom. 'Just as soon as I get served here.'

'OK. We can have a bit crack afterwards if you want to hang about.'

'Cheers, Mick. I'd like that.'

The barmaid took his order, and as he stood waiting for his pint to arrive, Dom recalled the first time Northern Circle had played The Bison Head. He smiled to himself and cringed; he

289

had been so naive back then, believing the gig to be a major step forward on the road to pop stardom.

From downstairs, Dom heard a smattering of applause, closely followed by a rendition of an early Rolling Stones album track, the name of which eluded him.

Paying for his drink, he exited the bar and began to descend the wide, thickly carpeted staircase that gently spiralled to the floor below.

Halfway down, Dom heard the door behind him at the main entrance to the pub open and close, accompanied by an icy blast of air.

'Dominic Blackburn.'

Dom froze when he heard his name called out; the discomfort caused by the brief intrusion of the wintry elements into the pub interior paled into insignificance next to the shiver that went down his spine as he recognised the voice.

Spinning round on his heels, Dom discovered Matty Parker gazing impassively down at him from the landing.

'Dominic bloody Blackburn,' said Matty coldly.

Dom was speechless. Judging by his countenance, it appeared time had not mellowed Matty since the last time they had been in a room together. He prepared himself for an unpleasant confrontation, the hammering of the final nail into the coffin of their friendship.

Matty walked slowly down the stairs, only halting when there was barely half a metre's space between them, his piercing gaze boring into Dom.

'Come here, you bloody sod,' shouted Matty, breaking into a huge grin and wrapping his lengthy thin arms around the unsuspecting Dom who, caught off balance, had no choice but to reciprocate or risk taking a tumble down the stairs.

After a weighty hug, Matty relinquished his hold.

'Right, whose bloody round is it?' he said boisterously, already walking back upstairs. 'We can have a chinwag in the bar and head back down to watch Mick's band in a bit.'

Once Matty had bought himself a drink, the pair sat down at the table Dom had just vacated.

'So,' began Dom awkwardly, 'why the reunion? You never struck me as the sentimental type.'

'You're barking up the wrong tree if you think this is all down to me,' protested Matty. 'This is news to me, too. Mick rang my parents' house on the off chance I'd be there over Christmas and told me about tonight, but never mentioned anything about anyone else turning up. I'm guessing he did the same with you?'

Dom nodded.

'So, he's the one who fancies himself as a *Surprise Surprise* presenter, the little bugger,' said Matty drolly.

Dom removed his packet of cigarettes from the pocket of his jacket and offered one to Matty.

'Thanks, but I've given up.'

'Never,' said an astonished Dom. 'You used to smoke like a chimney.'

'People change.'

'Obviously.'

'I still miss it, but I don't want to smoke around Francois. I couldn't inflict that on him.'

'How's he doing?'

A look of unembarrassed pride lit up Matty's features.

'Great. He's nearly walking already. He's a flighty little sod, though. You can't take your eyes off him for a second.'

'And Monique?' asked Dom.

'Fine. She's a fantastic mother. She's got the patience of a saint.'

'So, when do you go back down south?'

'Tomorrow,' replied Matty, wiping froth from his top lip. 'It's been nice for my parents to spend time with the little 'un, but I've been bored out of my skull, to be honest. I'm not one for sitting about the place for too long doing nothing.'

The thought suddenly struck Dom that Matty would have had numerous opportunities to look him up over the past week, if he had felt inclined to do so. Obviously, Matty was not that keen on seizing the initiative in mending old wounds.

'Are you still at Donnelly's?' said Matty.

'Yeah.'

'And how's Sara?'

Dom briefly brought Matty up to date on his broken relationship.

'I always thought the two of you weren't that compatible. You were bloody stupid to lose Katy.'

'I realise that now,' admitted Dom.

'Have you ever thought about looking Katy up again?'

Dom shook his head. 'That would be a great conversation, wouldn't it? "Hi Katy, fancy making a go of it again because the girl I chose over you buggered off and left me". Anyway, she's living away from Durham now, according to the women at Donnelly's who still keep in touch with her. She's assistant manageress of a bank in Birmingham, apparently.'

'What about music?' said Matty, aware that he was steering the conversation dangerously close to uncomfortable territory. 'Done any gigs recently?'

'Can't be bothered anymore,' said an indifferent sounding Dom. 'Not after everything that happened, with the single not getting anywhere and ... you know ...'

'Me pissing off and leaving you all in the lurch,' added Matty, bluntly finishing the sentence off for him. 'Look, Dom, I need to apologise for the way I acted back then. I was annoyed with you, and then a few days later I received this amazing offer to join the Milton Keynes branch of the company. If I hadn't taken the opportunity it might never have arisen again, but I realise now I shouldn't have gone away without telling anyone.

'And while we're clearing the air about the past, I just want you to know that I do believe your reasons for meeting up with Piers. In fact, now I think you're bloody mental for not signing to his record company. You wouldn't be grafting your bollocks off for peanuts now, that's for sure.'

'I don't regret it,' countered Dom. 'I came into music with you and the band, and it was either the band or nothing. I didn't fancy becoming a fabricated idol for teenyboppers, singing other people's songs that don't mean a thing to me.'

'Well, mate, I have to say I respect you for your principles. And I have to admit, I do miss being in Northern Circle. They were some of the happiest days of my life, especially when we were promoting the single. Just for a few weeks, I really felt like someone and not a nobody. Even if we did fall flat on our faces in the end.'

'They were good times. Let's drink to them,' said Dom, raising his glass in an act of conciliation.

'To good days,' said Matty, chinking his glass against Dom's.

'Shall we go and watch Mick, then?' said Dom, relieved to have finally made his peace with Matty.

'Aye, go on.'

'We can stand and heckle from the back.'

'The back?' remarked Matty, with a twinkle in his eye. 'I'm going to the front, mate, to throw my boxers at him.'

'I hope they're clean.'

'They were when I first put them on a week ago.'

After the gig, Dom, Matty and Mick chatted fondly about the old days, conveniently avoiding any areas that might cause old tensions to rise to the fore.

After they said their farewells to Mick, the duo went on to a nightclub to extend their unexpected reunion; several hours later, both men were extremely drunk as they waited at the taxi rank in the Market Place.

'Hey, why don't you come down and visit sometime? Monique would love to see you again, and just wait until you see Francois. He's amazing.'

Dom was taken aback by the offer. 'If you mean it, I'd love to.'

'Of course, I mean it,' bellowed Matty. 'You're my mate, Dom. The best friend anyone could have. We've a lot of lost time to make up for.'

A lone taxi drove into the cobbled street and stopped at the head of the rank.

'You take this one, Matty,' offered Dom. 'You're the one with the long drive home ahead of you tomorrow.'

'Cheers, Dom,' said Matty, walking to the passenger side of the vehicle. 'I'll give you a ring in a week and we'll sort something out,' he shouted, before disappearing inside the taxi.

CHAPTER 41

When Matty failed to contact him in the days that followed, Dom was disappointed but unsurprised. In hindsight, he assumed that Matty's offer had simply been the beer talking and that nothing further would come of it. If that proved to be the case, Dom had the consolation of knowing he had taken the opportunity to end their friendship on a positive note.

However, a month later Matty did finally get in touch, apologising down the telephone line for the delay in making contact and inviting Dom to visit him that weekend.

It was the revitalising shot in the arm Dom needed, a mini-break away from the tedium of work and mid-winter blues. He booked off some time from work, bought his bus tickets and looked forward to seeing his old friend again.

After a tiring journey on the overnight bus to Milton Keynes, much delayed by sporadic snow flurries and difficult driving conditions, Dom arrived at his destination the next morning to find Matty waiting for him when he stepped off the coach.

Although he was warm in his greeting, Matty did not appear to Dom to be his usual self; he was subdued, a little distant and definitely not the forthright Matty of old.

His physical appearance had also altered, appearing thinner than was normal even for him, with sunken eyes and black circles underneath. As if second-guessing Dom's thoughts, Matty attributed this transformation to a constant string of sleepless nights with Francois.

'Dom, lovely to see you again,' said Monique kindly, giving Dom a hug on the doorstep of their mock Tudor house. 'How was your journey?'

'As comfortable as could be expected trying to sleep next to a twenty-stone bloke with bad breath, who snores,' he moaned.

Monique placed a hand over her mouth in an attempt to smother a giggle.

'Never mind,' she said sympathetically. 'I will make you some breakfast and a cup of coffee. You must be really hungry.'

'That would be fantastic, thank you.'

'Come and meet the little fella,' said Matty, leading Dom into a large living room.

Sitting on the plain brown carpet, surrounded by a plethora of toys, was Francois.

'Francois, say hello to Dom.'

With his dummy firmly in his mouth and a serious, uninterested expression on his face, Francois briefly glanced up at Dom, before returning his attention to his cars and multi-coloured building blocks.

Dom smiled, unable to believe the uncanny resemblance between father and son.

'He's a dead ringer for you, mate,' said Dom.

'That's what everyone says,' admitted Matty. 'It drives Monique crackers.'

'Is he walking yet? You told me the last time I saw you that he wasn't quite there yet.'

'Yes, although he's still a little unbalanced on his feet.'

'Like his dad after a skinful,' Dom joked.

Matty laughed lightly.

'Right, I'll show you to your room, and you can freshen up if you like.'

'Great.'

Over the next two days, Dom enjoyed the full range of Matty and Monique's hospitality, including Monique's delightful cuisine, a guided tour of the local area by Matty, and the run of their house to do as he pleased.

For an hour or so each day, Dom made time to play with Francois, and the pair swiftly established a pattern of interaction. Enthusiastically implored by Francois to build a wall of building blocks, Dom would happily oblige, only for the infant to crash his toy cars into it. Collapsing into fits of hysterics as pieces went flying everywhere, Francois would then tirelessly gesture for Dom to rebuild the wall again and the whole process repeated itself.

On the Saturday evening, after a sumptuous homemade Beef Bourguignon, followed by Crème Brulee and several bottles of wine to wash it all down, the host was unable to resist producing his acoustic guitar. With Monique comprising an audience of one, Dom and Matty ran through numerous songs from their Northern Circle days, finishing off with a slowed-down version of a song that was a firm favourite of them all: The Style Council's "A Solid Bond In Your Heart".

At the end of their intimate performance, Monique stood up, clapping joyfully, before embracing them both and giving them a peck on the cheek.

Dom and Matty looked at each other and smiled softly. No words were necessary; both knew the other had experienced the same feeling of unadulterated happiness at playing together once again, and felt a golden flickering of the old magic that existed musically between them.

On Sunday morning, after a cooked breakfast and an hour's lazy conversation, with a heavy heart Dom bid farewell to Monique and Francois, before Matty drove him back to the bus station for his return journey.

'I've had a really great time, Matty,' said Dom, standing beside his coach.

'That's good. I was afraid you'd find spending time with us a bit boring.'

'Don't be daft. It was nice to catch up with Monique and to see Francois.'

'Oh, he's loved having a new face about the place. I bet he spends all today asking where you've gone.'

'Anyway, we can always fit a pub in next time I come

down, can't we? That'll raise the excitement stakes,' joked Dom.

'Of course, we can,' agreed Matty.

An awkward pause ensued as they looked uncertainly at each other, before Matty took a step towards him.

'Come here, you big puff,' said Matty, giving him a parting hug and a heartfelt pat on the back. 'I'll see you soon.'

'OK, mate.'

'Do you mind if I sod off before the bus pulls away,' said Matty. 'I'm not one for goodbyes. So, until the next time.'

'Until the next time,' repeated Dom, before reluctantly climbing onto the bus.

CHAPTER 42

Dom had spent all of Easter Monday making his flat as welcoming as possible: dusting and polishing, vacuuming throughout, washing dirty dishes and cleaning the bathroom. Fastidiousness was not a trait usually attributed to Dom when it came to cleanliness in his home environment, but he was prepared to break the habit of a lifetime for his guests.

As Matty and his family were in Durham visiting his parents for a few days, Dom had invited them over that evening for a Chinese takeaway to repay the kindness shown to him on his trip to Milton Keynes.

It had just gone five o'clock when an exhausted Dom finally finished his chores, leaving him just enough time to grab a shower, have a shave, and get dressed before his guests arrived.

When the expected time for their arrival came and went, Dom was not too concerned; punctuality had never been one of Matty's strong points.

When they were an hour late, Dom began to wonder if he should give Matty a telephone call; the hurtful thought crossed his mind that his friend had either completely forgotten or had a last-minute change of heart. However, Dom knew Monique would not be so thoughtless as to renege without first letting him know.

When they were two hours late, alarm bells began to ring.

Dom tried calling the home of Matty's parents three times in quick succession but received no answer.

Now he was worried.

Where were they?

Dom was just about to call for a fourth time when his doorbell rang. Through his living room window he saw Matty's car parked outside. Allowing himself to relax, he went to open the door.

He was completely unprepared for the sight that greeted him: Monique, standing alone on the doorstep, staring disconsolately down at the ground.

'Monique,' said Dom, baffled as to why there was no sign of Matty or Francois; a feeling of dread engulfed him.

She looked up to face Dom. Her skin was blotchy, and tears were streaming down her face. She was trying to speak, but was struggling to get her words out.

Eventually, she managed to blurt out, 'M … M … M … Matty's dead!'

CHAPTER 43

Matty had died of a suspected brain haemorrhage at the age of twenty-four, collapsing on the bathroom floor of his parents' home that morning.

Although the doctors could not say with absolute certainty, an examination of Matty's historical medical records led them to surmise the blow he had suffered to his head the previous year may have been a contributory factor in his untimely demise, and probably explained the severe migraines Matty had suffered from in recent months.

The results of the post-mortem several days later confirmed the doctors' initial suspicions.

The period leading up to the funeral was one of stunned disbelief for Dom, the worst living nightmare imaginable; he kept hoping it was not real, just one big joke, and that he was going to see Matty come walking through his front door at any moment with that familiar grin on his face.

Shock soon turned to raging anger, as Dom thought how cruel it was for Monique to be left without a husband, Francois without the father he adored, and his parents to suffer the anguish of having to bury their only child.

On a bright but cold April morning, Matty's funeral took place at his parents' local church in Gilesgate.

As Dom entered the service to the sound of "A Solid Bond In Your Heart" being played, the last song he and Matty had ever performed together in front of Monique, the reality of the occasion became all too much and he broke down in floods of tears.

Everyone Dom spoke to at the gathering afterwards all bore the same shocked expression and uttered the same words: 'I just can't believe it.'

As people eventually began to drift away, Monique took Dom to one side to tell him that she was returning with

Francois to France for an indefinite period the following day. Asking if he would drive them to the local airport, Dom agreed without hesitation.

'Are you sure you are going to be OK?' said Monique.

She had checked in her suitcase, and with a little time to spare before heading to the departures lounge, had insisted Dom join her in the airport cafe.

'Isn't it me meant to be asking you that?'

Monique smiled sadly and placed a comforting hand on his shoulder.

'We are all hurting, Dom, not just me.'

'I'll be fine,' Dom said weakly, swiping at a stray tear on his cheek, touched by how Monique could find time to be concerned about other people's feelings and not just her own. 'So, what will you do now?'

'Oh, I will sit in my parents' house and be fussed over,' she replied, raising an eyebrow wearily, suggesting that was the last thing she needed. 'However, so will Francois, and it will be a nice distraction for him to have. He has many aunts, uncles and cousins who cannot wait to see him again.'

'Ah, that's good. And what about your home here?'

'It will have to be sold. I'm afraid there is no way I can afford the mortgage payments by myself. I have no job, and because of Francois there is no way I can work. I really hope it sells quickly as I also have so many bills to pay on the furniture, the television set, video recorder … the list is endless. We bought nearly everything for the house on hire purchase.'

It was the first time Dom had considered the practical implications of Matty's death for Monique; he knew it was heart breaking enough for her, but to have the additional worry of a mountain of debt on her shoulders was not what she deserved.

'I'm guessing Matty had no life or mortgage insurance?'

302

probed Dom gently.

Monique shook her head. 'Who thinks of such things at our age? We were so excited at building a home and a life together that we never gave it a second thought.'

'Well, if there's anything I can do ...' offered Dom, knowing it was a hollow, clichéd expression, but it was all he could think of to say.

For five minutes they sat in silence, both dreading the moment that was fast approaching. Finally, Monique rose to her feet, with Francois clinging to her.

'Come on, Francois,' she said gently.

'Let me get that for you,' said Dom, picking up her hand luggage.

They walked towards the escalator that carried passengers up to passport control and the departures lounge. Upon reaching the point where they had to part, Monique turned to Dom and wrapped her free arm around him.

'You will look after yourself, Dom, won't you?' she said quietly, burying her teary face into his chest.

Dom was too overwhelmed to speak; it took all of his effort just to be able to nod unconvincingly.

'Well,' she said, letting go of him and wiping her tears with the back of her hand, 'we must be going.'

Dom handed Monique her hand luggage, together with a plastic bag he had brought with him.

'What is this?' asked Monique.

'A little present for Francois.'

Monique put down Francois and removed the item from the bag. It was a Newcastle United football shirt.

'It's a little big for him,' said Dom, struggling to find his voice. 'But age four to five was the smallest size I could find.'

Monique smiled. 'He will grow into it.'

'I'll take him to the match one day when he's older, although he'll probably be supporting Paris Saint-Germain or another team by then.'

'Don't worry, Dom, we will be back one day, and I'm sure he would like to do that. It is only natural he will ask questions about his father, and want to find out more about him.'

'That's a date. Right, get yourselves up there,' said Dom, with forced cheeriness. 'Don't want you missing your plane.'

'Goodbye, Dom, and thank you for everything.'

Monique picked up Francois once more and stepped onto the ascending escalator.

Dom watched despondently.

And then, they were gone.

CHAPTER 44

Rupe walked into Sweet Dreams, one of his favourite haunts in London's Covent Garden, and ordered a gin and tonic. He had just finished presenting his Saturday evening show for Radio WestEnd, and it was his custom to unwind afterwards with a few drinks.

On this occasion, he had arranged to meet up with David Babbelstein, an old school friend. It had been six months since Rupe had last seen him, and he suspected there had been an underlying motive behind Babbelstein's insistence on the telephone the previous day that a night out on the town was long overdue. Time would tell.

Life had been good to Rupe in the last year, beginning when he had landed a prestigious job at Radio WestEnd as a stand-in presenter within weeks of leaving university. Such vacancies always attracted hundreds of applications from aspiring disc jockeys who regarded the radio station as the ideal forum in which to learn their trade and gain valuable experience, before moving on to better things; in the previous two years, three presenters had departed for national radio stations. However, Rupe's father was an old friend of the radio station owner and had, unbeknown to his son, naturally put in a good word.

Despite Rupe's desire to succeed in life on his own merits, he was not so naïve as to think that nepotism had not played a major part in his appointment. Rupe had justified this good fortune to himself by reasoning that, although favourable circumstances had aided him on this occasion, he would just as swiftly be shown the door should he fail to deliver the goods. Fortunately, the reviews and ratings for his initial shows had been positive, so much so that four months ago he had landed his own permanent weekend show. That, too, had been a hit, and he was the current station golden boy, touted as one to watch by industry insiders.

'Hey, David,' greeted Rupe affably, when his friend arrived a short time later. 'How are you?'

'Bloody run off my feet, as per,' said a hassled looking Babbelstein. 'The MD has got us all working flat out on our latest campaign. He's labouring under the miscomprehension that we can compete with other companies on the jeans front.'

Babbelstein worked in the marketing department of a small but rapidly expanding clothing company.

'I thought you liked a challenge?' said Rupe. '"Think big", isn't that one of your sayings?'

Babbelstein caught the attention of the barman and ordered a drink before responding.

'There's thinking big, but there's also having your head in the clouds.'

'Tell me more,' Rupe said invitingly, aware he was going to get the full story regardless.

'He wants us to produce a similar type of television advert to Levi's, to launch our latest fashion range. Something along the lines of pretty girl out on the town, two guys fall for her, and she goes for the one wearing the cool clothes.'

'Sounds great. I'm sure there are plenty of young unknown actors out there dying to take part.'

'Oh, that's not the problem. It's finding the song to go with it. The MD doesn't want someone of the calibre of Marvin Gaye, in case we get accused of copying our rivals. Any bad publicity, the whole campaign backfires and the product goes down the pan, taking me with it,' he said, taking a sip from his bright green cocktail. 'I could accept losing the apartment, the girlfriend and the clothes, but not my beloved sports car.'

Rupe could see where this was leading. 'So, where do I come in?'

Babbelstein laughed guiltily, like a child caught stealing ice cream from the freezer by his parents in the middle of the night.

'Ah ha. You know what I'm going to ask, don't you?'
Rupe smiled perceptively.

'I thought of you straight away,' continued Babbelstein.
'You're at the heart of the music industry, and you must have
your ear to the ground. What the MD is after is a piece of
unknown music, by an unsigned act. That way …'

'…they'll be naïve about the business they're getting
themselves involved in, and you'll get them on the cheap.'

Babbelstein straightened his tie, appearing mildly offended
by Rupe's straight talking.

'Well, I wouldn't use those exact words, but, yes, you're
correct. But that's only because my hands are tied with the
budget they've given me to work with. And I'm sure you get
mountains of tapes from would-be pop stars who would sell
their souls for a sniff of the high life.'

Rupe sighed. 'As it happens, I do, David. And most of
them are unsigned for one good reason: they're rubbish.'

'What, all of them?'

'Not all of them. There is the occasional song that I think is
OK, but a song I like may not necessarily be to anyone else's
taste, and to find such a song would mean sifting through
hundreds of tapes. I really don't think I have the time. I've got
shows to prepare for, I'm looking for a new apartment and
…'

'Please, Rupe. I'll get down on my knees and humiliate
myself in public if you say you'll help.'

Rupe held out a stalling hand as a sudden thought struck
him.

'Hang on a minute,' he said. 'I think I know just the song
you're looking for.'

Babbelstein grinned uncertainly, unsure if Rupe was being
serious. 'You do?'

'Yes. Recorded by old friends of mine from up north.'

'The north?' said Babbelstein, with visible distaste. 'Are
you sure? I thought the three years you spent up there had

been cleansed from your soul.'

Rupe laughed at his friend's lazy prejudice, thinking Babbelstein really did need to get out more.

'Don't be so condescending,' said Rupe, good-naturedly chastising his friend. 'Go up there yourself one day and have a good look around. You might get a surprise. Durham is a beautiful part of the country.'

'OK, Judith Chalmers, I believe you. But you were saying about these friends of yours.'

'Yes. I met them towards the end of my second year.'

'Academics?'

'No, on the contrary, they were locals. Their band was called Northern Circle, and there was this one track of theirs I absolutely loved, "Obsession", which they released as a single.'

'Really,' said Babbelstein, arching an eyebrow in interest. 'Tell me more.'

'I got to know them when I was on the students' union entertainment committee, and even roadied for them for a little while.'

'Roadied!' repeated Babbelstein. 'My word, you are a dark horse, Rupe.'

'It wasn't as glamorous as it sounds. Basically, it involved driving them and their equipment to gigs in a van I'd borrowed from the university. You should have seen the state of some of the pubs and clubs they played. It was a real eye-opener, I can tell you.

'But they were a good bunch, particularly Dom, the singer, and Matty, the guitar player, who could be hilarious together. Dom even ended up going out with my girlfriend.'

'He sounds like a really good man to have next to you in the trenches,' said Babbelstein sarcastically.

'Sara and I had grown apart by then and just split up. It was bound to happen sooner or later; Dom just happened to be the one who caught her eye. I harbour no grudges.'

'Very mature of you, Rupe. I don't think I'd have been quite so understanding.'

'Anyway, to get back to the point, I always thought it was a real shame that "Obsession" wasn't a success. It has a real cinematic quality to it. With a little more airplay, it really could have been a hit. I can categorically say that the song matches your requirements.'

'Will I be able to buy a copy from the high street? I need to move fast on this.'

Rupe shook his head. 'I very much doubt it. But, don't worry, I can let you have one of my copies. I'll drop it in tomorrow.'

'OK, but my mind's made up already. If it's come on the recommendation of London's hottest DJ, then who am I to disagree? Rupe, you're a star. If this is a success, I'll not be ungrateful.'

'That's OK, David. Just make sure you treat them fairly on royalties. There'll be a good chance it'll make the charts, and I don't want them getting a raw deal on this.'

'Of course, my word is my bond. So, any idea where I can get in touch with them?'

Rupe smiled to himself as an idea took hold.

'Actually, could I give them the good news? I'd love to see the expression on their faces.'

'Be my guest. The idea of travelling up there myself doesn't appeal, if I'm being brutally honest. Just going north of Watford Gap gives me a nosebleed.'

'I'll get the first train up there on Monday. I've nothing on for a couple of days, and it would be quite nice to see the old city again.'

'Fantastic. I'll have my secretary fax further details to your hotel when you get up there. Of course, that's assuming such technology has reached the wilder fringes of our country,' said Babbelstein snootily.

'David,' warned Rupe.

CHAPTER 45

Rupe checked in to his hotel, dumped his overnight bag in his room and dashed straight back out. His first port of call was Donnelly's, the department store where Rupe hoped Dom still worked.

'Hello,' he said politely, to the female member of staff standing behind the counter. 'I'm looking for someone who I believe works here. Dom Blackburn.'

'Sorry, love. Dom's off work at the moment.'

'Is he away on holiday?'

Only now did it occur to Rupe that, with July being the height of the holiday season, it was possible Dom could be away sunning himself on some far-flung Mediterranean beach.

The woman looked over her shoulder to check no one else was in earshot before replying.

'Well, I shouldn't really be telling you this, staff confidentiality and all that, but he's on the sick at the moment. Has been for weeks.'

'Oh dear. I hope it's nothing too serious?'

The woman glanced behind once more, before leaning in closer to Rupe.

'He's had problems,' she whispered.

'Well, I'll try and catch him at home, then,' Rupe said, before thanking her and exiting the store.

Ten minutes later, he stepped out of a taxi onto the footpath outside Dom's flat in Newton Moor. Asking the driver to wait a moment, Rupe opened the rusted garden gate and walked down the short path to the front door. As he rang the doorbell, Rupe noticed both the living room and front bedroom windows had their curtains drawn.

Getting no response, he pressed the doorbell again.

When Dom failed to appear, Rupe returned to the taxi and

asked the driver for a pen and scrap of paper. Offered a bookmaker's pencil and an envelope that had contained a gas bill, Rupe gratefully accepted them and scribbled a brief message:

Hello Dom,

It's Rupe here. Look, sorry to show up out of the blue, but I have some really great news to tell you about. I'm only up here for today, so I will be in The Oak Tree at eight o'clock tonight if you would like to catch up with me there.

If for any reason you don't get this message in time, I'll post you a letter or give you a call, but I'd really love to tell you face to face. I've travelled up from London especially.

See you later (hopefully!)
Rupe

To fill in the afternoon, Rupe decided to go on a nostalgic tour of his old haunts: his college campus, the riverside walk in the shadow of the cathedral, and a couple of his favourite shops. Nothing much appeared to have changed in the year he had been away, the gentle and relaxed pace of life a stark contrast to the non-stop urgency of London.

After a shower, change of clothing and a bite to eat back at the hotel, Rupe made his way over to The Oak Tree. Arriving half an hour early, he was keen to sample once more the local bitter that had been his regular tipple in his university days. Delighted to discover the brew was still available, Rupe ordered a drink and chatted with Dave the publican, who was pleased to meet one of his old quiz regulars again.

When Dave was drawn away to serve an influx of new customers, Rupe settled at a table, impatient now for Dom to arrive.

He did not have long to wait.

When Dom walked through the door exactly on the hour,

Rupe was immediately alarmed by his physical appearance. Gone was the tidy, clean-shaven and smartly dressed person who always had an optimistic spring in his step. The Dom he now observed was approximately two stone heavier than Rupe remembered him being, unshaven, and with hair that was greasy and unkempt.

Rupe stood up to greet him. 'Dom, you got my message. It's great to see you. What can I get you?'

'The usual,' said Dom listlessly, displaying no sign that he was pleased to see his old friend.

'Well, shall we sit down?' said Rupe, once Dave had served him.

Dom shuffled over to a table at the rear of the pub and sat down with his back to the window.

Choosing the chair opposite, Rupe sensed something was seriously amiss; he felt as if he was in the company of a stranger who had begrudgingly allowed him to share his table. The usual spark was missing from Dom's eyes, with no spirit in his personality.

'No Sara tonight, then?' asked Rupe civilly, once it was obvious Dom was not going to be the one to speak first.

'She left me ages ago,' Dom mumbled, gazing down at the floor.

'Oh, I'm sorry,' replied Rupe.

'Don't be,' said Dom gruffly. 'We weren't right for each other.'

Attributing Dom's dour demeanour to the breakdown in his relationship with Sara, Rupe hoped his good news would act as a much-needed tonic.

'Once I've told you what all the fuss is about, then we'll have to tell Matty as we're going to require his guitar playing talents. We can always telephone him, but I would love for us to travel down to Milton Keynes together to tell him to his face. I trust you two patched up your differences after that unnecessary spat? These things happen between friends from

312

time to time, and there's nothing that can't be …'

'He's dead, Rupe,' said Dom, stopping him in his tracks.

'Dead?' a stunned Rupe managed to say, after a long pause. 'How?'

Dom shakily relayed the tragic events of over three months ago.

'I'm speechless,' said Rupe, shaking his head sadly once Dom had finished speaking. 'Jesus, it's so not right,' he protested, forcibly banging his fist on the table.

In that instant, everything Rupe was witnessing in Dom suddenly made sense: the haunted, distant gaze; the dark shadows lurking underneath his eyes; his lack of attention in his appearance. Understandably, Matty's sudden death was continuing to torment him.

'How is Monique?' said Rupe.

'Back in France, living with Francois at her parents' home. It's all a mess. She has a large mortgage on a house in Milton Keynes she's struggling to sell, and a load of other debts hanging around her neck.'

'Poor Monique. Poor Francois.'

'He's far too young to understand. He knows his daddy is in heaven, but doesn't realise what that means.'

'I'll get some more drinks in,' said a bewildered Rupe, swiftly returning with some whisky chasers. Not accustomed to seeking solace in alcohol, this was one of the few occasions in Rupe's life when such action was deemed essential.

For the rest of the evening, the pair chatted and reminisced about Matty; it was only with the calling of last orders that Dom returned the conversation to the reason for Rupe's visit.

'This news of yours,' said Dom, placing Rupe's crumpled note on the table in front of him.

Rupe's drunken state of mind searched for the correct words to begin.

'Someone wants to sign you,' he eventually managed to say. 'Your music career's got a real chance to take off at long

313

last.'

'Music career?' scoffed Dom. 'Rupe, the old days are gone. Matty's gone. It's over. I'm destined to be nothing more in life than a crappy stockroom assistant in a crappy shop, if I can ever pull myself together enough to sign off the sick and return to work. This whole thing has knocked me for six. I don't know if I'm coming or going.'

'Don't be too dismissive until you hear what I have to say,' said Rupe.

Rupe proceeded to enlighten him about his conversation with David Babbelstein the previous weekend, believing once Dom heard what he had to say, his attitude would change.

'This is the break you've been looking for,' concluded Rupe, handing Dom the faxed copy of the details. 'A re-recorded version of "Obsession" released as a single on the back of a jeans commercial, meaning lots of radio airplay and widespread publicity. Dom, it's a once in a lifetime opportunity, and you look like you could do with a change of luck.'

'I don't think so, Rupe,' said Dom coldly.

'Listen, Dom, I know at this moment in time you're still hurting. That's understandable. Matty's death has been a massive shock and there'll always be a hole in your life that can't be replaced, but think about what Matty would say if he was here. He would want you to grasp the chance with both hands.'

Dom looked thoughtful. 'Did you mention re-recording the song? I haven't sung a note in months. When do they want to do it?'

'As soon as possible. There's a recording studio in London booked, with a host of session musicians and a producer on standby as we speak, waiting for the honour of your presence.'

'Really?'

'Yes, really, and there's not another minute to waste. But if you need convincing further, how about we get the producer to retain some of Matty's guitar playing on the new version, if possible, then that way it's still the two of you together, living the dream. He would have loved that, wouldn't he?'

'I suppose so.'

Rupe sensed he was starting to win Dom over.

'What you've got to realise, Dom, is you're the main man at the minute, but time is money with these guys and if you don't get in there now and grab this opportunity, you may just wake up one morning and find it's passed you by.'

'If you could get them to do that for me, I'd be in.'

'Fantastic. So, here's what I propose. Get a good night's sleep, and then first thing tomorrow you're going to have a hot bath, a shave, and then go for a haircut. While you're doing that, I'll drop in on Jez and try to get the master tapes. Then, I'll meet you at the train station, and we'll jump on the first train to King's Cross. The company want this record signed, sealed and delivered by the weekend. They need to move quickly to get this on their autumn promotional campaign. And if you want me to, I'll act as your unpaid advisor. You'll need someone to go through all of the contracts for you, to check they are all above board.'

'Thanks, Rupe. You know I trust you.'

Rupe smiled at the faith shown in him. 'Now that's decided, I propose we have one more for the road before beginning a period of sobriety from tomorrow.'

'I'll drink to that,' slurred Dom.

CHAPTER 46

'Come on, Dom. Wakey wakey.'

'Ah, do me a favour,' Dom grumbled, as Rupe viciously pulled the curtains apart to reveal the early stages of what promised to be a glorious summer's day in the capital. 'What time is it?'

'Nearly half six,' smirked Rupe, dripping with sweat from his early morning jog. 'There's fresh coffee brewing in the percolator and grapefruit in the fridge. We need to be out of here in the hour, so chop chop.'

'I don't suppose there's any sugar puffs or bacon sarnies on the go?' shouted Dom, as Rupe disappeared out of the room.

'Sorry, I'm a bran type of guy these days,' came the muffled reply from somewhere within the apartment. 'I've got to keep an eye on my waistline.'

'Bran? I'm nervous enough without a load of fibre hitting my bowels.'

'Best stick to the coffee, then,' said Rupe, popping his head back inside the bedroom. 'It's going to be a long day, though, so do try and eat something. By the way, I've arranged for you to meet David at the recording studio. The plan is to do the recording first, and afterwards read and sign the contracts. Some of the jargon may be confusing, so, as promised, I'll hang around and help out.'

'Cheers, Rupe. All that legal baloney will go right over my head otherwise.'

'No worries. OK, I'm off to grab a quick shower.'

Travelling on the Underground through rush hour London, Dom and Rupe alighted at Marble Arch. A brisk five minute walk ensued, ending when Rupe came to an abrupt halt outside a grandiose four-storey townhouse, the end property in a long line of impressive Georgian buildings.

The pair ascended the steep flight of steps and passed through the arched entrance into the building's main reception area.

'Dom, I'd like to introduce you to David Babbelstein,' said Rupe, gesturing in the direction of a tense looking, suited male leaning against the receptionist's desk. 'He's in charge of the marketing campaign.'

Hurriedly stubbing out his cigarette in the ashtray behind him, Babbelstein approached them and shook Dom's hand.

'Pleased to meet you. We're all big fans of your song and think it's going to be a huge success.'

'Thank you,' Dom muttered humbly, feeling slightly overawed as the reality of the occasion hit him for the first time.

'Well,' said Rupe to Dom, 'I'll leave you in David's capable hands, and see you later when you're finished.'

'Thanks, Rupe. OK, Dom, follow me this way and let's meet the musical team we've assembled,' said an immediately business-like Babbelstein, leading the singer through an exit at the far end of the room and down a spiralling flight of wooden stairs.

Ushered through a door on the lower ground floor, Dom found himself inside a commodious recording studio that was a hive of activity. A handful of musicians were loosely jamming a Chuck Berry classic in one corner of the room; in another, a mini-orchestra was removing an array of brass and string instruments from their protective cases.

'I'm about to introduce you to your producer,' said Babbelstein. 'He'll guide you through the recording process this morning. Just do as he says and everyone will be happy.'

Dom followed Babbelstein through yet another door into an adjoining room. Seated at an enormous console, keeping an eye on proceedings in the main studio through a large glass panel, was a nerdy looking man in his late forties, with long,

317

silver-flecked hair and granny glasses.

'Guy, this is our singer, Dom.'

The producer stood up and shook Dom's hand, smiling warmly.

'Pleased to meet you, Dom,' he said calmly, before turning to Babbelstein. 'OK, David, I'll take over from here.'

Once the two were alone, Guy immediately set out to make Dom feel at ease.

'Right, Dom. Please try not to be too daunted by everything going on around you. I appreciate how nervous you must be feeling, but everyone is nice and friendly here.

'I've assembled a team of musicians who are consummate professionals. They have been rehearsing "Obsession" for the past two days, so the song is second nature to them. I'm sure they will do it justice. David mentioned you would like the guitar from the original version to be utilised. I'm sure I can add it into the final mix, as I fully appreciate the sentiments behind your request.

'OK, first things first. Let me introduce you to everybody, and then we'll do a couple of run-throughs before getting something down on tape. How does that sound?'

'Great.'

Dom took a deep breath and followed Guy into the studio.

Five hours later, with Dom having long since lost count of the number of takes, the session came to a halt when Guy declared himself ecstatic with what they had recorded.

As well as completing "Obsession" to his satisfaction, the producer had the unexpected bonus of a new track for the B-side of the single.

Guy's original brief had been to use an instrumental version of "Obsession" for the flipside, a common and cost effective tactic in the business. However, Guy decided to deviate from this plan after overhearing Dom, during a brief break in proceedings, sing a cappella to himself a rousing song with which he was not familiar. When Dom informed him he had only written it the previous day, an enamoured Guy immediately gathered the session musicians around so that they could learn the chords and melody. Within an hour, they had a second song recorded.

Once he had said his farewells to everyone, Dom returned to the reception area to find Rupe waiting patiently for him alone.

'Well?' enquired the DJ, folding his copy of The *Guardian* and dropping it onto the chair next to him.

'All done and dusted,' said a visibly relieved Dom.

'Great stuff. Shall we go for some food to the bistro over the road to celebrate? David has entrusted to me the contracts that you have to sign, as he had business to attend to across town.'

'Sounds good to me,' said Dom.

Settled at a table in the eatery, Rupe swiftly got down to business.

'I've studied the contracts in fine detail for you. This first one,' he said, handing the document and a pen across the table to Dom, 'is basically an agreement to pay you the fee, stated within, for your services as singer.'

Allowing a small whistle to escape his lips at the figure listed, Dom signed and printed his name where stipulated; he slid it back across to Rupe.

'Great,' said Rupe. 'Now, this second one tells you how much, as the sole songwriter, you will be paid per record sold. This contract is the real money spinner, Dom, I promise you that.'

Taking it from Rupe, Dom scanned the terms and conditions.

'The percentages appear fine, Rupe, but I can't sign this contract,' declared Dom plainly.

'But … but why ever not?' said Rupe, clearly bemused.

'It needs a minor alteration making to it. My name needs to be taken off and replaced with that of Matthew Parker, or

319

should I say the estate of Matthew Parker.'

Rupe's forehead creased in confusion. 'Dom, are you sure? I was there the first time you performed it, when you announced you had written it …'

'Rupe,' interrupted Dom firmly, a knowing look in his eye, 'history will now record it as Matty having written the song.'

It was then that the penny finally dropped with Rupe; he smiled in admiration for one of the most selfless acts he had ever witnessed.

'Of course, how could I have forgotten?' said Rupe, smacking the palm of his hand off his head, an exaggerated gesture that inferred he had displayed classic stupidity in ever suggesting Dom was the composer. 'I'll have this sent over to David immediately to be retyped. I trust you will inform Matty's wife that she will be required to give her permission to use the song?'

'No problem. I'll call her later from your apartment.'

'You're a good man, Dom Blackburn … a good man.'

CHAPTER 47

Dom was enjoying an early evening drink in the sedate atmosphere of The Newton Moor pub while engrossed in the latest edition of the *New Musical Express*. Holding the inky pages up in front of his attentive gaze, he was oblivious to the world beyond.

A female in her early twenties entered, spied the solitary figure sitting in the far corner of the lounge, and allowed herself a slight smile before walking towards him.

'Is the famous pop star going to buy the lady a drink, or must the lady pay for one herself?'

Dom stopped reading his article and peered uneasily over the top of his magazine.

'I'll buy you one, as long as you promise not to immediately tip it over my head.'

Katy laughed. 'I come in peace. I promise.'

An awkward pause ensued as Dom and Katy both struggled to think of something further to say. It had been a long time since they had last seen each other, and even then, their parting had been far from amicable.

'How did you know I would be here?' asked Dom finally, casting his reading material to one side.

'When there was no answer from the flat, I knocked on Mrs Higgins's door. She said you would probably be here.'

'I never used to like the place, being surrounded by geriatrics and allotment club members, but it's kind of grown on me these last few months. The beers well kept, there's no worrying about missing the last bus home, and the chippy's a stone's throw away.'

They both laughed nervously; with the ice beginning to break between them, Dom felt slightly more at ease.

'Well, it's good to see you again,' said Dom. 'You're looking really well.'

'It's good to see you, too. I was in the area, so I thought I'd look you up while I was passing, so to speak. Of course, if that's a problem I can always …'

Dom stood up quickly. 'Don't be daft,' he said. 'You sit yourself down while I go to the bar. The usual?'

'Yes, dry cider, please.'

'So, are you still living in the Midlands?' asked Dom upon his return, placing Katy's glass carefully down on the table in front of her.

'Yes, still with the same bank. I'm assistant manageress now.'

'I'd heard that. That's good news. I always knew you'd go far.'

'And what about you?' enquired Katy. 'I guess you've left Donnelly's far behind now that you're a bona fide pop star?'

'I was out of there like a shot,' said Dom. 'You should have seen Ramsgate's face when I told him why I was leaving. He had a face like he was sucking on a lemon. He made my life a living hell all the time I worked there. Still, he who laughs last …'

'I read about you in the newspapers when your song was in the charts. It did very well in the end, didn't it?'

'It reached number nineteen in October,' said Dom modestly.

'Of course, I also found out about Matty,' she added hesitantly, her tone growing serious. 'I wish I'd known at the time, Dom. I would have come straight back to see you. How are you coping now?'

A lump caught in Dom's throat. 'It's getting a little better, Katy,' he began shakily. 'It all happened so suddenly that I couldn't really function or think straight for a long time. It was only when the song took off that I began to sort my head out and try to be more positive about life again.'

'Well, if you ever need me for anything, I'm here.'

'Thanks. Anyway, what brings you back north? Visiting

family, are you?' said Dom, keen to steer the conversation onto a lighter note.

'I had a job interview yesterday at our Newcastle branch. There was a temporary vacancy because someone is going off on maternity leave, and I was fortunate enough to be offered the post.'

'Hey, congratulations,' said Dom.

'Thank you. It'll be good experience, and it'll also be nice to be living back at home for a while. My mother's over the moon about it. So, that's my next step in life. What do you have planned?'

Dom looked away thoughtfully for a moment.

'Do you know, I haven't got a clue, to be honest. I quite like the idea of writing for other artists. There are one or two offers on the table from some people down in London.'

'Sounds very glamorous,' said Katy. 'Is there no chance of your band making a comeback?'

'No, it wouldn't be Northern Circle without Matty.'

An hour and several more drinks later, Katy said, 'Well, I don't know about you, but I am absolutely famished. Would you like to go out for a meal somewhere? It would be nice to catch up further with you.'

'Only if you allow me to pay. It's the least I can do after all the grief I've caused you in the past.'

Katy pretended to mull over Dom's offer. 'I agree on one condition,' she said finally.

'What's that?'

'That you let me pay the time after.'

'You're on,' said Dom, draining his glass and standing up.

As they exited the pub, Katy noticed Dom was carrying his coat under his arm.

'Dom, put your coat on, otherwise you'll freeze. It's the middle of December.'

'No need, Katy,' said Dom mischievously. 'We're only going there.'

'Where?' she said, through chattering teeth.

Dom pointed ahead. 'Look closer.'

'Pete's Chippy?'

'Hey, it's a lot more plush these days than you might imagine,' he said, beginning to walk towards the takeaway. 'They have proper two course meals on the menu now, you know. And two tables to sit at and eat your food.'

'Two courses? You're pulling my leg.'

'I'm not. Tonight, Katy, we will be dining on no less than chips and sauce.'

Katy nudged him playfully in the ribs. 'Dom, that joke was terrible the first time you ever told me it, and time hasn't improved it. But, why not,' she said, putting her arm through his. 'Why not indeed.'